Praise for *The Tannery*

"Riveting. . . . In his debut novel, Michael Almond has given us a page-turner. Far more than a legal thriller, though it is that, *The Tannery* is historical fiction at its finest—a story set near the turn of the twentieth century in North Carolina. The state, still reeling from defeat in the Civil War, is torn by the violent politics of race, all of which Almond weaves through the mystery of a murder. Some of this tale will sound disturbingly familiar to readers in the twenty-first century—all the more reason to consider its lessons. History can come alive in a work of great fiction. This is one of those times."

—**FRYE GAILLARD**, Civil Rights Historian, Author of *A Hard Rain: America in the 1960s*

"Michael Almond's *The Tannery* is a remarkably drawn and richly detailed whodunnit. A uniquely American tale of the quest for justice, this search takes place at the crossroads of a nation's struggle for equal protection under the law. Full of beguiling and captivating characters, exciting plot twists and turns, *The Tannery* is a literary gem for lovers of mystery and historical fiction."

—**JEFFREY BLOUNT**, Author of *The Emancipation of Evan Walls*

"Michael Almond has produced a stunning, significant, page-turning masterpiece of historical fiction. Though *The Tannery* is Almond's debut novel, the reader falls immediately under the spell of this consummate storyteller. Almond weaves the rich detail of the post-Reconstruction South with delicious character development and gut-wrenching plot twists. The book chronicles lawyer Ben Waterman's crusade in defense of Virgil Wade, a mixed-race boy accused of the brutal murder of a prominent young White woman in the turbulent politics and social conditions of

North Carolina at the turn of the twentieth century. Though set in the past, this novel is a must-read for a country combatting the enduring racism and voter suppression of the present. The Faulkner quote on *The Tannery*'s first page resonates: 'All of us labor in webs spun long before we were born . . .'"

—**FREDERICK KEMPE**, Best-selling Author of *Berlin 1961: Kennedy, Khrushchev and the World's Most Dangerous Place*, Pulitzer Prize-nominated *Wall Street Journal* editor and Reporter, and Atlantic Council President and CEO

"In his debut novel, Michael Almond turns a penetrating and sympathetic eye to one of the darker, less-known chapters in North Carolina history. You'll feel like you're in the courtroom with young Virgil Wade as his attorney Ben Waterman fights for justice against seemingly impossible odds."

—**KIM WRIGHT**, Author of *Last Ride to Graceland*, Winner of the Willie Morris Award for Southern Fiction

"Michael Almond has created a fascinating and timely historical whodunit that evokes the era and ethos of Jim Crow North Carolina at the turn of the twentieth century as lawyer Ben Waterman confronts the scars of racism and white supremacy in post-Reconstruction Wilkes County. Almond's research is solid, and rich historical detail runs throughout this impressive debut novel."

—**DR. WILLIAM THOMPSON**, Emeritus Professor of History, Queens University

"For fans of historical fiction, *The Tannery* mixes solid research with powerful and suspenseful storytelling in this look back at early twentieth century North Carolina and the post-Reconstruction South. First-time author Michael Almond faithfully recreates a sense of time and place where memorable characters struggle with murder, bigotry, and injustice in the turbulent early days of Jim Crow."

—JAMES CAUGHMAN, Author of *Addison Mizner: The Architect Whose Genius Defined Palm Beach*

"*The Tannery* will not disappoint you. Michael Almond has fleshed out a cast of thoroughly believable characters and placed them in the history of the Blue Ridge Mountains on a quest that will engage the reader's interest to the very last page."

—BOB BAMBERG, Editor, *The Alleghany News*

"This fast-paced courtroom drama is laced with the truth of an early 1900's past gone backward. Set against the political birth of North Carolina's Jim Crow era, *The Tannery* will have readers fully engaged but shaking their heads at the twists and turns of history's impact on justice in a small mountain community, wondering until the very end whether there is any hope for a sixteen-year-old Black boy on trial for murder and the young White lawyer who represents him."

—LANDIS WADE, trial lawyer, host of *Charlotte Readers Podcast*, and author of *The Christmas Courtroom Trilogy*

"*The Tannery* has so many wonderful characters. Not just people and relationships, but also challenging dilemmas and little details of time and place that stay with you. Woven together, the story sweeps through so many questions about early Jim Crow North Carolina, but also about now. From time to time, I stopped reading to ponder today's world and the challenges facing us. *The Tannery* is a rich and thoughtful journey. And a fun read too!"

—VINCENT LOVOI, publisher *This Land Press* and board member of *Oxford American* and *Texas Observer*

"With the heart of a storyteller and the mind of a historian, Michael Almond has written a passionate novel about murder, race, and justice (or lack thereof) in the early days of the Jim Crow South. This is a vexing tale, vivid and haunting. You'll be transported far beyond your reading chair."

—JUDY GOLDMAN, author of *Together: A Memoir of a Marriage and a Medical Mishap* and the forthcoming memoir, Child

"It might not seem fair to compare *The Tannery* to Harper Lee's *To Kill a Mockingbird* since Lee's novel is recognized as one of the most important novels in the history of Southern literature, but *The Tannery* stands up to the comparison. . . . Michael Almond's depiction of North Carolina's bigoted past is unflinching and disturbing, but his portrait of his native state is not entirely negative. His story has its bigots, but it also has its heroes."

—DR. MARK I. WEST, Bonnie E. Cone Professor in Civic Engagement and Professor of English, University of North Carolina at Charlotte

"*The Tannery* is tough to put down because the storytelling is so compelling. . . . This book is timely, in that we can reflect on how far we have come today and see the tangible progress we have made. But it also glaringly reminds us that the issues of racism, voter suppression, and economic inequality are still with us . . . ."

—HARVEY B. GANTT, former mayor of Charlotte, first African American student accepted by Clemson University, inspiration for the Harvey B. Gantt Center for African American Arts + Culture

The Tannery
by Michael A. Almond

ISBN 978-1-64663-487-3

This is a work of fiction. The characters are both actual and fictitious. With the exception of verified historical events and persons, all incidents, descriptions, dialogue and opinions expressed are the products of the author's imagination and are not to be construed as real.

Published by

 köehlerbooks ™

3705 Shore Drive
Virginia Beach, VA 23455
800-435-4811
www.koehlerbooks.com

Used with permission of the Wilkes Heritage Museum

The
Tannery

Michael A. Almond

VIRGINIA BEACH
CAPE CHARLES

This is for Helen Ruth,
my loving, constant companion and
partner in all things.

"*The past is never dead. It's not even past. All of us labor in webs spun long before we were born, webs of heredity and environment, of desire and consequence, of history and eternity.*"

—William Faulkner, *Requiem for a Nun*, 1951

"*What has been will be again, what has been done will be done again; there is nothing new under the sun.*"

—*Ecclesiastes 1:9 NIV*

"*History, despite its wrenching pain, cannot be unlived, but if faced with courage, need not be lived again.*"

—Maya Angelou, *On the Pulse of Morning*

Prologue

T
he sky was the color of sour milk, the late-afternoon sun a crystal marble burning through it. In the stately oaks that grace the cemetery, cicadas buzzed like bacon frying. The Wilcox & Sons tent provided some relief for the family seated beneath it, none for the black-clad mourners standing nearby.

Damn, it's hot, thought Roscoe Elwood "R.E." McGee, as Reverend Dr. Jonathan Whitehead, rector of St. Paul's Episcopal Church, droned on through the *Burial of the Dead: Rite I,* holding the congregation fast to the *Book of Common Prayer.* McGee was partial to the more freewheeling send-offs at Baptist funerals. *I'm sweating through my clothes in this infernal heat.*

The late-summer air lay hazy, thick, and sticky. Looking up, McGee mused, *gonna have to move along to beat the storm.* As if on cue, Reverend Whitehead's litany wound down. And the people said, *"Amen."*

"And, finally, dear friends, the family has requested that R.E. McGee be permitted to say a few words of remembrance." McGee rose from the end of the family row and began to speak.

"Reverend Whitehead, friends. On behalf of the Waterman family, I would like to express their thanks and appreciation, and my own, for your many words of sympathy and consolation as we all grieve the passing of Benjamin Gordon Waterman.

"As Ben would certainly remind me at a time like this, and in heat like this, a eulogy, in order to be immortal, need not be eternal." A few men in the crowd chuckled, quickly elbowed into silence by their wives. "Ben

1

Waterman was my friend. His life's work, his commitment to justice and fairness to all whose path crossed his, his *story* is known to and admired by us all and need not be repeated here.

"Ben and I grew up together here in Wilkes, as close as two boys and, later, men could be. One of the happiest days of my life was the day that Ben, his beloved wife Emily, and their son Michael moved back to Wilkesboro. Emily, whose mortal remains also lie here, left us far too soon, but Ben devoted the remainder of his life to Michael and his family." McGee paused, wiping his brow with a handkerchief.

"Most of you may know that Ben was a lifelong learner, a student of the law, history, and philosophy. Above all, Ben was a man of honor, and, as the Roman lawyer and philosopher Marcus Tullius Cicero would say, *gravitas*. Two thousand years ago Cicero wrote an essay titled *On Old Age*. It was Ben's favorite, and today I believe Ben would want us to remember Cicero's words:

"'Souls with a keener and wider vision perceive that they are going to a better state, while others cannot see beyond death . . . . If I err in believing men's souls to be immortal, I do so willingly, and as long as I live I do not wish that which gives me so much satisfaction to be wrested from me. . . . O, glorious day when I shall go to join that divine company and conclave of souls and depart from these turmoils and impurities!'

"Ben Waterman has now transcended to that better state. And for us remaining, remember these words from the Second Book of Samuel: 'Know ye not that there is a prince and a great man fallen this day in Israel.'"

All were quiet as McGee again took his seat. Reverend Whitehead blinked away the thought that he had just been bested by an unschooled country layman and a pagan Roman lawyer. Sweltering under his ceremonial regalia and close to heat stroke, he cut things short. "O God, whose blessed Son was laid in a sepulcher in the garden. Bless, we pray, this grave, and grant that he whose body is to be buried here may dwell with Christ in paradise and may come to thy heavenly kingdom; through thy Son Jesus Christ our Lord."

And the people said, "Amen."

As clouds began to gather, the mourners patiently formed a line to pay their respects, watched by a pair of gravediggers eager to finish their work before the first rumble of thunder. The last hand shaken, the last murmur of sympathy uttered, the last tear shed, Michael Waterman, flanked by his wife, Ruth, and their teenaged son Gordon, walked hand-in-hand toward McGee.

"Ros, we cannot thank you enough. What you said about Daddy was just right." Smiling, he said, "I thought ol' Whitehead would have a stroke when you quoted from Cicero. Daddy would have loved it."

"Thanks, Michael," replied McGee. *Forty years-old and he still calls him "Daddy,"* he thought. Leaning forward, taking Gordon's hands in both of his, McGee said to the boy, "Son, I want you to know that I meant what I said about a great man passing. Your grandfather was the finest man I ever knew. As you live your life, as you face whatever troubles come your way, just ask yourself, 'What would Ben Waterman do?' You'll never go wrong."

Looking up at the sky, Michael said to Ruth, "Sweetheart, it looks like it's going to storm soon. Why don't you and Gordon take the car back to the house? Folks'll be dropping in. Ros and I need to go by Daddy's office for a minute. I'll be along directly."

W

St. Paul's Episcopal Church, a handsome brick structure in the Gothic Revival style, was built on the crest of a high hill near the center of town in Wilkesboro. To the north, the hill dropped sharply to the Yadkin River and Mulberry Fields below; beyond rose the Blue Ridge Mountains. To the south, the church and its cemetery overlooked the town, Cub Creek, and the low range of the Brushy Mountains.

Looking up, Michael pointed and said, "Daddy always liked that church, but he could never get comfortable being an Episcopalian. Too much kneeling and reading out loud. He always said that if folks could just read the liturgy to themselves instead of all that back and forth, the service could be over in fifteen minutes, and everybody could get home for Sunday dinner. He was a born-again Baptist, but Momma came from a big Episcopalian family, so that was that."

McGee smiled. "Where your mother was concerned, Ben always grinned and did what he had to do. But what's up at the office? What's on your mind?"

"Come on," Michael said. "Walk with me."

Michael led McGee back up to the gravesite where two Black men were hard at work shoveling rich and fragrant earth onto the lowered coffin. As Michael reached for his wallet, they stopped and removed their caps.

"Silas, Leon, y'all take this," Michael said, holding out two one-dollar bills.

"Naw, Mr. Waterman," said Silas Frye. "No need for that. The church, Preacher Whitehead, he done already paid us. 'Sides, your daddy was a fine man, always done right by us, stood up for us. Was an honor to help y'all out."

"No, no," replied Michael. "Daddy would want you to have this." Nodding their thanks, Silas and Leon accepted the money.

"We mighty sorry for your loss, Mr. Waterman."

Side by side, reminiscing along the way, Michael and McGee strolled through the tombstones, curving down the hill past the jail, the courthouse, and the Tory Oak, and stopped at a small, whitewashed clapboard building on the corner of North and Broad Streets.

Known to everyone as the Finley Law Office, the structure was located just across from the county courthouse. Built in the Carpenter Gothic style, the building was one room wide and two rooms deep. Plenty of light was provided by four six-over-six sash windows, and its steeply pitched gables were decorated with drop-shaped bargeboards and sawn work finials. But the building was coveted by lawyers as much for its location as its architecture.

Ben had moved his family from Wilmington to Wilkesboro, accepting an offer from his Wilkes County mentor, former Governor "Cotton Bob" Maxwell, to join him as his law partner. Maxwell owned a large white-frame house, walking distance from the courthouse, that provided ample space for two lawyers and their growing practice. After Maxwell died in his sleep at age eighty, Ben bought the house from his heirs, moved his family in, and continued to practice from there.

When Thomas Finley was elected superior court judge, his law office became available. Ben, eager at Emily's urging to "get out of the house," bought the Finley building and moved his practice. Later, Ben's son Michael graduated from the University of North Carolina School of Law in Chapel Hill and moved back to Wilkesboro to practice law with his father. They shared space in the Finley building until, bowing to changing times, Waterman & Waterman relocated to North Wilkesboro, the booming sister town across the river. Ben, looking to his retirement, held on to the small white building.

Climbing the stairs to the front porch, McGee asked, "What will you do with this place now that Ben is gone?"

"Keep it," Michael replied firmly. "I'll rent it to some lawyer. But who knows? Like Daddy, someday I may need it, too. Ruth and I are also keeping the house. Could never sell it. North Wilkesboro is good for business, but Wilkesboro will always be home."

Michael unlocked the door. "Come on in, Ros, there's something I want you to see." Entering the front room, Michael stopped, looked up to the ceiling. "Damn, it's hot," he said, flipping the wall switch that turned on the five-blade Hunter ceiling fan.

McGee glanced at the familiar worktable in the middle of the room, flanked by two ladder back chairs with cane seats. On the table was a chessboard with carved wooden pieces, the game now and forever unfinished, the black queen in imminent peril.

"That's better," said Michael. Taking in the familiar scene around him, he sighed. "After he retired back in January, said that he might piddle a little, take a *pro bono* case now and then. Converted my old office here into his law library. Brought a couple of old Persian rugs with him. Said they would *soften up* the place."

McGee, of course, knew all this. He and Ben had shared many a glass of whiskey and fine cigars in this comfortable space in the months before his death. But Michael was, for a moment, lost in time as he gazed around the room. "Let's go back to Daddy's office."

The room was dominated by a large, hand-carved mahogany partners desk made by an Italian craftsman who had worked on the Biltmore House near Asheville. A high-backed burgundy leather swivel chair faced the desk, a black cast iron woodstove to the left. Both the desk and the chair were left to Ben in Maxwell's will.

By the window on the north side sat a treasured extravagance, a polished cherry wood floor model radio, flanked by an antique grandfather clock, the only remaining link to Ben's early years in Pilot Mountain. In the corner rested an overstuffed dark blue leather club chair and ottoman.

To the left of the desk, the door leading from the front room had been permanently sealed. Tacked onto it was a 1940 red-and-white Ramon's Old Fashioned Almanac Calendar, distributed free of charge to customers of Brame's Drug Store in North Wilkesboro. Beneath it sat a small wooden bookcase with glass doors, housing Ben's personal library, including a maroon leather-bound collection of *The Complete Works of Marcus Tullius Cicero* and a well-thumbed copy of Virgil's *The Aeneid* in Latin. To the right, a tall, black walnut two-door chifforobe with a keyhole lock.

On the desk rested an Underwood No. 5 typewriter, gleaming black and smelling of machine oil, with round white porcelain keys. A birthday-retirement gift from McGee back in January. On either side lay scattered papers and files ready for Ben's attention.

Michael took a deep breath. "It smells like him," he said. "Can you smell it, Ros?"

"I sure can. Fine cigars and costly pipe tobacco. Ben liked a good smoke."

Michael walked over to the club chair, placed his hand on its back. "Hard to believe that he was here, working, just last Friday." Pausing, clearing his throat, Michael said, "I halfway expect him to come storming in here right now, wanting to know what in the Sam Hill we are up to in his *sanctum sanctorum*. I guess nobody is ever really ready or prepared to bury your father."

McGee had found him there last Friday afternoon, in the blue chair, feet up on the ottoman. Ben had died peacefully in his sleep, never waking from his afternoon nap. *Must've been a heart attack. Had to be,* McGee thought.

Michael walked to the chifforobe. Unlocking it, he opened the wooden doors and lifted a small cardboard box with a separate lid, like the ones lawyers use to store important files. It was light. He pushed aside the papers on the right side of the desk and set the box on top.

"After I got things square with Wilcox on Saturday morning, I came by here to look for Daddy's will. I found the key taped inside the lid of his tobacco box. The will was in his metal strongbox, along with some deeds and other things. But I also found this." Michael gestured for McGee to look. "I have no idea what this is, Ros, or what's inside it. It's obviously an old box, taped shut. And look here—"

On the top of the box, taped tightly to it on either side, was a cream-colored envelope bearing a typewritten message, *"For Roscoe E. McGee, to be opened only in the event of my death."* Beneath that was Ben's familiar scrawled signature. No date.

"Strange," said McGee. "The box is old, but the envelope looks pretty new. There's no date on it, but it's typewritten. So, the message must have been typed on that machine," pointing first to the envelope and then to the Underwood, "And then taped to this box. Shall we open it? See what's in the box?"

"No, Ros, I think not. For whatever reason, Daddy meant for that envelope and that box to be opened by you and only you. You and Daddy were the closest of friends, Ros, like brothers. Whatever private message he left for you . . . well, I have to respect that."

"Who else knows about this, Michael?"

"Nobody, Ros. This is just between you and me . . . and Daddy."

Just then the south window flooded the room with a burst of brilliant light, like a photographer's flashbulb. Several seconds later the sky exploded in a violent *CRACK* and a follow-on rumble like cannon fire. Both Michael and McGee involuntarily shrank and ducked their heads.

"Jesus!" shouted Michael. "Lightning, pretty close by. I need to get to the house, Ros. Ruth is expecting a passel of folks coming to pay respects and bringing food. If I scoot now, I can beat the storm."

"Go on, then," agreed McGee. "I saw some umbrellas in that stand in the front room, so grab one and get going."

"But what about you?" asked Michael.

Pointing at the box, McGee said, "I'll ride it out here. My car is up at the church, so I'll need to wait until the worst of it passes. And I have work to do here."

Heading for the door, Michael said, "After this blows over, come on by the house. We'll fix a plate for you. Nothing like a funeral to bring out the best in Southern cooking!"

W

Alone in Ben's office, McGee sat in the big high-back chair. The thunderclouds had cooled the air but had also darkened the late-afternoon sky, making it hard to see. He reached over and switched on the Tiffany desk lamp, which cast a pool of warm light over the Underwood and the mysterious box.

McGee then had a thought and strode into the front room where he left his suit jacket. *Might as well have a smoke*, he thought. As he reached for his pipe and tobacco pouch, he heard the first pitter-patter of rain on the tin roof. Back at the desk, the rain rattled loud as a snare drum roll, punctuated by kettle drums of thunder and flashes of lightning and the whistling of bending trees in the wind.

McGee stared at the box, running his fingers over the envelope, back and forth. The paper was off-white and smooth and without blemish. Stalling, McGee walked to the grandfather clock. Opening the glass door, he adjusted the weights, set the time, and gently nudged the pendulum into action. *Tick-tock.* Then he strolled back to the desk, his eyes never leaving the box. *What the hell*, thought McGee, reaching for it.

But then he had another thought. He opened a fine inlaid-wood box on the left side of the desk. Impressed onto the lid under a coat of gleaming varnish was a perfect yellow leaf of cured tobacco. The box was about half full of imported Danish pipe tobacco and two slices of green apple, browning but still fresh enough to keep the tobacco moist and fragrant.

McGee was about to load his pipe, but then noticed two fine Cuban cigars. He smiled. Taking one in hand, he pinched it—*fresh!*—moistened it with his tongue, and bit off the end, spitting the stub into a waste basket. From another, smaller box he took out a long safety match and struck it into life along the smooth surface of a Cub Creek river rock.

McGee fired up the cigar while reaching down to the bottom drawer on the left side of the desk. He knew what he would find there—a bottle of Geo. A. Dickel's Cascade Tennessee Whiskey and two cut crystal glasses. Pouring two fingers into each and drawing deeply on the cigar, McGee blew a ring of blue smoke. He wiped his face to clear his eyes, lifted his glass, and saluted its twin. "Here's to you, old friend, one last time." The sipping whiskey went down smooth and easy.

All right, then. McGee unfolded his bone-handled pocketknife and cut away the tape holding the envelope to the box. He slit it open and removed a single sheet of stationery.

Ben's message, in his loopy handwriting, was short and to the point:

Dear Ros,

If you are reading this, then I am dead. This means that you are the last one, the last man standing.

He doesn't know, Ros. He doesn't know anything.

It's all in here. I trust you. You decide . . . .

Your friend,

Benjamin Gordon Waterman

Oh, my God, thought McGee, the awful implications of Ben's message becoming clear in his mind. *Jesus, spare me this.* With trembling hands, Ben stood, sliced through the yellowed tape, lifted the lid, and opened the box fearing, yet knowing, what he would find there.

PART I

THE MURDER

Chapter 1

North Wilkesboro, North Carolina, Thursday, July 5, 1900

Hazel "Tink" Beasley awoke at eight to pounding on the front door. Tink was not a particularly modest woman and favored sleeping in the nude, especially during sultry summer nights when even the slightest breath of cooling breeze could bring blessed relief. Clutching the bedsheets to her chest, she reached across Roscoe McGee's still slumbering figure, checked the clock on his bedside table, and groaned.

"Ros!" she whispered, shaking him by the shoulders, "Wake up! There's somebody at the door!"

McGee's small but tidy apartment was squeezed into a larger space on the third floor of the Trogdon Opera House at the corner of 5th and D streets in the newly established town of North Wilkesboro. McGee had configured things to accommodate the office and printing press for his newspaper, *The Lost Province*, with separate living quarters in the rear. A smart and successful entrepreneur, McGee also kept a thriving business on the floor below. McGee's Emporium was a miscellany of saloon, chop house, dance hall, bookshop, tobacco and liquor store, and six-chair barbershop with shoeshine stand.

The pounding grew louder.

"Just a goddamned minute!" McGee shouted, hastily pulling on pants, shirt, and suspenders. "I'm coming!"

The pair were sleeping late. After attending the fireworks their peace had been disturbed by a racket coming from down near the river. A blast from Old Sam had summoned the fire brigade to the tannery, and McGee had rushed to investigate the commotion, hunting news.

"Close the door behind you!" hissed Tink.

Tink Beasley was an interesting woman. Years earlier she had married an ugly man with good prospects. Her husband owned a funeral home and a casket factory, but soon proved to be better at embalming than matrimony. Violent when drunk, he would turn on Tink. During one of his more serious attacks, and fed up, Tink reached under their bed, pulled out a double-barreled carriage gun, and shot him dead through the heart. *Self-defense*, Sheriff Poindexter agreed, aware of the man's intemperate proclivities. And so widow Beasley inherited a thriving business, which she sold, and a sizeable estate, including a small, paid-for house a few doors down D Street.

Bored, educated, liberated, and intrigued by the newspaper business, Tink had responded to an advertisement in *The Lost Province* for a job as McGee's copyeditor, jack-of-all trades assistant, and sometimes reporter. McGee, not unmindful of the widow's obvious charms, hired her on the spot. The rest, of course, was predictable, with Tink still residing in her own home, but a frequent overnight guest on the third floor of the opera house. There was no talk of marriage. McGee never proposed, and Tink never suggested it. The town soon shrugged off the arrangement.

McGee stumbled to the door and there stood his friend Oliver "Olly" Overby, about to deliver another knock. Overby owned a photography studio just down 5th Street and regularly provided halftone pictures for *The Lost Province*.

"What?!" shouted McGee, stepping into the hallway and closing the door behind him. Overby looked McGee up and down, focusing on his bare feet. "Sorry to disturb you, R.E., but I have news."

"What's up?"

"Well, Crip Goins just rode over, said Redbone had a job for me. Told me to grab my Kodak and get on over to the iron bridge lickety-split."

Jimmy "Redbone" Poindexter was sheriff of Wilkes County. Cobey "Crip" Goins was his deputy, whose halting limp came courtesy of a sawmill accident. McGee often observed that *ol' Crip stumbles around like a three-legged dog.*

"I'm supposed to get on over there and meet up at the river. I thought you might like to know."

McGee stroked his chin and thought about that. "Thanks for the tip," said McGee, reaching into his pocket. *Empty.* "Wait here."

McGee disappeared into the apartment and quickly returned nattily dressed, with shoes on his feet and money in his hand. McGee was a slim, dapper man of medium height, whose friendly face was accented with a parted pencil moustache and jet-black hair slicked back from a prominent widow's peak. He saw irony and humor in most things, and his nasal laugh sounded something like *naarh, naarh, naarh!*

"Here's five dollars, Olly. You know the deal. I don't know what's going on, but I want copies of whatever pictures you take over there. And I want them today. Whatever Redbone gets, I get."

"Understood, boss," said Overby, smiling and taking the money. "Whatever Redbone gets, you get."

"Listen, Olly. You'll get there quicker if I take you. Go downstairs and tell Sammy to get Rex and the Phaeton ready to go. I'll be along directly." Rex was McGee's Cleveland Bay gelding, the Phaeton, his magnificent, gleaming black carriage sporting four oversized yellow wheels.

"Got it, see you down there."

McGee entered the apartment, combed back his thinning hair, gave Tink a peck on the cheek, and hurried out the door, eager to see what trouble awaited down at the Yadkin River.

W

Riding high in the Phaeton, the men raced down to the iron bridge at Mulberry Fields near the confluence of the Yadkin and Reddies rivers.

"Whoa!" shouted McGee, pulling back on the reins. "What's going on down there?" Below the bridge on the north side of the river a group of dismounted men were milling about. As McGee and Overby climbed from the carriage Sheriff Poindexter walked slowly up to meet them.

"Overby," he nodded, not offering to shake hands. "Took you long enough." Pointing to McGee, Poindexter, arms akimbo, shifted his chaw with his tongue, spat tobacco juice, and said, "What the hell 'you doin' here, McGee?"

"Overby here needed a ride."

Shaking his head, Poindexter replied, "You, Overby, bring your stuff and come with me. McGee, you go on now. Nothin' here concerns you."

Overby retrieved his prized Kodak flat-folding camera and tripod from the rear seat of the Phaeton. "Thanks for the ride, R.E. See you later."

McGee, looking first at Overby and then to the Sheriff, said, "You'll need a ride back. I'll wait for you at the hotel." As Overby and Poindexter walked away, McGee snapped the reins, got the Phaeton going, crossed the Yadkin, and headed up the hill to the Schumann Hotel in Wilkesboro.

W

The Schumann Hotel was an attractive red brick building located on the courthouse square, just south of the Finley Law Office. The three-story structure featured several retail businesses on the ground level and a second-story wraparound porch. Like the tannery, the hotel was owned by Jakob Schumann, and visiting lawyers and businessmen found the food and lodgings most agreeable.

McGee stopped the Phaeton, tethered the horse, and walked into the lobby. Wiping her hands on a towel, Jewel Ponder, the Black housemaid, greeted him.

"Mornin', Mistah McGee," she said, her normally cheerful voice soft and trembling. "Nice surprise to see you over here."

"Good to see you, too, Jewel." He noticed her quivering hands, stricken expression, halting demeanor. "What's wrong? Trouble?"

Jewel clasped her hands to stop them shaking and looked away. "I best go get Miz Claire Elise," she decided, turning and walking back into the kitchen. Soon hotel manager Claire Elise Montgomery appeared, uneasy and unable to meet McGee's inquiring gaze.

"Mrs. Montgomery," he began. "What's wrong?"

Again, she looked away. Wiping her eyes with her handkerchief, Claire Elise said, "I . . . I am afraid there has been some trouble, Mr. McGee." She spoke quietly, but precisely, in her native British accent.

"Come, let's sit down," McGee replied, leading her to the dining area off the lobby. Morning sunlight poured through the windows. "Please, tell me about it."

Seated, Claire Elise looked up. "Sheriff Poindexter has already been here. I told him all I know. He told me not to talk about it. And you . . . you're a newspaperman."

"Mrs. Montgomery," said McGee, reaching to take her hands. "You're right, I am in the news business. But that means I hear things, see things. Maybe I can be of some help? You and I are friends. Tell me, and I promise that what you say will go no further unless Redbone allows it."

"I have your word?"

"You have it."

She began slowly, searching for the right words, arranging things

in her mind. *She needs to do this*, thought McGee. *She needs to tell it
. . . again, out loud.*

"Well, I guess it all began yesterday afternoon, down at the
fairgrounds. Mr. Schumann came up and told me that his daughter Leah
was celebrating her sixteenth birthday—yesterday—and he wanted to
organize a party for her and some friends. She wanted to have a *grown-up*
slumber party at the hotel. He apologized for the late notice and asked
me if I could arrange it.

"Well, we had no guests booked into the hotel, you know, no court
during the summer and no tannery visitors, so I said of course. He said
that he would bring Leah and her friends over to the hotel after the
fireworks, and that Jewel and I could chaperone.

"Then later I saw his elder daughter, Rachel. She said that she and
a friend of hers wanted to help with the party, and I said fine. She told
me that she had asked Virgil Wade to bring over her horse and another
from the tannery stable to the livery behind the hotel. She and her friend
wanted to ride up the Reddies River this morning to see the Flume."

She stopped, rose, fanned her face. "I could use a glass of sweet tea.
Would you like some?"

"That would be very nice."

Claire Elise disappeared into the kitchen and returned with a
tray bearing a pitcher of iced tea and two glasses. *Ice. In July*, McGee
marveled. She poured, drank deeply, and with a sigh continued.

"So, I left right away to get back to the hotel and began preparing
for the party. I was busy baking the cake, and Jewel made the beds and
set things up here in the dining room. She said that Virgil had arrived
earlier with the horses and was planning to spend the night in the livery,
to take care of the horses and get them ready for the ride this morning.
That was fine with me. He helps out around the stable and often sleeps
over on a cot in one of the horse stalls.

"Well, about ten o'clock, after the fireworks, Mr. Schumann arrived
with Rachel and her friend and a carriage full of chattering girls." She
paused, looked into the distance. "They were so happy."

"What then?" McGee asked, encouraging her.

"The party was a great success, brilliant. Birthday cake, candles, ice
cream, singing, laughing. About eleven-thirty I suggested that it was
bedtime and sent them all off. Jewel and I walked them to their rooms
and tucked them in.

"Rachel and her friend Eloise said that they were also ready to retire since they wanted to get an early start in the morning. I reminded Rachel that Jewel and I would be just downstairs in case they needed anything. I, in my room off the kitchen, and Jewel in her quarters downstairs in the basement.

"About seven o'clock this morning, Jewel and I were in the kitchen making breakfast. Eloise appeared, still in her nightclothes. She asked if I had seen Rachel. I said, 'No, why?'

"Eloise was plainly concerned. She said that sometime in the middle of the night she was awakened by movement in their room. She saw Rachel, dressed in riding gear, moving toward the door. Eloise asked her what she was doing. Rachel said that she had trouble sleeping, heard noise down the hall, and was going to check on the girls. She asked her why she was fully dressed, and Rachel replied that she thought she would also check on the horses to make sure that Virgil Wade had properly fed and watered them. I assume that Rachel was unaware that Virgil was sleeping over.

"Eloise said she was sleepy and went back to bed as Rachel left the room, wrapping herself in a quilt she brought over with her. I thought this was odd given how warm it was but thought little more of it."

Claire Elise again paused, took another sip of tea. "So, I sent Jewel to look for Rachel. I thought perhaps she had joined Leah in her bed. Jewel soon reported that Rachel was not to be found in any of the girls' rooms. I myself then searched the hotel but could find no sign of Rachel.

"I was beside myself with worry, didn't know what to do. So, I used the hotel telephone to call Sheriff Poindexter at his home." Looking up, she added, "He has a telephone, you know. For his . . . business. He answered right away, and I told him that Rachel Schumann was missing. He was concerned . . . said that he would be right over.

"Pretty soon the sheriff and Cobey Goins from the jail arrived. They searched the premises and the livery stable and confirmed that Rachel was missing, as were her horse and riding tack. Virgil Wade was also not to be found. The sheriff then spoke to Jewel and me, Eloise, and the rest of the girls. Together we all confirmed the story I've just told you."

Claire Elise paused a moment, then continued. "The sheriff asked to borrow the hotel telephone. He called Schumann Village to ask Mr. Schumann if Rachel had perhaps returned home for some reason during the night. Mr. Schumann was naturally alarmed and went to check Rachel's room. He confirmed that Rachel was not there. Sheriff Poindexter assured

Mr. Schumann that he had matters well in hand and would telephone him as soon as Rachel was located. He told Mr. Schumann to stay put and asked if he might send a carriage over to return Eloise and the girls to Schumann Village. He did, and they left about twenty minutes ago."

Tears again. Composing herself, Claire Elise continued. "Sheriff Poindexter was very . . . professional. He asked if I could provide something, clothing or something like that, that would have Rachel's scent. I sent Jewel upstairs to fetch the pillowcase from Rachel's bed and gave it to him.

"Mr. Poindexter took the pillowcase, told me not to worry, that he would find Rachel. As he was leaving, he told me not to speak of this to anyone. About ten minutes later I heard several horses and barking bloodhounds from over near the jail." She then began sobbing uncontrollably. "Poor Rachel! What has become of her, Mr. McGee? What has happened to that poor girl?"

McGee reached to comfort her but was interrupted by the clatter of the entrance door opening. Claire Elise and McGee stood as Olly Overby strode into the lobby, sweating and clumsily carrying his precious camera by its strap in one hand, the ungainly tripod in the other.

W

"Whiskey, please," whispered Overby as he walked up to the hotel reception, his face as white as Rachel's pillowcase.

"My God, Overby," cried McGee, "It's ten o'clock in the morning!"

"Please, a whiskey," Overby repeated, cradling his face in his hands and wiping away the sweat. Claire Elise moved toward the bar behind the reception desk, but McGee gently stopped her with his hand. "I'll get it."

McGee poured a shot, and Overby knocked it back. "Another, please." McGee obliged.

"What's going on, Olly?"

Shaking his head, Overby solemnly began, "Rachel Schumann is—"

"Yes," interrupted McGee. "She's gone missing, we know. Redbone rounded up a bunch of boys and got out the dogs. Mrs. Montgomery heard them ride off a little while ago."

"Surely they will find her!" cried Claire Elise.

Olly's eyes dropped to the floor, and it was a moment before he spoke. "I'm sure they will, Mrs. Montgomery," was all he said. Overby looked to McGee. "R.E., I need to get back to the shop. I got work to do."

McGee nodded. "Let's go then." Placing his hands on Claire Elise's shoulders, he said gently, "Try not to worry, Mrs. Montgomery. Everything will be all right. You'll see."

Dropping her head to her chest, Claire Elise wept as Olly and McGee left the hotel, climbed into the Phaeton, and drove away toward the river and the iron bridge.

For a while they rode in silence. Overby stared straight ahead, and McGee did not press him. As they approached the iron bridge, they could see Sheriff Poindexter and his crew still down by the riverbank. McGee moved to draw in the reins.

"Don't stop, R.E.," commanded Olly. "Do not stop here. Just keep on going." McGee snapped the reins, Rex's hooves clattering across the bridge and back to North Wilkesboro.

Finally, Olly spoke again, shaking his head. "The dogs. The dogs, R.E. The dogs are not looking for Rachel. They already found her."

"What?" asked McGee, eyes widening.

Olly again buried his face in his hands, looked up. "Rachel Schumann is *dead*. Her body is a-layin' on that flat by the river with a knife through her heart."

McGee dropped the reins. "What are you talking about?"

"She's dead, sure enough, R.E. Cold as marble. I saw it for myself. Doc Burleson showed me what photographs to take." Noah Burleson was a doctor and part-time county coroner in Wilkesboro. "Redbone says I'm to get those photos to him and Burleson PDQ."

"Well," said McGee, "If the dogs are not looking for Rachel Schumann, then who in the hell are they looking for? What about the pillowcase?"

Olly turned to face McGee. "What pillowcase?" McGee explained. Waving his hand, Olly continued. "Well, that must be how they found her down by the river. But now they're trying to tree a different critter." He paused. "R.E., what I'm about to tell you, well, it can never get back to me. Redbone told me to keep my pie hole shut. And you know Redbone. He can be rough as a cob if you cross him. Far as I know even ol' man Schumann doesn't know yet. It'll all come out pretty soon anyway, but I need your word on this."

McGee slowly nodded agreement. *The scoop of the decade, and I'm all clammed up.*

"Crip and the boys and the dogs are looking for Virgil Wade, R.E., and their blood is up."

"Virgil Wade!" McGee exclaimed. "What does Virgil Wade have to do with this? He's just a boy!"

"Well, boy or not, that high-yeller no-account killed her! Her body . . . well, it looks like he first beat the shit out of her. And then he stabbed her to death. His skinning knife, buried to the hilt in her chest. It had his initials on it! A *V* and a *W* carved on top of each other on the handle, formed a kinda diamond in the middle. No doubt about it. One of the boys down by the river works at the tannery and says that's the knife Virgil Wade uses skinning hides."

McGee thought about that, trying to absorb all he had just heard. "So, what else, Olly? What else did you see?"

"Well, one thing I didn't see was Rachel's horse."

"Her horse? What's that got to do with anything?"

"Well, when the dogs found Rachel, she was all dressed out in riding britches. We all wondered about that. Redbone, he said he talked to Mrs. Montgomery up at the hotel. Said the Wade boy was stablin' her horse at the livery behind the hotel, was sleepin' there last night. Seems Rachel got up in the middle of the night, got dressed, and went down to check on her horse. She and that friend of hers were going riding up the Reddies this morning early.

"Well, anyways, Redbone, he thinks that Rachel didn't know about Wade sleeping over and surprised him in the stable. Pretty girl like that, he took his shot and kidnapped her, bound her up, saddled her horse, and took her down to the river. Redbone figures he maybe raped her there, murdered her, and then skedaddled away on her horse. Stole it!" Shaking his head, Olly mumbled, "This is just going to kill ol' man Schumann and his wife. Ain't nobody done more for Wilkes, hired more men, paid them good, too. It's a goddamned shame is what it is."

"What else did you see, Olly?"

"Well, I did notice there was a bottle of whiskey down beside the body."

"*Whiskey!* Why, Virgil Wade can't be more than fifteen, sixteen years old. Moonshine, maybe, but where would he get whiskey like that?"

"Redbone figures he stole it."

McGee remembered an empty space on the liquor rack behind the reception desk. Recalling his talk with Claire Elise, McGee then asked, "Anything else down there, Olly? Maybe something like a blanket, or a quilt?"

Olly, impressed, said, "How'd you know about that? No matter.

Well, yeah. There was a fancy quilt there, all laid out like a picnic or something. Rachel's body was a'layin' on it, face up to the sky, eyes wide open." Olly shook his head and shuddered. "You should'a seen her face, R.E. Damn, what a sight!"

Drawing up to the photography studio, McGee reined in his horse. Olly stepped down from the Phaeton, retrieved his gear, and said, "Gotta go, R.E., Redbone is waitin'. And Burleson wants me back at his place to take pictures of the body . . . for the coroner's report."

McGee looked him square in the eye. "Remember—"

Olly smiled and winked. "I know, I know. What Redbone gets, you get."

Chapter 2

State Capitol, Raleigh, North Carolina, Thursday, July 5, 1900

North Carolina Governor Robert Rousseau "Cotton Bob" Maxwell sat back in his big leather chair, deep in thought. Seated across from him, his lawyer friend, US Congressman George Henry White, waited patiently.

Maxwell was a tall, heavyset bull of a man whose stocky frame was crowned by an unruly mop of hair the color of clotted cream. More rugged than handsome, his face was defined by a prominent nose, full lips, and animated bushy eyebrows that lifted when surprised, danced when amused, and tightened when vexed.

His nickname came courtesy of a professor early in Maxwell's first year at The Citadel in Charleston. "Who among you can state the *casus belli* of The First Barbary War of 1801?" he asked, his eyes moving over the nervous cohort of knobs whose names were as yet unknown to him. "What about, ah . . . you," he said, pointing at Maxwell. "Yes, you, Cotton, step up here and enlighten us." The cognomen stuck.

Finally, Maxwell spoke. "George, I appreciate your coming by. But are you sure I can't change your mind?"

"No, sir, 'fraid not. The handwriting is on the wall. I won't be running for re-election this fall, and I wanted to let you know."

"So, it's as bad as all that?"

"It appears so," replied White.

Maxwell fiddled with his pipe, struck a match, got it going. Rising from his chair he walked over to the big window overlooking the green and leafy capitol square and Salisbury Street beyond. The North Carolina

State Capitol, built of locally quarried granite, was a fine, extravagant example of Greek Revival public architecture that housed all branches of state government, including the governor's office.

"Give it to me one more time, George. Paint me a picture."

W

Born in Rosindale, North Carolina, George Henry White was the son of a free Black farmer; his mother Mary was born a slave. Graduating from Howard University in 1877, White returned to a state utterly devastated by defeat on the battlefield and occupied by federal troops. White, like many other newly enfranchised Blacks in the South, became a champion for equal rights and launched a career in politics in the legendary *Black Second,* a gerrymandered congressional district with a large Black majority. Heavy Black voter registration and turnout elected White as the only Black member of the United States Congress in 1896 and then again in 1898. Staunch Republicans, Maxwell and White were strong political allies.

"You know all this, Judge," frowned White, using the moniker Maxwell preferred.

"Humor me, George," replied Maxwell, staring out the window. "I do so love to hear it."

"Well," White began, "after the Democrats got back in by a whisker in '92, we could see that the combined vote of the Populists and the Republicans was bigger than the Democrats. So, we got to talking to folks about joining up next time. *Fusion* politics, people called it. Sure enough, when we teamed up in '94, we beat those sorry Democrats like a drum. We got you elected to the supreme court, 'swept the General Assembly, ran the table. A real ass-whupping to be sure."

Maxwell nodded, smiling. "And next?"

"Well, hell, Judge," White continued, "'Next was '96, bigger and better than '94. Fused again. Kept the General Assembly, got me elected to Congress. Got you elected governor!"

"And then," muttered Maxwell, turning to face White.

"Well, Judge, things were pretty good for a while, you got some good things done. And we made some progress for Black folks in Washington. And then things began to turn sour."

"And then things began to turn sour," repeated Maxwell, moving back to his desk. His pipe had gone out, so he fiddled with it again, relit it, blowing fragrant smoke toward the ceiling. "Go on."

"Well, that's when your *friend* Charles Brantley Aycock and that son-of-a-bitch Furnifold Simmons . . . excuse my French, Judge . . . got together and dreamed up their so-called *White Supremacy* strategy for '98. Aycock has had his eyes on your chair for years, wants it bad, and means to have it.

"Simmons and his kind started riling up White people, talking about *nigger* rule and *nigger* domination, *nigger* this and *nigger* that. Got the Red Shirts and the Klan to back them up, riding around in robes and hoods, burning crosses, lynching people, telling Black folks that if they tried to vote in '98 they would torch their houses and rape their women."

"I know," Maxwell nodded sadly. "I tried to tell our Populist friends to hold fast, that we could beat them again if we would just stick together. But they got scared. And then they *ran* scared, trying to 'out-nigger' the Democrats." Looking up, he added, "No offense intended."

"None taken, Judge. You're right. Our common front blew itself up in '98, and Democrats swept the state, claimed that North Carolina had at last been 'redeemed'. I was able to squeak by, got re-elected in a four-way race. But Simmons turned out to be a damned political genius, I'll give him that. And once they took over the legislature, they started to undo everything."

"And don't forget Wilmington," said Maxwell.

"How could I forget Wilmington?" said White.

In 1898, the port city of Wilmington was North Carolina's largest, with a majority-Black population. On Election Day, thanks to strong-arm tactics by Democrats and the Red Shirts, Democrats in Wilmington won the city by more than six thousand votes as terrified Black voters stayed away from the polls. Members of the biracial city government, however, had not been up for re-election in 1898. Two days later, not content with stealing the election, White supremacist Democrats led a mob of more than two thousand armed insurgents in a bloody *coup d'etat* that torched Black homes and businesses, murdered dozens of Black citizens, and overthrew the duly elected local government, replacing it with an all-White Democratic city council and mayor. Appeals to President McKinley for federal intervention proved futile. More than two thousand Black citizens, fearing for their lives, fled permanently.

"Bad as it was, Judge," continued White, "It could have been a whole lot worse if you hadn't sent Ben Waterman down there. A lot of folks in Wilmington, Black and White, owe their lives to Ben's work getting them out of town in time."

Maxwell thought about this. "So, what's next, George?" he asked, leaning forward. "How do you see things?"

White sat back, laughed, and said, "Why, Judge, like you always say, 'It's as plain as a rat turd in a sugar bowl.' You can't run again. And me, well, let me put it this way. Black registration in North Carolina in 1896, when you were elected, was over one hundred and twenty-five thousand and most everybody turned out to vote. I talked to Albi Tourgee yesterday, and he says today it's certainly less than ten thousand and falling every day. Even in Black Second, I can't make the numbers work. Old Jim Crow has done me in."

The reference was to Albion W. Tourgee, an Ohio-born transplant (*"Carpetbagger!"* sneered Democrats), a former Reconstruction-era superior court judge from Greensboro who was a pioneer equal rights activist and fearless crusader against the Ku Klux Klan.

"So, the way I see it, Judge, you and I, well, we are political dead men walking. And there is no help coming from the federals. *Plessy v. Ferguson* settled that."

Tourgee had taken a case to the United States Supreme Court challenging a Louisiana statute requiring railroads "to provide equal but separate accommodations for the White and colored races" on passenger trains. He represented Homer Plessy, an *octoroon* resident of New Orleans, who had firmly refused to move to a *colored* car.

He lost. The Supreme Court affirmed state-mandated segregation under the separate-but-equal doctrine that would thwart the progress of the Black race in America for decades.

"The last straw, Judge, is the Suffrage Amendment. The vote is coming up next month, and it's sure to pass. The poll tax and the literacy test will kill the Black vote."

Riding high after their 1898 landslide, Democrats in the General Assembly had passed a constitutional Suffrage Amendment designed and intended to curb, if not eliminate, Black voting. To soften the blow to their White base, the amendment cleverly and cynically included a grandfather clause waiving the literacy requirement for any illiterate person whose ancestor had been a registered voter before 1867—prior to federal Reconstruction mandates.

"So, it's like this. Election Day in November will be a train wreck for Republicans. I can't beat Claude Kitchin, so I won't try. The Suffrage

Amendment will pass. Aycock will take over after you're gone in January. And then everything that you and I have worked so hard for will be thrown on the trash heap. The Republican Party in this state is dead, Judge. Jim Crow, Furnifold Simmons, and the Democrats have murdered it and will hang its carcass from a tree for all to witness for a hundred years.

"There is no future for me here, Judge. I'm done. I'll go back to Washington, deliver my swan song to the House, and start new."

The two men shook hands across the desk. Maxwell looked White in the eye and said, "Goodbye, George. Thank you for your friendship. I'm sorry. I'm sorry for all of it. Good luck to you."

Without a word, White nodded, retrieved his hat from the wall hook, and with a last glance backward and with a wry smile, he departed.

W

Deep in thought and feeling in his bones each of his sixty-five years, Maxwell rose and again gazed out the window, flooded by memories.

In 1861, surrounded by secessionist states, North Carolina joined the Confederate States of America, the last state to do so. Maxwell, like most in Wilkes, had opposed secession. Compared to wealthy plantations in the eastern part of the state, the mountainous counties of western North Carolina had relatively few slaves, and pro-Union sentiment was strong. But once the decision was made, Maxwell, like most young men in Wilkes, felt duty-bound to do his part. He was recruited by Major James B. Gordon, a Wilkes native and captain of the 1st North Carolina Cavalry Regiment under legendary Confederate General J.E.B. Stuart.

Gordon was promoted to brigadier general commanding the 1st North Carolina Cavalry Brigade, and Maxwell had risen to the rank of captain. On May 11, 1864, General Stuart was killed at the Battle of Yellow Tavern, and Gordon assumed command of Confederate cavalry units defending Richmond. The next day Gordon himself was mortally wounded at the Battle of Meadow Bridge, just north of the city.

During the battle, Maxwell's horse was shot from under him. He survived, but less than a quarter of Wilkes' soldiers sent off to war returned, many disabled and disfigured. After Appomattox, Maxwell turned his attention to post-war politics, determined to help repair the broken spirit of a vanquished state. Wilkes County emerged from the conflict a committed Republican stronghold.

The disenfranchisement of many Confederate veterans and the rise of Black voter registration, propelled by Reconstruction Amendments to the United States Constitution, created political opportunity, and Maxwell moved to take advantage, guided by Lincoln's appeal "to the better angels of our nature." Blacks registered and turned out to vote in droves, and many were elected across the state.

But the progress would not last. In 1870, Democrats regained control of state government and immediately began to reverse many Reconstruction-era reforms. Six years later, Maxwell, running as a Republican, was nevertheless elected to an eight-year term as superior court judge in Wilkes, and was re-elected in 1884 and 1892.

In the 1880s, much of the nation, including North Carolina, was suffering a severe economic depression that hit small farmers hard. Their misery was compounded by the Panic of 1893. The national Farmers Alliance was formed to promote agricultural and monetary reforms, and in North Carolina the movement gave rise to a new political party, the Populists.

Democrats were able to prevail statewide in three-way races, but in 1892 could only claim a plurality of votes, leading to a Fusion of Populists and Republicans, an uneasy marriage of convenience that swept the state in 1894 and again in 1896.

Maxwell was deeply disturbed by his conversation with George White. *What kind of state are we that has no room for George White in it?* he mused. *So much accomplished. So much left to do. It seemed for a time that we could escape our past, that we held the future in the palm of our hand. North Carolina could have led the building of a truly New South, free, democratic, and cleansed of bigotry, prejudice, and hatred. For a glorious moment, it all seemed possible. And now, here we are at the abyss, sure to fall once again into darkness. And I am helpless to prevent it. What could I have done better, sooner?*

He walked to the large oak credenza behind his desk, flanked on either side by the flags of the United States and the State of North Carolina. Displayed on a small wooden rack were his officer's sword and scabbard. Maxwell picked up the weapon, its steel blade, polished to a mirror finish, curved and gleaming, a menacing killing machine unmarred by rust or tarnish. Engraved on its blade were the words, *1st North Carolina Cavalry Brigade Capt. R.R. Maxwell.* Beside the display was the brigade's tri-folded ceremonial colors, a gift from General Gordon's beloved sister.

What must someone like George White think, walking in here and seeing these trophies so proudly on display? Maxwell thought. Enough. A powerful truth overcame him. For North Carolina to fight the War was its inescapable destiny. To lose it, a moral necessity.

Maxwell picked up the scabbard and sheathed the sword one final time. Cradling the weapon in his arms, he retrieved the colors and walked to his closet, opened the doors, and gently placed the objects inside. *The last casualties*, he thought, closing the doors. *It's over, behind me now. I will do all that I can for as long as I can.*

Straightening, returning to the present, Maxwell bellowed, "Peggy! Please go get Ben for me! I need to see him."

The pretty face of Imogene Alexander, Maxwell's secretary, appeared through a crack in his office door. She was a fixture in Maxwell's office, and everyone called her Peggy.

"Yes, sir, right away," she said and went to fetch Benjamin Gordon Waterman, Maxwell's chief of staff, chief legal officer, and political fixer.

Chapter 3

July in Raleigh is hot. Always. Ben Waterman, daydreaming, reclined in his swivel chair, put his feet up on his desk, crossed his legs, and closed his eyes. In truth there was not much official business to attend to. The General Assembly had gone home to campaign. No one paid much attention anymore to Governor Maxwell, who would soon be retired and, with his Republican and Populist fellow travelers, run out of town by the Democrats.

His peaceful, late-afternoon dozing was interrupted by the urgent voice of Peggy Alexander. "Ben!" she cried, shaking his shoulder. "Wake up! Governor Maxwell wants to see you. Right now!"

Ben roused himself, unfolded his lanky frame, and ran his fingers through his headful of black hair. "Okay, Peggy, thanks." Picking up his notebook and pencil, Ben muttered, "I'll be right there."

Captain "Cotton Bob" Maxwell and his wounded runner, Thomas Sydney "Syd" Waterman, had been shipped by train, with other walking wounded, from Richmond back to North Carolina. Falling from his gut-shot blue roan and breaking his leg, Maxwell had lain helpless as a Yankee took deadly aim from point-blank range. Waterman leaped from his own horse onto the Yankee's back and wrestled him to the ground, taking the minie ball meant for Maxwell through his left arm as the terrified enemy scrambled away.

As the war drew to a close, Maxwell recovered and resumed his law practice in Wilkes. Waterman was not so fortunate. Doctors were able to save his arm, now but a withered and mostly useless appendage.

Before enlisting, Waterman had courted and married Martha Jane Flippin from nearby Surry County. He bought a run-down tobacco farm on a ridge above Tom's Creek with a fine view of Pilot Mountain. Waterman borrowed the money, and his father-in-law co-signed the note. Jane proved to be a frail and temperamental woman, constantly complaining of her ailments. Nevertheless, after Waterman's return, a son was born, named for Revolutionary War hero Colonel Benjamin Cleveland and the recently martyred Confederate General James B. Gordon.

The son thrived, but the farm did not. Several poor seasons left Waterman deep in debt and the farm mortgaged to the hilt. On a cold February morning in 1875, Waterman was in the barn with his young son Ben, the two wrestling to shoe a stubborn and moody mare.

"Goddammit!" shouted Waterman, who knelt, cursed again, spat tobacco juice, and jerked hard with his good right arm on the mare's hind leg. The mare snorted and kicked back sharply, striking Waterman square in the temple and killing him instantly.

Waterman's funeral and CSA tombstone consumed the last of the cash money. Spring came and went with no crops planted, and Jane suffered a nervous breakdown. By the fall, it was over. The bank foreclosed on the farm and a local land shark bought it for a song. Soon the sheriff served Jane with an eviction notice. Worse, Jane's parents lost their own home and her father's barber shop to pay Waterman's debts. There was no choice. The family committed Jane to Dix Hill, the state mental hospital in Raleigh, where she died three years later.

Word of the family crisis reached Maxwell in Wilkesboro. Mindful of his debt to Syd Waterman, Maxwell brought the orphan to Wilkesboro, and with his wife raised him, along with their own three daughters, as his own. Maxwell sent Ben to study at Chapel Hill. Early in the fall semester of his senior year, he was approached by Dr. James Burton, a visiting faculty member from Oxford University, with an astonishing proposition.

"Your Latin professor, Dean Russell, informs me that you are an excellent student, Waterman," Burton began, steepling his fingers as he sat in his comfortable office in South Building. "He also tells me that you intend to study law, to become a lawyer here in North Carolina."

"That's right, sir," Ben replied. "My aim is to read law under my mentor Robert Maxwell in Wilkes County after I graduate."

"Very good, Waterman, a reasonable plan," nodded Burton. "Russell thinks that you have great promise and could benefit from a . . . broader . . . exposure to the legal world beyond North Carolina. I have spoken to Russell about you, reviewed your academic record here, read some of your papers, and I am inclined to agree. Therefore, I have an idea that may appeal to you."

"Yes, sir?"

"My sabbatical here expires at the end of the current semester, and my family and I will return to England soon after the Christmas holidays. At Oxford I hold the professorship of jurisprudence. I will be working on a treatise on comparative international law, focusing on historical antecedents of English Common Law and civil law systems in France and Germany.

"Oxford has provided me with funds to engage a clerk, a research assistant, if you will. Russell thinks that you might be a good candidate, that a bright young American like you might bring a new, refreshing perspective to my work.

"You will not, of course, be enrolled as an Oxford student, but you will have the opportunity to attend lectures in law there. You will also have access to our fine library. Dean Russell has assured me that your service with me will earn full academic credit here. And your time at Oxford would doubtless be excellent preparation for your studies with Mr. Maxwell." He paused, studying Ben's face. "So, Waterman, there it is. What say you?"

Stunned, Ben blurted, "Sir, are you serious? How would it work?"

"Well, you would sail with my family and me to England. We have a large home in Oxford, and you could lodge with us there. I have already booked springtime lectures at the University of Freiburg and at the Sorbonne in Paris. You would, of course, accompany me on these excursions, so some travel would be involved."

Eyes widening, Ben said, "I am . . . most honored that you would consider me, Dr. Burton, but I am afraid that I cannot accept. I fear I lack the means—"

Burton interrupted. "Don't worry about that. As I said, funds are in place. It's a meager stipend, but I think sufficient for your needs. You would only need to cover your transportation costs. Can you manage that, Waterman?"

"I . . . I would have to ask Mr. Maxwell."

"Yes, do that, please. Right away. I would have an answer, if you please, at your earliest convenience. Presuming that the financial details can be worked out, would you accept?"

Grinning from ear to ear, Ben replied, *"Res ipsa loquitur,* Professor Burton. I would be delighted."

"Then it's settled," said Burton, with a dismissive wave. "Go now. Talk to Maxwell. I'm sure he will see things my way."

And he did. Maxwell immediately understood the opportunity and wired funds to cover Ben's journey.

W

Soon after the New Year, Ben and the Burtons stepped off their train in New York City and embarked on a ship bound for Liverpool. Having never ventured beyond North Carolina, Ben celebrated his twenty-first birthday in the middle of the North Atlantic with a glass of champagne and the captain's hearty best wishes aboard the White Star Line *SS Britannic.*

Dr. Burton was as good as his word. During his time at Oxford, Ben was exposed to some of the finest legal minds in the English-speaking world. Under Burton's mentorship he read voraciously from the library, paid close attention to the lectures Burton recommended, and was meticulous in his research. His work was interesting and challenging, and Burton pronounced Ben's contributions "Excellent. Terse, precise, thorough."

Most rewarding were his occasional trips with Burton to the Inns of Court in London and his lecture tours to the Sorbonne and Freiburg. Ben marveled at previously unimaginable sights, incomprehensible languages, new and strange customs, and the often-flamboyant personalities that populated Burton's professional circle of friendship.

Ben missed home, but Maxwell proved a faithful and frequent correspondent. As Ben complained in a letter to the judge, experience in the university dining hall soon convinced him that boiled beef and cabbage could never replace fried chicken and collard greens.

Dr. Burton and his wife, Dorothy, treated Ben most kindly in their spacious and comfortable home in Oxford. Mrs. Burton, chair of the music faculty at nearby Lady Margaret Hall, a finishing school for young women, was charming, a talented pianist, and an accomplished educator. She managed the Burton household with a light touch but a keen eye for detail.

Evenings in the Burton dining room often included interesting guests and were memorable occasions, full of laughter, word games, witty banter, take-no-prisoners philosophical debates, and spirited political discussions, all enjoyed over fine food and superb wines. Many times, after dessert, the Burtons would entertain in the music room, Mrs. Burton at the piano and Dr. Burton, port wine glass in hand, serenading Schubert *Lieder* or silly songs from Gilbert and Sullivan in his fine baritone voice. The time passed very quickly.

And then, of course, there was the Burtons' daughter.

Her name was Julia.

Julia Charlotte Burton, an only child, was named after Julius Caesar's beloved daughter (her father's idea) and the German-born consort of the late-King George III (her mother's).

Julia's childhood was one of wealth and privilege. Yet, and perhaps despite the indulgence and infinite patience of her parents, the girl grew into a delightful, polite, and even-tempered young woman. Self-aware, but in no sense self-absorbed, Julia pursued her interests with independence and commitment. She was intelligent and focused on her studies, but carefree and charming in society.

Julia was a student of European art and painting at Lady Margaret Hall when her father was invited to spend a semester-long sabbatical in Chapel Hill. It would be the family's first visit to the New World, and Dr. Burton declared it a capital idea. In the summer of 1885, the family closed their home and eagerly embarked on their American adventure.

Ben had been introduced to Julia by the Burtons on the platform in Raleigh as they awaited their train to New York City in January. Ben's experience with the fairer sex had been limited to fleeting and surreptitious peeks of the female form in the Maxwells' house full of daughters and a few stolen kisses and clandestine fondlings with willing girls in Wilkesboro.

As he gently took Julia's hand in polite greeting, it was as if, for a moment, time stood still. Standing before him Ben saw only perfection. He would later be unable to describe any aspect of her clothing or anything she might have said to him or he to her. But he would never forget her smiling, oval face, her skin smooth and pure as cream, her hand small and delicate in his own, her voice soft as vellum in greeting. Her auburn hair, held back by combs of mother of pearl, fell in a riot of curls against her long, thin neck, and her astonishing, deep green eyes, set off by dark and full eyebrows, promised mischievous good humor.

Aboard the *Britannic* their acquaintance blossomed into friendship during long walks on the promenade deck. In Oxford, both were soon preoccupied with their work, Ben with Dr. Burton, Julia at Lady Margaret Hall. But evenings brought opportunity for more relaxed companionship, particularly those nights when the Burtons' social calendar required their presence elsewhere. Friendship deepened into romance, romance into passion, passion inevitably into intimacy.

Ben realized he was in love, and it seemed that Julia shared his passion. He began to think of the future. One evening near the end of his time in Oxford, Ben asked Julia to join him in the Burtons' drawing room, where he dropped to one knee, declared his love, and proposed marriage.

Julia, tears forming, took his hands and brought him to his feet. "Oh, Ben," she began, slowly shaking her head. "I am honored, truly I am. But surely you see that this is impossible."

Ben, eyes widening, blurted, "Impossible? But why, dear Julia? Surely you must love me, too? Surely—"

"Ben. Dear Ben," interrupted Julia softly, dropping his hands and turning away. "I do. I do . . . love you. You must never doubt that."

"Then come with me, back to America. Be my wife, Julia."

"I cannot, Ben. I . . . I cannot do that."

"But why, Julia? Tell me why."

"Your life is in America, Ben. And mine . . . well, mine is here, surely you see that. My life is art, painting," she continued, spreading her arms wide. "Everything you see on the walls of this house, everything you saw in the museums of Paris. I cannot leave all that behind."

"Then I will stay here!" Ben cried. "I will stay with you, and we will build a life together here!"

Taking his face in her hands, Julia whispered, "No, Ben. No. I know you, I know your ambitions, your dreams. You must return to America, Ben, you must realize that."

"Nothing is worth losing you, Julia! Nothing!" pleaded Ben.

"I fear the decision is already made, Ben."

"What do you mean, Julia?"

Grasping the arms of her chair, Julia explained. "My father asked to see me this morning. He and Mother must surely suspect how . . . how close we have become. They are immensely fond of you, Ben, and under different circumstances—"

"But—" interrupted Ben.

"Please, Ben. Let me finish." Composing herself, Julia continued. "Father realizes that I have my own work, my own goals. He has a friend, a professor, Rodolfo Scaglione, who teaches painting and art history at the University of Florence. Father has arranged an apprenticeship in Professor Scaglione's studio, beginning in the fall. He is prepared to do for me what Father has done for you here at Oxford, Ben. Please understand that I cannot refuse. This is not only something that I *must* do, Ben. It is something that I very much *want* to do."

Ben, defeated and helpless, could only nod.

"Ben, I will never forget you or our time together. You found me an innocent young girl and made me into . . . a woman. You taught me to love, Ben." She gently put her hand on Ben's chest. "Carry that with you, Ben. In your heart." Pulling Ben's hand to her chest, Julia whispered, "As I will carry you in mine."

Looking into her eyes, Ben said softly, "I love you, Julia. I always will."

Julia smiled gently, took his face in her hands, kissed him softly, and murmured through her tears, *"Sunt lacrimae rerum, et mentem mortalia tangunt."* Trembling, holding her close, Ben recalled the ancient words of the poet Virgil and whispered in her ear, "There are tears for things, which touch the hearts of mortal men."

And they parted.

Ben returned to Wilkes with a confused mind and a broken heart.

As planned, he read law under Maxwell, passed the bar, and later worked as the judge's law clerk. As Maxwell's attention turned to politics, Ben found he also had a knack for the game. Ben managed Maxwell's successful Fusionist campaigns for the North Carolina Supreme Court and later for governor. He proved his mettle during the Wilmington Massacre of 1898 when he courageously stood up to the insurgents there and arranged the safe evacuation of the city's deposed mayor and city council, an act of heroism that Maxwell and his followers would never forget.

Ben thought of himself as gangly and awkward, but in fact he was a handsome young man, tall, erect, serious, and with an unmistakable command presence that appealed to all who entered his orbit. Ben also came to very much enjoy and welcome the presence and comfort of women in his life. But he remained single. As Roscoe McGee would say, "There's been many a good dog put on him, but ain't 'nary a one treed him yet."

W

Ben, notebook and pencil in hand, entered Maxwell's office and took a seat. "What's up, Judge? Peggy said you wanted to see me."

"That's right, Ben. We need to talk."

Maxwell explained his conversation with George White and recounted White's bleak outlook for the election and beyond. "Me, I'll be fine. I'm going back to Wilkes. Retire, maybe. Maybe practice a little law now and then. But what about you, Ben?"

"'Tell you the truth, Judge, I haven't thought much about it. You have something in mind?"

Maxwell rose and paced the room. "Well, you're sure as hell done in Raleigh. No Democrat will come within ten miles of you, particularly after what you did down in Wilmington."

"Fair enough," nodded Ben.

"So, we're both done in politics. That's clear. And good goddamned riddance!" Maxwell boomed, slapping his desk. "So, what I was thinking was, what about you coming back to Wilkes with me? We could practice law together, maybe make some money. There's for damn sure been none in politics."

"So, just me and you, like always?" asked Ben, raising an eyebrow.

"Something like that," nodded Maxwell.

"Well—" Ben was about to respond, when Peggy Alexander stormed into the office, flustered and excited.

"Governor!" she cried. "Roscoe McGee is on the telephone from Wilkes. Says it's urgent!"

"McGee? Telephone? I didn't know McGee had a telephone."

"Well, I don't know about that. But he's got one now!" answered Peggy. "And he says to put you on the line right . . . well, right now!"

Maxwell stared at the ungainly wooden contraption hanging on the wall by his desk. *I will never get used to this infernal machine. Two people, hundreds of miles apart, jabbering away at a box full of wires like it was the most natural thing in the world.*

"All right, Peggy. Put him through in here. Ben, you stay put."

In a minute Peggy shouted from her desk, "He's on the line, sir!"

Maxwell hesitantly picked up the black earpiece, moved close to the box, and bellowed in a voice loud enough to carry to Wilkes, "All right, then, Ros! What's so goddamned important?"

Chapter 4

Colmar, German-Occupied Alsace, Friday, January 17, 1873

Moshe ben Itzhak walked slowly from his home and workshop in the *Rue des Tanneurs* up the *Place de l'Ancienne Douane* to the old customs house. Standing before the entrance to the *Koifhus,* he felt a powerful sense of dread. In his hand was an official summons, signed, stamped, and demanding his presence at this place, on this day, at this time.

Entering the building, Moshe asked for directions, and the clerk pointed down the hall. He knocked softly under a sign reading *Prefecture de Police.* "HEREIN!" came a guttural shout from within. Moshe entered cautiously and stood before the desk of what could only be a German policeman. The man ignored him, absorbed in the papers before him. Moshe waited. At last, the man lifted his eyes, looked squarely at Moshe, and demanded, *"Und? Was denn?"*

Perhaps he wants my name, thought Moshe.

Holding the summons out for inspection, Moshe replied, *"Je m'appel—"*

"Nein! Nein! Nein! Hier bist du im Deutschen Reich, und hier wird deutsch geredet!" "No! No! No! You are in the German Empire, and German is spoken here!"

Moshe obeyed as best he could, answering haltingly in the unfamiliar language. "I am Moshe ben Itzhak, and I have been summoned here."

Snatching the summons from Moshe's hands, the officer reviewed it, scowling.

"Moshe ben Itzhak. What sort of name is that?"

"I am . . . Jewish, sir. It is a Jewish name."

"Ah, that explains it." Reaching into a drawer, the prefect withdrew a printed form and presented it to Moshe. "Can you read that?"

Moshe looked at the document. "It . . . it is difficult for me."

"*Ach*! As I thought! I will explain it to you. Pay attention to me!" The prefect stood, stiff, as if about to salute, and read from the paper.

"*'By Universal Decree of Joseph II Habsburg, Holy Roman Emperor, dated 28th of August, 1787, in the 24th year of Our Roman Rule over the Hereditary Countries, it is hereby demanded that, beginning January 1, 1788, every Jewish head of household under Our jurisdiction shall adopt a Constant German Surname and, without exception, shall never change it in his or her lifetime.'*

"Do you understand what I have just read to you?"

"I understand the words, sir," answered Moshe. "But what has this to do with me? Emperor Joseph has been dead for many years. This document," Moshe pointed, "this decree was issued almost one hundred years ago."

"Silence! Not another word from you! Do you not know that your former Emperor Louis Napoleon stupidly started a war with Prussia in 1870? That Prussia and its German allies *crushed* the French like an egg!" he shouted, reaching out and triumphantly snapping his fist closed.

"We *occupied* Paris, *Gott sei Dank!* Have you forgotten the Treaty of Frankfurt? Alsace belongs to *Germany,* my Jewish friend, and you and your miserable Alsatian countrymen are all now *GERMANS,* fully subject to the authority of Otto von Bismarck, chancellor of the unified Empire of Germany!" He paused to catch his breath.

Drawing himself up to his full height, he resumed. "As prefecture of police in the City of Colmar, the power and dictates of the German Empire are exercised and enforced here through *ME!*" Pushing the official paper toward Moshe's face, he declared, "And that includes the Universal Decree of Joseph II, which has now been adopted in all German states!" He sat.

After a few moments of silence, Moshe timidly offered, "What is to be done?"

The prefect waved his arms in exasperation. "Why, your name, of course!" Looking at the summons, he sneered sarcastically, "Moshe ben Itzhak." Looking up at Moshe, he taunted, "Doesn't sound very *Germanic,* eh?"

Helpless, Moshe repeated, "What is to be done?"

"Change it, of course! You must change it!"

"Change it? To what? It is my name—"

Impatient, the prefect blurted, "The Decree requires a constant *German* surname. So that's what you shall have." Reaching into his desk drawer, he retrieved another official form. "You must choose a new name, today, here and now. And I will record it in the official census."

Slowly nodding, Moshe asked, "Do you have any . . . suggestions?"

Looking past Moshe out the window, the prefect paused. "Well, what about your occupation? Many of the Jews take their new name from what they do. So, what do you do?"

"I own a tannery here in Colmar, sir. In the *Rue des Tanneurs*."

"Tannery?" The prefect sneered, pulling a face. "Filthy business."

"It can be, sir," Moshe agreed. "But my family has been in the tanning and leather business for many generations."

"*Ledergerber,*" grimaced the Prefect, the German word for *leather tanner* slowly emerging from his mouth. "Nasty word. Who would want to go through life with a name like that? Think of your children!"

Moshe shrugged.

Looking down at the form, the prefect shook his head. "And it's *eleven letters long!* There's hardly enough room on the form for that. No, *Ledergerber* won't do." Thinking for a moment, the prefect then inquired, "So what do you do with the leather?"

"Some I sell to other artisans in the town. They make saddles, leather bags, things like that. But I am also a cobbler. The rest I use to makes shoes and boots."

The prefect clapped his hands. "So, you are a *shoe man!* Yes! That will work. "*Schumann!*" he exclaimed, repeating the German word. Picking up his pen, he scribbled on the form, selected the appropriate item from the rack on his desk, and with a flourish stamped the document.

At last smiling, the prefect asked, "Anything else, *Herr Schumann?*"

Again, Moshe shrugged.

"Dismissed!" said the Prefect curtly, already turning his attention to other papers.

And so, the man who had entered the *Koifhus* as Moshe ben Itzhak departed as Moshe Schumann, a name never to be changed in his lifetime.

W

Life as a Jew in German-occupied Alsace in 1890 under the Germans was difficult. But Moshe worked hard, perfected his German, stayed out of trouble, and, as he grew older, his business grew and prospered. He bought a large house in the *Rue des Juifs* in nearby Ingersheim for his growing family and moved his business to a new and expanded factory there.

One of Moshe's largest customers was a boot and leather goods factory in Gruenwald, across the Rhine in the Grand Duchy of Baden. The company was owned by a Jewish family headed by the German nobleman, businessman, and financier Solomon *Freiherr von Gruenwald im Breisgau.*

One afternoon, Moshe's work at the tannery was interrupted by his wife Sarah. "Mo . . . Moshe!" she stammered. "You have a visitor! At the house!"

"A visitor?" Moshe asked, cross at the intrusion. "Who is it?"

"It's Baron von Gruenwald!" she said. "He's come all the way from Germany to see you. I think you should come right away."

Wiping his hands on his apron, Moshe thought, *Trouble. Maybe some problem with the leather.* "All right. I'm coming." Looking across the shop floor, Moshe called to his son. "Jakob! Come! We have a visitor."

As it turned out, there was no problem with the leather. Baron von Gruenwald had instead come to Ingersheim with a business proposition that was astonishing in its vision, scope, and global reach.

The von Gruenwald family had grown rich providing high-quality boots, shoes, saddles, harnesses, and other leather goods to Grand Duke Frederick of Baden for his various military adventures. Solomon, son of the founder, expanded his business operations to include a small but very discreet and very profitable private bank located in the spa town of Baden-Baden, where he moved his family into an elegant mansion on the Lichtenthaler Allee facing the Oos River.

Baden-Baden had long been a favorite resort among wealthy German elites, and, beginning with the marriage of Princess Louise of Baden to future Tsar Alexander I, the town emerged as a preferred playground for Russian royalty, businessmen, and emigres.

Solomon cultivated these well-heeled visitors, and, leveraging these connections and his personal relationship with the Grand Duke, Solomon was introduced to the Frankfurt banking house M.A. Rothschild und Soehne. During the Franco-Prussian War of 1870, Solomon's bank was an important partner in a number of syndicated Rothschild loans to the North German Federation under Otto von Bismarck. After the peace, and in gratitude, Grand Duke Frederick conferred the noble hereditary title of *Freiherr* upon his loyal Jewish vendor and banker. Baron Solomon von Gruenwald emerged an extraordinarily wealthy man.

As Moshe and Jakob entered the comfortable parlor of their large home in the *Rue des Juifs*, two well-dressed gentlemen seated at a table sipping tea awaited them.

"Welcome to our home," said Moshe, bowing.

Both men rose. The elder man approached Moshe and returned the bow. "Good day, Herr Schumann. I am Solomon von Gruenwald, and this is my son, Gabriel." The younger gentleman nodded in greeting.

"It is an honor to have you in our home, Baron von Gruenwald," replied Moshe. "This is my son Jakob. I apologize for our appearance, but we have just come from the factory."

The Baron was a small but imposing man in his early sixties with a bald head and full moustache, formal in dress and manner. The son was more relaxed. He was taller, dark-complected and strikingly handsome, with a clean-shaven face that seemed just on the verge of a smile. His eyes were a piercing blue, his perfect teeth brilliant white.

"My son and I have come a long way to meet you, Herr Schumann. I apologize for disturbing you without notice, but I have an important matter to discuss."

"I do hope that there is not a problem with the leather," said Moshe cautiously.

Von Gruenwald waved his hand. "No, no, Herr Schumann, nothing like that. To the contrary. Your family over the years has proven to be one of our very best and most reliable suppliers. In fact, that is why we are here."

Moshe replied, "We, too, value our relationship very highly, and I appreciate your kind words. How may we be of service, sir?"

Raising an index finger, von Gruenwald cautioned, "First of all, I must emphasize that this conversation must be held in strictest confidence. This is very important." Moshe and Jakob nodded.

"My family and I have been rewarded in life and business almost beyond imagination, Herr Schumann. Fortune has indeed smiled generously upon us. But as we have prospered, I am acutely aware that thousands of our Jewish brethren throughout Europe have not." Shaking his head, he continued. "In Russia, particularly, life has become most difficult. Pogroms, persecution, oppression. I am determined to offer some relief to these people, to assist them in overcoming these challenges."

"To that end, I plan to devote a substantial portion of my estate to philanthropy. Through various contacts it has come to my attention that there are promising opportunities for Jewish settlement in the New World, in South America, particularly in Argentina where reports suggest that Jewish colonization is welcomed and encouraged by the government."

Intrigued, Moshe nodded. Von Gruenwald continued. "Last year a large group of Russian Jewish emigres travelled to Buenos Aires, intending to start an agricultural colony there. I have taken an interest in this effort, Herr Schumann. There are reports that the colonization effort has encountered serious difficulties purchasing land in Argentina and is in great need of assistance."

Jakob offered to refill their teacups and did so. Von Gruenwald resumed his story.

"This effort cannot fail, Herr Schumann. I will personally ensure that it does not. I have therefore formed and funded a private charity, the Foundation for the Preservation and Propagation of the Jewish Faith, to support this colonization effort, which will be referred to as the New Canaan Project. Funds will be used to purchase grazing land in Argentina, near Buenos Aires. The colonists will become cattle farmers." He smiled. "What some refer to as *Gauchos Judios*.

"My son, Gabriel, who has just finished his legal studies at Freiburg, will relocate to Argentina to manage the project on behalf of the Foundation."

Moshe considered this before asking, "I congratulate you, sir, and I sincerely admire your commitment. I wish you every success, but what, sir, has this to do with us?"

Here von Gruenwald extended a hand toward Gabriel. "Perhaps it is better if my son explains."

Gabriel smiled and began. "Meat from the cattle operations will, of course, be sold into the local market in Argentina. The bigger question is, what to do with the hides?

"Our research indicates that there is tremendous opportunity in the United States. The market for factory-made shoes there is exploding, as is the population, and the extensive rail network now makes it possible to supply most of America from the industry base of operations in the northern state of Massachusetts. But the problem is the supply chain.

Shoe factories there lack access to a sufficient supply of tanned leather. The shortfall is becoming critical.

"We have done our calculations, and we believe it is possible to profitably export cattle hides from Argentina to a tannery in the eastern part of the United States where the hides can be made into finished leather for further shipment to Massachusetts. But first we need a tannery with ready access to raw materials such as tanbark and a good water supply, and, of course, we need a railroad connection."

Moshe and Jakob looked at each other, perplexed. For the first time, Jakob spoke. "As my father says, what, sir, does this have to do with us?"

Gabriel looked to his father, who took up the narrative. "Gentlemen, I will speak directly. Surely you both have read about the tremendous economic and social opportunities available in the United States. Literally millions of Europeans, and thousands of Jews, are emigrating to America. The promise of America is real and waiting for those with a good head for business and an appetite for hard work. The New Canaan Project will provide an enormous opportunity in America. We would like to offer this opportunity to you, to the Schumann family."

Still uncomprehending, Moshe and Jakob exchanged a glance, but remained silent.

"We need a first-class tannery partner in the United States, owned and run by someone we can trust. The Schumann family has proved to be our most capable and reliable source of premium-grade finished leather in Germany over many years.

"We therefore propose, Herr Schumann, that your son Jakob relocate to America and build a new tannery there to process hides that Gabriel will ship from Argentina. I have excellent contacts in America who have already provided information about a potential location.

"Finished leather would then be shipped to shoe factories in the north. My bank in Baden-Baden will provide all needed financing on very attractive terms, backed by the assets of the Foundation. You," he said, gesturing toward Jakob, "your new tannery will be paid a processing fee per hide that will cover all costs and a handsome profit. You," he repeated, now pointing, "are likely to become a very rich man."

The Gabriel von Gruenwald piece of the New Canaan Project was already settled, and soon after the Ingersheim meeting, the Baron's young son was aboard a steamer bound for Buenos Aires.

For the Schumanns, it took a little longer. After weeks of weeping, wailing, gnashing of teeth, and fierce family debates, a consensus was reached—the baron was correct. The opportunity was too promising to refuse.

Moshe, a still vigorous but now older man, would remain in Ingersheim as the Schumann *pater familias* and would, together with his other sons, continue to run the business there. Jakob, the eldest, would emigrate to America, build a new tannery, and play his part in the grandiose New Canaan Project. Jakob and his family would make a new life for themselves in America.

Financing was arranged, the contracts were signed, and in May of 1891, Jakob Schumann, his wife Rebekah, and their children Rachel, Leah, and young Amos boarded a steamship to New York City and all the unknowns that awaited them there.

Baron von Gruenwald had arranged a meeting in the financial district with his friend Dannie Heineman, a native of Charlotte, North Carolina, a booming commercial, textile, and railroad center. Heineman had made his fortune in New York City in banking and finance, but never cut ties to Charlotte, where he remained a respected philanthropist and supporter of Jewish causes.

Jakob was admitted to Heineman's opulent office, where they discussed the New Canaan Project in great detail. At one point, Heineman switched languages. "How is your English?"

Jakob shrugged, "*Es geht.*" Then in halting English he said, "I am learning. So is the family. The Baron . . . got . . . a . . . tutor for us in Ingersheim, and we were . . . lucky . . . to meet a nice woman English teacher on the ship. She was also very helpful." Again, he shrugged, "We will survive."

"Very good. This is important."

Coming to the point, Jakob said, "Baron von Gruenwald told me that you have an idea about where we might put the tannery?"

Heineman reached into his desk drawer, withdrew a business card, and handed it to Jakob. It read, "*William Franklin Trogdon, President, Winston Land & Improvement Company.*"

"Take the train to Charlotte," Heineman instructed. "Meet with Trogdon. He's a friend of mine, and we have done business together. He's building a new town in North Carolina and has a proposal you should hear. I'll send him a telegram and set things up for you." He scribbled his Charlotte lawyer's name and address on the back of Trogdon's card and handed it to Jakob. "Good luck, Jakob," he said, and with a smile and a handshake Jakob was on his way.

Arriving in Charlotte by train on a Sunday afternoon, Jakob spent some time strolling the streets of the attractive small city, locating the building where the meeting was to be held. The next morning, arriving promptly at eleven o'clock, Jakob was admitted to the law office at the corner of Trade and Tryon streets in the center of town. A kind receptionist escorted him into a small conference room.

Seated at the conference table was a large man, radiating energy and strength. Rising and reaching across the table to pump Jakob's hand in both of his, the man smiled broadly and introduced himself in a loud voice, "Hello, Mr. Schumann. I'm Bill Trogdon. Let me tell you about North Wilkesboro . . . "

Chapter 5

Claire Elise sat alone in the dining area off the hotel reception. The half-eaten remnants of her light lunch, poached Blue Ridge Mountain trout with lemon sauce and boiled new potatoes, lay before her. She had little appetite.

In truth, she was exhausted. The adrenaline rush had subsided, her head pounded, and she felt aching fatigue deep in her bones. Overhead fans did little to dissipate the afternoon heat as rivulets of sweat trickled down her back. Tilting her head slightly, she gazed out at the ornate cast-iron façade of Ferguson's Store across Main Street. But her eyes were focused on a vision that only she could see.

Rising, she walked to the west-facing window and looked out toward the jail. She reviewed in her mind the calamitous events of the day. The turmoil surrounding the search for Rachel Schumann, the awful realization that the girl had gone missing, her meeting with Sheriff Poindexter, the panicked telephone call to Schumann Village, the excited men on horses, the dogs . . . the howling, barking dogs. And her conversation with R.E. McGee.

Her reverie was broken by the sight of a tall man walking quickly toward the hotel. *Sheriff Poindexter*. He made his way to the hotel door and entered, removing his broad-brimmed hat. Approaching Claire Elise, he motioned her to the dining table. "Come, Mrs. Montgomery, please have a seat. I am afraid I have some bad news to report." Fear in her eyes, she quickly complied.

Sheriff Poindexter broke the news and manner of Rachel's murder as gently as he could. Claire Elise dropped her head, her eyes full of tears, her body trembling uncontrollably. She had no words.

"I know this comes as a terrible shock, Mrs. Montgomery, and I shore am sorry to bring you this news. If there's any good in it, we caught the high-yeller bastard Virgil Wade. He was hidin' out in the old Cleveland place west of town, near Purlear. Rode out there on Rachel's horse. Crip and the boys 'rested him without any trouble and brought him and the horse back to the jail. Was all Crip could do to keep the boys from stringing him up on the Tory Oak right then and there. But we got him under lock and key, and Crip's a-keepin' watch. Anythin' I can do for you, Mrs. Montgomery? You need anythin', you just say the word."

Claire Elise raised her head to meet Poindexter's inquiring eyes. "No. No thank you, Sheriff. I really do not know quite what to say. What awful news! Has Mr. Schumann been informed?"

"I'm 'bout to ride over there now." Shaking his head Poindexter said simply, "He and Mrs. Schumann need to hear it from me."

"Yes, please do that right away, Sheriff. Tell them that Jewel and I will prepare food for them and bring it over in time for supper." Tears again filling her eyes, she sighed, "Go now. Go tell them now, please."

W

It was a cool, late-August winter day in 1892 when Claire Elise Montgomery and her father, John Russell Fleming, were seated in the parlor of the official residence of Her Majesty's Minister for Economic Affairs, near the British Embassy in Buenos Aires, finishing up a long and difficult conversation.

Minister Fleming reached across the table and took Claire Elise's hands in his. "It's for the best, my dear. Surely you must see that. The last year has brought you so much unexpected and undeserved misfortune. You and Randall are no longer . . . welcome . . . here in BA. Nasty, nasty business, that, and I am due to be seconded to my next post, Lord knows where. Most likely Canada, if rumors can be believed.

"That we will be separated is a given, so we must all make the best of an . . . unfortunate situation. Gabriel von Gruenwald has come up with an ideal solution, one that enables you and Randall to start over, start a new life for yourselves in America."

Claire Elise withdrew her hands, looked away, and then back. "But Father," she pleaded, "I appreciate and respect all you say, and you are correct. We must leave here.

"But America!" she cried. "So far away, such a strange place for us! And we know nothing about this town in North Carolina, this North Wilkesboro. From all reports it is nothing but a frontier village in the middle of nowhere! A wilderness! How will we survive there? How will we ever see you again?"

"There, there, Claire Elise," Fleming comforted. "It will be all right, you will see. Randall will be headmaster at a new academy there, with the full backing of Jakob Schumann. He is building an enormous tannery in North Wilkesboro, which by all accounts is a booming new city full of prospects and potential. Schumann's own children will be among your pupils, and he will provide a house for you on his property and build a new schoolhouse for Randall."

Claire Elise remained silent, unconvinced.

"As far as you and I are concerned, the thought of such a separation pains me greatly, dear Claire Elise. Indeed, the prospect is nigh unbearable. But every father must accept the fact that his daughter and son-in-law must make a new life for themselves in a place where opportunity presents itself. I know not where my next posting will be, but I make you my solemn promise that I will visit you—and your *family*—as soon and as often as circumstances permit." He smiled. "Ottawa is, after all, not so far away."

Spreading his arms wide, Fleming pleaded, "I implore you, Claire Elise, please see the good in this. Please take advantage of this unique opportunity. Please accept von Gruenwald's most generous offer.

"Schumann is a formidable businessman, a widely-travelled European with a refined circle of friends and contacts. He has Baron von Gruenwald's full backing and support. Why, Gabriel told me yesterday that he himself will soon be moving to North Carolina, to the port city of Wilmington on the Atlantic Coast."

Claire Elise straightened her back, came to full attention, her eyes widening. "What did you just say, Father?"

"The New Canaan Project here in Argentina is well along and running smoothly now. And the tannery in North Wilkesboro is about to open soon. So, Gabriel is moving to Wilmington to supervise the receipt of cattle hides from New Canaan and arrange for their further transport to the tannery in North Wilkesboro and the finished leather thence to

Massachusetts, to the shoe factories there."

Fleming smiled. "He plans to regularly be in North Wilkesboro to monitor the tanning process there. You and he are already good friends, so you will often see a familiar face in your new city."

"Really? Gabriel von Gruenwald will visit North Wilkesboro?"

Fleming nodded slowly. "Indeed, he will. One week every month, or so he says."

Her heart racing, Claire Elise struggled to remain calm. For several minutes she did not speak, looking out the window at the bustling streets of Buenos Aires. Her father did not break the silence. Finally, she said, "Well, then. I will agree to discuss all this with Randall. It is, after all, his professional future we are talking about. I am not sure he will agree."

Her father, a bit ashamed, confessed, "Please do not be cross with me, Claire Elise, but I have already taken the liberty of discussing von Gruenwald's proposal with Randall. He is fully informed and understands the pros and cons. But on balance, he is prepared to accept, providing you agree. Randall suggested that perhaps it would be best for me to have this conversation with you privately. He is a good man and respects how this resolution of our respective issues would tear at the fabric of our dear, dear relationship, Claire Elise. But, again, he sees the wisdom in it, as do I.

"So, my dear Claire Elise, it is up to you."

Looking directly into her father's eyes, tears came to her own. Her shoulders sagged as she ran into her father's warm embrace.

"Then it's settled," she sobbed, holding him tight.

Claire Elise Fleming, born in Cairo, Egypt, was the only child of John Russell Fleming and his wife, Muriel.

A native of Lytham St. Annes on the Lancashire coast, Fleming came from solid middle-class stock and worked as a career civil servant in Her Majesty's diplomatic service, rising through the ranks to ministerial level. Through a series of successful postings throughout the Empire, his professional portfolio steadily expanded to include increasingly important matters of international trade, business, and investment.

Great tragedy struck the Fleming family when, during a posting to India, Claire Elise's mother Muriel died of malaria. Fleming never remarried, and going forward his beautiful young daughter dutifully served as his official consort at Embassy functions.

Despite his talents and diplomatic and business skills, Fleming lacked the family resources and political connections needed to secure an ambassadorial appointment in the late-Victorian years. As minister for economic affairs, however, Fleming's position was important. British businesses, bankers, and traders had become essential sources of investment capital, machinery and equipment, and other goods needed to fuel and finance Argentina's expanding economy and infrastructure. Fleming emerged as a significant and influential person in the Argentine capital.

For Claire Elise, Buenos Aires was an exciting new adventure as she transitioned from adolescence to womanhood. Always at her father's side, well-educated, well-traveled, and charming, she was widely regarded as a most attractive and eligible young woman, but had yet to be connected seriously with any of the willing suitors of diverse nationalities who regularly attended the many elegant receptions, banquets, and balls on the diplomatic circuit.

Among the most earnest and persistent of her admirers was Professor Charles Randall Montgomery, a handsome and unmarried master of European languages, history, and philosophy who had been headmaster of a prestigious public school for boys in London. The increasing number of British expatriates created demand in Buenos Aires for a similar school, and Montgomery had been recruited to establish the British School for Boys in the Argentine capital. Ten years older than Claire Elise, Montgomery came from a good family of acceptable rank in the Midlands and was clearly smitten with the minister's daughter.

Claire Elise turned twenty-two in 1891, an age at which most of her contemporaries had long since found suitable marriage partners, and Minister Fleming was eager to make an appropriate match for his lovely daughter and only child. *Why not the professor?*

Fleming followed the development of the New Canaan Project closely and with great interest. He made frequent visits there and often organized business meetings and receptions in Buenos Aires for delegations from the colony. At one of these events, Claire Elise was introduced to the leader of the New Canaan Project, Gabriel von Gruenwald. She fell at once for the handsome, dashing bachelor and imagined a fairy-tale romance and life together colonizing the *Pampas*. Sadly, given religious differences, these flights of fancy were the hopeless, romantic dreams of an infatuated young woman.

All the while, Montgomery continued to press his case, and Claire Elise concluded that she could not reasonably refuse such a fine match. She consented to marry the professor, while her heart secretly pined for the dark and handsome Jew from New Canaan.

Soon after the wedding, things suddenly and unexpectedly began to turn sour for Montgomery. A disciplinary matter involving alcohol and inappropriate sexual contact between two male classmates put Montgomery at odds with the aristocratic father and insufferably arrogant mother of one of the spoiled pupils. Complaints about Montgomery's handling of the issue and other minor nits found their way to the ambassador, and Montgomery's position in British society slowly slipped away.

Fleming could not defend his son-in-law without risk to his own career, and soon the campaign of whispers and innuendo took its toll. Montgomery was smoothly and discreetly relieved of his position as headmaster, suddenly unwanted and unemployable within the British community in Argentina.

To be effectively shunned and cast out of British society stunned Claire Elise. She felt hopelessly adrift, ostracized by friends and acquaintances, her place and role in the community irretrievably lost. The damage was equally great to the young couple's finances.

All this put incredible stress on a marriage built upon an already flimsy foundation of convention and convenience. Claire Elise began to withdraw personally and physically from Montgomery. The couple remained childless.

Montgomery was compelled to face the plain truth of it; they needed to leave Argentina, and they needed a place to make a new start if their marriage was to be saved.

Gabriel von Gruenwald witnessed all of this with concern. He had grown fond of Claire Elise and felt great sympathy for her situation. He recalled a conversation with Jakob Schumann during his most recent trip to North Wilkesboro to inspect the tannery under construction. Schumann complained that there were, in his judgment, no suitable schools or tutors available in the town for his three children.

"Would the Foundation consider supporting a new school or academy here?" he asked Gabriel. "Other children from the area could also attend, and hopefully once established, the academy would be self-sustaining."

Gabriel thought about this. *Could a new academy in North Wilkesboro led by Randall Montgomery solve Schumann's problem while also providing a new opportunity, a fresh start for Claire Elise and her husband?* He would write to his father about this. *Yes. I will do that right away.*

Chapter 6

Interim Solicitor and Prosecutor George Vincent Taliaferro—pronounced *TOLLIVER*, he would quickly correct—was seated at his desk on the first floor of the new Wilkes County Courthouse. A solid red-brick structure built in the neoclassical revival style with four tall white Doric columns supporting a dominant pediment, the courthouse had government offices on the ground level and an imposing ceremonial courtroom upstairs.

From his windows, Taliaferro could see the Schumann Hotel just across Broad Street. The legendary Tory Oak, used by Revolutionary War patriot Colonel Benjamin Cleveland to hang hardheaded and unyielding British loyalists, provided welcome shade. Elbows on his desk, hands clenched, Taliaferro eyed Wilkes County Sheriff Jimmy "Redbone" Poindexter, seated opposite him. Poindexter spoke first.

"Crip just got back with the boy. They found him out at the Cleveland place near Purlear. He was hidin' out there, but the dogs found him, and Rachel's horse. He was a-shakin' like a thorn bush in a cyclone. Didn't give us no trouble."

"Where is he now?" asked Taliaferro in his thin and reedy voice.

"Crip's got him locked up. But I gotta tell you, boss, the boys are not happy about that. Their blood is up, and they want his neck in a noose. The word is out, and folks're gatherin' outside the jail. They're in a black mood, and that fool Roscoe McGee is back over here asking questions. Damn, what a mess."

Taliaferro bit his fingernails, thinking. His gaze drifted up to a fluttering sticky fly-tape hung from an overhead ceiling fan. Poindexter waited patiently.

Taliaferro was a short, corpulent, balding, middle-aged bachelor with limited interests, few friends, and no hobbies. His skin was the color of fatback, and his shaven face, set off by a well-groomed handlebar moustache, bore a bluish five-o-clock shadow visible through a thin sheen of sweat. A fastidious dresser, he insisted on wearing a three-piece suit in all seasons and refused to remove his jacket even in the most oppressive heat.

Folks who bothered to think about it would describe him as more clever than intelligent, a driven but preening, ambitious yet cautious man. Ruthless and merciless in the courtroom, he could be fawning and unctuous in chambers, reliably prone to kissing up and kicking down—traits that inspired in many who encountered him an instantaneous and, for most, permanent sense of dislike. Behind his back, victims of his sharp and cutting tongue, especially defendants and their counsel, called him *Razor.*

Taliaferro's predecessor as solicitor and chief prosecutor was local lawyer Calvin Hauser. Hauser had signed up for military service in the run-up to the Spanish American War, and in 1898, he was killed instantly when a special train on the Florida Central and Peninsula Railroad carrying North Carolina volunteers to Florida collided with a northbound vegetable train.

A rare and slim Democratic majority on the Wilkes Board of County Commissioners set about finding a temporary replacement for Hauser until the general election in 1900. Furnifold Simmons, chairman of the state Democratic Party and architect of its White Supremacy campaign, recommended Vincent Taliaferro.

Taliaferro's family had moved to North Carolina from Virginia and settled in Surry County. He also had Wilkes County connections, having attended the Blackstone Law School near Elkville before returning to Dobson, the Surry County seat, as an assistant prosecutor. More importantly, Taliaferro was a committed Democrat and Simmons supporter.

Wilkes commissioners, eager to remain in Furnifold Simmons' good graces, appointed Taliaferro interim solicitor and prosecutor in late-spring 1898. He declared his candidacy for the permanent position in June of 1900, running against Republican Charlie Odell. Democrats including Taliaferro, buoyed by the White Supremacy campaign, seemed destined to win, but, in traditionally Republican Wilkes, you could never be sure.

Hmmm, thought Taliaferro. *Bad as it is, this Rachel Schumann thing could be a godsend. I can drag things out, hang Virgil Wade, and ride that all the way to November. Yes. That will work.*

"Okay, Redbone, here's the deal. I need you to keep this Wade boy alive until I can bring him to trial, understand? We need the trial to convince people that Wilkes County justice will not tolerate a half-breed high-yeller boy murdering a virtuous young White woman. That's how we will do it."

Taliaferro was getting wound up now, his index fingers moving fast in circles, like reeling in a catfish. He spoke precisely and in rapid staccato bursts. "Folks need to see him hang, and I will be proud, you hear me, *proud* to be the awful instrument of their revenge! I will be their eager hangman, the defender of precious White womanhood against the depredations of merciless Black savages *et cetera, et cetera, et cetera.*" He paused to catch his breath. "You follow?"

Poindexter nodded. "I hear you, boss. I'll do my best. But like I said, things are iffy. What if the Klan gets involved?"

Taliaferro responded, his black, hooded eyes focused on the sheriff. "That can't happen, Redbone, you hear me? You've got friends in the Klan. Talk to them. I need that boy alive. I need a trial, got it?"

"I understand. Just know it's just me'n Crip over at the jail. I'll make sure he understands the plan. But still, just how far are you prepared to go?"

Rising, Taliaferro pointed at Poindexter. "Make it happen, Sheriff. Take care of it."

Nodding, Poindexter rose and prepared to leave.

"What now, Redbone? What's next?" asked Taliaferro.

"I'm off to Schumann Village to inform the family. I'll stop by the hotel on the way to fill in Mrs. Montgomery. She needs to know."

With that, Sheriff Poindexter departed on his wretched mission.

Taliaferro considered his options. *I need to tell Simmons about this. He will know what to do, how best to handle this.* He picked up the black earpiece from his desk telephone and jiggled the handle several times.

"Hello, this is Central. Number, please?"

"Good afternoon, Betty," spoke Taliaferro. "Please connect me with Mr. Furnifold Simmons at Democratic State Party Headquarters in Raleigh."

"Right away, Mr. Taliaferro. I'll ring you back when I have him on the line."

"I'll be right here, Betty. Thank you."

Taliaferro sat back, stroked his moustache. Gazing out at the Tory Oak, he daydreamed of a packed courtroom upstairs, full of locals, out-of-towners, newspaper people. He could see Redbone in the witness box, Wade in chains, looking small and pitiful with Crip Goins guarding him. He could hear his own thundering summation and final plea for justice, the somber jury foreman speaking the electrifying word "*GUILTY*," the judge hammering his gavel and pronouncing the inevitable righteous sentence. He could see it all, clear as day in his mind's eye. *The trial*. A vulpine smile splitting the sheen of his face, he waited for his telephone to ring.

Chapter 7

Wilkes County, 1750-1900

The life force of Wilkes County is the Yadkin River, its headwaters burbling up from a hidden spring in Watauga County near Blowing Rock. The river enters Wilkes near Elkville, and, flowing east, carves a green and bucolic valley nestled between the Blue Ridge to the north and the Brushy Mountains to the south. Most important for Jakob Schumann, the virgin forests of the Yadkin Valley were dominated by majestic chestnut trees, whose tanbark would be essential for the success of his tannery.

Legend has it that the first White settler was Christopher Gist, a celebrated frontiersman who moved his family from Baltimore to a homestead just west of Wilkesboro in 1750. Most notably, Gist's son and Cherokee wife had a child, George Gist, who would, under the name Sequoyah, achieve fame as the inventor of the Cherokee alphabet and written language.

The famous backwoodsman and pioneer Daniel Boone was also an early resident of Wilkes. Boone and his wife Rebecca lived many years in the county before departing for Kentucky in a huff after losing a bitter lawsuit relating to a land title.

Wilkes County, with Wilkesboro as its county seat, was established in 1778, named for British Parliamentarian John Wilkes, a fervent and passionate supporter of American independence during the Revolutionary War. Wilkes was then the home of the American patriot Colonel Benjamin Cleveland, the *Terror of the Tories*, who hanged many an unrepentant British loyalist from the Tory Oak on the courthouse square in Wilkesboro.

Cleveland also collected a large company of patriots at Rendezvous Mountain and led these Overmountain Men to the Battle of Kings Mountain, a decisive victory in the fight for American independence.

The most unusual and perhaps most famous of Wilkes County residents were Eng and Chang Bunker, the original Siamese Twins. Born in Thailand, these brothers, joined by a strip of cartilage at the chest, became an international sensation, performing at venues throughout the world. In 1829 they emigrated to the United States and, wealthy and weary of their travels, settled in Wilkes County, bought a farm in Traphill, and became US citizens. They wooed and then married twin sisters, Sarah and Adelaide Yates, and no doubt awkwardly sired twenty-one children between them. They died within minutes of one another in 1874.

The Civil War was a time of crisis for Wilkes. Prior to secession, sentiment in Wilkes was strongly pro-Union. After North Carolina joined the Confederacy, however, Wilkes sent many of its sons to fight against the Yankees. Of all who served, scarcely a quarter would return.

Wilkes' most infamous veteran was Tom Dula, pronounced *Dooley* by the locals. Returning from the War, Dula was involved in a lovers' triangle with Ann Melton, a married woman, and Laura Foster. When Dula discovered that he had contracted a venereal disease, he blamed Foster and made several public threats against her. Soon she disappeared, and Dula was arrested for her murder and put in the Wilkes County Jail, awaiting trial. In August, Foster's body was recovered, its location disclosed by Ann Melton, who was also charged with the murder. The resulting trial claimed national attention. Dula was ultimately convicted and hanged on May 1, 1868. Before his execution he wrote a note stating that Ann Melton was not involved in Foster's murder, and she was acquitted. It is said that, in a wagon on the way to the scaffold, Dula sat atop his coffin, playing a fiddle.

Other Wilkes veterans would return to a county in chaos, first suffering Union General George Stoneman's brutal occupation, and later the depredations of the renegade Fort Hamby Gang. Led by a renegade Union deserter named Major Wade, the half-dozen or so members of the gang commenced an unrestrained reign of terror against the population of Wilkes, robbing, raping, and killing seemingly at will. They established their headquarters at Meg Hamby's house, located on a high bluff overlooking the Yadkin Valley and the Valley Road north of the river, a highly defensible position. Hamby, well-known in Wilkes as an attractive and shapely woman of questionable morals, was most recently Wade's concubine. Men from Caldwell, Alexander, Iredell, and Wilkes counties finally joined forces to attack Fort Hamby. Four of Wade's henchmen were captured, tied to stakes, and shot on the spot. Wade and Meg Hamby were able to escape, fled the county, and were never heard from again. They left behind an illegitimate infant son, to be raised by others.

His mother named him Luther Wade.

Chapter 8

Jakob Schumann cleaned his lips on a starched white napkin as he finished his hearty American breakfast—coffee, toast and rhubarb jam, a small beefsteak, fried eggs, and something the locals called *grits*—in the sun-filled dining room of the newly-constructed Hotel Gordon on B Street, the main thoroughfare of the town. He was ready for a walk.

It was a lovely day. An early morning shower had given way to deep blue skies and white puffy clouds. As he stood on the wide board sidewalk, he could see hills and peaks bracketing the village north and south, filled with the precious chestnut trees that had brought Schumann to the place.

North Wilkesboro was, as W.F. Trogdon promised, a town on the move. Schumann had spent the last few days in Trogdon's company as he proudly presented the town and promoted its bright future. Schumann had been impressed, but today he wanted to explore alone. He had a tannery to build, and he was behind schedule.

As he stepped from the quiet lobby of the hotel, he entered a maelstrom of noise, smells, and enterprise. The morning rain had made B Street a sea of mud, filled with horses, mules, oxen, wagons, and buggies, all in a hurry. Board sidewalks on both sides of the street were filled with fast-walking men and sturdy women shopping and running errands.

The pleasant scent of fresh-sawn lumber and the aroma of baking bread were no match for the tangy stink of horse manure and the odor from public privies here and there along the street. Small Black boys, fighting away flies, were busy shoveling away horse droppings and cleaning outhouses.

And there were the sounds—the clamor of carpenters hammering frameworks of new buildings, shouting as they worked, the shrieking of the sawmill, the rattle of ox-drawn lumber wagons, the metallic clanging of the blacksmith at the livery stable, the spirited notes of Gay Nineties piano tunes from the saloon, the barking of shopkeepers inviting customers to buy the tobacco, produce, watermelons, fresh meat, and salt-cured country hams on offer, the cacophony of flocks of wild turkeys being herded from the Reddies River covered bridge through town to the depot, wide-eyed Bible-thumping street preachers on the corners proclaiming the Gospel in rhythmic cadences, warning of the wages of sin and the eternal hell fire and damnation awaiting the unrepentant.

Jakob Schumann shook his head. *Ach!* he thought. *Look at this! There is nothing like this in Alsace.* There was indeed a sense of frontier energy, a New World dynamism about the place, unlike anything Schumann had experienced.

Squinting into the sun, Schumann carefully made his way across wide boards laid in the mud to the corner of 9th and B, site of Brame Drug Company, the first brick building in the new town. From there he continued downhill to the terminus of the Northwestern North Carolina Railroad, the vital link from North Wilkesboro to the port of Wilmington and the haciendas of New Canaan beyond.

As related to Jakob Schumann by Trogdon, the coming of the railroad was a story of enlightened civic leadership, entrepreneurial vision, and, to hear the people of Wilkesboro tell it, abominable deception, treachery, and grand larceny.

In the late nineteenth century, Wilkes was a poor, isolated, mostly inaccessible rural backwater with a tiny county seat, Wilkesboro, near its center. There were few roads, and those that existed were poorly constructed and maintained. Narrow, rutted, and curvy, the roads generated clouds of red dust in fair weather, axle-deep rivers of mud after a rain. Transportation into and out of Wilkes was so poor that the county was commonly referred to as *The Lost Province.*

Determined to improve things, the people of Wilkes passed a $100,000 bond issue in 1888 to recruit a railroad to the county, and later that year Wilkes County commissioners and the Northwestern North Carolina Railroad signed a contract to bring rail service from Rural Hall, near Winston, to Wilkes, with the terminus to be located within one mile of the Wilkes County Courthouse. Residents of Wilkesboro and the commissioners naturally assumed that the rail line would cross the Yadkin River and end on the south bank in Wilkesboro. Trogdon, however, had other plans.

Trogdon explained to NWNCRR that the cost of bridging the Yadkin to Wilkesboro would add thousands of dollars to the total cost of the rail line. Pointing to a map, Trogdon noted that the open farmland on the north side of the Yadkin, east of the Reddies River and just across from Wilkesboro, met the one-mile from the courthouse bond requirement. Ending the line there would both comply with the contract and save the company money. NWNCRR liked the idea very much.

Once the deal was struck, Trogdon formed the Winston Land and Improvement Company and began buying up farms on the north side of the river. Leveraging the potential of the railroad, Trogdon quickly set about realizing his ambitious plans to build a completely new town around the rail terminal at the corner of what would become 9th and A Streets in North Wilkesboro, North Carolina.

And so, on August 30, 1890, Colonel A.B. Andrews, president of the parent company of the NWNCRR, arrived in his private railroad car at the terminal in North Wilkesboro. Wilkes commissioners, seething at what they regarded as Trogdon's underhanded treachery, boarded the train, gritted their teeth, smiled, and dutifully signed the documents that released the $100,000 bond.

And thus began an enduring rivalry between "The Wilkesboros" that, built on bitterness and resentment, continues to this day. Schumann smiled as he remembered Trogdon slapping his knee and bellowing a hearty laugh as he finished the story.

Trogdon proved an irrepressible promoter of his new town. Schumann smiled as he recalled an advertisement the businessman had placed in today's edition of *The Lost Province*.

> *North Wilkesboro has done more in just a few years than Greensboro did in fifty years, and with the railroad and the great turnpike road completed, factories of all sorts, and work for everybody, it will outgrow every other town in the State.*
>
> *More than three hundred wagons come into North Wilkesboro daily, loaded with tan bark, lumber, mountain and country produce of all kinds. North Wilkesboro has the largest steam tannery in North Carolina, Jakob Schumann owner.*

North Wilkesboro has a local and long-distance telephone system, also a Western Union Telegraph office. North Wilkesboro owns its own electric light system.

North Wilkesboro was not on the map ten years ago, see what it is today.

DEAR READER, WILL YOU MOVE TO NORTH WILKESBORO OR WASTE YOUR TIME WHERE YOU ARE, LET YOUR CHILDREN GROW UP IN IGNORANCE AND NOT GIVE THEM A CHANCE TO DO SOMETHING AND BE SOMEBODY? WHICH? **DECIDE NOW! TIME IS MONEY!**

—W.F. Trogdon

W

The NWNCRR terminal and depot was a long, squat, one-story red brick building with a low hipped roof with overhanging eves. A hissing black locomotive sat on a sidetrack as box cars were being loaded with timber, turkeys, chickens, herbs, produce, cases of wine, furniture, bricks, caskets, and other Wilkes products.

The scene at and around the depot was utter bedlam. A hundred or more ox carts and mule wagons fought for position at the loading dock, their drivers shouting orders and insults to all and sundry. A hundred more were waiting at the wagon camp just west of the terminal just as William Blackburn, broadcasting corn from a pail to move the birds along, arrived with his cackling and gobbling wild turkeys.

Well-dressed eastbound passengers waited in lines along the main platform as food and drink purveyors hawked their wares, and buggies with latecomers sought passage through the crowd.

From the depot, Schumann made his way farther south, passing several coal and ice companies, walking toward the Yadkin and the new iron bridge that had finally spanned the river, connecting the two rival towns. Schumann laughed as he read the sign prominently posted at the entrance to the bridge:

NOTICE

Walk your horse and save fine.
Fine not less than $5.00 nor more than $25.00.
Imprisonment not more than 30 days.

J. Poindexter, Sheriff

At the bridge, Schumann turned left and took the footpath east along the green and leafy north bank of the Yadkin. Passing Blair Island to his right, Schumann looked left to the flat bottomland where Trogdon had proposed he build his tannery. *This is good,* he thought. *Here the westerly winds and the river will push the stink, the smoke, and the waste from the tannery east, downstream and downwind, away from the town. Very good.*

Following a sharp bend in the river to the north, Schumann made his way up a gentle rise to a point just south of Cherry Street. Looking to his left, Schumann mused, *High ground. Perfect for a home for Rebekah and the children. Space for other houses for supervisors and foremen. Ja. We will call it Schumann Village!* Ja, prima. Perfekt! *We have the chestnut trees, the tan bark, the water, the railroad.* Nodding, Schumann pronounced out loud, "I will build my tannery here."

Chapter 9

Cotton Bob Maxwell slowly replaced the telephone earpiece in its cradle. He was silent for several moments. He turned to Ben Waterman and spoke slowly, in a quiet voice. "McGee has terrible news, Ben. Jakob Schumann's daughter Rachel has been murdered."

"What do you mean, Judge? Murdered?"

"Ros says that she went missing somehow from the Schumann Hotel, in the middle of the night. Redbone found her body early this morning, horribly beaten and stabbed to death down by the river."

"What? . . . How? . . . Why?"

"Unclear at the moment."

"But who . . . who would do such a thing?"

"Ros says Redbone arrested a young colored boy, Virgil Wade. Says that his skinning knife was plunged deep in her heart. Crip Goins and the dogs found him out by the Cleveland cabin. Rachel's horse outside. He's in the county jail now. God almighty, Ben, think of the Schumanns! Ros says that folks're up in arms. Big crowd milling around, calling for his head. Somehow Ros has gotten hold of photographs. Awful!"

"Is the boy safe? Can Redbone control things?"

"Ros says no. People want him strung up right now."

"So, what can be done, Judge?"

Maxwell looked into Ben's eyes. "Ros thinks that I need to intervene, put a stop to it. Thinks you need to get to Wilkes right away. Take charge."

Ben nodded. "Wilmington."

"That's right, Ben. He says it's that bad."

"Well, so I go to Wilkes. Then what?"

"Well, here's how I see it, Ben. I'll be goddamned if there's going to be a lynching if I can stop it. No more Wilmingtons while I'm governor . . . not on my watch. Not in my hometown."

Rising from his chair and pointing at Ben, Maxwell continued in a firm voice. "Get to Wilkes, Ben, fast as you can. Take the morning train. I'll send a telegram to Redbone and Taliaferro, let them know you're on the way. That you speak and act for me. I'll have Peggy contact the Schumann Hotel and book a room. It's near the jail, so you can keep an eye on things. I'll also let Ros know, tell him to meet you at the station."

Pausing a moment, Maxwell shifted gears. "Go see Schumann, Ben. Tell him how sorry, how deeply sorry I am. He's a good friend, and I owe him a lot. Damnation, Ben, what a tragedy!"

Winding up, Maxwell said, "Do what you need to do, Ben. Mark my words, if that boy is convicted of killing Rachel Schumann, I'll gladly put the noose around his neck myself. But not until justice takes its course, Ben. You understand me? Keep him alive!"

"Yes, sir. Understood. I will do my best."

"If it turns out you can't control it, Ben, you let me know. I'll send the Guard if I have to."

"I'm on my way, Judge. I'll keep you informed."

Maxwell slumped heavily in his big leather chair, swiveled to face the window, and gazed out at the giant oaks on the Capitol square. *Wilmington. Not again. Not in my town. Not on my watch . . .*

Chapter 10

Even early in the morning, the air was warm, thick, and humid. Struggling with his valise, Ben could feel his sweat as he made his way down the platform. Checking his ticket against the numbered cars of the train, Ben stopped and prepared to board. A friendly porter walked up and pointed at his grip. "'Mornin', sir," said the smiling Black man. "Lemme he'p you with that."

"Thanks," replied Ben, handing off the case and pressing a coin into the porter's hand. "Much obliged."

"So, where're y'all headed this fine day?" Ben climbed up into the passenger car and held out his ticket. The porter inspected it and said, "Looks like you're traveling west, way west."

"That's correct. North Wilkesboro."

Lifting Ben's suitcase and placing it in the overhead luggage rack, the porter said, "Now, mind you, don'chu fall asleep and miss your connection in Rural Hall. This here's your seat. Enjoy your journey, mister. You'll prob'ly get there 'bout noon."

The passenger car rattled, and the train began to move. As the locomotive cleared the station, Ben rose and joined several other passengers in the dining car. Soon his breakfast was served, and he relaxed and enjoyed his meal as the Piedmont countryside passed by. Returning to his seat, Ben dozed off, sleeping through the train's stop in Greensboro. It had been a long night.

Ben was awakened by a gentle touch on his shoulder. "Excuse me, sir," said the uniformed conductor. "We're about five minutes out from

Rural Hall. You'll need to change trains there." Nodding his thanks, Ben roused himself, retrieved his suitcase from the rack above, and moved to the rear of the cabin, ready to disembark.

Rural Hall station was busy with passengers, workmen, and wagon drivers milling about. Ben located the NWNCRR train waiting on the westbound track, boarded it, and took a window seat on the left side of the aisle. *Going home*, Ben mused, as the train slowly picked up steam on its way to North Wilkesboro, sixty-three miles west.

The countryside rose into green, rolling hills, the train following the north bank of the Yadkin River, stopping at small villages and way stations along the route. Ben knew them all. *Tobaccoville, Donnaha, Siloam, Rockford, Crutchfield, Burch.*

The train huffed and chugged its way west, crossing the county line at Elkin, bound for Ronda, Roaring River, and finally, North Wilkesboro, end of the line. Soon the engine began to slow. Looking left toward the river, Ben could see the tall, red brick chimney of the tannery, standing tall amid the curving tanbark sheds and sprawling workshops, its black smoke drifting slowly east on the breeze. The smokestack proudly bore the letters S-C-H-U-M-A-N-N in tall white letters down its length.

A few moments later, the engineer blew a series of whistle blasts and with a clatter and bang the train stopped as the conductor shouted, "North Wilkesboro! North Wilkesboro! End of the line! All passengers disembark here!"

Ben stepped down into a scene of utter chaos. The locomotive, a breathing black Leviathan, hissed and coughed clouds of smoke and steam, porters with their carts cried for business, passengers rushed to and fro, a crowd heading for the exits, pushing against those rushing toward the waiting rail cars. On both sides of the track shouting stevedores and their mule-drawn wagons fought for position, some to unload the train, others to take their place loading goods and produce for the eastbound return run.

Ben searched left and right, looking for Roscoe McGee. Finally, through the din and murk, Ben spotted his friend strutting toward him, a wide smile on his face. "Ben!" he shouted, holding out his hand and pumping Ben's up and down. "Damn good to see you!"

"Same to you, Ros," Ben replied, returning the smile. "Been a long time."

"Too long, Ben."

"I haven't been back to Wilkes since the judge's campaign in '96." Ben looked around. "God Almighty, Ros, this place is booming!"

"I heard that!" McGee agreed. "More'n a thousand people living over here now. 'Putting poor Wilkesboro to shame. When ol' man Trogdon stole the railroad and started buying up land over here, why, there couldn't have been more than ten or twenty folks living on this side of the river." Pointing at the locomotive, McGee said, "And we can thank that big black monster there for all of it. Looks like the 'Lost Province' ain't so 'lost' anymore. *Naarh, naarh, naarh!*"

Ben laughed, too. Turning serious, he asked, "So what's the plan, Ros. What's going on, and how can I help?"

Looking from side to side, Ros whispered, "Not here, Ben. Let's load you up and get to my office. We can talk in peace there." The two men worked their way through the crowd to the hitching post where Rex waited patiently. McGee loaded Ben's luggage, and they set off for the Trogdon Opera House. Looking south across the Yadkin, Ben spotted a collection of wooden buildings and simple houses, almost hidden by a layer of smoke from cooking fires.

"What's all that over there, Ros?"

"Well, that's Cairo, Ben. When they were building the rail line, Northwestern brought in, oh, three hundred or so colored workers to do the heavy work. Some of them liked it here, so they settled over yonder across the river. It's grown a lot since then."

"'*Kay-ro,*' you say?" asked Ben. "Like the corn syrup?"

McGee laughed. "Nope. It's pronounced that way, but folks spell it C-A-I-R-O, you know, like in Egypt. It's quite a thing, impressive. Like a whole 'nother town. They've got a rooming house, a church, a beauty shop, a poolroom, a café, and Isaiah Watkins built himself a fine grocery store. Why, even some of the White women shop there when fresh produce comes in."

McGee snapped the reins, and Rex pulled the Phaeton, its big yellow wheels gleaming in the sunlight, up 9th Street to D, where they turned right and made their way to the Trogdon Opera House, home of *The Lost Province* newspaper and its owner, editor, and publisher. The two men had a lot to discuss.

W

McGee, Ben, and Tink Beasley sat at the kitchen table in McGee's apartment, finishing up lunch brought in from McGee's saloon on the floor below. Fried chicken, mashed potatoes, collard greens, biscuits, and peach sonker for dessert, all washed down with large, ice cold draught beers.

Gathering up the plates and utensils, Tink said, "Let me get these things out of your way, boys. I'll clean up and get back to work. Got three obituaries to finish. And you," she said, pointing at McGee, "You need to write up the one for Rachel Schumann." Her arms full, Tink smiled at Ben. "Real good to see you, Ben. Real good. I 'spect I'll see more of you before you go back to Raleigh?"

"Count on it, Tink. I'll be around."

Lifting his mug for a swig of beer, Ben turned to McGee. "Okay, Ros, let's get to it. Tell me what you know."

Shaking his head, McGee said, "Ben, I've gotta tell you, this is the damndest thing I've ever seen."

"So, start at the beginning. Bring me up to date."

"Well, it all started yesterday morning when Olly Overby came by."

McGee recounted the events of Thursday, July 5, beginning with his trip with Overby to the river, his conversation with Claire Elise Montgomery, the awful truth of Rachel Schumann's murder, the search for Virgil Wade, and his capture.

"What about this Wade fellow?" Ben asked. "Who is he?"

"He's just a boy, Ben. Maybe fifteen, sixteen years old. Small, skinny guy, light-skinned, curly red hair, freckles. Folks say he's nice, respectful, never caused any trouble. Mrs. Montgomery uses him to help out in the hotel livery when the lawyers come to town. Hard to figure how he got messed up in something like this."

"So, who're his people?"

"Well, that's complicated," said McGee. "You know about Fort Hamby? The gang that caused such a ruckus after the War?"

"Sure, I know about it, Ros. But what's that got to do with Virgil Wade?"

"Like I said, complicated. When Colonel Wade and Meg Hamby ran off after the big fight, they left behind a bastard baby boy, named him Luther Wade. Turned out to be a bad seed, like his daddy. Several people took him in, tried to raise him right, but it was no good. Nobody could handle him. Wouldn't go to school, always getting into trouble and starting fights, drunk or on dope half the time. When he was scarce old enough, he went out on his own, taking odd jobs here and there. He's still around, working up at the sawmill by the Flume on the Reddies River."

McGee paused, took a sip of beer. "There's a colored woman in town,

Pauline Oxendine, married a Lumbee Indian come up here looking for work. Old-timers say that she was a good-looking woman, Ben, and before Oxendine came along, she got pregnant. She says Luther Wade came by her house one night, three sheets to the wind and drunk as a skunk, pulled a pistol, tied up her momma and daddy, and raped her. Well, the baby came, and Pauline named him Virgil Wade. Really pissed Luther off. He never owned up to it, never had anything to do with the boy. Pauline and her husband, they raised him."

"So, Virgil Wade is Luther Wade's illegitimate son, the gangster Wade's grandson?"

"Well, that's what Pauline Oxendine says."

"My God, Ros, what a story. So, what next?"

"Well, Redbone and his posse found Rachel's body down by the river, and then Crip Goins and the dogs went looking for Virgil. Found him out near Purlear, Rachel's horse tied up outside. Brought him to the jail. Well, word got out, Ben, and there was a big mob around the jail, all worked up. Half of 'em work for Jakob Schumann at the tannery, and they were out for blood. I'll swanney, Ben, it's a wonder that boy got through the night. Redbone and Crip were standing guard, but they were plenty nervous, and it was two against twenty, maybe thirty. Finally, Vince Taliaferro showed up, told the crowd that if they didn't get on home, he would have Redbone arrest every last one of them. Finally, they left, but more'n one shouted 'We'll be back!'"

"So that's when you called the judge?" asked Ben.

"That's right. I didn't know what else to do. I know what you did down in Wilmington, so I asked him to send you right away. I'll tell you what, Ben, those fellers may be standing down for now, but they aren't done with this. I hope I did the right thing."

"You did right, Ros. I was in the room with the judge when you called. He was really shaken up. Right after he hung up with you, he gave me my marching orders. Told me to get to Wilkes right away. So," Ben spread his arms wide, "here I am, Ros. Now I just need to figure out how to deal with this thing."

"Well, there's more." McGee offered. "After I got off the phone with the judge, I drove back over to Wilkesboro. Redbone had taken Rachel's body over to Doc Burleson's, you know, for the autopsy. I guess they have to do that in a case like this?"

"That's right," Ben confirmed. "Always in murder cases, to confirm the legal cause of death."

"Well, anyways, this South American Jewish guy, Gruenwald I think his name is, the guy who brings in the hides for the tannery, well, pretty soon he shows up, says that Schumann sent him over to identify the body. Said that Schumann was a mess, just not up to it. So, he does his thing and then tells Burleson to hurry up."

"Why the rush?"

"Well, as I understand it, Jewish people are pretty partic'lar about funerals. They like to get their people into the ground real quick. So, he was pushing Doc Burleson to finish up, release the body. Burleson didn't want to cause trouble. Told Gruenwald that the cause of death was pretty obvious—Virgil Wade's skinning knife stuck through Rachel's heart, so deep that the point pushed through her back. So, Burleson signed the papers and released the body. Gruenwald loaded her up in his wagon and brought her back to Schumann Village. Tannery workers had already dug her grave, and the family buried her this mornin'."

"How do you know all this, Ros?" asked Ben, frowning.

McGee paused. "Well, Olly Overby was there, taking pictures of the body. You know, for the record. Olly said that Taliaferro told him to do it. Said he would need them for the trial."

"So, there are photographs of the body?" asked Ben.

"That's right. Not only at Burleson's office. Redbone called Olly over earlier to take pictures at the river, too. I brought him over in the Phaeton."

Something clicked in Ben's mind. "The judge told me something about photographs. Said *you* had some pictures."

Sheepishly, McGee replied. "Well, I did say that, Ben. Actually, I have an . . . an arrangement with Olly. I have copies of all the photographs, at the scene and at Doc Burleson's."

Ben pondered this. "I need to see them, Ros."

McGee rose, walked to a cabinet, and took out a thin brown manila envelope. He placed ten, eight-by-ten-inch photographs on the kitchen table. Ben examined each of the gruesome photographs, wincing at each new horror.

The photographs at the small sandy beach by the river were taken from different angles. Several captured the entire scene, Rachel on her back, eyes wide open, her shirt torn apart, the knife through her heart.

"And look here, Ben." McGee pointed at several slashing wounds on her chest and stomach. "That boy must'a been plenty pissed off about something."

Virgil Wade's knife handle stood upright at an awkward angle, the overlapping *V* and *W* clearly visible, forming a diamond pattern in the middle.

"And you can see that big bruise there, on the left side of her face. Jesus, he must'a knocked her plumb out!"

Ben nodded. "Is that a rock under her head? Looks like maybe she hit her head on that, too."

McGee bent for a closer look. "I didn't notice that before."

"And what about that fancy quilt? Laid out nice and proper," said Ben.

"And that's not all that's strange, Ben. Look'a here," McGee said, pointing at a kerosene lantern overturned on the quilt. "And here," indicating a half-full whiskey bottle on the ground beside a small canvas bag. "And here—" McGee gestured to two small, clear, round objects on the quilt, beside the whiskey bottle.

Ben squinted, drew closer for a better view. "Looks like a couple of marbles, maybe?"

"I couldn't figure it out either. So, I got this," said McGee, reaching for a small magnifying glass. "Now, take another look."

Ben moved the glass back and forth, trying to bring the blurry image into focus. Then he looked up at McGee. "I see it now. It's shot glasses! For the whiskey—"

"You got it."

"Are you telling me that Virgil Wade, a skinny young boy with rape and murder on his mind, kidnapped Rachel Schumann on impulse in the middle of the night, bound and gagged her to keep her quiet, saddled her horse, picked up a quilt and a lantern, and then took the time to break into the hotel and steal a bottle of whiskey and two shot glasses? Put all this stuff into a canvas bag, lifted Rachel Schumann up onto her horse, got himself up in the saddle, and trotted off to the Yadkin River bridge? All without making a sound, without waking anybody up?"

McGee spread his arms wide, shrugged. "But for a dead body layin' there, looks like a *party* goin' on, Ben." McGee then pointed at Rachel's throat. "See there, Ben? See that necklace? Looks expensive, gold, with a jeweled locket. And Olly says that Redbone found money in her pocket, too, twenty or thirty dollars."

"So why would Virgil Wade leave all that behind? You'd think that if he was going to murder her, he would at least have made off with the necklace and the money, poor boy like him."

"Beats me," said McGee.

Reaching for the second stack, McGee paused. "These are the photographs from Doc Burleson's office, Ben. There're worse than the others."

And they were. Rachel's unwashed, unclothed body lay face-up on a table in Burleson's office, her face darkly bruised, the knife still deep in her chest. The brutal, obscene indignity of it struck Ben like a fist to the stomach. How had a beautiful young woman, her whole life ahead of her, come to end up like this, cold and lifeless, unseeing, unfeeling, her naked breasts and private parts uncovered for all to see, unaware of her tragic and senseless insult and humiliation? Burleson had, at least, closed her pleading, terrified eyes.

The final photographs showed Rachel face-down on the table. Burleson had obviously removed the knife, leaving the gaping exit wound clearly visible high on her back.

Stricken, Ben looked up at McGee. "Ros, these are just . . . just terrible. The Schumanns must never be permitted to see these, Ros. Never."

McGee grimaced, shrugged. "I hear you, Ben. Nobody but you, Olly, and Tink know I have these. But Redbone and Taliaferro have the originals. What they plan to do with them, well I guess that's up to Taliaferro."

Ben made a decision, said firmly, "Ros, I need you to give me the photographs. You don't ever want them to be traced back to you. I need to make sure they stay private and secret. You follow me?"

McGee considered that. "Okay, Ben. I hear you. You know what's best," he said, replacing the photographs in the manila envelope and handing it over to Ben.

Ben took the envelope and shook McGee's hand. "Thanks for understanding, Ros. It's the right thing."

Ben rose and said, "Okay, then. Let's go see this man Taliaferro. Let's go right now."

W

McGee and Ben crossed the Yadkin at the iron bridge, stopping briefly to inspect the spit of beach on the north bank below the bridge. Rex then pulled the Phaeton up the road to the Wilkes County Jail, set on a gently sloping hillside diagonally across from the courthouse and the Schumann Hotel beyond.

Several sullen men were loitering, muttering quietly among themselves. Deputy Sheriff Cobey "Crip" Goins sat chewing tobacco in a rocking chair in the shade, a sawed-off twelve-gauge shotgun across his lap.

The building that once confined Tom Dula was a two-story brick structure with a low hipped roof with overhanging eaves. Goins lived in rooms on the south side, and four iron-barred cells were on the north side, two up and two down. Bars covered the windows, and come election time, Sheriff Poindexter liked reminding voters that no prisoner had ever escaped from his jail.

Drawing Rex to a halt, McGee and Ben stepped down from the Phaeton and walked slowly toward Goins. Rising from his chair, and favoring his unsteady leg, Goins worked his mouth, turned his head, and spat.

"Afternoon, McGee," he nodded, breaking the breech and cradling the weapon in his arms.

"Same to you, Crip," replied McGee. "Hot today."

"Ain't it, though?" Crip answered, removing his hat and wiping his brow with his sleeve. Moving the shotgun in Ben's direction, Goins said, "Looks like you brought a visitor, R.E. Nice to see you, Ben. Been a while."

"You, too, Crip," smiled Ben. "Too long."

"What can I do f'you gentlemen this fine Friday afternoon? Redbone told me you might turn up."

"That's right, Crip. Governor Maxwell sent me over to see if you and Redbone needed any help with your new prisoner."

"You mean the Wade boy?" asked Goins. "'Looks like you come a long way for nothin', Ben. We got that scalawag locked up in there," pointing a thumb back at the jail. "Chains and handcuffs, yessir, bound up tighter'n a tick."

"What about them?" Ben asked, pointing to the group of men standing by. "McGee here tells me that folks're mighty stirred up about this Rachel Schumann thing."

"Naw, naw. McGee here needs to learn to mind his own damned business. Me'n Redbone, we got it covered. Terrible thing happened to that girl, Ben. Terrible. But anybody gets out of line," he smiled, patting the shotgun, "me'n ol' Gladys here can handle it." Snapping the breech shut with a click, he added, "Twelve gauge, sawed off, buckshot."

"Glad to hear it, Crip. That thing legal?"

"Well, Ben, not in your hands. But for me, one hundred percent. O-fficial gov'ment issue," smiled Goins, stroking the shotgun's barrels.

"Looks like Gladys here could sure enough ruin somebody's day."

Goins laughed, spat again, nodded. "You got that right, Ben."

Ben smiled back. "But you're right, Crip. I have come a long way. Mind if I talk to the Wade boy a minute, just check up on him? Would go a long way to getting Governor Maxwell off my back."

Shaking his head, Goins replied, "Nope. Not gonna happen, Ben. Taliaferro, Razor, he gave me'n Redbone strict orders. Nobody gets near the Wade boy. No visitors, nothin', nobody. Not even his momma, done already been down here cryin' and all, not them," pointing at the men standing by, "and not you."

"So maybe I need to talk to Taliaferro."

"Do what you gotta do, Ben," he shrugged. Gesturing toward the courthouse, Goins continued. "I 'spect you can find him in his office over yonder. But you better hurry. Ol' Razor likes to cut out early on Friday afternoon."

"I hear you, Crip. Thanks for your time. Good to see you. You stay . . . cool . . . now, you hear?"

"I heard that!" Crip laughed, again patting the shotgun, and taking his seat. "Cool as a Cub Creek river rock, that's me."

Walking back to the Phaeton, Ben looked at McGee. "Ros, I'm going to try to see Taliaferro now. Probably better if I do that alone."

McGee nodded. "I'll take your bag over to the hotel. You can check in when you're done at the courthouse. I'll feel better, knowing you're there, close by."

"Thanks, Ros. Look, let's put it to bed for today. I've got to go see Schumann tomorrow. I'll drop by later and we can talk."

"Good idea," agreed McGee. "See you in the mornin'."

Ben made his way around to the front of the courthouse, climbed the steps and entered the coolness of the vestibule. Ceiling fans pushed a breeze along the hallway. Finding the office he sought, Ben knocked on the closed door.

Taliaferro in his three-piece bespoke suit and Sheriff Poindexter were discussing the Rachel Schumann case. Taliaferro reclined and asked, "So, then, how'd it go over at Schumann Village yesterday?"

Poindexter shook his head. "Tough, boss. Real tough. How do you tell a fam'ly their daughter's dead? Murdered at the hands of a—" The sheriff stopped, took a breath. "Ol' man Schumann and his wife, well, they were all tore up. Schumann, he tried to keep it together, but his wife, well, she was all to pieces. Thought I might have to call Doc Burleson."

"Did you express my condolences, tell them how sorry I am for their loss?" Taliaferro asked eagerly, spinning his fingers.

"Yessir, just like you told me to. I told them that we had the Wade bastard in the jail, and that you aim to hang him. Real soon like."

Taliaferro nodded. "Good, Redbone, that's good."

"I told Schumann that we needed somebody to come over to Doc Burleson's to identify the body. Well, Schumann just collapsed in his chair, started cryin' like a baby. 'Bout that time that fella Gruenwald, the guy brings the hides in, well he came in. Seems like him and Schumann are real tight. Schumann asked him if he would go on over to Doc's place and . . . take care of it. Gruenwald said he would.

"Mrs. Schumann, well, she spoke up and told Schumann that they needed to get the body back over there. Said they needed to bury Rachel quick. Some Jewish thing. Gruenwald said he would handle all of it. 'Fore he left he got some tannery hands busy digging the grave over in the yard, by the bandstand, told the superintendent to get on over to Wilcox & Sons for a casket. I rode with Gruenwald back over to Doc's house."

"What about Burleson? He get his job done?"

"Yessir. Olly Overby was there takin' pictures while Doc did his work. God what a sight! Burleson finished up real quick, signed some papers, and Gruenwald left with the body. I hear they got a rabbi over from Greensboro and buried her first thing this mornin'. Burleson said he would have the autopsy report and the photographs over to you right away."

Taliaferro took all this in. "Yes, I got a package from him." Changing the subject, he asked, "What about the Wade boy?"

"Well, after you and I got through talking him through the thing this morning," Poindexter rolled his eyes, "I chained him up in the jail. Crip's standing guard."

"And that horse shit fairy tale he told us!" shouted Taliaferro. "What does he take us for, Redbone, a couple of morons? That boy is dumber than a bagful of hammers! I do think we put the fear of God into that curly red head of his. I don't expect to hear his *story* repeated," he said, looking at the sheriff. "As long as you can keep your trap shut, Redbone."

"No problem, boss."

"That's what I like to hear, Redbone. You just remember that." Moving on, Taliaferro asked, "Is he safe?"

"I gotta tell you, boss. Last night was a close call. Twenty or thirty boys, likkered up and calling for blood. Good thing you showed up and chased them off. Tonight? Weekend?" he said, spreading his hands wide. "Hard to say."

"I'm counting on you, Redbone. Like I said, I need that boy living and breathing so I can get him in front of a jury. We clear?"

Sheriff Poindexter just nodded.

"And, like I didn't have enough to deal with, I got this first thing this morning," fumed Taliaferro, reaching for a yellow paper on his desk.

"What's that?" asked the sheriff.

"It's a goddamned telegram! From that no account Republican governor of ours. Maxwell says he's concerned about the safety of the boy. Says he's sending this guy Ben Waterman here to snoop around. Says he 'will not accept' a Wilmington repeat. Says Waterman will get here *today!* Son of a bitch, Redbone!" Taliaferro exploded. "Can't he see I'm with him on this? I need Virgil Wade alive even more'n he does!"

Taliaferro tossed the message back onto his desk. "And who in the hell is this Ben Waterman? Far as I know, he's just a hey-boy for Maxwell, been carrying his water for years. And how could Maxwell hear about this so quick?" he mused. "I see R.E. McGee's hand in this. Folks say he and Waterman are thick as thieves."

"That's shore 'nuff right, boss. I've knowed 'em both all my life. They're like brothers. And Waterman, well the Republicans think he's the Second Coming for what he did down in Wilmington. And he's from here, knows the Schumanns real well, knows ever'body, really." Poindexter paused and said softly, "Well, boss, ever'body 'cept you. So, no surprise that Maxwell would send him. Question is, what do we do about it?"

"I'm thinking about that. For sure this means trouble, Redbone, trouble I don't need."

Just then there were three loud knocks on the office door. The two men looked at each other as Taliaferro shouted, "Come in!"

Taliaferro turned to Poindexter. "If it's Waterman, you let me do the talking."

Ben entered the office. Visible were two dark, standing silhouettes backlit from the window. Closing the door behind him, Ben's eyes adjusted to the light.

"Yes? Who are you? What do you want?" demanded Taliaferro.

So it's going to be like this, thought Ben.

"I am Ben Waterman, sir, and I assume you must be Solicitor Taliaferro?"

"Correct. What can I do for you?"

"Well, sir, I work for Governor Maxwell in Raleigh. He asked me to come to Wilkesboro, to pay you a visit and—"

"Yes, yes," interrupted Taliaferro, waving the telegram. "I got his message. So why are you here, Waterman?"

The three men stood awkwardly in the room. Ben glanced at Redbone Poindexter, whom he had known since childhood. The sheriff nodded to Ben but remained silent. Gesturing at the desk and chairs, Ben suggested, "Perhaps it would be better if we all took a seat?"

Taliaferro hesitated, snorted, sat. Ben and Poindexter followed suit.

"I'm waiting, Waterman. Make it quick. I'm a busy man. Sheriff Poindexter and I have work to do."

"First of all," Ben began slowly, "I am here to pay Governor Maxwell's respects—and mine—to the Schumann family. We have known them since they came to Wilkes and are fortunate to count them as good friends."

No shit, thought Taliaferro. *Schumann and his Jewish buddies have given thousands of dollars supporting Maxwell and his Fusionist friends.*

"Second, Governor Maxwell has heard about Rachel Schumann's murder and the Wade boy's possible role in it. Also heard about the mob outside the jail, calling for his head yesterday."

"Bah!" spat Taliaferro. "*Mob!* Lord have mercy, Redbone, you hear that? . . . Let me tell you, Waterman, that lovely girl, Rachel Schumann, well, she's stone-cold dead in the ground, murdered! So yes, folks're in high dudgeon about that. Why wouldn't they be? And all the while that Wade boy is over there in the jail, locked up safe and sound, getting three squares a day, probably sleeping like a baby, right Redbone? You don't believe it, just go on over to the jail and see for yourself," said Taliaferro, pointing in the direction of the jailhouse.

"I tried that," replied Ben evenly. "All I got for my trouble was Crip Goins waving a sawed-off shotgun in my face."

Taken aback, Taliaferro paused, looked over to Poindexter. "Well, that . . . that could be," he nodded. "He's got his orders. What of it?"

"Let me be perfectly clear about this, Mr. Taliaferro. You have an awful murder on your hands that has riled up the whole county. You have a young colored boy in custody and a bunch of vigilantes just itching to get their hands around his neck. And you have two—*two*—lawmen, one a cripple, to look after him twenty-four hours a day, seven days a week, until the trial starts.

"Governor Maxwell thinks that Wilkes, his home county, mind you, is a powder keg about to explode. And he is determined to prevent that from happening, Mr. Taliaferro, with or without your cooperation.

"Now, as you must know, I work for the governor. If you read the telegram, then you will also know that I have full authority to investigate this situation and take whatever action I think is necessary to keep the peace here and protect the prisoner." Easing back in his chair and softening his tone, Ben continued. "You have a hell of a mess on your hands, you and Sheriff Poindexter. I understand the fix you're in. I did not come here to cause trouble for you or get in your way. My mission is to *help you*, Solicitor, to help you defuse the situation so justice comes to Virgil Wade . . . by the book."

Taliaferro was silent for a long minute. Then he leaned forward, sneered, and slowly clapped his hands in sarcastic cadence. "Bravo, Waterman, bravo! What a lovely speech!" Rising, scowling, he pointed at Ben. "Now, my turn. Now, *you* listen to *me*."

Counting on his fingers, Taliaferro made his points in his rapid-fire high-pitched voice.

"*First*, I don't *need* your help.

"*Second*, I don't *want* your help.

"*Third*, I have everything I need to go to trial. Right now! I have the Wade boy at the scene, I have his knife through Rachel Schumann's heart, I have him in possession of her stolen horse, and, most important, *I have the boy*.

"*Fourth*, in Wilkes County, I *am* the law, and what I say here goes.

"And *fifth*, what I say is this—you will *not* enter my jail, nor will you be permitted to visit or speak with my prisoner.

"Now, I hope that I have made *myself* clear, Mr. Waterman, unless you have some questions or need additional clarification?"

Ben did not speak.

Shaking with fury, Taliaferro again pointed his finger. Now you, sir," he thundered. "You may now by God get the hell out of my office! Crawl your own bootlicking sorry self back to Raleigh, deliver my message to your lame duck has been, and tell him to put that in his pipe and smoke it!"

Without a word, Ben closed the door behind him and made his way across the street to the Schumann Hotel.

Chapter 11

His head spinning, Ben took a deep breath and entered the hotel. Jewel Ponder, a large, friendly Black woman, was busy tidying up the reception desk and the bar behind it. Jewel was the head housekeeper, and during busy court weeks she was assisted by her three daughters, Ruby, Opal and Pearl. She greeted him with a wide smile.

"Afternoon, suh. You must be Mistah Waterman? Your name is on the list."

"That's me, ma'am."

"I'll go fetch Miz Claire Elise. Your bag is over there where Mistah McGee left it. You can go ahead and put your name and address in here," she said, pushing a red leather-bound registration book across the desk.

Ben retrieved his bag and began filling out the information required.

Claire Elise Montgomery quietly made her way to the front desk. She was wearing the typical Gibson Girl ensemble of the day—a black A-line pleated skirt, closely fitted at the waist and held by a wide matching belt and silver buckle, paired with a white embroidered lace gigot summer blouse. Its wide, puffy sleeves reached down from her shoulders to just above her elbows. A high white collar was adorned with a carved Italian cameo. Her long auburn hair was pulled back on the sides and up, providing some relief from the heat, held by opalescent mother of pearl combs.

"Good afternoon, Mr. Waterman," smiled Claire Elise, and, in her lovely British accent, said, "Welcome to the Schumann Hotel. I am Claire Elise Montgomery, the hotel manager. We've been expecting you. Miss Alexander in Governor Maxwell's office was kind enough to telephone us.

"Jewel has prepared a nice corner room for you on the second floor, two windows to catch the breeze, plus a ceiling fan. It should be very quiet during your stay. In fact, you are our only guest this week, so you will have the run of the place."

As he glanced up from the registration book, Ben stared into Claire Elise's startling green eyes. For a moment, he was speechless, stunned.

Julia.

Waiting for Ben to reply, Claire Elise tilted her head, raising an eyebrow. "Mr. Waterman? Are you quite all right?"

"Uh, yes, yes, of course," Ben stuttered. "Sorry. It's been a long day, and I've just come from a . . . difficult meeting." He clumsily held out his hand, and they shook. "Ben Waterman."

Her face. The eyes. The hair. The voice. The touch.

Julia . . . Julia Charlotte Burton. His mind flashed back to Oxford.

"I understand. You've had a long journey. And in this heat . . . let's get you checked into your room. Perhaps you would enjoy a nice cool bath? Shall I have Jewel prepare it for you?"

"That would be . . . would be wonderful, Mrs. Montgomery. Thank you. Very kind."

"Good then! I'm sure you will feel much refreshed afterward. Dinner is served about six o'clock, here in the dining area, if that suits you?"

"Six o'clock is just fine, thanks."

Ben climbed the stairs to his pleasant, spacious room overlooking the courthouse, the Tory Oak, and the Wilkes County Jail. *Perfect.* It appeared the group of men milling about the jail had gone home for supper. *That's good.*

Ben was unpacking his valise and hanging his clothes in the chifforobe when there came a soft knock.

"Mistah Waterman?" called Jewel.

"Yes, Jewel?" answered Ben through the closed door.

"I got your bath ready. Nice and cool, suh. Just right!"

"Thanks, Jewel."

"Bathroom and johnny are just down the hall on the left. Towels'n everythin' all laid out."

"Very good, Jewel, I'll be right along."

Ben removed his clothing and stood looking into the mirror above the washbasin. *God, I'm a mess,* he thought as he took out his straight razor and whetstone. *Need a haircut, too.* Wiping his clean-shaven face on the hand towel, Ben eased his lanky frame into the cool water of the claw foot bathtub. *Ah, that's more like it,* he thought, lathering up. He rinsed himself, submerged his head, shook away the water, smoothed back his hair, and sat low in the tub, up to his chin, relaxing and enjoying the peace and quiet.

He may have dozed off. His thoughts were of Julia, but the face he saw in his mind was that of Claire Elise Montgomery.

W

One floor below, Claire Elise was busy preparing Ben's evening meal. Pork chops, sweet potatoes, green beans, biscuits and gravy, and Jewel's famous banana pudding.

What a handsome, charming man, she thought. *Sent by the governor. Surely, he is here about Rachel Schumann. What to make of that?*

Chapter 12

After their long sea voyage from Buenos Aires, Charles Randall Montgomery and Claire Elise had arrived on a beautiful fall day. The summer heat had finally broken, and the afternoon air was cool and crisp, the cloudless sky a deep blue.

To Claire Elise's delight, they were met at the wharf by a smiling Gabriel von Gruenwald. "Welcome to North Carolina, dear friends, your new home!" he said as he supervised the loading of their baggage into the wagon that would deliver them to the train station.

From Wilmington, the three travelers proceeded to Raleigh, Greensboro, Rural Hall, and finally North Wilkesboro. Along the route Gruenwald produced photographs and spoke with great enthusiasm about the new Schumann Tannery, the hustling, bustling new town of North Wilkesboro, the small cottage Jakob Schumann had built for them, the new clapboard schoolhouse not a stone's throw away.

"It is such an opportunity for you," he said to Montgomery, "I think you and Claire Elise will love it there. The Schumanns are wonderful people, and their children are most charming and intelligent. And the town is growing so rapidly! Full of interesting people, too."

"And we will see you there from time to time?" asked Claire Elise.

"Why, of course. As you know, I live in Wilmington with my two small sons." Gruenwald bowed his head. "Just the three of us since . . . since my wife passed away earlier this year. In childbirth." Seated across the aisle, Claire Elise reached her hand to Gruenwald, touched his forearm.

"Yes, Gabriel, we heard about that. A terrible tragedy. We are so sorry for your loss."

"Thank you, thank you both. It was quite a blow, but we are adjusting, surviving. So, the answer, Claire Elise, is yes, you will see me in Wilkes. I need to be there to manage the processing of the hides."

"It will be very nice, Gabriel, to see a friendly face now and then."

Gruenwald smiled. "I could not agree more, Claire Elise."

W

Things did not go well for the Montgomerys in Wilkes.

The new cottage provided by Schumann was comfortable, and the schoolhouse was perfectly suited for its purpose. Schumann Village was an interesting mix of tannery managers and supervisors and their families and children, some from faraway places in the United States and beyond.

Claire Elise made every effort to adapt and fit into her strange and sometimes bewildering new community, and she enjoyed her growing friendship with the Schumanns and their children. She made some friends among the townspeople, too, mostly mothers of children attending the academy. But there were drawbacks. North Wilkesboro was no doubt a lively new town, full of promise and potential. But given their backgrounds, it often seemed they were living as pioneers in a muddy, rude, and rustic Wild West frontier town.

And there was the tannery. Soon to become the driving economic force in Wilkes County, the tannery was also the source of breathtaking and inescapable stink, vile black smoke, and putrid waste, odors that seemed to overwhelm and permeate the very timbers of Schumann Village and the surrounding workshops and factory buildings. "The smell of money!" Jakob Schumann would lecture to any who complained, but Claire Elise and her husband, unlike other residents of Schumann Village, were never able to adjust to it.

W

As for Randall Montgomery, he had never fully come to grips with the disgrace of his sudden and, in his view, unfair dismissal from his school in Buenos Aires and his and Claire Elise's ostracization. He had grudgingly accepted Gruenwald's proposal, supported by Claire Elise's father, because he felt he had no choice. He despised his new *home*, his new life. He made no friends.

Montgomery's burning resentment soon undermined his work. Schumann had recruited a cohort of a dozen or so pupils for the Academy, including his own children, Rachel, Leah, and Amos. The children were bright and eager enough, but, in Montgomery's view, they were no match for his former students in England and Argentina. He found his job boring, unfulfilling. He regarded himself much as a convicted felon, exiled to a remote and forgotten island barren of all culture and refinement.

Montgomery began drinking heavily and would sometimes buy opium, readily available from local dealers lurking in the dark alleyways near the train depot. Many nights Claire Elise would softly cry herself to sleep as her distraught and shattered husband paced the floors of the small cottage.

Their marriage was a union in name only. Claire Elise craved a child, knowing her chances were daily slipping away, but she could not bring herself to conceive *his* child. They fought, quarreling over small things and large. They were, in a word, miserable. And there were no comforting visits from her father. Sadly, John Russell Fleming passed away from a heart attack two months after assuming his new position in Ottawa. Claire Elise, heartbroken, felt alone and abandoned, an orphan in a strange land.

A year passed, then two, and then five. Each month, from a distance unbridgeable in so many ways, Claire Elise would watch as the handsome and dashing widower Gabriel von Gruenwald visited North Wilkesboro. She would see him here and there around the town, everywhere it seemed, busy buying, selling, doing business, striding about the tannery grounds, enjoying a meal, laughing with friends. *Happy,* she thought. *Enjoying life.* His strength and vitality, his confidence and carefree spirit contrasted poorly with the wreck of a man her husband had become.

On Christmas Eve 1897, Charles Randall Montgomery drained the last drop of Irish whiskey from its bottle, tossed it aside. He took a final, forlorn look around his small, unhappy home, unadorned with holiday trappings. Without a word or note to anyone, he strode purposefully through the cold wind to the barn behind the house. There he climbed into the rafters, strung a rope from a hook in the ridgepole, knotted it securely around his neck, closed his eyes, spread his arms, and fell into space.

Montgomery's suicide was a disaster for Claire Elise. Suddenly she had no money, no prospects, her future uncertain. Soon a new schoolmaster was recruited, and the small cottage on the grounds of Schumann Village was needed for him and his young family. What was to be done?

Genuinely fond of Claire Elise, Gabriel von Gruenwald had yet another idea. He asked for a meeting with Jakob Schumann.

Gruenwald and Schumann sat in the comfortable parlor of Tanner's Rest, the Schumann home, enjoying a glass of cool, golden Alsatian Riesling.

"So, Gabriel, what can I do for you today?" asked Schumann.

"Well, sir, I have been thinking about Mrs. Montgomery."

"*Ach, mein Gott,* what a tragedy!"

"She is in a terrible situation. No husband, no family, no source of income."

"*Ja, ja.* She has been much on my mind," nodded Schumann. "Rebekah and I and the children have grown very fond of her. I wonder what I might do to help her."

"I have an idea about that, sir."

"Please continue, Gabriel. I am eager to hear it."

"Last month you closed your purchase of the hotel in Wilkesboro." Baron von Gruenwald's prophecy had come true. The tannery project made Jakob Schumann a wealthy man. The elderly husband and wife owners of the Hotel Wilkesboro had died recently, only days apart, leaving the property to their children. Uninterested in the business, the heirs quarreled among themselves, unable to agree on what should be done with the hotel or how to manage it.

The hotel was important to Schumann. Visiting business associates, vendors, and customers needed a place to stay during their frequent visits, and Schumann preferred to house them in Wilkesboro, far enough away to escape the malodorous pollution of the tannery, but close and convenient enough for business meetings. During court weeks the hotel was also favored by judges, lawyers, and clients who appreciated its comfort, food, and service. Gruenwald had stayed there many times.

Schumann made the heirs an offer and became the new owner of the renamed Schumann Hotel. What he lacked was someone to run it for him.

"You mentioned to me that you are searching for someone to manage the hotel," Gruenwald said.

"Yes?"

"What about Mrs. Montgomery? She is pretty and charming and quite capable. She has traveled the world, sir, speaks several languages, and is most comfortable in the presence of businessmen and others of high rank. I have seen firsthand the supportive role she played for her father in Buenos Aires. She has experience in the hospitality field, having organized many elegant receptions and dinners there. She certainly has the poise and confidence necessary to manage an enterprise such as your hotel."

"*Ach, Gabriel!*" exclaimed Schumann, slapping the arm of his chair. "*Was fuer eine hervorragende Idee!*"

"She could live on site in the owner's quarters. That would solve the issue with the cottage. And the job would provide her with a steady income."

Schumann nodded enthusiastically. "*Ja, ja. Einverstanden! Danke, Gabriel. I will send for her right away!*"

Claire Elise accepted Schumann's proposal with enthusiasm and relief. She moved into the two-room apartment behind the hotel reception and began her new life. Jewel had been a fixture at the hotel for years and was most helpful during the transition.

Claire Elise enjoyed her new job immensely. Having moved on from her bleak existence at Schumann Village, her renewed engagement with interesting people from all walks of life, from all over the world, restored her natural vibrancy and vitality, and the light and sparkle returned to her striking green eyes. Her impeccable British manners, cheerful disposition, and warm personality soon won the admiration and respect of hotel guests and Wilkesboro townspeople alike. For the first time in Wilkes, she was happy.

And, once a month, regular as clockwork, tannery business brought her friend Gabriel von Gruenwald to town. One of Schumann's men would meet him at the depot in North Wilkesboro and deliver him to the Schumann Hotel—now under new management.

How interesting, mused Claire Elise, that both she and Gabriel Gruenwald should both end up widowed and once again regularly in each other's company.

Chapter 13

Ben removed his spare shirt, pants, and suit jacket from the chifforobe and hurriedly dressed, checked the mirror, and strode to the door. Checking himself, he returned to the bed, picked up his journey-worn clothes, and placed them the small wicker basket for Jewel to brush and press. Leaving the basket in the hallway, Ben made his way down the stairs.

Separate from the reception was a comfortable dining area with several round tables covered with starched white linens. Claire Elise's smiling face appeared from the kitchen. "Welcome, Mr. Waterman. I hope you found your room and the bath satisfactory?"

"Perfect," said Ben. "Very sorry to be late, but I must confess the bath was so pleasant I may have napped for a few minutes."

"Think nothing of it. I can only imagine how tired you must be from your journey. All the way from Raleigh, and then straight into meetings." Tilting her head, she again smiled. "But I must say, you look much more . . . refreshed than when you arrived. But see here, you must be famished after your long day. May I offer you refreshment before dinner?"

"Well, I would not refuse a whiskey if you have it."

"Certainly," she replied, moving toward the bar behind the reception desk. "Any particular brand?"

"I will leave that in your capable hands, Mrs. Montgomery. Whatever you think best. But I do hate to drink alone. Will you join me?"

She returned to the table, two glasses in her hand. "For you, fine George Dickel Tennessee sipping whiskey, sir," she said, setting the glass at his place setting, gesturing for him to sit. Claire Elise poured amber liquor into his glass. "Ice?"

"Why, yes, if you have it. How, may I ask, do you have ice in July? I've seen it in Raleigh, but I didn't expect it here."

"In wintertime, Negro gentlemen from Cairo cut blocks of it from the Reddies River. They bring it back to their icehouse, cover it with straw, and keep it in the dark. They deliver ice all summer long, coal in the winter."

"And you?" asked Ben, taking his seat and eyeing the cut crystal wine glass in her hand.

Sweeping her skirt aside, Claire Elise sat across from Ben. "A nice claret from France. Bordeaux. An indulgence, I realize. Mr. Schumann keeps me stocked. Mr. Gruenwald brings it when he comes from Wilmington."

Raising an eyebrow, Ben asked, "Medoc?"

Surprised, Claire Elise replied, "Actually, no. Saint-Emilion. Do you know wines?"

"I have some experience. I learned to enjoy French reds during my stay in Oxford, back during my university days."

"Oxford? I am impressed, I must say!"

"It was a long time ago. But not so long that I cannot recognize a British accent when I hear one," smiled Ben.

"You have a good ear, Mr. Waterman. I am indeed from England, daughter of a British diplomat, but I have spent time in various countries during my father's postings abroad. But look, your ice is melting, watering your drink. Shall we?"

Ben raised his glass, "To Claire Elise Montgomery and the excellent hospitality she provides."

Grasping her glass by its stem, Claire Elise touched it to Ben's with a gentle, clear chime. "And to your health, Ben Waterman, and to a successful sojourn in Wilkesboro." They drank.

"And now, your meal," said Claire Elise, rising from her chair. "I will be back shortly." She soon returned with a tray and set the meal before him.

"But surely you will join me?" asked Ben.

"I would be delighted, but I have already dined this evening. Perhaps another time? While you are here?"

Disappointed, Ben said, "I look forward to it."

"When you are finished, just leave everything here. Jewel will clear it all away. And do remember breakfast at seven tomorrow morning.

Right here, in this room."

Nodding, Ben smiled and said, "I will be here. And I promise to be here promptly at seven.

"Speaking of tomorrow, Mrs. Montgomery, I wonder if I might ask you to set aside some time for me. You see, I am here on business, business having to do with the . . . incident here in Wilkes yesterday. I understand that you had the misfortune to be somehow involved in discovering the awful crime committed against the Schumann girl?"

Claire Elise's face clouded, her face suddenly betraying her strain and exhaustion. "Yes. It has truly been a terrible experience . . . horrible." Smiling again, she said, "But I am so pleased that your arrival has provided me with a reason to put it out of my mind for a while. We will have plenty of time to talk, Mr. Waterman. I promise. But now, your food is getting cold. Please, enjoy. I must retire. I, too, have had a long, long day."

With that, Claire Elise turned and disappeared behind the curtain, leaving Ben to finish his supper alone. The banana pudding was excellent.

Chapter 14

Ben arrived right on time. Outside was overcast, gray, threatening rain, but cooler. Jewel Ponder looked up from her work, smiled. "Morning' Mistah Waterman. You sleep good?"

"Like a baby, Jewel, thank you."

"You must be hungry, suh. Let me get your breakfast."

Raising a hand, Ben said, "Jewel, I know that you and Mrs. Montgomery have had a difficult couple of days, what with the Rachel Schumann thing and all."

"That's right, Mistah Waterman. Been a tough patch."

"Did you know Rachel?"

Jewel hesitated. "I knowed her pretty good I guess, yessir, pretty good."

Filing this away, Ben asked, "What was she like, Jewel? 'Friendly? Treat you right?"

Jewel frowned. "Not f'me to say, suh. I'll go fetch your breakfast now."

Ben quickly added, "What about the Wade boy, Jewel? Virgil Wade?"

Jewel slowly shook her head, sighed. "He always been a good boy, Mistah Waterman. Skinny, quiet. Pauline Oxendine, she raised him right. He was good help 'round here, too, cleanin' out the stables, runnin' errands for me'n Miz Claire Elise. I still just cain't believe it. No suh, I just cain't." She returned to the kitchen.

A few minutes later, Claire Elise appeared, smiling, with a tray. "Good morning, Mr. Waterman! Jewel says you had a restful night, so I expect you are ready for breakfast."

"And good morning to you, Mrs. Montgomery. What have we here?"

Claire Elise set the items before him. "Fresh orange juice to start. Mr. Schumann brings them in from Florida. Next, Jewel's specialty, sausage gravy over buttermilk biscuits, and fresh strawberries and cantaloupe on the side. Coffee?"

"Yes, please. This looks wonderful and smells great!"

"So, please enjoy." She started to turn away, but Ben stopped her.

"Say, I was wondering. I have several things to do today, across the river and back here in Wilkesboro. I wonder if you might know somewhere nearby where I might hire a horse for the day?"

Pointing out the window, Claire Elise replied, "I can do better than that. It looks like rain today. I have a sulky in the livery that would keep you dry or shade you from the sun, either way. You are welcome to borrow it. I use my little pony Maybelle to pull it. She is very gentle and knows every street and byway in the Wilkesboros."

"Much appreciated, Mrs. Montgomery, thank you."

"After breakfast, I'll walk you to the livery out back. Since Virgil Wade is . . . unavailable, I've asked Jewel's daughter Ruby to help out in the stable. She loves to be around the animals. She can get everything ready so you can be on your way."

"Most kind. I appreciate it very much."

Claire Elise held up a cautionary finger. "Just be sure to slow down over the iron bridge. Sheriff Poindexter is very strict about that."

Laughing, Ben said, "Yes, I saw his sign yesterday."

W

Ben looked around while Ruby harnessed up the pony. *There it is. That's the stall with Virgil Wade's cot in it. And that must be the stall where Rachel Schumann's horse was stabled. What could the boy have been thinking?*

Snapping the reins, Ben set off for the bridge. Pulling Maybelle to a halt, he dismounted on the north side of the river. The pony waited patiently in the shade, nibbling at the grass. Holding Olly Overby's photographs, Ben made his way carefully down several stone steps through a tunnel of overhanging branches shading a mostly hidden stretch of sandy beach.

So, this is the place, thought Ben, pacing off the ground, a level space about ten yards long and two deep. All traces of the murder had been removed. The place was once again quiet and peaceful, the Yadkin River flowing slowly downstream. He compared the tranquil scene to Overby's awful photographs, shaking his head. *What in God's name happened here?*

Ben returned to the sulky, snapped the reins, and headed east, past the depot and lumber yards, toward the tannery.

Schumann Village was a collection of tidy frame houses, built on high ground just north of the tannery complex. On the highest point stood Tanner's Rest, Jakob Schumann's Victorian mansion. Next to it was a green and leafy village square, dominated by a raised, eight-sided white gazebo. Close by was a scar of freshly turned and mounded earth. A simple wooden stake bearing a Star of David marked the spot. *Rachel's grave.*

Beneath the clouded sky, the air was still, heavy. The noise and business of the tannery were missing, the factory shut down. Not a soul disturbed the silence. But the sour stench still hit Ben hard. *My God*, he thought. *How do they live with this?*

Ben recalled his first and only experience inside the tannery. Bill Trogdon, eager to display his new economic development trophy, had invited Judge Maxwell to take a tour. Ben tagged along.

Stacks of pungent chestnut oak and tanbark from the railhead were stacked in curving bark sheds before it and hundreds of cords of American chestnut were fed into an enormous grinder (the *hog*) to crush tannin for the tanning vats. *You could hear that grinder all over town*, Ben remembered. Jakob Schumann met the delegation and led them inside.

More than a hundred men, many of them Black, worked in a hot, steamy, noisy, hellhole of a factory reeking of putrid cattle hides. They were summoned to their labors each morning at five o'clock by the shriek of Old Sam, the factory steam whistle. The hides, most of them from the New Canaan Project, were unloaded by hand, a job shunned by White workers. They were washed and soaked in unslaked lime water vats to loosen the hair, and workers then skinned them using long, sharp skinning knives. Hair from the hides was sold to local carriage makers for seat padding.

Schumann, beaming and oblivious to the overpowering stench, explained that the stripped hides were then taken to "the yard" for immersion in a solution of tan liquor. The tanned hides were then dried, finished, and oiled to make durable shoe leather. The entire process, a dark, dangerous, and dirty business, could take several months. Factory waste was dumped into the Yadkin River, flowing east, away from town. No one complained.

W

Tethering the pony, and with a heavy heart, Ben knocked gently on the front door. A solemn, but pretty, young Black woman dressed in mourning clothes opened it.

"Yes?" she asked. "Can I help you?"

Removing his hat, Ben said, "Good morning, ma'am. You must be Pearl?"

"That's right, sir. And you are?"

"My name is Ben Waterman, a friend of the Schumanns. I am sorry to disturb you under the circumstances, but Governor Maxwell has sent me here from Raleigh to pay his respects to Mr. and Mrs. Schumann. We are both so very sorry for their loss."

Pearl glanced over her shoulder. "That's very kind of you, Mr. Waterman. You've come quite a ways. But I'm not sure—"

Suddenly a voice came from within the house. "Who is that, Pearl? Who is at the door?" asked Jakob Schumann, his grim face appearing behind Pearl in the doorway. Blinking in surprise, Schumann stared at Ben. In his heavily accented voice Schumann whispered, "Ben? Ben Waterman? Is that you?"

Pearl withdrew and quietly disappeared.

Hat in hand, Ben answered, "Yes, Mr. Schumann, it's Ben." He held out his hand to shake, but Schumann's big arms folded Ben in a tight embrace.

"Ben. Ben," he said, shaking his head, backing away, tears forming. "How wonderful that you have come. Please. Please come in," he said, gesturing for Ben to enter.

Schumann led Ben into the large, well-appointed parlor, the light dimmed by closed, heavy curtains. A large mirror above the fireplace was draped and covered with a simple bedsheet. A candle burned on the mantle. They sat. Schumann, as always, was formally dressed. On the lapel of his suit coat was pinned a small piece of torn, black fabric. With the back of his hand, Schumann wiped away his tears.

"Ben, it is so very good to see you again after all this time. Surely you have heard—"

"Yes," Ben gently interrupted. "Roscoe McGee was kind enough to call Governor Maxwell soon after it . . . it happened. He asked me to come to Wilkesboro immediately, to tell you and Mrs. Schumann how very . . . very sorry we are. I cannot imagine your pain, Mr. Schumann. There are no words—"

"*Ja. Ja*, Ben. I so much appreciate the gesture." Looking away, Schumann's eyes again moistened. "I am sorry, Ben, but I hope you can understand that Rebekah . . . poor Rebekah . . . "

"No, no, Mr. Schumann, please. I do not wish to disturb her. Please, when the time is right, tell her that I was here, that you and your family are in Governor Maxwell's thoughts and prayers. And mine."

Schumann sighed, taking a deep breath. "After . . . after Rachel was . . . released, it was important to us to have the funeral as soon as possible. That is our custom. Perhaps you saw . . . outside—"

"Yes," Ben said. "I saw."

"We were fortunate that Rabbi Levy was able to come so quickly from Greensboro. We buried Rachel yesterday morning, before *Shabbat*. Tomorrow we will begin to sit *Shiva* for Rachel."

Suddenly Schumann exclaimed, "*Ach, was fuer ein Gastgeber bin ich?* Where are my manners? May I offer you something to drink, Ben?" He raised his sad eyes, a faint smile crossing his lips. "Perhaps a nice cool glass of *Gewurtztraminer*, from Riquewihr?"

Shaking his head, Ben rose. "No, no thank you, Mr. Schumann. I have imposed on you long enough. I am sorry to have disturbed you on the Sabbath. I should be on my way."

Rising to meet him, Schumann said, "I am so very pleased to see you, Ben, even under these terrible . . . circumstances. Please tell Governor Maxwell how much this thoughtful gesture means to me and to Rebekah."

"I will certainly do that, sir."

Walking back to the entranceway, Schumann stopped, thought a moment, and spoke in a voice filled with sadness. "Ben, I must also tell you something, something that I would also ask that you pass along to Governor Maxwell. The terrible . . . shock . . . of this, this *thing*, has opened my eyes, Ben, forced me to make a decision, a very sad decision, Ben."

Ben waited for him to continue.

"Rebekah and I have discussed it. North Wilkesboro has been good to us, Ben. We have, for the most part, been happy here, successful. But things have changed, Ben, are still changing.

"When we first came here and started up the tannery, everyone welcomed us with open arms. We brought jobs for the men, paid them well, created a market for the woodcutters, brought prosperity to this new city. We were, of course, the first Jews in North Wilkesboro, but nobody seemed to notice or care. We were surprised, thrilled. Much different from the nasty looks the Germans gave us back in Alsace.

"But, as I said, things are changing. In recent years it seems that there is something different, something . . . ugly in the air. We feel it, Ben. It is hard to explain, but it is there. Politics is now full of hatred and anger, mostly aimed at the Negroes, but now we feel it, too. We sense that people are sometimes talking about us, behind our backs, little things, Ben, hurtful things. It is usually very subtle, but we suddenly feel their . . . *contempt*." Shaking his head, he continued, "And now we have felt their *violence.*

"These people, Ben, these terrible members of the Red Shirts and the Ku Klux Klan . . . they openly declare their hatred for Blacks and Jews, Ben. There have been . . . incidents at the tannery, among the workers. They seem sullen, resentful.

"In truth, Ben, and for some months now, Rebekah and I, and the children, we no longer feel *at home* here. I hear about the pogroms in Russia and Eastern Europe, Ben, and I fear that this . . . disease may be crossing the Atlantic."

This was the longest speech Ben had ever heard from Jakob Schumann.

"I understand what you are saying, Mr. Schumann. And I cannot disagree that life in North Carolina is . . . changing, and not for the better, particularly for Negroes, but also, I confess, for Jewish people here. I wish I could tell you that your fears are unfounded, but—"

Schumann held up a hand. "It's not your fault, Ben, nor Governor Maxwell's. I know you have done your best. But you—"

"Yes, Mr. Schumann, I know." Ben bowed his head. "We are losing, sir. We may well yet lose it all. And for that, and for *you,* I am so sorry. But what can I say? Do? What does all this mean for you, sir?

Schumann smiled and said softly, "In Europe it is often said that Jews live their lives seated on packed suitcases. So, Ben, we are packing ours, preparing to leave."

Shocked, Ben asked, "What do you mean?"

Schumann took a deep breath. "You must understand, Ben, that the knife blade that ended Rachel's life also pierced the hearts of all of us.

Rebekah. Leah. Amos. And me. I have decided to sell the tannery, Ben. There is no longer a place for us here, I can see that now. I will not allow my . . . my *remaining* children to grow up in this hateful place."

"But what . . . what will you do? Where will you go?"

"We will return home, Ben, to Alsace. My father is old, and he and my brothers need my help with the business. And we will take Rachel with us. We will take Rachel . . . home. Away from here."

Ben was about to protest, but just then a tall, handsome, dark-complected man strode up the front steps of Tanner's Rest. Looking first at Schumann, then to Ben, Gabriel von Gruenwald said, "Good morning, Mr. Schumann. I hope I am not interrupting?"

Waving his hand, Schumann said, "No, no, Gabriel. We were just finishing. Ben, this is my good friend Gabriel von Gruenwald. Gabriel, this is another good friend, Ben Waterman."

The two men looked at one another, shook hands.

"Ben, once again, I cannot thank you enough for your visit. Please give Governor Maxwell my best wishes and thank him for his concern." Raising a finger, Schumann concluded, "And please, Ben, keep the last part of our conversation confidential. I must make certain arrangements before my plans become known."

"Of course, sir. You have my word."

"Very good, Ben. I am certain that we will see each other again before . . . well, you know. And now, Gabriel, please come in. I was just explaining to Ben something that will interest you as well."

Puzzled and intrigued, Gabriel looked at Schumann. *Business? On Shabbat?* Turning to Ben, he said, "It was a pleasure to meet you, Mr. Waterman. I look forward to seeing you again as well."

As Ben walked away, a deep sadness filled his heart. Reaching the sulky, a gentle rain began to fall.

Chapter 15

Interim Solicitor and Chief Prosecutor Vincent Taliaferro and Sheriff Jimmy "Redbone" Poindexter were again seated in Taliaferro's office.

"So," Taliaferro began, "How'd it go last night?"

"Pretty quiet, boss. Things cleared out about suppertime. Crip says no trouble."

"Good, good, Redbone. Now listen up. I've talked to Furnifold Simmons in Raleigh by telephone a couple of times since Thursday, asked him how he thought we should play it, you know, politically."

Poindexter nodded.

"He thinks we need to get ahead, get out front of this thing, with the public and in the press. He likes it and thinks it could go statewide. Said I should make a big announcement Monday morning, call all the reporters, give them our take on the Schumann murder, *et cetera, et cetera, et cetera.* You follow?"

"Yessir, boss. Fine with me. Where do you want to do it? What time?"

"Right on the front steps of the jail, Redbone. Let's say, ten o'clock. I want a big crowd there, and all the newspaper people. Simmons says he'll send some people from Greensboro, maybe Winston. You'n Crip should both be there, on either side of me. I'll do the talking. Tell Crip to bring his shotgun. There will be some photographers there. Will make a good picture for the papers. I'll explain everything. How you led the search, found the Schumann girl by the river, how Crip and the dogs found Virgil Wade, tell about Doc Burleson's autopsy report."

"I'll get the word out, boss. So, Burleson got back to you?"

"Yes. I got his report—and the photographs—yesterday. Confirms the obvious." He sneered, "A dagger through the heart will do the trick every time."

"You gonna put out those pictures? Let folks see 'em?" Shaking his head, Poindexter said, "Not sure I would do that, boss. Folks see 'em, they'll get really riled up. Will make it harder to protect the Wade boy. And think of the Schumanns."

Grinning, Taliaferro answered, "No, no, Redbone. No worries. We'll keep the photographs under lock and key for now. I'll need them later. For the trial."

"Understood."

"Now, Simmons says we should make a lot of noise about how we will protect the Wade boy until the trial, so we can hang his ass fair and square for all to see, blah, blah, blah. Can you handle that?"

"Like I said, boss, it's just me'n Crip."

"Yes, yes. But I want you to put the word out, Redbone. No vigilante stuff. Hear me?" Moving on, Taliaferro continued, "Simmons also had another idea about the Wade boy, something that might help us."

Taliaferro paused. Poindexter waited. "Now, listen to me very carefully, Redbone. I'm not saying that you shouldn't expect some sort of . . . demonstration at the jail, maybe sometime after the announcement Monday. Some understandable, let's say . . . *expression* of the righteous indignation and outrage felt by the good people of Wilkes. Something to put the fear of God into that boy's heart. Not a riot, mind you. Just maybe a little trouble? Then I could show up just in the nick of time. Save the day, follow?"

Hesitating, Poindexter replied, "Yessir, boss. I understand. I'll take care of it."

"Very good, Redbone. I knew I could count on you. Anything else?"

"No sir, not right now. I'll get right on it."

Alone in his office, Taliaferro sat back, satisfied with his morning's work. Suddenly, he remembered his second telephone conversation with Furnifold Simmons.

Simmons didn't like it when I called him back and told him about Ben Waterman showing up here. No, he didn't like that one little bit. Said Waterman is a troublemaker, a first-class asshole. Told me to watch him, watch him every minute.

Rising from his chair, Taliaferro nodded to himself.

I need information.

W

Looking out the window, Claire Elise could see the short, stubby-legged figure of Vincent Taliaferro, his moustache twitching, making his way quickly to the hotel. She made a face. *Taliaferro. What can he want?* She opened the door, and Taliaferro walked in. "Good morning, Mrs. Montgomery. A word?" Looking around, he whispered, "In private?"

"Of course, Mr. Taliaferro." They were alone in the lobby. Claire Elise led him to one of the dining tables. "What can I do for you, sir?"

Leaning forward, his hands clasped before him, Taliaferro explained in a low, conspiratorial voice, "I apologize for my bluntness, but I have a favor to ask of you, Mrs. Montgomery. An important favor, one that will require some . . . discretion."

Claire Elise tilted her head, waited.

"You have a guest in your hotel. A Mr. Ben Waterman?"

Surprised, Claire Elise nodded.

"Are you aware of why he is here?"

"How is that my concern, Mr. Taliaferro? Or yours?" she asked archly.

"Trust me, Mrs. Montgomery, his presence here is very much of concern to me. And perhaps to you as well."

"Whatever can you mean?"

"Ben Waterman has been sent here by Governor Maxwell to investigate the murder of Rachel Schumann. His friend Roscoe McGee has been raising a ruckus up in Raleigh about the Wade boy. So, the governor sent Waterman here to make trouble *for me.*"

"For you? How?"

"He came by my office yesterday, asking questions about the murder, about the Wade boy, wanting to talk to him, pointing his finger at me and telling *me* what I can and cannot do, *warning* me. Can you imagine?"

Confused, Claire Elise said, "I was not aware of all that. But, surely, Mr. Taliaferro, his concern—and the governor's—can only be for the safety of the Wade boy, until you, sir, can bring him before a jury for his crime? I myself have seen the angry men milling about the jail, shouting and calling for vigilante justice."

SMACK! Taliaferro slapped the tabletop with his open hand. "Stop!" he shouted. Taliaferro struggled to catch his breath, to compose himself. After a moment, he said softly, "I must apologize for my intemperate outburst, Mrs. Montgomery. I am sorry."

Claire Elise, wide-eyed, said nothing.

"You see, Mrs. Montgomery, my political views and those of Mr. Waterman and the governor are, well, very different. The Republicans' love for the colored race is well known and well documented. To them, a colored man can do no wrong, though you and I realize what nonsense that is."

Claire Elise held up a hand. "Please, Mr. Taliaferro, I am not a political person. Do not project your views or opinions onto me."

Chastened, Taliaferro replied, "Again, I must apologize. Let me put it this way: It is clear that Waterman has come here to undermine and interfere with my investigation of the Schumann murder and my prosecution of the boy who committed this wanton and savage offense. And I will not have it!"

"Surely you exaggerate, Mr. Taliaferro. Keeping the Wade boy safe must certainly *support* your efforts to see justice done, no? How is this interference?"

Exasperated, Taliaferro responded, "Mrs. Montgomery, now it is I who must beg you not to impose your opinions on me about the administration of my office. I have this situation totally under control. I do not seek, need, or welcome outside interference or *assistance* from a government in Raleigh in which I have no confidence and for which I have no respect!"

Claire Elise pondered that. "Well, then, it seems we are at an impasse, Mr. Taliaferro. So, what about this *favor* you came to ask?"

Taliaferro began slowly. "Waterman. He is a guest in your hotel, your only guest it appears. While he is here, you will interact with him, hear things, see things. I need to know what he is up to, Mrs. Montgomery, where he goes, who he is talking to, what he knows. I need to be prepared for whatever moves he makes."

Claire Elise's eyes widened in astonishment. "So, you want me to what? To *spy* on my own hotel guest? To feed you information about his comings and goings, to pass along details about purely personal matters? Listen to yourself talking, sir! I run a respectable establishment here, dedicated to the comfort and privacy of my guests. Discretion is the foundation of my business, Mr. Taliaferro, and I am amazed that you would suggest that I compromise myself or that principle!"

Rising abruptly, Taliaferro snapped, "Very well then, Mrs. Montgomery. You have made your unwise position perfectly clear. Rest assured that I will remember it. Thank you for your time. I do indeed regret disturbing you."

Chapter 16

Tink Beasley opened the door at noon, hand-rolled cigarette in hand. "Why, Ben! What a nice surprise. Come on in."

Ben found McGee at the kitchen table, a foamy mug of draught beer in his hand. "Well, howdy, Ben. Just in time for lunch!"

"Thanks, Ros. Don't mind if I do. What in the world are you eating?"

"You must try this, Ben. *Dee*-licious!"

Tink rolled her eyes, took another drag off her cigarette. "He's gone plumb crazy, Ben."

Ben looked at the large, circular dish in front of McGee. "What is that, Ros?"

"Pizza!" exclaimed McGee.

"What in the world is pizza?"

"Well, I hired this guy, Antonio Moretti, *Tony*, to cook for me in the saloon downstairs. He's from Italy. Stonecutter by trade. Worked for ol' man Vanderbilt building his big house up in Asheville. Liked it down here and wanted to stay. Came looking for a job. Said he could cook, so I gave him a try.

"This here thing is called pizza. He calls it a *pie*. Nice bread crust underneath, cheese and tomato sauce and some other stuff on top, baked in the oven. 'Never tasted anything like it. *Dee*-licious! Here, have a slice."

McGee handed over a piece of the strange new food. Ben bit off a small mouthful. "This is really good!"

"Told you!" cried McGee. "And he makes all kinds of other good stuff, too. I tell you, Ben, these Eye-talians know what they're doing in the kitchen! Business is up ten percent since ol' Tony showed up."

Ben finished the slice, reached for another.

"Been waiting for you to come by, Ben. What's up?"

"Well, I've been busy since I left you yesterday, Ros." Ben explained his heated discussion with the prosecutor. "This Taliaferro, he's something else, Ros. Really into this Schumann thing. Personal like. Refused to let me talk to Virgil Wade. Got all upset when I told him why I was here. I told him I was just trying to help him. He didn't see it that way."

"He's running for office, Ben. Aims to ride this murder case to the permanent job. You, well, he prob'ly sees you as just getting in his way."

"I get that, but still—"

"Look, Ben, I never liked the man since I first laid eyes on him. He's meaner than a striped snake, and when he gives you that possum-toothed grin of his, there ain't a speck of humor in it. Watch your back. He's not a good man to have as an enemy, Ben."

Changing the subject, McGee asked, "Did you meet Mrs. Montgomery? Talk to her?"

"Yes, I met her. Nice lady. But it was late. She said that she would talk to me today or tomorrow, you know, about Rachel Schumann."

"Okay, fair enough. What else?"

"This morning I went over to see Jakob Schumann, pay my respects. Told him that Judge Maxwell sent his condolences."

"That must have been tough."

"He was a mess, sure enough. Oh, and just as I was leaving, this fellow Gruenwald came by for a visit. Interesting guy."

McGee smiled. "Interesting ain't the half of it, Ben. Good looking, too. Half the single women in Wilkes got their eyes on him."

"This afternoon I'll visit Doc Burleson, see what I can find out from him."

McGee nodded. "Anything else?"

Ben paused, thinking about Schumann and his decision to sell the tannery. "Look, Ros. As I get into this thing, we need to have an understanding about how we work it."

Eyebrows raised, McGee said, "Go on."

"There're a lot of moving parts here, Ros. You can be a big help to me."

McGee smiled. "I hear a big *but* coming."

Ben nodded. "But—it's likely that I . . . *we* will hear things, Ros. Secret things. Things that I wouldn't like to see in the paper. And you, well, you're in the newspaper business—"

Holding up a hand, McGee interrupted, "I've been thinking about that, too. That's how I earn my living, against plenty of competition. It's a small town, Ben, and I depend on my advertisers, and most of them are convinced that the Wade boy is guilty as hell. They won't take kindly to me poking around, stirring things up.

"But this Schumann thing, well there's something off here. Call it reporter's intuition, but my gut tells me something doesn't smell right, Ben. Everybody's got the Wade boy tried, convicted, and standing on the gallows already. I know things look bad for him, but—"

"Yes," said Ben. "I agree. The quilt, the lantern, the whiskey bottle, the shot glasses. Leaving the necklace and the money behind. Rachel Schumann all dressed up in her riding clothes in the middle of the night—"

"Right," McGee interjected. "There's more to it, Ben, more than meets the eye. So, let's make a deal. I'll play this on the straight and narrow, publish only things that're public record. And behind the scenes, I'll help you any way I can. I've already given you the photographs, and we've agreed to keep that just between us. So, anything that I pick up, or that you pick up that needs to stay private, will stay that way. I won't publish any of it 'til you give me the go ahead, Ben. And maybe together we can make some sense out of it. Fair enough?"

Ben smiled. "Just what I wanted to hear, Ros." And they shook on it.

Ben then told McGee about Jakob Schumann's decision to sell the tannery and move back to Alsace. McGee shook his head and whistled. "Boy, that's big news, Ben. Sorry to hear that."

"It won't be a secret long, Ros. I think he was fixing to tell Gruenwald. You'll be able to publish it soon enough."

"There's something else *you* should know, Ben. Redbone called here this morning to tell me that Taliaferro plans to make some sort of public announcement about the Schumann case Monday morning, at the jail. Wanted to make sure I would be there. Just in time for me to get the news into next Wednesday's paper."

Surprised, Ben said, "Well now, that should be quite a show. I guess I will see you there?"

"Count on it."

Ben paused, thinking. "Now, Ros, we have to be smart about this. Taliaferro will surely make his case against Wade in the best light possible for himself and in the worst light for Virgil Wade."

"And?"

"Well, he will never tell the whole story, you know that. But remember, Ros, he doesn't know we have the *photographs*. *He* doesn't know that *we* know what we know. Follow me?"

McGee snapped his fingers. "Got it. We let him talk, give him plenty of rope."

"That's it. Get him on record. And then we'll see where things go from there."

McGee nodded, smiled. "I like it."

Glancing at his pocket watch, Ben said, "I better get on over to Doc Burleson's. See what he's come up with."

Rising from his chair, McGee asked, "So, what're you doing for supper tonight?"

Ben shrugged, "I'll eat at the hotel, I guess."

"Aw, don't do that. It's Saturday night! Come on back over here. We always have a big shindig on Saturday night, music, dancing, all that."

"I don't know."

"Come on, Ben. Let loose a little. You can check on the Wade boy on your way over and back. I would bet a three-dollar bill that nothing will happen 'tween now and the big show next Monday morning. Taliaferro will see to it that nothing ruins his chance to shine."

Ben thought about it. "Okay, Ros. I'll do it. What time?"

"Well, the steaks will be ready around six-thirty. Then we haul away the tables and start in with the music and dancing 'round eight. Bar's open the whole time. Look forward to seeing you 'trip the light fantastic,' Ben! *Naarh, naarh, naarh!*"

Ben laughed, too. "I'll drop by the hotel to let Mrs. Montgomery know not to expect me for supper. I expect she'll let me borrow the sulky again."

"That's good, Ben. You'll enjoy it!" Pausing a moment and looking closely at Ben, McGee said, "Come early. You need a haircut."

Chapter 17

Claire Elise looked up from her work and smiled. "Good afternoon, Mr. Waterman. Productive day so far?"

"Very," said Ben. "Thanks so much for the sulky. It kept me dry in the rain. I wanted to let you know that I will be having supper tonight over across the river. Roscoe McGee has invited me. Would it be possible to borrow Maybelle and the sulky again?"

"Of course. I'll tell Ruby."

"I've already arranged things with her, thanks. I'll put Maybelle in her stall when I get back."

"Very good, then. Thanks for telling me. I can give Jewel the night off. I'll leave the front door key under the mat in case you're late." Claire Elise paused for a moment. "There's something you should know, Mr. Waterman."

"Yes?"

"I had a visitor this morning. Mr. Taliaferro. He wanted to talk."

"And?"

"Well, he wanted . . . information."

"Information? About what?"

"Information about . . . you."

"What?"

"It appears you have gotten under his skin. He wanted me to . . . well, *spy* on you. Tell him what you're up to, who you're talking to, that sort of thing."

"I see. So how did you respond?"

"Well, I rather impolitely and firmly declined," she said in her precise English accent, pointing at the entrance. "And I then showed him the door."

Ben considered this. "Thank you, Mrs. Montgomery. I appreciate that very much. Let's keep this between the two of us, okay?"

"Of course."

Ben turned back to the entrance, stopped, spun around. "Yesterday I asked you for a meeting to talk about—"

"Yes, I know. Rachel Schumann. But it seems you are quite busy today. Perhaps tomorrow? Jewel leaves for church after breakfast. It should be quiet then. Would that be all right with you?"

Ben smiled. "Perfect. Tomorrow, then." Looking out the front door, he remarked, "I see the rain has quit. Look at the sunshine!"

Frowning and thinking about Vincent Taliaferro, Ben made the short walk across East Main Street to the home and office of Doctor Noah Burleson.

W

Burleson lived in a two-story home with a wide front porch and an unobstructed view of the courthouse square. He modestly referred to himself as "just a country doctor," but he had married well. The money for the house and his lifestyle came from his wife, a tobacco heiress from Durham.

Burleson, a thick-waisted man with a friendly face framed by wire-rimmed spectacles, acted as the part-time coroner for Wilkes County, a position that contributed little to his income. He was universally admired, highly respected, and had delivered more than a generation of infants throughout the county.

Burleson stood on the front porch, hands on his hips, in his shirtsleeves, his trousers held up by bright red suspenders. "Hello, Ben. Nice to see you back in Wilkes. Long time."

"Afternoon, Doc." They shook hands. "Hope I'm not disturbing you."

"Not at all, not at all. Come in, please."

Burleson led them into the elegantly appointed parlor, invited Ben to sit. "Can I offer you something to drink? Lemonade, sweet tea?"

"Thank you, no. I shouldn't be here long."

"Well then, let's get right to it. What can I do for you?"

"Well, it's about Rachel Schumann." Ben explained his mission to protect Virgil Wade, Governor Maxwell's concerns.

Pushing his eyeglasses up on his nose, Burleson said, "I figured as much. Taliaferro dropped by, told me you might be visiting. Told me that you were here causing trouble. Told me that I shouldn't talk to you, can you imagine?"

"I can't explain Taliaferro's agenda, Doc. And I'm not here to cause trouble. If he would just listen to reason, I could help him. He's got a dangerous situation on his hands."

"Well, Ben," Burleson smiled. "Let's just say that I don't need Razor to tell me who I can and can't talk to. Just leave it at that. So, again, how can I help you?"

"Well, Doc, as you well know, violent crimes like this require an autopsy. I'm told the case came to you."

Nodding, Burleson began in a solemn tone. "Of course, you are correct, Ben. The law requires it. I had a hell of a time convincing that Gruenwald fellow that it had to be done. He identified the body, said Schumann asked him to, and then he started in about Jewish customs, funerals, all that.

"I told him that the law is the law, and that, as coroner, I am bound to comply. He knew he was beat, Ben, but he was all over me to finish the thing quick and release the body. Something about Jewish burial ritual. That made sense to me, I respect that, so I got done and turned the body over to him."

"So, what were the results, Doc? Did you confirm a cause of death?"

"I did. I completed the autopsy Thursday afternoon, released the body, finished my report, and sent it over to Taliaferro."

"I understand there are photographs?"

Surprised, Burleson nodded. "You are very well informed, Ben. Yes, there are pictures. Olly Overby took some down by the river, and I asked him to come over and take pictures of . . . the body."

"Why?"

Spreading his hands wide, Burleson answered, "Taliaferro told me to. Said he would need a complete record, you know, for the trial. Not my business. So, I sent all the photographs over with my report."

"And the COD?"

"Well, wasn't too hard. Now, mind you, I had that Gruenwald fellow breathing down my neck the whole time, fidgety, pressing me to hurry up." Waving a hand, he continued. "This'll all come out soon enough. Razor says he's making a public announcement on Monday, so I might as well tell you now.

"First of all, her clothing, her shirt had been ripped apart, exposing her chest and . . . breasts. My examination revealed that the girl had been attacked and badly beaten. Her upper arms were both badly bruised, as was her face, looked like a blow from a closed fist, big purple bruise on the left side of her head."

Consistent with the photographs, thought Ben. "Left side?" he asked. Closing his hand and swinging it in a wide circle, Ben said, "So right hand fist?"

"Correct," Burleson agreed. "And then there were the knife wounds." Here Burleson paused, took a breath. "There were a number of slashing cuts on her chest and abdomen, none fatal, but trust me, extremely painful. It was like the Wade boy was . . . was *possessed*, furious, wanting to *hurt* her, make her feel pain before . . . killing her." He took another deep breath.

"And, finally, there was Virgil Wade's skinning knife buried to the hilt in her chest, right through the heart." Shaking his head, he continued. "Ben, it was just awful. The point of the knife protruded an inch or two out her back. Terrible!"

"So, what about the knife? I assumed you removed it?"

"Of course."

"So, what happened to it?"

"Well, I did like Taliaferro said. I withdrew it carefully, put it in a paper sack, sealed it up with tape, and wrote *Schumann Murder Weapon* and the date on a label, stuck it on the bag, and gave it to Taliaferro along with my report and the photographs. Procedure."

"And your report? The cause of death?" reminded Ben.

"Well, it didn't take long to write it up. Page-and-a-half. Cause of death: knife wound through the heart. It's all in the report."

"Did you sign the report? Before sending it over to Taliaferro?"

"Of course, Ben, signed and dated. That's required."

"So, then it's an official document, public record. May I have a copy?"

Curious, Burleson stared at Ben. "Look here, Ben, what's your interest in all this? What's my report got to do with keeping Virgil Wade safe in the jail?"

Ben paused. "Listen, Doc. Judge Maxwell is scared to death of this thing, coming up right here at the end of his term, in his own hometown. He sent me here to see to it that the Wade boy is kept safe, that's true enough. But his concern is broader than that. He wants me to look at this thing from the very beginning, top to bottom, make sure everything is done by the book, dot all the I's and cross all the T's. And that includes Taliaferro's investigation. There must be no rush to judgment here, Doc. So, I would appreciate your cooperation."

Burleson looked at Ben, square in the eyes. "Razor will not like that, Ben. He won't like it a-tall."

"So, your report?"

Burleson made a face. "Look, Ben, you know the law better than me. If my report is indeed a public document as you say, well then you need to get it from Taliaferro. I've told you what's in it, told you more than I should, and that's that."

Ben nodded slowly. "Okay, then." He hesitated. "So, what about other things, Doc? Things you saw but maybe left out of your report?"

Burleson nervously looked away, licked his lips, head down. Turning back to Ben he muttered, "I don't know what you could be talking about, Ben. And I don't appreciate your insinuation."

Ben looked at Burleson for a long moment through the silence, felt the doubt growing in his gut, and made a decision. *He knows something. Something he's not telling me. But he doesn't know what I know, doesn't know whether I maybe know it already. Take the chance. Play the hunch.*

Ben came up close to Burleson, placed an index finger gently against his chest. "Let's stop playing games, Doc. Like you said, I am indeed *well informed* about this case. We've known each other too long for this, Doc, been through too much. You're holding something back. You know it, and I know it. I just need to hear it from you."

Frantic, Burleson protested. "Ben, remember I am a doctor! A physician! I took an oath! There are some things that you are not meant to know . . . not *entitled* to know. Please."

So. There it is. With growing confidence, Ben replied in a firm voice, "Doc, the only person in this world with the right to assert that privilege is lying dead and buried in a fresh grave in Schumann Village. You know that."

Burleson whispered, "What do you want from me?"

"I want the truth, Doc. I want the truth about Rachel Schumann."

Straightening himself, shoulders back, Burleson replied, "No, Ben. It is simply out of the question. The Schumanns—"

"There's a lot about this case that the Schumanns should never see or hear about, Doc. I do not intend to add to their suffering and grief. You can count on that."

"I said no, Ben!" shouted Burleson. "Please leave now. Please leave my house."

Ben made no move to depart. In a slow, steady voice he played his final card.

"I am very sorry to hear that, Doc. I came here to ask you a favor, and you've turned me down. But I remember very well the time not long ago that you came to Judge Maxwell, hat in hand, asking *him* for a favor. A big one. And he was there for you. *I* was there for you, Doc."

Burleson replied uneasily, "What are you talking about?"

Ben uttered two words. "Louise. Triplett."

Suddenly the warm and humid air fell on Burleson like a soggy blanket, pinning his arms to his sides, leaving him rigid, unmoving.

"You *bastard!*" was all he could say.

W

Two years before, in the middle of Maxwell's term as governor, a young, unmarried Wilkesboro woman named Louise Triplett unfortunately and unexpectedly found herself in the family way. Despite intense pressure from her parents, she never named the father.

Louise Triplett's father was a prominent, short-tempered businessman, proud and protective of his reputation and the honor of his family name. He was unhappy about this inconvenient new development in his well-ordered life. He was determined to fix the problem, permanently.

He quietly approached his good friend Noah Burleson for help. When he explained what he had in mind, Burleson was at first aghast, refusing even to consider the proposition. Triplett put intense pressure on Burleson, leveraging their long friendship. Burleson resisted until Triplett put a sum of money into play that captured Burleson's undivided attention. Rationalizing that the procedure would be best for the young girl and, of course, the Triplett family name, he agreed.

Burleson performed the abortion alone in his clinic on a cold, sleeting Sunday morning while his wife and family were away at church. The young girl arrived, frightened and alone. For reasons never fully explained, the operation went badly wrong. Louise Triplett's punctured uterus became septic, and she developed a raging fever. Two days later, she died in terrible pain. Burleson listed the cause of death as "respiratory complications from influenza."

Wracked with guilt and shame, Louise Triplett's distraught father raged at Burleson in private, blaming him for the botched procedure. He threatened criminal proceedings and a civil lawsuit. He even went so far as to schedule a meeting with the president of the North Carolina State Board of Medical Examiners to demand revocation of Burleson's medical license.

Panicked, Burleson hurried to Raleigh to ask his good friend "Cotton Bob" Maxwell for assistance. Maxwell listened patiently and sympathetically to Burleson's desperate pleas for help. He then gave Burleson what he later described to Ben as "a first-class ass whuppin." Winning Burleson's pledge never to repeat his offense, or speak of it again, and mindful that the overbearing Triplett father was not without blame in the matter, Maxwell told Burleson that he would look into it.

As in many similar situations, the task of sorting things out fell to Ben Waterman. Ben arranged to meet with Triplett in his hotel room during one of the man's frequent business trips to Raleigh. Triplett was to meet later the same day with the Board of Medical Examiners.

Triplett was full of piss and vinegar and spoiling for a fight. Ben heard him out. "But what," Ben asked, "what would taking things to court accomplish?" Litigation would bring the entire tawdry story into public view. The gossip ladies in Wilkes would be thrilled. And what of Triplett's own culpability in the matter? He must know that, once the cat was out of the bag, he would surely be prosecuted alongside Burleson and would certainly be convicted as an accessory to Burleson's crime?

"Have you thought this through? Are you sure this is what you want? And this business at the Medical Examiner's Office. Do you really want to be responsible for bringing down the most prominent, most revered doctor in Wilkes County?" Ben raised a cautionary finger. "Remember. The president and all of the other Medical Board members are appointed by . . . Governor Maxwell, who has taken a personal interest in the matter. Surely it would be best, hard as it may be, to put this ugly episode behind you, leave it in the past. Nothing can be done to bring your poor Louise back to life. And revenge, says the Good Book, belongs to a higher power. Better to let sleeping dogs lie, no?"

In the end, Triplett gave way, moved mightily by the realization that his own freedom could be at stake. He certainly would not risk subjecting himself to Vincent Taliaferro's tender mercies, much as he would like to see Noah Burleson die in Central Prison. Having come to that sober conclusion, Triplett hurriedly called the Board of Medical Examiners, cancelled his meeting, and took the next train back to Wilkes.

Not my finest hour, thought Ben as he walked back to the Capitol. *No, not at all.*

The episode was never spoken of again. Until today.

W

"You sorry *bastard!*" Burleson repeated, shaking with fury.

Ben spread his hands, shrugged, unyielding. "I'm sorry to bring this up, Doc. Truly I am. But you must know that actions have consequences. Favors, like debts, must be repaid."

"So, what do you want to know, Ben?" Burleson sneered. "How can I best satisfy your perverse, morbid curiosity?"

"I want to know," Ben said evenly, "whatever was not included in your report to Taliaferro. I want to know it all. And, if humanly possible, I will see to it that Jakob and Rebekah Schumann never hear a word of it."

Nodding and raising himself up to full height, Burleson began to tell his story, once again a man of science, all business, a medical professional reciting clinical data.

"Even though the cause of death was obvious, nevertheless state law requires a full pelvic examination of women who have been . . . *assaulted* in such a violent manner."

"Yes, I am aware—"

"Do not interrupt me again, Ben!" Burleson shot back. "My examination thankfully revealed no evidence of rape or sexual assault. At least there's that. However, the hymen was not intact. Rachel Schumann was not . . . a virgin.

"Close examination also revealed a slight, but unusual roundness of the abdomen. This led me to conduct an examination of her cervix, as is standard procedure. The normal cervix of a woman of her age should exhibit firmness, much like touching the side of one's nose," he explained, touching his index finger to his own. "In this case, the cervix was not firm, but was rather soft in texture. Much like the surrounding tissues of the labia and vagina."

"So, what does that mean" asked Ben, fearing he already knew the answer.

Burleson dropped his head, closed his eyes tight, and whispered, "I have seen this many times before. At the time of her death, Rachel

Schumann was about three months pregnant."

Nodding gravely, Ben said, "I see." As he turned to leave, Burleson's voice, now a snarl, stopped him.

"This makes us even, Ben. We are all square now, you hear me? You be sure to tell that to your boss in Raleigh."

Ben let himself out.

W

Thunderstruck by Burleson's revelation, Ben made his way quickly back to the livery stable. "Ruby, I need to get on back over the river sooner than I expected."

"Yessir, that's no problem. Gimme a minute, and I'll get Maybelle hitched up for you."

As he waited, Ben replayed in his mind his conversation with Burleson. *Pregnant! Hard to believe. A lovely, young, unmarried girl. Daughter of a rich man, a business giant and community leader. An unexpected and surely unwanted pregnancy. Who in the world could the father be? Somebody in Wilkes, obviously. Somebody who would not want the . . . situation to come out? Somebody with too much to lose? Maybe a motive . . . maybe a powerful motive . . . for murder? I need to talk to Maxwell.*

Chapter 18

Back in McGee's apartment, the two men huddled around the kitchen table. Ben again swore McGee to secrecy and summarized his meeting with Noah Burleson.

"*Pregnant?* Well, shit fire and save matches, Ben, this changes everything!"

"That it does," Ben said, nodding. "The father of Rachel Schumann's unborn child is out there, Ros, somewhere here in Wilkes."

"And maybe Mr. Somebody wasn't too happy about it, Ben. So, how do you think it went down?"

"Well, like you said, Ros, the scene at the river looked . . . staged. Like Rachel Schumann laid things out for a secret meeting? Maybe she arranged to meet with someone at the river. Got dressed and rode her horse down there . . . set things up. So she could deliver her news?"

"Let's say she told the daddy about the baby," said McGee, in full brainstorming mode. "And maybe when she did, Mr. Somebody didn't take kindly to it. Decided that he would just take care of things, right then and there?"

"It could've played out that way, Ros. But what about the boy? How does he figure into this?"

"Well, we know he must'a been there. It was his knife, after all. Surely you don't think that Rachel was messin' around with the likes of Virgil Wade, do you?"

Spreading his hands wide, Ben replied, "Damn if I know, Ros. I can't figure that out. I really can't see Rachel Schumann and the Wade boy together, but . . . damn Vincent Taliaferro! I need to talk to that boy!"

"So, how're you gonna do that, Ben? How're you gonna get past Crip Goins and his *friend* Gladys?"

Ben paused. "I need to talk to Judge Maxwell, Ros. Right now."

"So, let's see if we can get him on the horn."

In McGee's office, Ben rang up Central and asked Betty to please connect him with the Governor's Mansion. "The number in Raleigh is 2-5-5-J." While they waited for the callback, Ben said, "It's late Saturday afternoon. No chance the judge will be in his office. I expect he's home getting ready for a snort or two before supper."

The jangling ring of the telephone startled them both. Ben picked up the earpiece. Betty, the operator, said breathlessly, "Mr. Waterman? I have . . . I have the *governor* on the line!"

W

"So, Ben. Good to hear from you!" Maxwell boomed. Ben winced and held the receiver away from his ear, permitting Roscoe McGee to hear. "I've been waiting for you to report back. What's the story?"

"Good afternoon, Judge. Sorry to disturb you, but I have some news that you will want to hear."

"Go on."

"First, I've got Roscoe McGee here with me. We're working on this thing together."

Silence from Raleigh.

"Judge? You there?"

"Of course I'm here, Ben! I'm just thinking, that's all. What's McGee got to do with this?"

Ben explained his conversation with McGee, his production of the photographs, his pledge of confidentiality, the need for his cooperation.

"Put McGee on the line, Ben."

Ben handed him the earpiece. "Now see here, Roscoe McGee!" Maxwell bellowed, loud enough for Ben to hear every word. "You help Ben however you can, but if I see a single goddamned word in your newspaper that Ben hasn't ok'd, I will kick your sorry ass plumb into next week. You got that?"

"Yes, Governor. We're on the same page."

"Just so we're clear then. And I mean what I say, Ros! Now, put Ben back on the line." McGee did, and Maxwell said, "So, first of all, Ben, did you go see the Schumanns like I told you to? Pay my respects?"

Ben told Maxwell about his visit to Schumann Village, ending with Jakob Schumann's decision to sell the tannery and move back to Alsace.

"Damn." Maxwell muttered. "Now, that's a real surprise."

Ben then reviewed his time in Wilkes since arriving Thursday afternoon. He explained his conversation with McGee, the unexpected and secret cache of photographs, their encounter with Crip Goins, the tense situation surrounding the jail, and his acrimonious meeting with Vincent Taliaferro and Sheriff Poindexter.

"He won't let me see the Wade boy, Judge. Just flatly refused."

"Why do you need to see the boy, Ben? If Taliaferro and Redbone say they can keep him safe until his trial, and if you're satisfied that they can, what else is there for you to do?"

"That's just it, Judge. Folks're mighty riled up about this thing, bunch-a surly guys hanging around the jail, up to no good. With guns. They were there all day today. I can see them from my hotel room. Even Redbone admits that it's just him and Crip Goins to guard the boy. There's a black mood loose in Wilkes, Judge, and I don't know if they can keep a lid on it. Long time until court comes back in September."

"I see."

"And there's more." Ben explained about the photographs of the scene by the river. The riding clothes, the quilt, the lantern, the whiskey and shot glasses, Rachel's necklace, and the money. "Something's off, Judge. Ros agrees."

"But the knife? The pictures show it belongs to the Wade boy, right?"

"True enough, Judge. It sure looks like the boy was there. I can't see any other explanation for it."

"Well, why not just let Taliaferro handle it? That's his job. All I care about is keeping the boy alive, Ben."

"Well, Judge, there's one more thing." Ben told the judge about his meeting with Noah Burleson, ending with the news of Rachel Schumann's pregnancy.

Again, a long silence. Finally, Maxwell said in a much quieter voice, "Say it again, Ben. Tell me that last part again."

Ben did so. More silence, the long-distance line hissing and crackling, and then a heavy sigh from the Raleigh end.

"Well, this changes everything, Ben." McGee looked at Ben and smiled. "First thing, Ben, you too, Ros, not a word of this to the Schumanns, you hear me? *Not one single word!*"

"Yes, Judge, we are very clear on that."

"So, what do you boys make of this new . . . development?"

"Well, Ros and I have been knocking around a few ideas." Ben then repeated their thinking about what *might* have happened at the river, taking into account Rachel Schumann's pregnancy.

"Well, Ben, that seems like a stretch to me. But if you're right about the daddy being there, in Wilkes, and if Virgil Wade is *not* the father, that means—"

"Exactly, Judge. That means that there must have been *two people* under the bridge that night."

"Yes, I see that," said Maxwell slowly. "But you got any proof? Any evidence?"

"Pure speculation, Judge. So far. But the *circumstantial* evidence, and what we know from the photographs and from Burleson, well they could very well point in another direction."

"Understood. And I understand now why you need to talk to the Wade boy. Get his story."

"But Taliaferro is in the way. Won't let me see him."

"Give me a minute," said Maxwell. After a few moments he came back on the line. "Taliaferro refuses to let you speak to the boy, Ben, because you have no *right* to. No *status*, you follow? I can't blame Taliaferro for that. And even if you got in to see him, Ben, why should he talk to you? Any lawyer worth his salt would tell him to sit tight and shut up. So, a conversation with the boy would almost certainly not be in his best interests. Taliaferro will insist on listening in, and anything he told you would be admissible against him. Unless—"

"I'm listening."

"Well, Ben, all that would change if you should be, well, act as his *lawyer.* That way he would be your *client,* and anything he said to you would be privileged, confidential. Taliaferro would have to let you talk to him—in private."

"What do you mean, Judge?"

Another heavy sigh from Raleigh. "Look, Ben. I sent you to Wilkes to *protect* Virgil Wade. But the things that you and Roscoe have uncovered, may still uncover, well, all that raises at least some possibility that the boy may not have been in on this thing *alone.* That somebody *else* may very well have been under the bridge that night. And that bothers me, Ben, that bothers me a lot.

"So, Ben, in addition to *protecting* Virgil Wade, maybe you should consider *defending* him. Take his case. Be his lawyer. Raise some hell, throw some dirt in the air. Worst case, you keep him alive for a while longer, get him a fair trial, maybe make a deal with Taliaferro. Best case . . . well, hell, Ben, who knows what the best case could be?"

"But how would that work, Judge? After all, I work for you. In the governor's office."

"Not anymore, Ben. Well, not if you don't *want* to, that is. Now look, Ben. We've talked about this. We're done and out of here come January anyway. I'd hate to lose you, but maybe you should take advantage of the situation, resign now, take on this *hopeless* case, get back in the game. That way you could have everything ready for me to join you after Aycock's *coronation.*"

"Judge, think about it. If I take on the Wade boy's case, why, nobody in Wilkes will speak to me again! And Jakob Schumann? Well, how do you think he will feel about his friend the governor's hey-boy standing up for the murderer who put a knife through his daughter's heart and drove him out of town? And what about you? Why would you want to be associated with a pariah like me come January?"

"You let me worry about me, Ben. I can take care of myself. But you? Think it through. Just how strongly do *you* feel about this *hunch* of yours? What really happened on the riverbank that night? How bad do you want to know the real truth, the whole truth, all of it? And what are you prepared to do, to *sacrifice*, to learn it?

"If you stand by and do nothing, why, Taliaferro will convict the Wade boy and hang him, just like he's promising. And then what? You and McGee have raised some good questions, hard questions, questions that deserve answers, Ben. And if you don't pursue this thing, if you don't run it to ground, all those unanswered questions will be forever buried in Virgil Wade's grave with him.

"*Think*, Ben. Put that good mind of yours to work. Think about what we've stood for all these years, the good we have tried to accomplish. Forget about *the law*, forget about what people might say, hell, even forget about what lawyers jabber about as *justice*. Follow your heart on this, Ben. Cross your own Rubicon. Do the right thing."

Silence came from the Wilkes end of the line. McGee stared at Ben, eyes wide, jaw slack.

"I hear you, Judge. I hear you," said Ben slowly. "I will. I will think about this. Think about it hard, Judge."

"That's all I can ask, son. You let me know what you decide."

The line went dead.

W

Looking at Ben for a long moment, McGee whistled and looked at his watch. "Well, I sure as hell didn't see *that* coming. But look-a here, Ben. You've had a bitch of a day. Take the rest of the day off, come to the saloon, have some fun. Forget about all this stuff for a night. Tink can't wait to pull you out on the dance floor. *Naarh, naarh, naarh!*"

Ben smiled. "Okay, Ros, you win. Just one more thing."

"What's that?"

Pointing to McGee's work desk, Ben exhaled and said, "I need to borrow your machine for a minute. Won't take long. I have a letter to write."

McGee stopped, stared. "Well, then." Pointing at the Underwood, he said, "Help yourself, Ben. Paper's in the drawer. But hurry up. We need to get on down there now, Ben, early. Like I said, you need a haircut."

W

While Ben was having his hair trimmed and his face shaved in one of the big barber chairs in McGee's Emporium, the phone rang in Vincent Taliaferro's office.

Irritated at the interruption, Taliaferro snapped, "Yes!"

"Mr. Taliaferro? This is Betty over at Central."

"Yes?" he repeated, more gently this time.

"Well, sir, like you asked, I wanted you to know that I placed a long-distance telephone call this afternoon from Roscoe McGee's telephone over at the paper."

"Yes, yes?" he eagerly replied. "And?"

"Well, sir, it was that Mr. Waterman on the line. I connected him with . . . well, with the *Governor's Mansion.* You know, in Raleigh."

"Yes, Betty, I know where the Governor's Mansion is."

"Well, wouldn't you know it, but he came right on the line! Governor Maxwell, I mean. The governor himself! I never in my life—"

"Yes, Betty, yes."

"Well, sir, they talked for a long time. Yes, sir, for quite a while."

Taliaferro posed his next question carefully. "Now, Betty, did you happen to . . . pick up on any of their conversation? Hear what they were talking about?"

"Oh, *no*, sir! That would be *wrong*, not right a-tall. Why, I could lose my job."

Taliaferro winced, closed his eyes. "Of course, Betty, quite right. You are quite right. You did the proper thing. Thank you so much for the information, Betty."

"Now, you're sure this has to do with that awful Rachel Schumann thing, right?"

"Of course, Betty. You are providing a very great service to law enforcement in this terrible case. And I am very grateful to you."

"Always glad to help the law, Mr. Taliaferro."

"Thank you, Betty. Goodbye."

"Bye!" said Betty in her always cheerful voice.

Maxwell, thought Taliaferro. *Waterman. Calling from McGee's place. Now what?*

W

Shortly before 11pm Saturday evening, Ben guided Maybelle and the sulky into the livery stable behind the hotel. All was quiet at the jail. He was in a fine mood, whistling and humming the tunes he had enjoyed during the evening. The "Hillbilly Hoedown and Honky-Tonk Sing Along" at McGee's Emporium had indeed lifted his spirits.

Ben struck a match and lit a kerosene lantern hanging from a hook. He unhitched the harness and led Maybelle into her stall. He smiled to see the manger full of golden hay, buckets filled with grain and fresh water. Ruby had mucked the stall and spread fresh pine shavings on the floor. *I must remember to tip her tomorrow.*

W

McGee's Emporium was a large, open space occupying most of the second floor of the Trogdon Opera House. Six barber chairs and a shoeshine stand lined the far wall. In one corner was a small tobacco kiosk with cigars, cigarettes, snuff, and pipe and chewing tobacco. Beside that stood well-stocked bookshelves sporting all the latest novels, illustrated magazines, and local newspapers. Along the wall nearest the entrance ran a long zinc-topped bar. Behind it were colorful bottles of whiskey and other spirits, reflected in the framed mirror that ran the bar's full length. Oil lamps hung from the rafters, providing warm, yellow light.

For an admission price of one dollar per head, the one hundred or so patrons this Saturday night were treated to a fine meal of grilled T-bone steaks with Tony Moretti's spaghetti and sauce and an open bar. The crowd was in a good mood, men and women flirting and laughing, animated conversation filling the room as an old-time string band played in the background.

After the tables were cleared, the men shoved the tables and the chairs back against the wall to make way for dancing, while the musicians retuned their instruments. Roscoe McGee mounted an empty liquor box and shouted, "Here we go! Hillbilly Hoedown! Grab your partners and dosey-doe!"

The floor swarmed with people, pairing off for the square dance. Led by a grinning fiddle player, backed up by a banjo and a stand-up bass, the band struck up a lively mountain tune, and McGee called the jigs and reels. For those not dancing, the bar did a good business.

Tink Beasley grabbed Ben by the hands, pulled him up, and cried, "Come on, lawyer man, let's see you strut your stuff!" Ben joined in, laughing as their circle moved through the calls.

After a while, McGee motioned for the music to stop and shouted, "Well done, y'all! Now it's time for the cloggers!"

On cue, about twenty men and women in fancy dress ran onto the dance floor, wearing tap dancing shoes. The fiddle man led another fast-paced Scottish reel, and the buck dancers began their rhythmic stomping and gyrations to the delight of the crowd. The men and women smiled broadly, holding their arms tight against their hips while their legs and feet whirled around in wide arcs, like puppets on strings.

The fiddler ended with a snappy "shave and a haircut, two bits," and the saloon erupted in hoots, hollers, and whistles. "All right then!" cried McGee. "Well done, cloggers! And let's hear it for the Overmountain Men!" More applause, and the musicians grinned, bowed, and acknowledged the praise.

As the band packed up their instruments and sat down to their supper, McGee stepped down from the wooden crate and walked over to a beat up and battered upright piano at the end of the bar. Sitting on the stool,

McGee looked over his shoulder and, with a devilish grin, hollered, "Who's ready for some Honky Tonk? Y'all know the rules. Sing it if you know it!" The crowd again roared its approval, lifting their beer mugs and whiskey shots to the sky.

McGee ran through a few piano riffs, warming up the room. Ben turned to Tink and asked, "How does he make the piano sound like that? Sounds like a Wild West saloon."

Tink rolled her eyes, leaned in close to Ben. "It's his secret. He pushes thumbtacks in the hammers. Says it puts the *Tonk* in Honky-Tonk."

McGee then pounded the keys through a series of popular Gay Nineties tunes, singing at the top of his voice, accompanied by a chorus of eager revelers. Beginning with "Bill Bailey Won't You Please Come Home," McGee followed up with lively renditions of "Sidewalks of New York," "The Band Played on," "A Hot Time in the Old Town Tonight," "A Bicycle Built for Two," "Frankie and Johnny," "In the Good Old Summertime," and "Oh, You Beautiful Doll." As he finished with a flourish, *"Ta-Ra-Ra-BOOM-De-Ay!"* the crowd erupted amidst shouts of *"encore, encore!"*

McGee stood, spread his arms. "You want some more?" More applause, whistles, cries of "After the Ball! After the Ball!" McGee motioned for quiet, nodding his head toward Tink. "Come on up, Tink! This is your song!"

Shooting McGee a deadly look, Tink slowly rose and approached the piano. "Damn you, McGee!" she whispered in his ear. McGee trilled through the opening bars, and then Tink sang the sad, mournful tune in a clear and moving voice. When she finished, the room again resounded with clapping hands, stomping feet, shrill whistles of approval.

McGee grinned, his eyes full of mischief. "But y'all know, there's another verse, right? Wanna hear it?"

More noise. "Sing it, R.E.! Sing it!"

And so, he sang his own silly parody.

> *"After the ball was over,*
> *Alice took out her glass eye,*
> *Put her false teeth on the table,*
> *Hung up her wig out to dry,*
> *Stood her peg leg in the corner,*
> *Turned out the light in the hall,*
> *The rest of her hopped off to slumber,*
> *After the ball . . . ."*

Once more, pandemonium in the room. McGee stood, took a bow. "Well, folks, thank y'all for coming out tonight. Tink tells me it's about time to wrap things up so y'all can get home and get some sleep before church tomorrow mornin.' We always like to end things with praise for the Lord, so please join with me in singing a hymn we all know well."

Standing in the stable, Ben thought back to that last piece of music. He did not consider himself a religious man, but the lyrics seemed to comfort him, giving him guidance for the days ahead. He began to hum the tune to himself, remembering the words from his Baptist childhood.

"Life is like a mountain railway,
With an engineer that's brave.
We must make the run successful,
From the cradle to the grave.
Watch the curves, the fills, the tunnels,
Never falter, never fail.
Keep your hands upon the throttle,
And your eyes upon the rail."

Closing Maybelle's stall, Ben blew out the lantern and made his way around to the hotel, lit by a lamp within. Reaching under the doormat, Ben retrieved the key left there by Claire Elise. Locking the door behind him, Ben placed the key on the reception desk. He reached inside his suit jacket and pulled out a long, slim envelope. It was addressed to:

Honorable Robert Rousseau Maxwell
Governor's Mansion
200 North Blount Street
Raleigh, North Carolina

For a long moment Ben stared at the letter, holding it in his hands. With a sigh, he slid it through the slot in the polished brass box with engraved letters *U.S. Post Office, Outgoing Mail.*

Chapter 19

On Sundays, breakfast at the Schumann Hotel was served an hour later than normal. Ben Waterman, refreshed and feeling fine, walked to a dining room table.

"Mornin' Mistah Waterman," said a smiling Jewel Ponder, dressed in her Sunday best. "Got somethin' special for you today. Miz Claire Elise calls it *French toast.* Got some really good blackstrap molasses to go with it, plus fresh sausage and fruit."

Ben gleefully eyed the morning feast. He poured dark, sweet syrup over the fried bread, took a bite, and said, "Why, this is delicious! Compliments to the chef!"

"You can thank Miz Claire Elise, suh. It was her idea."

As she turned away, Ben stopped her. "Jewel, I need to speak with you about something. Please, have a seat."

Frowning, Jewel said, "Naw, suh, I druther stand." So, Ben also rose.

"Well, as you may know, Jewel, I have been sent here by Governor Maxwell to take care of the Wade boy, to protect him. I need to speak with him, but Mr. Taliaferro won't let me. I have an idea, Jewel, a way to help the boy. I would like to talk with his mother, Mrs. Oxendine. Can you help me arrange it?"

"You want to talk to Pauline? 'Bout Virgil?"

Ben nodded. "That's right, Jewel. Can you help me?"

Jewel thought about it. Slowly she said, "Mebbe. Mebbe I can." She paused, continued. "Best thing would be for me to talk to Preacher Bondurant about it. He's real close with Pauline. Close to all of us, really. He's looking after Pauline, 'specially during this thing with Rachel Schumann. Pauline, well, she's all tore up about it. Yessir, Preacher, he'll know what's best. I'll see him at church this mornin'. I'll pass along your message and see what he says. If he agrees to it, he'll talk to Pauline and see if she'll talk to you. That be all right?"

"I understand, Jewel. I think that's a fine idea. Be sure to tell the preacher that I am very eager to help the Wade boy, and I think I know a good way to do it."

Jewel smiled. "All right then. I'll take care of it. Count on me, Mistah Waterman. If you can help Virgil, I know that Preacher and Pauline will be mighty grateful. Now, you finish up your breakfast."

"Thank you, Jewel. I appreciate it very much. Very much indeed."

Jewel returned to the kitchen, and Ben cleaned his plate, using the last bite of toast to sop up the sweet molasses. Soon Claire Elise appeared.

"Good morning, Mr. Waterman." Pointing at his clean plate, she said, "I see that my culinary surprise was well received?"

"Very much so, Mrs. Montgomery, delicious!"

"Good, good," she replied. "Now, let me clear all this away. I'll be right back. And then we can talk."

Ben considered how he would handle the conversation. He would need to be careful. Soon Claire Elise returned and sat opposite Ben.

"I just got off the telephone with Mr. Schumann. He asked me to come over to the Village, invited me to lunch. He said he has something important to speak to me about, so I told him I would be there soon. I can't imagine what's on his mind."

I think I know, mused Ben. *I wonder how he will explain things to her. Surely, he will sell the hotel, too.*

"Jewel and I have already planned to help Mr. and Mrs. Schumann later today and this evening with the services for Rachel. *Shiva*, I think they call it. So, I'm afraid you will be on your own tonight. Jewel will make your dinner and leave it on the stove for later. You can make yourself at home, heat it up on the cookstove. Help yourself to the bar. I apologize for the inconvenience, and I hope you understand?"

"Certainly, Mrs. Montgomery. That will be no problem at all. It is important to help the Schumanns any way you can. I am sure they will appreciate it." Changing the subject, Ben pointed to the shelf behind the reception desk. "I notice you have a typewriter there. I wonder if I might borrow it? I have some paperwork to catch up on this afternoon."

"Of course, Mr. Waterman. Be my guest. There is paper in the drawer under the counter."

And then it was her turn to change the subject. "So, Mr. Waterman, it appears that we have some business to discuss. I assume from what Mr. Taliaferro tells me that it has something to do with Rachel Schumann and the Wade boy?"

Ben began with a sigh. "That's right, Mrs. Montgomery, it does. I expect Taliaferro explained—in his own way—that I have been sent here by Governor Maxwell to look into the Rachel Schumann murder. In particular, the governor is concerned about the safety of the Wade boy. I have myself seen the men milling around the jail, and they are not in a good mood.

"Governor Maxwell—and I—we are determined to see to it that Virgil Wade is protected until he can be brought to trial. I have my doubts that Sheriff Poindexter and Mr. Goins can handle this volatile situation. I offered to provide support to them, but Taliaferro rejected my offer out of hand. Unfortunately, I remain convinced that the danger of violence to the boy remains very real."

Claire Elise listened with great interest. "Yes, that is what Mr. Taliaferro told me, too. He said you were here to make trouble. I told him I thought your offer of assistance should be regarded as a helpful gesture, not interference. He reacted very badly to that." Here she smiled. "And that is when I showed him the door. It appears, Mr. Waterman, that Mr. Taliaferro is not your friend."

Ben laughed. "I am getting that impression, too, Mrs. Montgomery."

Spreading her hands, focusing on Ben, Claire Elise asked, "But what does this have to do with me? How can I help you protect the Wade boy?"

"Well, you see, it's more complicated. It appears that there are some aspects of the Schumann murder that require further clarification. So, to be on the safe side, the governor has asked me to take a fresh look at things. From the beginning. For good order's sake."

Claire Elise raised an eyebrow. "*Aspects?* What *aspects*?"

Ben hesitated. "I'd rather not say, not just now. I would ask for your understanding and patience with me as I work through this."

Claire Elise pressed her lips together and replied in a formal tone. "All right, then. As you wish. How may I help you?"

"Please tell me about your role in this. From the beginning."

"But I . . . I have already been through this with Sheriff Poindexter.

And, of course, I spoke about it with Mr. McGee, as I'm sure he told you. What more can I add?"

"Please," Ben said.

"Well, then, if I must."

"Please," Ben repeated.

With a sigh, Claire Elise began her story. "I suppose it began on July 4th, the day of the fireworks display at the fairgrounds. Early in the afternoon I saw Mr. Schumann there, I guess about two o'clock. He explained that he would like to organize a birthday celebration that night at the hotel for his daughter Leah, a girls' slumber party he called it. He apologized for the short notice and asked if I would be able to organize it. Of course, I agreed.

"Later, I saw Rachel speaking with the Wade boy. A short conversation. And then she walked over and asked if I was aware of the party her father was planning. I told her I was and would soon need to return to the hotel to begin preparations. She then informed me that she had asked Virgil to bring her horse and one other to the livery stable. She explained that she and her friend Eloise intended to take a ride up the Reddies River the next morning. Jewel later told me that Virgil arrived at the hotel with the horses about three o'clock in the afternoon, put them in their stalls, and then left again."

"Did you see Rachel speaking with anyone else at the fairgrounds?" asked Ben, now a lawyer cross-examining.

Claire Elise thought for a moment. Her face clouded, eyebrows furrowed. "Well, yes, now that you mention it, I did."

"And who was that?"

Again, the pressed lips, the formal tone. "I saw her speaking with Gabriel von Gruenwald. Yes, they talked for quite a while. Very animated. It appeared that Rachel was angry about something."

"Angry? About what?"

"I'm quite sure I do not know, Mr. Waterman. But there was most definitely heat in the conversation."

Ben nodded. "Please, continue."

Claire Elise then repeated her story. The birthday party, Eloise looking for Rachel, the frantic search of the hotel, the telephone calls to Sheriff Poindexter and Tanner's Rest, the men on horses, the dogs, and Poindexter's terrible news that Rachel's body had been found with Virgil Wade's knife deep in her chest.

This tracks what she told Roscoe, thought Ben. "So," he said, "Rachel, fully dressed in riding gear, left the hotel in the middle of the night?"

"That's what Sheriff Poindexter thinks. He thinks she went out to check on the horses, you know, before their morning ride." Claire Elise burst into tears. "But she never came back!"

"And you? Did you hear anything? Did Rachel make any noise that woke you up?"

Wiping her eyes with a handkerchief, Claire Elise sniffed, "Not a thing. Not a sound. If only I had! If I had awakened, why, perhaps I could have stopped her! Asked her to return to bed, to wait until morning. Oh, Mr. Waterman, perhaps I could have saved her!"

Ben reached across the table, gently patting her hand. "Now, now, Mrs. Montgomery. You mustn't think that. You cannot blame yourself for this terrible tragedy."

Composing herself, Claire Elise smiled weakly. "Thank you for that, Mr. Waterman. Your words are most comforting."

"I very much appreciate your patience in speaking with me, Mrs. Montgomery. I know it must be difficult for you to remember that awful day."

Claire Elise nodded.

"So, to wrap things up, is there anything else that you recall? Anything to add to your story?"

Claire Elise thought for a long moment, set her jaw. "You mentioned certain . . . *aspects* of the case that need to be clarified. Could it be that Mr. von Gruenwald is one of those *aspects*?"

Taken aback, Ben replied, "Why do you ask?"

"Well, as I mentioned, I witnessed an extended conversation between him and Rachel on the very day she was . . . murdered. Perhaps this is none of my business, Mr. Waterman, but I must emphasize that this was *not* a *friendly* chat between friends. Not at all. I thought you should know."

Intrigued, Ben asked, "What do you think it means? This conversation?"

Claire Elise hesitated. "I'm sure I do not know, Mr. Waterman. But all I can tell you is that in my opinion, Mr. Gruenwald has lately been very attentive to Rachel Schumann. I have known him for a long time, since before I came to Wilkes. And, you see, Gabriel von Gruenwald is an attractive, very charming man, at least in the eyes of the women in his life."

Claire Elise's mood darkened. "During his visits here, Mr. Gruenwald now stays at the guest house Mr. Schumann built in Schumann Village, right across the square from Tanner's Rest. He used to stay here in the hotel but moved on when the guest house was finished.

"Rachel Schumann, Mr. Waterman, was a complicated young lady—mature beyond her years. I do not mean to speak ill of the dead, especially Mr. Schumann's daughter, but, well, around men, and especially Mr. Gruenwald, she was coy, flirty, if you know what I mean."

Ben nodded.

"I have often seen her and Mr. Gruenwald together, arm in arm, walking around town, smiling, laughing. Almost like *lovers*. And as for Mr. Gruenwald, it was as if he was *courting* her! And this at a time when he is engaged to another woman, a Jewish woman in Wilmington!"

Engaged? thought Ben. *Interesting.* Gently, Ben asked, "And Mr. Schumann. Was he aware of this . . . behavior?"

Claire Elise waved her hand. "Rachel was his eldest child, Mr. Waterman. His cherished *daughter.* In his eyes, Rachel could do no wrong. As far as Gruenwald's attentions, Mr. Schumann remained blind to it all." Shaking her head, she finished, "There. I've said too much. I apologize, Mr. Waterman, forgive me. I am not normally such a gossip."

"No, no, Mrs. Montgomery. Not at all. I very much appreciate your candor. I will keep this information between the two of us."

Claire Elise nodded. "Thank you. Thank you for that."

"Of course."

Rising, Claire Elise asked, "Will that be all, Mr. Waterman? Do you have what you need from me? I need to be on my way to Schumann Village."

Standing, Ben looked into her eyes and shook her hand. "Yes, thank you. You have been most helpful, and I appreciate it. Again, I apologize for having you relive all this." With that, Claire Elise withdrew.

As Ben sat thinking, trying to make sense of the interview and Claire Elise's final observations, Jewel appeared once more. "Off to church now, Mistah Waterman. Cain't be late, y'know!" Snapping her fingers, she added, "Just about forgot about your lunch. You had a big breakfast, so I fixed you something light. Something special."

"And what might that be, Jewel?"

Leaning down to meet his eyes, Jewel grinned. "Cracklin' cornbread! In a pan on the stove. Made it fresh this mornin'. And fresh buttermilk from the springhouse, in a bottle in the ice box. Mmm, good!"

"That's wonderful, Jewel. Just right! I haven't had crackling cornbread and buttermilk in years. What a treat!"

"'Hope you like it! Gotta go now."

Chapter 20

Dressed in his freshly pressed suit, Ben came down the stairs, leather satchel hung from his shoulder. Carrying the heavy hotel typewriter, he placed it back behind the reception desk. He sat in the dining room, and soon Jewel appeared carrying a tray, humming to herself and smiling as always.

"Good Monday mornin', Mistah Waterman! Another fine day in Wilkes!"

"Indeed it is, Jewel," said Ben, looking out at the morning sunshine. "So, what have we here?"

"Got you some fried eggs, country ham with red-eye gravy, grits and butter, and homemade biscuits and strawberry jam."

As she poured the coffee, Jewel said, "Well, suh, like I promised, I talked to Preacher Bondurant after church. Told him what you had in mind. He says you should come on down to the church, down in Cairo, sometime today. Wants to talk to you about, you know, what you got in mind. Pauline and all."

"Thanks so much, Jewel. I can't tell you how much I appreciate it. I've got this thing at the jail this morning, but I can get down there sometime after that, late morning probably, maybe this afternoon."

"That'd be good, Mistah Waterman. You do that. He'll be around all day, 'cause Monday is wash day. It's the Mount Zion AME Church, like I said, down in Cairo, on the main street there. Big white church with a sign out front. Cain't miss it."

"Thanks, again, Jewel. I'll be there. But now I'm going to enjoy this wonderful breakfast!"

Smiling, nodding, humming, Jewel returned to the kitchen.

As Ben finished his breakfast, Claire Elise approached his table with a smile. Her mood seemed much improved from the day before. "Good morning, Mr. Waterman, another breakfast success?"

"Indeed, Mrs. Montgomery! You and Jewel are magicians in the kitchen." Curious, Ben asked, "So, how did things go at the Schumann's?"

Claire Elise looked away, a slight shift in mood. "Fine, fine. Mr. Schumann wanted to discuss . . . some business. About the hotel."

Ben let it go. "And the *Shiva?* For Rachel?"

Claire Elise shook her head. "So sad, Mr. Waterman. What can one say?" Changing the subject, she continued. "What about you? What's on your agenda for the day?"

"Well, later this morning Taliaferro is making some sort of announcement at the jail. You know, about the Schumann . . . incident. So, I will definitely be there for that."

"Yes, I heard about it. I may step over to hear what he has to say. I expect it will not be good news for the Wade boy."

"I'm sure you're right about that, Mrs. Montgomery. Absolutely sure."

"Let me get these dishes out of your way, Mr. Waterman. And tonight? Dinner?"

"Well, I expect I will have a full day. But I don't see why I couldn't have dinner here."

"Very good, then. I'll let Jewel know."

"And," Ben continued, "I would be most pleased if you would join me? You mentioned—"

"Yes, you're right," she smiled. "I did. That would be lovely. I'll arrange it. Say, half past six? Seven?"

"Wonderful! Let's make it seven, just to be safe. A lot is going on today."

"Seven it is. See you then. If not before."

After breakfast, Ben remained seated, reached into his satchel, and removed the sheaf of papers he had worked on the day before. First, he reviewed the detailed memorandum he had prepared, summarizing events and developments since his arrival in Wilkes, making small changes and edits. Then he read through the document he intended to discuss with Reverend Bondurant, and hopefully Pauline Oxendine, later in the day.

Good, he thought. *This will do. Now, I just need to get Pauline Oxendine to sign it.*

Ben was deep in thought, thumbing through his leather-bound copy of *North Carolina Criminal Law and Procedure*, when the hotel door opened and Roscoe McGee walked in. Ben smiled, looked at his pocket watch. "Well, good morning Ros. I figured you would turn up about now. Fun evening Saturday night. I never figured you for a vaudeville crooner."

"*Pffft*," muttered McGee, waving a hand. "So, *counselor*. Ready for the big show? At the jail?"

"I was born ready, Ros," grinned Ben. "You know that."

McGee smiled and nodded. "So, what's up? Any news?"

Ben filled him in about his conversation with Jewel the day before, his upcoming meeting with Reverend Bondurant, and the document he had prepared for Pauline Oxendine.

"So, you did it? The resignation letter?"

Ben pointed across the room to the brass letterbox. "On its way to the judge. I'll let him know directly the next time we talk on the telephone."

"Big step," said McGee, reaching out his hand to shake Ben's. "Proud of you."

"I just hope I don't live to regret this, Ros. But it's done, and so that's that."

"Time will tell, Ben, time will tell. But I expect we better get on over there, see what ol' Razor has to say. There's a big crowd waitin'."

Rising, Ben pointed to McGee. "Now you remember what we discussed."

McGee zipped his thumb and index finger across his lips. "Not a peep, Ben. Not a word from me."

W

Vincent Taliaferro looked out the window of the Wilkes County Jail. "Good job, Redbone. Must be fifty, sixty people out there. Newspapers?"

Sheriff Poindexter nodded. "I got in touch with most all of 'em. I also called Winston, Greensboro. Both said they would prob'ly send somebody over here on the mornin' train."

Taliaferro nodded. "Good, good. Photographers?"

"Olly Overby is all set up. I told him most likely he could sell some pictures to the Winston and Greensboro boys. Maybe locals, too. He liked that."

"The boy?"

"Upstairs, in his cell. Crip's with him."

"Chains?"

"Hands and feet."

"Cleaned up?"

"Crip took care of it. Got him washed up cleaner'n a choir boy."

"He knows to keep his trap shut?"

Poindexter nodded. "He damn well better."

Crip Goins limped down the stairs, shotgun in hand. "Ready when you are, Mr. Taliaferro."

Taliaferro looked at the clock on the jailhouse wall. "Ten on the dot." Reaching into his briefcase, he withdrew a stack of paper. "Bring the boy down here and let's go."

Chapter 21

Ben and McGee took in the scene. Fifty or sixty pairs of boots kicked up red dust that hung close to the ground in the muggy air. Muted grumbling and grousing compounded the tension and fueled an uneasy sense of anticipation. Morning sun promised another hot day.

The crowd was all men, some dressed in business suits, others in bib overalls, chewing tobacco and spitting thick brown juice on the ground. There were a few small boys, some playing marbles in the dust, others running around, excited, come to see the show. Here and there men held up cardboard signs reading *Elect Taliaferro!* and *Vote for Vince!* and the like.

Olly Overby stood nearby, his precious Kodak ready on its tripod. He was surrounded by several men with small notebooks, pencils behind their ears, shaded by black derby hats. McGee pointed at them. "Newspapermen. Mostly local, but some from out of town. Olly will do a good business today."

In the distance, Ben spotted Claire Elise Montgomery, standing on the porch of the hotel, a broad brimmed straw hat shielding her eyes and face from the sun.

Off to one side stood a knot of eight or ten surly men, armed with pistols, shotguns, and rifles, their horses tied to hitching posts. They were all wearing rough-knit, long-sleeved, collarless shirts in various shades of vermillion, looking like a flock of cardinals.

"Red Shirts," said Ben.

"I see them," nodded McGee. "Trouble."

W

The Red Shirts were an infamous White supremacist group founded in Mississippi in 1875. Chapters soon spread across the Post-Reconstruction South and, working openly, they used terror, intimidation, and, in many cases, violence to suppress Black civil and voting rights and to restore the Democratic Party to power. In North Carolina, Red Shirts served as the paramilitary wing of the Party and had been leaders of the Wilmington Massacre of 1898. Most were legacy members of the early Ku Klux Klan and donned white robes and hoods when their more serious transgressions required concealment.

"Take a look, Ros," said Ben. "Around their necks."

McGee squinted to see. "I'll be damned, Ben. Nooses!"

Ben nodded. "That's right. Saw that in Wilmington, too."

Each of the Red Shirts wore a twine lanyard woven into a miniature hangman's noose, a small silver Christian cross hanging from it. Leaning in, McGee whispered, "This could get ugly, Ben."

Ben said wryly, "I doubt it, Ros. They do their best work in the dark."

Pointing to the Red Shirts, McGee said to Ben, "You see that one over there? The guy in charge? The one with the red beard and the heavy gut? That's Luther Wade."

"Luther Wade?" asked Ben, eyes wide. "You mean Virgil Wade's daddy? Who raped Pauline Oxendine? Here?"

"In the flesh," nodded McGee.

A little past ten o'clock, the door of the jail opened, and Vincent Taliaferro and Sheriff Poindexter emerged. Taliaferro positioned himself behind a small wooden table, legs apart, feet firmly planted. Rising to full height, he stroked his moustache and set down a pile of papers and a brown paper bag on the tabletop. He motioned for quiet, and the crowd obliged. The newspapermen, including Roscoe McGee, were ready, pencils and notebooks in hand. "Take good notes, Ros," whispered Ben. "We may need them."

In a loud, but solemn voice, Taliaferro began.

"My name is G. Vincent Taliaferro, that's T-A-L-I-A-F-E-R-R-O, pronounced *Tolliver*. For those who do not know me, I am the interim solicitor and prosecutor for Wilkes County. I see some of you are aware," smiling and pointing at the signs, "that I am a candidate for the permanent position in this fall's election.

"Beside me is Mr. Jimmy Poindexter, Wilkes County sheriff, who is no doubt known to you all." Putting one hand on the stack of documents, he continued. "For those representing the newspapers, here are typed copies of my statement so that your reporting may be fully accurate. Once I have finished, I will take a few questions."

Taliaferro reached for the pince-nez hanging from a cord around his neck and pinched the spectacles firmly on the bridge of his nose. Holding the page in his hand, Taliaferro began to read.

"It is my sad duty to provide information about a horrendous crime that has been committed here. In the early morning hours of Thursday, July 5th, Miss Rachel Schumann, beloved young daughter of Jakob and Rebekah Schumann, was brutally attacked, bound, gagged, and abducted against her will from the Schumann Hotel, where she was an overnight guest. Her assailant stole her horse from the hotel livery stable and rode off with her to the north bank of the Yadkin River, just below the iron bridge.

"There, concealed from view, she was cruelly and savagely beaten and stabbed to death by a drunken, merciless monster who fled the scene. Thanks to the intrepid work of Sheriff Poindexter here, assisted by Deputy Sheriff Cobey Goins and several brave townspeople, Miss Schumann's body was recovered Thursday morning. Her attacker was soon identified and captured. He is now imprisoned here in the Wilkes County Jail, where he will remain until he can be tried, convicted by a jury of solid and sober Wilkes citizens, and hung by the neck until dead!"

"No, no!" shouted voices from the crowd. "Hang him now! Justice for Rachel Schumann! Bring him out here now!"

Taliaferro let the outburst take its course, then held up a hand and continued. "The perpetrator of this vile and vicious, pitiless, and barbaric murder has a name. He is Virgil Wade, the half-breed son of Pauline Oxendine, a resident of the Cairo community in Wilkesboro."

More angry shouts and calls for justice. The Red Shirts were quiet.

"The evidence against the Wade boy is overwhelming. In all my years as a prosecutor, I have never seen a more horrendous crime or a more solid case. We have him in conversation with the victim during the afternoon of July 4th at the fairgrounds. We can place him at the hotel, in the livery stable. We have him in possession of Rachel Schumann's stolen horse and tack. We can prove beyond the shadow of a doubt that he was present at the scene of the monstrous crime. And, most importantly," holding up the sealed paper bag, "We have the murder weapon—Virgil Wade's own skinning knife bearing his hand-carved initials! Plunged deep into the heart of poor, defenseless Rachel Schumann!"

Men in the crowd edged closer to Taliaferro, fists upraised, clamoring *"Justice! Justice now! String 'im up! Give 'im to us!"* Folding his statement and slipping it into his jacket pocket, Taliaferro removed his pince-nez and motioned for calm.

"No, no!" he cried, holding out his hands, raising his voice. "I understand your anger. I share your outrage. And I promise you this: *Justice will be done!* I pledge to you on my honor as your prosecutor that the Wade boy will hang for his crime. But we are a civilized people, my friends, and we must be patient. We must wait for the law to pronounce its righteous judgment and seek vengeance for this assault on our humanity! And I will be the awful instrument of your wrath, your fury, your horror and indignation! I beg you, let me do my work."

Those holding signs erupted, *"Hurrah for Vince! Hurrah for justice! God bless Taliaferro!"*

Nodding gravely, Taliaferro again motioned for quiet. "And now, I will entertain a few questions from the press."

Immediately a hand shot up. "Roy Sturgill," McGee whispered. "From *The Yellow Jacket*. Local. What about the knife, Vince? We need a picture."

Taliaferro paused, thought about it. He then reached for the paper sack and carefully removed the tape sealing it shut. He slowly and theatrically removed the knife, holding it high above his head by the hilt, turning it from side to side so that the sun glinted off the bloody blade, the interlocking initials *V* and *W* clearly visible.

Olly Overby was ready. As he plunged the shutter, the flash pan exploded in a burst of brilliant light, startling the crowd. "Got it!" he shouted. Taliaferro gently replaced the weapon in the bag and resealed it.

Another hand raised. "Rupert Snyder, Mr. Taliaferro. *Winston-Salem Journal*. What about the body?"

"The body of Rachel Schumann was released to the family last Thursday afternoon," replied Taliaferro sadly, "and, pursuant to Jewish custom and tradition, was buried in Schumann Village, next to the Schumann family home on Friday."

"So, what about the autopsy report?" asked Snyder. "When will you release it?"

Taliaferro nodded. "Doctor Noah Burleson, Wilkes County coroner, delivered his full report to me last Friday morning. This document will be an important piece of evidence at trial and will be available to you all then. In the meantime, suffice it to say that Doctor Burleson confirms the cause of death as the unspeakable wound inflicted by Virgil Wade's knife, the very weapon you have all just seen."

"It is my understanding that there are photographs," Snyder continued. "Aren't these a matter of public record? When may we expect you to release them?"

Taliaferro blinked, hesitated. "As you may know, sir, photographs are required by law in cases like this. These are far too horrible for public consumption, as I am sure you can understand, so no, out of respect for the Schumann family and the memory of Rachel Schumann, the photographs will not be released to the public or the press."

Not to be put off, Snyder pressed on. "You talk about being patient, waiting for the law to take its course. When can we expect a trial in this matter?"

Taliaferro, in his element, nodded. "Well, as you know, the courts are now in summer recess. It is my intention nevertheless to convene a grand jury as soon as possible, hopefully next week. Once we have the indictment, I expect to bring Virgil Wade to trial in the fall term of superior court here in Wilkes, most likely in early September. We have everything we need to convict him right now, and I wish it could be sooner."

Another hand up. "Johnny Flinchum, sir. *The Daily Evening Patriot.* Greensboro. Any chance we could see the murderer? Get a look at him?"

Taliaferro nodded to Sheriff Poindexter. The moment had come.

Poindexter disappeared into the jail and soon returned with Crip Goins, sawed-off shotgun in the crook of one arm, Virgil Wade held tight by the other. The boy looked small, weak, and pitiful, head down, legs and hands in heavy iron chains. He spoke not a word. There was first a gasp from the crowd, followed by a steady, angry, rumbling murmur.

"Don't look much like a monster to me," whispered McGee.

Taliaferro, Poindexter, Wade, and Goins stood in a line, facing the crowd, a rigid tableau captured by another flash from Overby's Kodak, a photograph that soon made its way into newspapers across Northwest North Carolina and beyond.

With a superb sense of timing, Taliaferro then brought the assembly to a close. As Poindexter, Goins, and their prisoner moved back inside the jail, Taliaferro spread his arms and said, "Now, gentlemen, if you will excuse me, we have important work to do. I will provide periodic reports to you as the case develops and as circumstances warrant."

As Taliaferro turned to leave, ignoring shouts from the newspapermen, the crowd began to disperse. Irritated, the newspapermen dutifully retrieved their copies of Taliaferro's statement. As they departed, a stiff breeze scattered the remaining papers across the open space between the jail and the courthouse, a sea of white covering the ground, a snowstorm in July.

Before Taliaferro could depart, Luther Wade approached him, and the two engaged in a short but intense whispered conversation. Nodding to Wade, Taliaferro turned and entered the jailhouse.

"See that?" said McGee, elbowing Ben and sliding his notebook into his side pocket. "I'd sure like to know what that was all about." Pointing, McGee said, "And look-a there, Ben."

Luther Wade slowly walked back to his group, and, without a word, the Red Shirts mounted up and rode quietly away.

W

McGee and Ben walked slowly to the Phaeton.

"Well, Ben, that was quite a performance."

"Indeed, it was. Listening to Taliaferro, the case against Wade is iron clad, open and shut. What in the hell have I gotten myself into, Ros?"

"Well, the way I see it, that little piece of political theatre was more about what ol' Razor *didn't* say. Nothing about the riding clothes, the quilt, the lantern, the whiskey and shot glasses. None of that. And he cleanly sidestepped the photographs, which show all of it. And don't forget, Ben. Razor doesn't know what we know, what we know about—*Rachel*. What Burleson told you."

"You're right, of course," Ben agreed. "Look, Ros, I really need to get over to Cairo. Talk to the preacher there. If I can get Pauline Oxendine to agree, there's no way Taliaferro can deny me access to the Wade boy. I need to hear what he has to say, get his side of things." Shaking his head, Ben said, "Maybe the boy has some sort of explanation? So, Cairo. Give me a ride?"

McGee grinned. "Climb aboard, buddy-ro."

Chapter 22

As he walked along the main street of the Cairo community in Wilkesboro, Ben realized that Jewel was right. Mount Zion AME Church was hard to miss, a simple, whitewashed box with three tall, arched windows on each side. Atop the high-pitched roof sat a hexagonal steeple crowned with a simple wooden cross. The building appeared freshly painted and was in pristine condition. The church sat on a wide green lawn, shaded by two tall, spreading oak trees flanking the entrance. Here and there in the cemetery, ancient magnolias perfumed the air.

Beneath one of the oaks, two large black kettles hung from iron frames over small wood fires, filled with laundry worked by young Black women churning the mix with short wooden poles. Closer to the street and in the sun hung lines of drying sheets, towels and bed linens, tended by more young women with sacks of clothespins around their necks.

Under the other shade tree sat three circles of women, chatting as they strung and sewed small cloth tobacco pouches. Two older women were busy churning butter from fresh Wilkes cream.

Along the street sat a row of elderly Black women in sunbonnets, some weaving intricate baskets, others offering colorful bunches of fresh cut summer flowers in tin buckets filled with water. The flower ladies passed around a yellow-labeled tin of Society Brand Sweet Snuff, dipping and massaging their gums with twig toothbrushes. Ben was surprised to see several well-dressed White women inspecting the goods and making their purchases.

As Ben approached the entrance, one of the red doors opened and a distinguished older man appeared, dressed all in black with a starched white clerical collar.

Reverend Napoleon Bondurant was born into slavery, his pregnant mother having been sold and "sent South" to the cotton fields of the Mississippi Delta by a hard-luck owner from Wilkes. After Emancipation, and recalling his mother's tales of her childhood, the young man made his way back to Wilkes. He soon found he had a knack for scripture and a calling to preach the Gospel.

Standing over six feet, slim and erect, Bondurant's skin was black as onyx, his features like finely-carved ebony. His dark brown eyes were friendly and set off by brilliant white sclera. His hair was cropped close in tight curls, the color of weathered steel. Bondurant held out his hand and flashed a dazzling smile.

"So, you must be Ben Waterman. Jewel told me that you would be stopping by today. Welcome to Mount Zion."

Shaking Bondurant's hand, Ben smiled. "That's correct, Reverend. Nice to meet you. I appreciate your taking the time to see me, sir."

Bondurant laughed. "I learned pretty quick to do what Jewel Ponder tells me to." Holding up a finger, he grinned, "We all know better, mind you, than to cross her, Mr. Waterman. She's a force of nature here. Her daughters Opal and Pearl are out there right now, helping out with the laundry. For the hotel and the Schumann place."

Looking around, Ben said, "What a beautiful church you have, Reverend. And look what's going on! Everybody's so busy, working hard."

"Thank you, Mr. Waterman. We do our best. Our congregation may be poor, but we believe in hard work. I have tried to create opportunities for our women folk. All this," he said, spreading his arms, "gives them ways to earn a little cash money. Every little bit helps."

"I can see that, Reverend. Your flock is lucky to have you."

"Thank you for that. 'Preciate it. But now, you are a busy man yourself, Mr. Waterman. Let's go inside. Much cooler in there."

The men sat in the front pew facing each other. It was, indeed, dark and cool. "Now, that's better," said Bondurant. "So, how can I help you?"

Ben explained his mission to Wilkes, his desire to protect Virgil Wade, Governor Maxwell's interest in the case.

Bondurant shook his head. "Terrible thing about that Schumann girl. Terrible. I know the Wade boy well, Mr. Waterman. His momma, too. Pauline. Nobody down here can believe he could be involved in something like this. He's always been a good boy, in church every Sunday, right here in this pew, right up front. I 'preciate your concern about him, Mr. Waterman, and Governor Maxwell's, too. He's always been a friend to our people, stood up for us. If I can help you get Virgil Wade through this thing, why, I will. But what can I do?"

"I need to speak with Virgil, Reverend. I need him to tell me what happened at the river that night. You see, since I have been here, I have uncovered what appear to be several irregularities, some inconsistencies in the story told by Mr. Taliaferro and Sheriff Poindexter."

Bondurant's eyes narrowed. "Go on."

"Well, I am mostly concerned about the boy's safety. He's locked up in the jailhouse now. Only the Sheriff and his deputy to guard him. There are some in town that don't want to wait until the trial. They want to take matters into their own hands."

Bondurant sighed. "Yes, Mr. Waterman. I know how that works."

"The night he was arrested, well, that was a close-run thing, Reverend. Taliaferro was able to call them off, just barely. But this morning he made a presentation at the jail. Big crowd. Taliaferro got them all worked up. I'm sorry to tell you that there was a bunch of Red Shirts there. Armed."

Bondurant frowned. "Red Shirts?"

"I'm afraid so, Reverend."

Bondurant moved on. "Jewel said you want to talk to Pauline. About Virgil."

"That's right, Reverend. I have an idea about how to protect Virgil, but I need her help. Virgil is, I understand, underage, a minor. That means I need her permission to proceed. Can you help me? Mrs. Oxendine, I expect, has no reason to trust me, but surely she would listen to you?"

Bondurant sat silent for a moment. "Pauline is outside sewing tobacco pouches, under the tree. Let me speak with her about this. Life has not been kind to Pauline Oxendine, Mr. Waterman, and if there is anything I can do to ease her burden, I will do it. But first I need to hear you say it. Hear you say that you will keep Virgil Wade out of the hands of those Red Shirt vigilantes."

Looking squarely into Bondurant's eyes, Ben said. "Reverend, that's why I'm here. Governor Maxwell has instructed me to do just that, and I swear to you that I aim to see it through. To the end. I will do my best."

Bondurant held his chin in one hand, thinking. "I'll be right back."

While he was waiting, Ben replayed the morning's events in his mind. *Taliaferro's got the bit in his teeth now. He won't back off. And what was he talking about with Luther Wade? Not good.*

Soon the door opened. Bondurant led a small, shy woman to the front pew. Ben stood.

"Mr. Waterman, this is Pauline Oxendine, Virgil Wade's mother. I have explained your mission and your willingness to help Virgil in this dark hour."

"Pleased to meet you, Mrs. Oxendine. I cannot imagine the pain you are going through. And I hope I can help you, and Virgil."

Her eyes moistened. "I 'preciate that, Mr. Waterman. Virgil, well, he is a good boy, and I just cain't believe all this," she whimpered, shaking her head. "They got him locked up in the jail, won't even let me see him. His momma! And him just a boy."

"I have told Pauline that I have looked into your soul, Mr. Waterman. That I trust you and believe that you will do all you can to help Virgil. And that she should, too."

Ben nodded. "Thank you, Reverend. Thank you for that."

"So, what do you need Pauline to do? What do you have in mind?"

Ben reached into his leather satchel and removed a typed document. "First, I need to speak with Virgil. Try to figure out just what happened that night. But Mr. Taliaferro refuses to let me see him, talk to him. Says I have no right.

"But there is a way around Taliaferro." Ben took a deep breath. "I have talked to Governor Maxwell about this, and we are agreed. I am prepared to take his case, Mrs. Oxendine, to be his lawyer. To defend him against Taliaferro's charges."

Eyes wide, Bondurant said, "You would do that? Be his lawyer? But we can't afford—"

Ben shook his head. "Don't worry about that. I will do this for free, Reverend. Virgil needs help, somebody to stand up for him. And I will gladly take the case."

"What can I do to help you, Mr. Waterman?" asked Pauline, wiping her tears.

"I need you to sign this paper, Mrs. Oxendine."

"What is it?"

"Virgil is underage, Mrs. Oxendine. That means I need your permission as his mother to take his case. So, I have prepared this paper for you to sign. It's your consent for me to represent Virgil. To act as his attorney. To defend him."

"That's all? That's all I have to do? Sign this paper?"

"That's right, Mrs. Oxendine. That's all," said Ben, holding out the form. "And I want you to know that anything Virgil and I talk about, all that will be strictly between the two of us. Confidential. Nobody, not Taliaferro, not the Sheriff, not even the judge can make me reveal what Virgil tells me. And likewise, I need you both to keep all this to yourself. Taliaferro won't like it a bit, and I need to pick the right time to tell him."

Pauline looked to Bondurant, eager, hopeful. He nodded slowly.

Taking the form from Ben's hand, she located the signature line, looked up. "Suh, do you have a pen?"

As he left Cairo, Ben had a choice to make. Return up the hill to the hotel or cross the river to the Trogdon Opera House. Something in the back of his mind had been troubling him. Something about the photographs. His conversation with Noah Burleson. He couldn't quite put his finger on it. Ben needed to talk to Roscoe McGee.

"Well, Ben! Bless your heart, just never know when you'll turn up!"

"Afternoon, Tink. Ros around? I need to speak with him."

Tink motioned with her head. "He's in the back room, working on the paper. Go on back."

Looking up from his desk, McGee put down his pen. "Howdy, Ben. Take a seat. How'd it go over in Cairo?"

"I had a good talk with Reverend Bondurant. He put in a good word for me with Pauline Oxendine, and she signed the paper. Got it right here," he said, patting his satchel.

"Well, that's good news, Ben. Real good. Now I reckon you've got what you need to raise a little hell with ol' Razor. Spoil his big day."

Ben smiled. "That's the plan, Ros. He won't be happy but if everything works out, I hope to talk to the Wade boy, too. But I need you to help me think through something. I know you're busy with the paper, but—"

"Naw, nothing that can't wait. What's on your mind?"

Ben reached into his satchel and took out the dreadful photographs of the Rachel Schumann crime scene and autopsy and spread them over the desk. "Something's been bothering me. I need another set of eyes on these pictures. Come here and take a look."

Ben selected several of the photographs, put them side by side. These were Olly Overby's close-up pictures of Rachel Schumann's body, on her back, taken at the river and on Burleson's operating table.

McGee examined the photographs carefully, looked up. "Okay, what am I supposed to be seeing different than before?"

"Get me that magnifying glass of yours, Ros." McGee opened a drawer, handed it to Ben. Bending over, Ben took the lens and closely examined two of the photographs. Then he rose and handed the glass to McGee. "Look carefully, Ros. Now what do you see?"

McGee took his time. "Why, same as before. Virgil Wade's skinning knife stuck in her chest, the handle—"

"Yes! The *handle*, Ros. That's it! You see the way it leans to the left, way left, at an angle?"

McGee took another look. "O . . . K . . . So what?"

"Think about it, Ros. Think about what that means!"

McGee held his chin in one hand, bent over, squinted through the lens, moving it back and forth, taking a longer look. Suddenly he stood, snapped his fingers. Making a stabbing motion in a wide arc with his left hand, he shouted, *"Left-handed!"*

"Exactly! Exactly right, Ros. No way a right-handed person could leave the knife at that angle. You see it?"

McGee repeated the stabbing motion, first with his right hand, then again with his left. "No doubt about it, Ben. Both pictures show it."

With growing excitement, Ben then shuffled through the photographs, pulled out a picture of Rachel's tortured face at the river, eyes wide open in terror. "Now, look at this."

McGee examined the photograph carefully, looked up. "Damn, Ben, her eyes."

"Never mind her eyes, Ros. Look at her *face*. Look at the *left side* of her face, beside her *left eye*, near her *left* temple, where that big dark bruise is. Now, what does that tell you?"

McGee looked up, made a fist with his right hand, swung wide and punched the air. "Right-handed!"

"You got it. Unless I'm missing something, the blow to Rachel Schumann's head came from a *right-handed* person. Even Doc Burleson agrees. Couldn't deliver a powerful punch like that, leaving that big a bruise, with your left hand!"

McGee nodded slowly. "And *that* means?"

Smiling, Ben said, "*Occam's razor*, Ros."

McGee grinned back, recited, "Occam's razor—the principle that, of two explanations that account for all the facts, the simpler one is most likely to be correct.'"

"And that would mean?"

McGee stood straight, spread his hands, and said, "The simplest answer, Ben, is that *two* people were at the river with her that night. One right-handed, the other left. That *two* people were involved in Rachel Schumann's murder!"

Nodding gravely, Ben repeated, "Two."

Still worked up from his meeting with McGee and suddenly hungry, Ben detoured back to Cairo. A smiling Black street-vendor was selling sandwiches from a cart shaded by a big umbrella. Ben chose chicken salad with freshly baked white bread, dressed with leaf lettuce and a thick slice of vine-ripened tomato. Sprinkling salt and pepper, he took a bite. *Delicious.*

Finishing up, Ben balled up the wax paper wrapping and dropped it into a trash bin. He then walked over to the flower ladies in front of the church and selected a large bouquet of sunflowers. Wrapping them in old newspaper, the elderly Black woman cautioned, "Now, suh, you better get these in some water pretty quick, 'fore they wilt. And carry them upside down 'til you get 'em home. Keeps 'em fresh."

Ben grinned, "Yes, ma'am, I'll do just that."

Ben was deep in thought as he walked up the hill, mulling over how he would handle his next conversation with Taliaferro. As he entered the hotel, Jewel Ponder was busy mopping the floor, humming. "Afternoon, Mistah Waterman. What you got there?"

Handing over the bouquet, Ben said, "Sunflowers, Jewel. For Mrs. Montgomery. She will be joining me for supper here this evening."

"Aw, that's real nice of you, Mistah Waterman. I'll get a vase and put 'em in some water. Set 'em right over there."

"Thanks, Jewel. And thank you again for arranging things with Reverend Bondurant."

"You see him? The Preacher? Down at the church?"

"I did, Jewel. And Mrs. Oxendine, too."

"Things go all right? Like you wanted?"

"Things went fine, Jewel. I think I have what I need to help Virgil Wade now."

"Bless you, Mistah Waterman, for what you doin'. Now, let me get that vase."

Ben walked to the courthouse across the street and down the corridor to Taliaferro's office. The door was closed. Ben knocked, waited. No response. Ben knocked again, this time gently turning the doorknob. Locked. He crossed the hallway to the Clerk of Court's office. The door was open.

A middle-aged woman working behind the counter looked up. "Can I help you?"

"Thank you, ma'am. I'm looking for Mr. Taliaferro, but his door is locked. Do you know when he will be back?"

Shaking her head, the woman replied, "Well, sir, he came over about noon, said he would be out the rest of the day. So, I doubt he will return. Anything I can do for you?"

"No, thank you, ma'am. I need to speak with him about . . . a case. I'll come back later." The woman returned to her work and Ben returned to the hotel.

Jewel, still busy tidying up, greeted him. "Why, Mistah Waterman. Back so soon?"

"Yes, Jewel, back again. Looks like I have the rest of the afternoon off. I was thinking, though. Another one of your cool baths might be nice. You know, 'freshen up before supper."

"Yessiree, Mistah Waterman. I'll fix it for you right away. And by the way, I brushed and pressed your other suit for you. Put it in your room, in the chifforobe."

"Thanks, Jewel, that's very kind of you."

As he approached the stairway, Ben noticed a tall cut crystal vase full of yellow sunflowers in the middle of one of the dining room tables. *Very nice*, he thought. *Just right.*

Freshly shaven and refreshed from his bath, Ben toweled himself dry, slipped on the white cotton bathrobe laid out for him by Jewel, and walked barefoot back to his room. He stretched out on the bed, hands behind his head on the soft feather pillows. *Well. Nothing more I can accomplish*

today. Might as well put Virgil Wade out of my mind and enjoy the evening. With Claire Elise. Maybe just close my eyes for a minute.

Ben awoke with a start, fragments of his dream dissolving, floating away. He struggled to remember. *Lovely green eyes, beautiful smiling face. Julia! No? Claire Elise.* Ben shook his head to clear it, reached across to the nightstand to look at his watch. *Almost seven! Gotta hurry!* Five minutes later, Ben was dressed and ready.

"Evenin', Mistah Waterman! You ready for supper? Miz Claire Elise made up somethin' special for you."

"Ready, Jewel. Hungry, too!"

"Well, you just set y'se'f down over there. I'll go get Miz Claire Elise."

Soon Claire Elise arrived, wearing a blouse the color of daffodils. Around her slim neck was a braided gold necklace and jeweled pendant that matched her eyes. Her lustrous auburn hair was pulled back into a bun, held by crossed sticks of carved ivory. Her smile was radiant. "Good evening, Mr. Waterman," she said, in her pleasant British accent. "You look very nice this evening."

Ben helped her to her chair and sat across from her. "And you, as well, Mrs. Montgomery. What a lovely necklace."

She touched it, smiled. "Thank you. It was a gift. From my father. A birthday present. While we were in Argentina."

"And the stone?"

"An emerald. Also from South America. Also from my father."

"Argentina, you say?"

And so, it began. Over drinks, Ben a whiskey, Claire Elise red wine, they shared their stories.

Claire Elise spoke of life and travels with her peripatetic parents, her time in Buenos Aires, her move to Wilkes, and how she came to the Schumann Hotel. Her marriage and the death of Charles Randall Montgomery were mentioned only briefly, and in passing, to explain her widowhood.

Ben reminisced about his childhood in Wilkes, his relationship with Governor Maxwell and his family, his studies in Chapel Hill, his remarkable semester in Oxford, and his experiences with Professor Burton in London, Paris, and Freiburg. About Julia Burton, he spoke not a word.

Gabriel von Gruenwald was not mentioned.

Shaking her head, Claire Elise said, "I venture to say, Mr. Waterman, that there are no other people in Wilkes County having a conversation such as this tonight. Amazing!"

Ben nodded, smiling. "I am sure you are correct, Mrs. Montgomery. I'd wager on it." Pausing a moment, Ben continued, "But I have a proposition for you."

She tilted her head, lifted her eyebrows. "Yes?"

"We should dispense with all this formality. I would much prefer it if you would call me Ben."

Her laugh was like music. "Why, of course, Mr. . . . I mean . . . Ben." She raised a cautionary finger. "But only if you call me Claire Elise. And no talk of . . . business tonight."

"Agreed!" said Ben, raising his glass.

Claire Elise touched her wineglass to his, and said cheerfully, "We are agreed then. But where are my manners? I must thank you for the beautiful flowers, Ben. They are quite lovely, and yellow is my favorite color."

Gesturing toward her blouse, Ben replied, "I can see that, Claire Elise," relishing the opportunity to say her given name aloud. "Yellow goes well. With the green of your eyes."

Bowing her head, she smiled shyly, "Why thank you, kind sir. They are my mother's gift to me."

Jewel appeared from the kitchen, wiping her hands on a towel. "You ready, Miz Claire Elise? Supper'll be done in about five minutes."

"Perfect timing, Jewel."

"So," Ben asked, "what culinary masterpiece have you two come up with tonight?"

"Well, yesterday you had French toast for breakfast. So, I thought we would continue the French theme. Tonight, it will be chicken in the French style, *coq au vin*, cooked in red wine sauce. My mother's recipe from our time in Paris."

Ben sniffed the air. "If it tastes as good as it smells, it'll be delicious!"

Claire Elise pointed at Ben's glass. "Will you stay with whiskey, Ben?"

Ben shook his head. "I think not, Claire Elise. French it is, all the way. I would love a glass of whatever you're having, if you don't mind."

"*Bien sur, monsieur!*" said Claire Elise. "*Tout de suite.*"

Jewel looked at them, back and forth. "I reckon that means he wants some of the red wine, too?"

Claire Elise laughed, "Yes, please. Thank you, Jewel."

"Comin' right up," said Jewel, disappearing into the kitchen.

Jewel soon returned with a large, covered tureen, set it on the table between Ben and Claire Elise, and lifted the lid with a flourish. "Chicken stew!" she exclaimed. "French style!"

Ben wafted his hands, sniffed the air as Claire Elise ladled portions into two deep bowls. "*Coq au vin!*" he marveled. "In Wilkesboro!"

The meal was a delicious and fragrant combination of chicken thighs and drumsticks cooked in a mixture of red wine, diced bacon, carrots, sweet pearl onions, mushrooms, garlic cloves, and a dash of apple brandy.

"It's a little heavy for summertime, but I thought you might enjoy something different," said Claire Elise, as Jewel reappeared with a tray bearing a basket of crusty sourdough bread and a bottle of red wine from Burgundy.

As Ben predicted, the flavors of the dish exceeded the promise of its savory aroma, the meal perfectly paired with the bouquet and smooth finish of the Pinot Noir. Finishing his meal, Ben sopped up the remaining sauce with a chunk of bread. "Wonderful! Simply delicious!" Claire Elise smiled and nodded in appreciation.

Jewel again appeared with a tray. "Apple pie!"

"*Tarte aux pommes,*" Claire Elise corrected, as Jewel cleared away the dinner plates and replaced them with dessert. As they were about to begin, there came a low, rumbling noise from outside the hotel in the direction of the jail.

Walking to the window, Jewel said, "Somethin' goin' on out there. Over't the jail." Curious, the three of them walked outside and stood on the covered porch, straining to see in the dark.

"Horses," Ben muttered. The night was indeed filled with the sound of hoofbeats. Soon they heard a different sound, the thud and clank of tools digging into the earth. Suddenly, the air exploded with a *whoomph.* A ball of yellow-orange light quickly resolved itself into a familiar symbol.

"It's a cross!" Ben shouted. "A burning cross! They've come for the boy!" Eyes wide in alarm, Ben exclaimed, "Claire Elise, do you have a weapon? A firearm? I need to get over there!"

Confused, her face illuminated by the blazing evil image, Claire Elise responded, "Weapon? No, Ben, I'm sorry! No!"

Ben grabbed her by the shoulders. "Get inside, Claire Elise! You and Jewel get back in the hotel. Right now!"

"What are you doing, Ben? Stay here!"

Shaking his head, Ben shouted, "Back! Back into the hotel!"

Running toward the jailhouse, the white robes and hoods of the mounted men became clearly visible. *Klan!* Ben realized.

Ben reached the jail just as Crip Goins limped clumsily through the open door, dressed only in his long johns. "What th' hell's goin' on here?!" he demanded, brandishing his shotgun.

The leader of the vigilantes slowly edged his horse forward, stopped directly in front of Goins and Ben. "Put that thing down, Crip." said the man, casually pointing at the shotgun, his voice muffled through the hood. "We've come for the boy. Now go inside and get him out here. Right now! And you, lawyer man," he said, pointing at Ben. "You git on outta here, you know what's good for you!" Ben did not move.

Trembling, Goins said, "Y'all . . . y'all know I cain't do that. I got orders!"

Suddenly a large brown dog, a long-eared Plott Hound, raced through the open jailhouse door, growling and snapping at the mob. "Git that goddamned dog back, Crip!" shouted the leader. The dog, fearless, teeth bared, kept coming. Without hesitation, the man removed his pistol from its holster, fired once, and shot the dog dead.

"Goddamn it, Luther!" cried Goins. "You've kill't my dog! You've done kill't poor Rufus!"

Luther, thought Ben. *Luther Wade. Come to lynch his own son!*

Without a word, Wade holstered his pistol and nodded to one of his men. The man dismounted, holding an ax handle, one end wrapped in rags. He ran to the burning cross, lit the cloth, and trotted back to the jailhouse. Swinging the roaring torch through the air, he threw it through the open door. Flames quickly spread across the pine floorboards and licked up the walls.

Virgil! Ben realized, his mind racing.

Ben reached over to Goins, grabbed the shotgun from his hands, and shouted, "Get in there, Crip! Get in there and put out that fire!"

Goins glared at Ben, hesitated for a moment, and then did as he was told. As Goins limped into the jailhouse, Ben turned to the crowd, pointed the shotgun into the air, and fired. A deafening *BOOM* shattered the night air. Several wild-eyed horses snorted and reared up in panic as buckshot pellets rattled back to earth.

"You're a fool, lawyer man," sneered Wade. "And stupid to boot!" he added, pointing down at the shotgun, leaning forward in the saddle. "Ol' Gladys there is a double barrel, and one of them is empty now. Whatcha gonna do, lawyer man?" Waving an arm at his mounted men, he grinned behind his hood. "You sure as hell cain't get us all!" The men laughed.

Leveling the shotgun, Ben cocked the second barrel and snarled through gritted teeth. "That's right, Luther Wade. But I sure as hell can get *you*, take *you* with me!"

Hearing his name said out loud, and wary of the shotgun, Wade hesitated for a moment. Just then another horse and rider slowly emerged from the darkness beyond the burning cross, from the direction of the courthouse.

Sheriff Jimmy "Redbone" Poindexter gripped the reins in his left hand, his right grasping a Winchester repeating rifle held upright against his hip. Poindexter drew his horse to a halt, dropped the reins, and coolly leveled the rifle at the hooded mob, working the lever, chambering a round.

"That's one in the chamber, Luther. Six more to go." He spat tobacco juice on the ground. "So, then, which of you sorry sons a bitches wants to be first?" Nobody moved.

Suddenly, yet another man came running and stumbling out of the gloom, sweating and panting. *Taliaferro!* Ben realized. Taliaferro stopped, hands on his knees to catch his breath. Standing, he shouted, "All right, then! All right! That's enough! Luther, I want you and your boys to stand down, right now! Go on! Get the hell out of here. Party's over. Git!"

Wade, weighing his options, eyes fixed on the weapons, spurred his whinnying mount upright on its hind legs and nodding to his crew, he spun the horse around and galloped off, his robed and masked men following him into the night in a thunder of hoofbeats and random pistol shots.

As the burning cross sputtered and waned, Crip Goins stumbled from inside the jail. "Fire's out!" he yelled.

"And the boy?" demanded Ben.

"Upstairs," Goins replied, wheezing. "He's okay."

Poindexter spoke. "Go on, Crip. Get inside and put some clothes on. You look a damn sight silly out here in your underwear."

"But, but—" Goins protested.

"Git!" shouted Poindexter.

"All right, Sheriff, all right. But can I have Gladys back?"

Sighing, Ben eased the hammer down and handed over the shotgun, and Goins disappeared. Turning to Taliaferro, Ben snarled, "What in the hell just happened here?"

Taliaferro said calmly, "Just some boys raisin' a little hell, Waterman.

Nothing we can't handle."

"The hell you say!" shouted Ben. "You're lucky there was not a lynching here tonight!"

"Calm down, Ben," said Poindexter. "Me'n Crip got this. They won't be back tonight. I'll set here a while. We'll trade off watchin' the boy 'til mornin'. It'll be all right."

"And what about tomorrow?" exclaimed Ben. "What about tomorrow night?" Ben twisted and pointed his finger at Taliaferro. "Damn you! I warned you about this!"

Taliaferro stared at Ben for a long moment. Without a word, he turned and walked slowly away, the night hiding his smile, back toward the courthouse.

W

Hands trembling, Ben made the slow walk back to the hotel. Claire Elise and Jewel ran down the steps to meet him. "Ben!" cried Claire Elise, grasping his arms, looking him over. "Are you all right? Are you hurt?" Jewel stood by, shaking and working her hands.

Taking a deep breath, Ben said, "No, no. I'm fine, Claire Elise. I'm fine."

Looking into his eyes, she suddenly embraced him tightly. "Ben, oh, Ben." She whispered into his ear. "That was very *brave*. What you did. I was so frightened!"

Exhausted, Ben gently stroked her hair. "It's okay, Claire Elise. It's all over." Disengaging, he took her hands in his, looked to Jewel. "Let's all settle down and get some sleep. Come on, let's all go back inside."

Ben knew there would be no sleep for him this night. He opened the door to the covered porch and sat down heavily in one of the rocking chairs. Blowing a breath, he stared into the darkness toward the jail, keeping watch, as the cursed cross finally collapsed in a shower of sparks and smoldering rubble.

Chapter 23

In the early morning light, leaning back in the rocking chair, Ben awoke with a start. Blinking, he gazed out toward the jail. Crip Goins appeared from behind the jailhouse, rolling a wheelbarrow. He removed a shovel and a rake and began to clear the charred remains of the fire, leaving an ugly black scar on the ground.

Stretching and rolling his shoulders, Ben entered his room, splashed water on his face, and looked in the mirror. *God, what a night,* he mused, his wet hands smoothing back his hair. *Well, this will have to do.*

He walked down the stairs and was greeted by Claire Elise, a concerned look on her face.

"Are you all right, Ben? Did you sleep?"

Shaking his head, Ben said, "Not much, I'm afraid. I was watching the jail. Maybe a few minutes just before dawn. In the rocking chair."

"Here now, Ben. Let me get you some breakfast."

Ben held up his hands. "No time, Claire Elise. I need to get over the river. See Roscoe McGee."

"I understand. Please take the sulky. Can you manage it? In the livery?"

"No problem. Thanks." Looking around, Ben said, "Where is Jewel? Is she—?"

"She's . . . she's as well as can be expected. She was very shaken by all *that,*" said Claire Elise, gesturing toward the jail. "I told her to take the day off. She wanted to go be with her daughter, Opal, down in Cairo."

Nodding, Ben replied, "I'm sure that's for the best, Claire Elise. I am so sorry that she had to see that last night. But now, if you will excuse me, I really do need to be on my way."

"Take care, Ben. Be careful."

As he turned to leave, she grasped his sleeve and added, "And please, join me for dinner again tonight."

"Thank you, Claire Elise. I'll try to do that. I hope to be back over here before dark. You know," he nodded toward the jail, "to watch things. Now, I would very much appreciate it if you would telephone Mr. McGee, let him know I'm on my way."

W

Ben could smell sizzling bacon wafting from McGee's apartment. Tink Beasley opened the door with a tight smile. "I do declare, Ben Waterman, we're going to have to start charging you rent! Come on in. Mrs. Montgomery called from the hotel, said you might appreciate some breakfast. I'll get coffee. You look like you could use some."

Ben realized he was ravenous. "That would be great, Tink. Thanks."

Looking into his tired eyes and serious face, Tink frowned. "Trouble, I hear?"

"I'm afraid so," Ben nodded.

"Let me go get Ros."

As the three of them finished up their breakfast, Ben recounted the events of the night before.

"Damnation, Ben!" exclaimed McGee. "What a thing! Hard to believe. The boy okay?"

"Yes," Ben nodded. "For now."

"And you say those boys, dressed up like the Klan, they were led by *Luther Wade*?"

"'Fraid so," said Ben. "Crip Goins called him out by name. Taliaferro, too."

McGee whistled softly. "So now we know what they were talking about, there at the jail yesterday morning?"

"Can't say for sure, Ros, but put two and two together."

"So, what now, Ben?"

"We need to get the judge on the phone, Ros. Right away." McGee jiggled the handle, got a connection, and told Betty what to do. Soon the telephone rang.

"Governor Maxwell is on the line for you, Mr. McGee," said Betty in her professional voice. "Please go ahead." There was a *click* as Betty left the line.

"Mighty damned early in the morning, Ben," thundered Maxwell. "What's going on?"

Ben held the earpiece between himself and McGee so that both could hear. Ben described the attack on the jail, the burning cross, the attempt to burn the jail and capture Virgil Wade, Poindexter's intervention, Taliaferro's late arrival.

"This Luther Wade," said Maxwell, astonished. "You say he's Virgil Wade's *daddy?* Come to lynch his own son?"

"That's right, Judge. He had a hood on, but Crip Goins and Taliaferro called him by name."

"Damn, Ben, that's just not right. So, what was Taliaferro's role in all of this?"

"Well, Judge, it was like he was in control. It was a real standoff when he showed up, pretty tense. So, he just struts into the middle of it like a banty rooster. He told Luther Wade that the party was over and for him and his men to ride off. And, just like that, they did."

"And they did not return?"

"No, sir. I sat up all night watching. No more trouble."

"Well, then. That settles it."

"Settles what, Judge?"

"So, Ben, now listen up. What did you do about, you know, what we talked about last time?"

"You mean Virgil Wade? Taking his case?"

"Yes."

"Well, I thought about it, Judge. Long and hard. And then I typed up my resignation letter like you suggested. Put it in the mail that very night, last Saturday."

"In the mail, you say? Saturday?"

"Yes, Judge."

"Well, that's good. It hasn't arrived here yet. So, who else knows about this, Ben?"

"Just me and McGee here, Judge."

"Good, very good. Now Ben, your resignation is not effective until I receive it and accept it. So, you still work for me. You two keep quiet about the letter, Ben. When it gets here, I'll put it in my pocket, and we can deal with it later, when the time is right. But right now, I've got another job for you."

"Sir?"

"Well, looks to me like that sorry-assed no-account Taliaferro has played right into our hands. Too clever by half. See, this attack proves that Taliaferro and Redbone are in over their heads, can't handle things, can't protect the Wade boy. Maybe even in on it."

"And?"

"That means I have just what I need, Ben. And I know exactly what to do."

"Yes?"

"I aim to call Bev Royster, declare an emergency, call up the Guard, send some boys to Wilkes and bring the Wade boy here to Raleigh. Put him in Central Prison. *Protective custody*, until the trial."

Beverly S. Royster, from Granville County, was the adjutant general of North Carolina, appointed by Maxwell, and, as such, commander of the North Carolina State Guard, the state militia subject to activation by the governor.

"The *Guard?*" asked Ben, incredulous. "Here?"

"You're damned right, Ben. The Guard. Hell fire, Ben, this is what they're *for!* I'll tell Bev to round up four or five volunteers, get 'em in uniform, issue weapons, and get their hind ends over to Wilkes. Take the boy and bring him back here, where we can keep him safe. From Taliaferro. And from his *daddy*."

Taken aback, Ben replied, "Well, that sounds like a plan, Judge. But I expect it will take you some time to get all this organized. So, what do we do until then?"

"That's where you come in, Ben. Why I need you to still be on my payroll."

"Yes, sir?"

"When I declare the emergency, I will designate you as my official representative in Wilkes, full power to act in my name and on my behalf. You are my chief of staff and chief legal officer, after all. I doubt the attorney general will give me any trouble about it. And Bev Royster sure as hell won't. He loves a good scrap."

Ben swallowed. "But how?"

"Don't worry. I'll wire a statement to you covering all of it. The declaration of emergency, the call-up of the Guard, your appointment. All of it. Everything you need to go see Taliaferro and shut him up. Shut him *down*. He's up for election in November, and he's too much of a coward to cross me on this."

Suddenly McGee piped up, "Say, Judge, what about—"

"McGee? That you?" boomed Maxwell. "I know what you want. You still publishing that little rag of yours on Wednesdays?"

"Why, yes, Judge."

"Good for you. So, here's the way it will work. I'm authorizing Ben here to release a copy of my statement to you, so you can put it in your paper tomorrow. I'll have it done and wired this afternoon, latest, so save some space in the paper for it. And I want a headline, McGee, a *humongous* headline that will put the fear of God into Taliaferro and his friends."

McGee grinned like the Cheshire cat. "Yes, *sir!* Leave it to me. I know just what to do."

"All right then, boys. Anything else?"

Ben hesitated. "Well, Judge, your plan takes care of *protecting* the Wade boy, but what about *defending* him?"

"One thing at a time, Ben. We'll work all that out. Taliaferro hasn't even got his indictment yet. He'll get on that soon, but for now we have some time. Let's get the boy to Raleigh now, and we then can deal with your resignation and your representation of Virgil Wade. All in good time."

"Yes, sir. Understood."

"Well, if y'all will excuse me, I need to get to work. Stick close to the telegraph office, Ben. Be right there when the ticker comes in. I'm not interested in some fool operator flapping his gums around town about this 'til you have a chance to lower the boom on Taliaferro."

Maxwell bellowed a laugh. "By *God*, Ben, but this is fun! Kickin' ass! Just like the old days, eh?"

Ben grinned. "Yes, Judge. Just like the old days."

W

Vincent Taliaferro arrived at his office early, still brooding over the turmoil at the jailhouse the night before. *Well, that was not all bad*, he thought. *All except that fool Ben Waterman, sticking his nose into things again. But this'll still make all the papers.*

The ringing telephone startled him. He lifted the receiver, listened to the voice on the other end, frowned. "Thank you, Betty. I appreciate the information." *Goddammit! Waterman again. Calling the governor. What's he up to now?*

Chapter 24

Sandwich in hand, Ben stood over the Western Union telegrapher as his machine began its staccato clacking. "Telegram coming in?"

The telegrapher nodded, stringing out the ticker tape in his hands as it emerged. "Looks like it's for you. From Raleigh."

"Let me see that, please," said Ben, reaching for the tape.

"But—" the telegrapher protested.

"Sorry," said Ben, "Confidential. Government business."

Shrugging, the telegrapher sat back as the clacking continued. Ben smiled as he threaded the tape through his hands. Finally, the noise stopped. "That whatcha waiting for?" asked the telegrapher.

"Oh, yes," said Ben. "Yes, indeed."

Suddenly the machine started up again. Busy rereading the original message, Ben paid no attention. "Looks like this one's for you, too," the man said, handing over the tape. "But shorter."

Ben read the message. *"CAVALRY ARRIVING SOONER STOP TMW NOON FM GBORO STOP BE READY STOP MAXWELL"*

"I need a Western Union form," demanded Ben. "And your paste pot."

"But, but that's *my* job!"

Ben put up a hand, and the telegrapher sighed and pointed across the room. Ben took scissors and cut the long telegram into short pieces, then pasted them in neat lines onto the first yellow form. It took several to complete the job. The second tape he folded and put in his pocket.

Finished, Ben looked at the telegrapher, placing several coins beside the machine.

"Like I said. *Confidential.* Official business. We clear?"

Pocketing them, the telegrapher nodded, and Ben was gone.

W

Looking up from his work, cigarette in hand, McGee asked, "Well, any news?"

Holding out the sheaf of yellow papers, Ben replied, "Got it, Ros. Got it right here. The judge has been busy."

Ben was quiet as McGee read through the telegram. "So, what now?" McGee asked.

"Well, first thing, you copy this telegram."

"For tomorrow's paper," finished McGee. "I've saved space for it. The boys in the Linotype room are waiting. And I've been working on the cover story."

"I'm going to see Taliaferro, read this to him."

"You realize, don't you Ben, this'll cause all hell to break loose?"

Ben nodded. "Get it over with, Ros, sooner the better." He pulled the second telegram from his pocket, handed it to McGee.

"So, it's all coming together, Ben. Quicker'n we thought."

"Looks like it. If the Guard boys get here around noon tomorrow, maybe they can get the Wade boy loose from the jail and ready to travel on the afternoon train."

"So, that covers tomorrow. But what about tonight, Ben?"

Ben thought about that. "So, Roscoe. I wonder if you might have a shotgun? Or a pistol? I'll have to handle this myself."

Grinning, McGee walked over to a tall cabinet and took out a small-gauge shotgun and a long-barreled hunting rifle, holding the weapons high in his hands.

"Two?" asked Ben.

"You sure as hell don't think I'm gonna let you do this alone, do you? You take the shotgun now, maybe wave it in Taliaferro's face to make your point. Here," he said, fumbling around in a drawer and handing over a box of .410 caliber shells. "Buckshot. If things turn to cheese tonight, you sure as hell won't be huntin' quail. I'll finish up here and be on over to join you later. Might be late, but I'll be there."

"But, Ros—"

"No buts about it, buddy-ro. Make a hell of a story for the paper. Like momma used to say, sometimes best to just shut up and say thank you."

Ben reached for the weapon. "Thank you, Ros, more than you know."

"It's settled then. You git on over the river now and give ol' Razor the what for."

W

Crip Goins was seated outside behind a table in front of the jail, not looking up from his game of solitaire as Ben drove by in the sulky. He unhitched Maybelle, put her in her stall. Shotgun in one hand, satchel in the other, Ben walked to the courthouse and gave Taliaferro's door three sharp knocks.

"It's open," came a voice from within.

Ben stood in front of Taliaferro's desk. "Well, then," snorted Taliaferro, pointing at the gun. "Mighty late in the day for bird hunting."

"Not exactly," replied Ben, breaking open the breech. "I have some news for you." He took out the sheaf of yellow papers and handed them over. Taliaferro took the papers and began to read. The color drained from his face as he worked his way through the telegram. As he finished, his face flushed, now crimson with anger.

"What in the hell is this?" he sneered, a speck of white spit forming in the corner of his mouth, his face breaking into a sheen of sweat. Throwing the papers back at Ben, hands trembling, he shouted, "What have you done, Waterman?"

"It means just what it says," replied Ben evenly. "Given the disturbance last night at the jail, Governor Maxwell has declared a state of emergency in Wilkes and mobilized the State Guard to protect the Wade boy, since you and Sheriff Poindexter are clearly unable to guarantee his safety. As you can see," said Ben, putting the telegram back in his satchel, "troops will be arriving tomorrow to escort the boy to Raleigh. Until then, I speak and act on Governor Maxwell's behalf, and I will do what I think is necessary to prevent another episode like last night."

"*Goddamn you, Waterman!* Just who in the hell do you think you are? Drag-assin' in here, shotgun in hand, like you own the goddamn place!"

"Well, that's the thing, you see. Until the Guard arrives tomorrow, I *do* own this place, Taliaferro, the jail *and* the boy. Poindexter and his deputy work for me now."

"You, you . . ." stuttered Taliaferro, searching for words.

Ben held up a hand. "Don't, Taliaferro. I don't want to hear it. It's done now, and you can't stop it. I warned you. I offered to help you. But you and your friend Luther Wade had other plans for the boy. So, shut up and keep out of my way."

Rising, Taliaferro pointed at Ben, thundered, "This will not stand! You can't do this! You'll never get away with it, Waterman!"

Ben stared back, closing the breech of the shotgun with a loud, metallic *click*. "I can and I will, Taliaferro. Don't mess with me. I'll be watching the jail tonight, and I will be armed. And I will have help. If I were you, I'd get the word out to your friends to stay well clear of Virgil Wade tonight. There'll be plenty of room in the prison car tomorrow if there's trouble. Room for you, too, if you interfere."

Slamming the flat of his hand on his desk, Taliaferro bellowed, "*Me? Prison car? Me?* Is that a threat, Waterman?"

With a sarcastic smile Ben said, "No, Taliaferro. Like they say, that's not a threat. That's a *promise*. Wouldn't look too good on your resume, would it? How to explain your arrest for obstruction of justice and violation of a lawful order from the governor? Right before the election? Might cause the State Bar to take a look at your law license, too. Charlie Odell will surely file a complaint. Don't press me on this, Taliaferro. I have the authority and the *power*, and I *will* use it. Raise all the hell you want, no matter. Just stay out of my way, and you'll be all right."

"Get the hell out of my office, Waterman! Now!"

Ben nodded. "I'll be off to see Poindexter now to tell him how things stand. I do not expect to see you or any of your sorry friends anywhere near the jailhouse, Taliaferro. I mean it."

"*Out! Now!*"

Alone again, Taliaferro, leaned back in his chair, thinking, breathing hard, trying to steady his blood pressure. Finally, he reached for his telephone and jiggled the handle. "Betty? Taliaferro here. Please connect me with Mr. Simmons again. In Raleigh. Right away, please."

W

Ben's meeting with Sheriff Poindexter went smoother. He read through the telegram slowly, shifting his chaw and launching tobacco juice into the spittoon at his feet.

"This for real?"

"Yes, Sheriff, it's for real. Just came through on the wire a little while ago."

"How'd Razor take it?"

"Not very well, I'm afraid. I didn't expect him to."

Sighing, Poindexter said, "Well, I was afraid-a somethin' like this. Last night . . . " shaking his head, "Last night was not good. I don't 'preciate being put in that position."

"So, I can count on you then? Tonight?"

Waving the yellow papers in the air, Poindexter said, "'Seems like your friend the governor has dotted his *I*'s and crossed his *T*'s, Ben. Way I read it, you're in charge now. Least 'til the boy is on the train. You tell me how you want to play it, and that's how it'll be."

Ben explained he wanted both Poindexter and Goins at the jail all night. He told him of his plan to keep watch from the hotel balcony across the way. He wanted the Wade boy cleaned up and ready to travel when the Guard arrived.

"Well, that's a plan, Ben. I 'spect ol' Razor will put the word out. I gotta think those boys shot their wad last night. I don't see 'em comin' back." He sighed. "But if they do, why then, Ben, me'n Crip will be ready."

W

Ben slumped into one of the big, overstuffed chairs in the hotel lobby and closed his eyes. Soon Claire Elise appeared. "Ben? Ben? Are you all right?"

Ben blew out a deep breath. "Yes, thank you, Claire Elise. Just been a long day."

"Let me get you a whiskey. Looks like you could use one."

Ben accepted the drink gratefully, took a long pull, ran his fingers through his hair. "Thanks. I needed that."

"So, what have you been up to today?" she said, eyeing the shotgun. "I mean, after last night."

"Well, first of all, Claire Elise, I'm afraid that I can't join you for dinner tonight." He explained the events of the day, including his plans to keep watch from the hotel balcony with Roscoe McGee.

Wide-eyed, Clair Elise said, "My goodness, Ben. State militia, coming to Wilkes! To take the Wade boy to Raleigh, you say?"

Ben nodded. "That's the plan. In and out on the train tomorrow."

"But tonight," she said, "here's what we'll do. I will fix a light supper for you and Mr. McGee. There's a table and chairs on the balcony. And I'll open the bedroom next to yours so that he can get some sleep, should you decide to keep watch in shifts. What about that?"

"That's a fine idea, Claire Elise. And listen. I want to be very clear about this. Whatever happens tonight, I want you to stay in the hotel. I want you safe."

Grasping his hands in hers, alarmed, Claire Elise replied, "Of course, Ben. I understand. You have my word." Squeezing his hands, she added, "But promise me, Ben, that you will be careful, too. I couldn't bear it if, if anything—"

Ben squeezed back. "Try not to worry, Claire Elise. Redbone and Crip will guard the jail, and Ros and I will just be backup. Redbone says he doesn't think there will be any more trouble. We just need to get through the night."

W

Taliaferro replaced the receiver, cutting the line. *Well, that settles it.* He quickly walked across the hall to the Clerk of Court's office. Linda Jessup looked up with a smile.

"Afternoon, Mr. Taliaferro. What can I do for you?" Looking at the clock on the wall, she said, "I was just about to close up."

"So glad I caught you, Linda. We've got a situation here that I need to talk to you about." He briefly explained the plan to take Virgil Wade to Raleigh, presenting it as his idea. "So, things are moving fast, Linda. And I need your help."

"What can I do for you?"

"Grand jury," replied Taliaferro quickly. Jessup tilted her head, confused. "We need to get the grand jury back in here, Linda. Right away. I need to get an indictment of the Wade boy as soon as possible. So, we can be sure to get him in front of a jury in the fall term. First case called."

"But Judge Transou—"

"Yes, yes, I know. He's out of town. Visiting relatives in Asheville. Won't be back 'til the end of the month."

"So, shouldn't we wait?"

"*No!*" he shouted, then calmed himself. "Sorry. You see, when the judge is away from the district, I have the authority to recall the grand jury, to convene them in his absence. They've already been sworn in, so it's just a matter of calling them back."

"I don't know."

"Linda, listen. This is something the governor needs. To hold the boy. Without an indictment, why, some fool lawyer might be able to spring him loose. And we don't want that, do we? What would Jakob Schumann think about that, Linda? So, to get a case filed, all nice and proper, to hold the boy 'til the trial, we need an indictment right away."

"So—"

"So, here's what I want you to do. Tomorrow morning, first thing, I want you to prepare the grand jury summonses. Give them to me, and I'll get Poindexter busy serving them. Once the Wade boy is on his way to Raleigh, Poindexter will have plenty of time to get it done."

She thought about it long and hard. Finally, she nodded. "I can do that, Mr. Taliaferro. I'll have them ready before noon tomorrow."

Taliaferro smiled. *She bought it!* "That would be great, Linda. Much appreciated. And I will be sure to tell Judge Transou how helpful you've been."

Jessup beamed, but then raised a finger. *Uh oh,* thought Taliaferro. "How much notice do you want me to give? You know, in the summonses?"

Relieved, Taliaferro thought about it. "One week, Linda," he said. "Get them back in here next Wednesday morning."

"Got it!" she said.

Chapter 25

It was full dark when McGee arrived. Ben, seated in a rocking chair, turned as the screen door opened. He was surprised to see two people there.

"Tink! What in the world are you doing here?"

McGee shook his head, rolled his eyes. "Her noggin's as hard as a pine knot, Ben. I tried to talk her out of it, but she—"

"Give me the carriage gun, Ben," demanded Tink, reaching for it.

"What?"

"Hand it over, Ben," she smiled. "I damn well know how to use it."

"You mean this is *the* gun?" Ben asked, suddenly realizing the instrument of her widowhood was cradled in his arms.

"The one and only!" Tink beamed. "Now, give it to me. Buckshot, right? Here, you can use this," she said, holding out a double-action six-shooter and a box of bullets. Ben exchanged the shotgun for the pistol, amazed.

McGee brandished his hunting rifle. "So, looks like we're ready. We saw Redbone and Crip sitting outside the jail. Both with shotguns. Bring it on! *Naarh, naarh, naarh!*"

"Well, okay then, but let's hope we have a quiet night." Looking up, Ben said, "At least we've got a good moon to see by."

"Yep," said Tink. "Looks 'purt near full to me."

Snapping his fingers, Ben said, "Say, you two get supper?"

"Naw," said McGee. "We just got done puttin' the paper to bed. The boys in the back room are printing and stacking it now. The runners will get it out pretty soon." Grinning, he said, "I think Cotton Bob will like it. And I think it will drive ol' Razor plumb crazy!"

"Well, look here, then," said Ben, gesturing to a table and chairs set up on the balcony. "Help yourself. Claire Elise fixed it for us." Atop the red checkered tablecloth sat a plateful of roast beef and cheese sandwiches, a bowl of coleslaw, and a dish of sliced, red ripe summer tomatoes. Beside a stack of plates was a full pitcher of fresh lemonade and glasses.

"Well, let's dig in!" cried Tink.

As they were finishing, a rumble and clatter made them look up toward the jail. "Uh, oh," said McGee. "What's that?" In the light of the moon, they could see what looked like three mule-drawn wagons, full of people, nearing the jail.

His jaw set firmly, Ben announced, "Come on. Let's go." Weapons in hand, the trio marched toward the jailhouse.

By the time they reached the jail, Sheriff Poindexter was already in conversation with the group's leader. "What's going on here?" Ben demanded, looking around.

Then he saw a face he recognized. "Reverend? Is that you? Here?"

Napoleon Bondurant stepped forward, tipped his hat. "Yes, Mr. Waterman. It's me. And some friends."

"But what are you doing here? Don't you realize—"

"Yes, sir, we know all about it," Bondurant interrupted. "All about last night, too. That's why we're here." Pointing to a small woman in one of the wagons, he continued, "You see, Mrs. Oxendine here, well, she was worried about her boy. In there," pointing at the jail. "We all figured that we would come on over, you know, help keep watch."

Alarmed, Ben blurted, "Are you armed, Reverend? Surely not."

"No, sir. Not a weapon among us. We just aim to keep a peaceful vigil here. 'Til morning. 'Til your friends get here. To move the boy."

"But how, how do you know—"

Bondurant smiled. "The boys running Mr. McGee's printing press, well, they thought we should know what's in his paper tomorrow. Big news. And so, here we are," he said, spreading his arms wide. "We'll just rest here a spell, pray for the boy, sing a few hymns."

Ben turned to Poindexter. "Sheriff?"

Poindexter lifted his shoulders, shrugged. "Free country, Ben. They got no weapons, not plannin' any trouble. I don't see I got any reason to clear 'em out, long as they don't get out of line. We on the same page, preacher?"

Bondurant bowed in agreement, turned, and motioned toward the wagons. A group of about twenty men, women, and children slowly and silently began to climb down. They put quilts on the ground in a circle surrounding the black ashes from the fire the night before and lit candles. Ben watched it with wonder in his eyes.

"You stay here, Reverend. All of you. Stay with the boy. And tomorrow—"

"Don't worry about tomorrow, Ben. Tomorrow will take care of itself. Each day has enough trouble of its own."

Ben smiled. "Matthew. Chapter 6."

"Verse 34. You know your scripture, Ben," Bondurant smiled. "And now, if you will excuse me, we need to pray. For the Wade boy and those who strive to protect him. For justice, Ben. And mercy."

W

Back on the balcony in rocking chairs, McGee was first to speak. "Now, *that*," he said, shaking his head, "that beats all I've ever seen. Colored folks coming over here, to the jail, like ol' Daniel in the lion's den. Hard to believe Redbone went along with it."

Tink snorted. "Razor will ream him a new one for this. Taliaferro gets elected, he'll make him pay, sure's I'm sittin' here."

They rocked for a while. Then Tink spoke. "So, Ben, you sure you've thought this through?"

"What do you mean?"

"Well, here we sit, armed to the teeth. And all for a boy we don't even know. You sure we're on the right side of this thing? You think about that, Ben?"

Ben pondered the truth of her words. "I hear you, Tink. Could well be that Virgil Wade is guilty as hell, but that's for a jury to decide, not me. He'll get his day in court, Tink, and that's all that matters to me right now."

Just then the sound of people singing wafted through the air, from near the jail.

"Nobody knows the trouble I've seen.
Nobody knows but Jesus.
Nobody knows the trouble I've seen.
Glory, Hallelujah!"

McGee smiled and began to sing along. Ben and Tink joined in.

"Sometimes I'm up,
Sometimes I'm down.
Ohh, yes Lord,
Sometimes I'm almost to the ground.
Ohh, yes Lord.
Nobody knows but Jesus.
Glory, Hallelujah!"

Reaching into a bag, Tink pulled out a pint-sized Mason jar. "Any of that lemonade left?" she asked.

"Plenty," said Ben.

"Time for a snort! Let's open up a keg of nails, boys!"

She opened the jar, laid the lid on the table, and poured a thimbleful of colorless liquid into it. She struck a match, and the alcohol burst into a clear blue flame. "Wilkes County moonshine! Best in the world! Pure and clean!"

They all laughed as she poured generous shots into each glass, then filled them with lemonade.

"Down the hatch, boys!" she cried, and they all took a long pull.

Chapter 26

B en checked his watch as the train from Rural Hall rattled to a stop in a cloud of hissing steam and smoke. He walked along the track to the end of the train. Instead of the normal caboose, the last car was painted completely black, the windows covered with a grid of sturdy iron bars. After a time, a uniformed officer appeared, followed by four soldiers in full military gear, rifles slung over their shoulders. Ben walked forward to greet the officer, held out his hand. "General Royster!" he said, greeting the Adjutant General of the North Carolina State Guard. Beverly Royster was an imposing, no-nonsense military man and Civil War veteran. "I wasn't expecting *you*. I assumed—"

"Yes, well. Good to see you, Waterman, very good indeed. When I got the call from Governor Maxwell yesterday, I decided to command this mission myself. So, what have we got here? Prisoner transport, I think?"

"That's right. Just one young boy. He's in the jail, across the river."

"Any trouble at the jail last night?"

"No sir. It was quiet. The prisoner was under armed guard, and there were no further disturbances."

"Very good," said Royster, nodding stiffly. "So, let's get on with it then. Need to get this done so we can be on the return train this afternoon. No time to spare."

"Sheriff Poindexter has a wagon waiting for your men," said Ben, pointing to the group of soldiers. "You can ride over with me in the sulky."

"Will you accompany us on the trip back, Mr. Waterman?"

"Do you need me, too?"

"No need, Mr. Waterman. My men and I will have the situation firmly under control, I assure you. The prisoner will be delivered without incident to Central in good order. And I should point out," he said, making a face, "accommodations in the prison car . . . primitive at best."

"Thank you, General. I have some things to wind up here, but I should be able to get back to Raleigh tomorrow latest."

W

As the wagon load of soldiers approached the jailhouse, Crip Goins met them, Gladys in hand. A sizable group of curious onlookers flooded the street, alerted by McGee's sensational headline and coverage in *The Lost Province*. Off to one side stood Roscoe McGee and Olly Overby, his Kodak set up and ready to go. Royster scanned the crowd with scorn. Ben made the introductions, and General Royster and Poindexter signed the paperwork. Taliaferro was nowhere to be seen. Crip appeared with Virgil Wade, hands and feet bound, eyes open wide in fear, a pitiful sight. Ben approached the prisoner and spoke to him for the first time.

"Virgil, my name is Ben Waterman. I want you to listen to me very carefully. These men," he said, pointing at the soldiers, "are here to take you to Raleigh. You will be held in Central Prison, under close guard to protect you, until we can get things sorted out here in Wilkes. No one will hurt you there. Do not be afraid. Do you understand me?"

Silent, the boy nodded.

"Very good. Now, I must warn you, Virgil. You are not to speak to anyone, and I mean *anyone*, about the Rachel Schumann thing. I will come see you about all this, and we can talk then, understood?"

Again, a nod.

Royster watched all this with impatience. He was ready to move. "All right, Sheriff. The prisoner is now my responsibility. Do you have any questions for me?"

"No sir, no questions."

Royster turned to Ben. "Mr. Waterman, pursuant to Governor Maxwell's order, the declaration of emergency remains in effect here until further notice, but you are now relieved." Royster snapped a quick salute and turned to his men. "Men, secure the prisoner. We will now proceed to the station for our return trip to Raleigh. My thanks to you, Sheriff Poindexter, for your helpful cooperation and assistance in this matter."

As Poindexter handed over the prisoner, there was a sudden

explosion of light from the flash pan of Overby's Kodak, capturing the scene for posterity. The soldiers put Virgil Wade on the floor of the wagon bed, then climbed in themselves. Royster sat beside Crip Goins on the driver's bench, and, with a snap of the reins, they were off. The wagon rumbled down toward the iron bridge.

"Well," said Poindexter. "That's over and done."

Ben, shoulders slumped, said, "I wish that were true, Sheriff. But somehow I believe things have only just begun."

W

Claire Elise met Ben in the lobby. "So, he's gone? The boy?"

"Yes. For now."

"And you, Ben? What of you?"

"Well, Claire Elise, first I need to borrow your telephone. Governor Maxwell will want to know that things came off here without a hitch. After that, well, I would like to get some sleep, take a bath. I also need to write up my final report for Governor Maxwell while things are fresh on my mind. And, tomorrow, well, I plan to be on the train back to Raleigh."

"Of course, Ben. You need a rest. You've certainly earned it. So, back tomorrow?"

"Yes."

"Well, then, surely you will join me this evening? For dinner before you leave? Sort of a farewell celebration? For all you have accomplished here. Why, you saved that boy's life!"

"That would be wonderful, Claire Elise. I look forward to it. Very much. Seven o'clock?"

"Seven it is, Ben. I have something special in mind."

W

Ben awoke from a long nap, bathed, shaved, refreshed and ready for the evening ahead. He had not eaten since breakfast, and the enticing aromas wafting up from the kitchen whetted his appetite.

Claire Elise and Jewel greeted him with big smiles.

"Jewel! I am so happy to see you!"

"Thanks, Mistah Waterman, good to see you, too!" Her mood shifted. "Now that the Wade boy is . . . gone, I figured it would be, you know . . . all right to come back."

"I don't think there will be any more trouble, Jewel. I appreciate you being here tonight."

"Wouldn't miss it, Mistah Waterman. Now, I better get on back in the kitchen 'lest somethin' burn up in there!"

Turning, Ben took in the vision before him. "Why, Claire Elise, you look . . . beautiful!"

And she did. Her usual Gibson Girl ensemble had been replaced by an elegant, long-sleeved watered silk gown of forest green, fitted at the waist, the dress matching her wide and lively emerald eyes. The low-cut bodice, trimmed in lace and the color of ivory, exposed her fine, long throat, wrapped in a necklace of woven gold. Her auburn hair, pulled up and away in tightly woven braids, shone in the fading light.

Smiling, she politely curtsied, dropped her head in appreciation. "I thank you for the kind compliment, Mr. Waterman. The dress is from my time in Argentina. Another gift from my father. I do not have many opportunities to wear it here in Wilkes. But tonight seemed to be appropriate. A special occasion, after all."

"I am honored, Mrs. Montgomery," said Ben, bowing from the waist. "You are a fair vision for these pitiful sore eyes."

"Enough of that, Ben," she blushed. "May I offer you a drink? Whiskey again?"

"What will you be having, Claire Elise?"

Smiling, she walked to the bar. "Again, something special. Will you join me? I think you will like it."

Atop the bar sat a silver wine bucket filled with chunks of summer ice, the neck of a tall green bottle protruding from it. Claire Elise poured lemon-yellow wine into two finely cut crystal goblets. Handing one to Ben, she raised her own. "A toast to you, Ben Waterman, champion and protector of the downtrodden and keeper of the peace!"

Ben clinked his glass to hers, nodded, and took a sip. "Wonderful!" he exclaimed, inhaling the floral bouquet and holding his glass to the light. "What is it?"

"It's called *Torrontes*, from Argentina. Mr. Gruenwald used to bring it from Wilmington. It's the last of the lot, I'm afraid, but what better time to enjoy it? Now, let's sit. I have something I want you to sample. You must be famished."

She gestured to a silver tray bearing what looked to be tiny, golden fried pies. "*Empanadas*," she explained. "An Argentine specialty. Turnovers with a crispy crust, filled with bits of ham and cheesy spinach. Be careful. They're hot."

Ben gingerly lifted one of the delicacies in his fingers and took a bite. "Why, these are delicious!" Taking a sip of the wine, he added, "And the wine is perfect with them!"

Claire Elise nodded her thanks.

"Argentina, eh?" said Ben. "I'm sensing a theme here."

"Patience, Ben," smiled Claire Elise.

Ben grinned and reached for another *empanada.* Then, looking across the room, his eyes fixed on something he had somehow not noticed before, a gleaming black grand piano. "Yours?"

"Yes. It's a Boesendorfer. From Vienna. It was my father's only extravagance. He told me that it was once played by Franz Liszt. This instrument followed us all over the world. I only agreed to come to Wilkes if the piano came with me. And here it sits."

"Do you play?" asked Ben. Claire Elise rose, walked to the piano, raised the lid, and sat on the bench. The room had dimmed in the twilight, illuminated now by candlelight. Soon the slow, haunting melody of Beethoven's *Piano Sonata Number 14 in C-Sharp Minor* filled the room. As she finished, Claire Elise closed her eyes, lifted her hands from the keyboard, and looked back to Ben.

Mesmerized, Ben said softly, "Beethoven. *Moonlight Sonata.* Lovely."

Claire Elise bowed her head in appreciation. "Your knowledge of music is as good as your ear for accents, Ben. I see you made the most of your time abroad."

With a sly grin, Ben crossed the room, sat to the left of Claire Elise on the piano bench, their hips and thighs touching. She made no move to slip away. Ben unlimbered his fingers and began to play, again Beethoven, *Bagatelle Number 25 in A Minor.* When he finished, Claire Elise clapped her hands in delight.

"*Fuer Elise!*" she cried. Waving a raised finger, she whispered conspiratorially, "You, Ben Waterman, are a dangerously charming man."

"Well, look-a here!" Jewel Ponder piped up, emerging from the kitchen with a wide smile. "What'chall up to?"

Claire Elise stood and returned the smile. "Just a little music before dinner, Jewel. Are things about ready in the kitchen?"

"Comin' right up! Steak! Just let me clear this all away." Jewel soon reappeared with an enormous tray loaded down with plates and dishes.

Ben looked on in amazement.

"Thank you, Jewel. Now, then, my dear, you have had a difficult couple of days, and you have been working hard all afternoon. I think Mr. Waterman and I can manage things the rest of the evening. What's undone we can finish tomorrow morning. Go on, now. Get your rest."

Looking first at Claire Elise, then at Ben, Jewel winked and said, "Gotcha, Miz Claire Elise. See y'all in the mornin'!"

When she was gone, Claire Elise and Ben both laughed. "She really is a *Jewel*," said Ben.

"I don't know what I would do without her, Ben. But see here, now, let's begin."

As she served the plates, she said, "This is a classic Argentine meal for special occasions. Beefsteak with green *chimichurri* sauce, fried potatoes, and grilled fresh peaches. I hope you like it."

"Outstanding, Claire Elise! You have gone to so much trouble."

"Oh, and I almost forgot." She walked back to the bar and returned with a tray with two fresh goblets and two open bottles of red wine.

Ben, eyebrows raised, said, "Two?"

"It's a celebration, Ben," she said firmly, but with a smile. Pouring a sip for him to sample, she explained, "It's a Malbec. From Argentina, of course." She hesitated. "Again, from Mr. Gruenwald. It's a Bordeaux style claret with a hint of spice. It was first brought to Argentina by French colonists in the 1850s."

Ben swirled the purple wine in his glass, took a sip. "Excellent!" he proclaimed.

And so it went. Their animated conversation moved around the world, touching on many subjects, many places and people, the many experiences that had enriched both their lives. There were easy smiles and much laughter. The first bottle finished, Ben poured from the second. The meal concluded with bowls of fresh strawberries topped with spoonfuls of thick *dulche de leche*.

Aware the evening was drawing to a close, they reluctantly rose, slowly and a bit awkwardly, feeling the wine. Claire Elise walked one last time to the bar, returned with another small tray.

"A last surprise, Ben. A bottle of old French Armagnac, brought from Argentina, and a fine cigar from Havana. Take these to your room, sit out on your balcony, and enjoy the night."

"Claire Elise," Ben began, looking into her eyes. "I cannot thank you enough for this evening. The magnificent feast, the wonderful wine. I will cherish the memory of this time with you, our time together here."

On impulse, Ben reached out and tenderly took her auburn hair in his hands, slowly loosening the braids and fanning his fingers through her long curling locks as they fell about her shoulders. "There," he whispered. "That's better."

She leaned into him, sighing, and he could feel her round, full breasts against him. As he caressed her hair, he inhaled the subtle fragrance of her perfume. She returned his embrace as they held each other tightly, wordlessly, for a long moment. Ben then gently took her hands in his own, bent his face to hers, and kissed her lightly on the lips. A powerful current passed through them as he released her, reluctantly.

"Good night, dear Claire Elise," he whispered hoarsely. "Sleep well."

Jacket removed, shirt collar open, Ben sat in the rocking chair outside his room. He poured a finger of the French brandy into the snifter Claire Elise provided, swirled it in the glass, breathed in the heady bouquet. *Excellent. Smooth,* he thought as the Armagnac warmed his throat. He reached for the cigar, a slim panatela, struck a match, puffed, and blew out a perfect ring of aromatic blue smoke.

It was a warm night, lit by a full summer moon casting dark shadows through the trees. As he stared into space, Ben leaned back, closed his eyes, and succumbed to night music in the air. Thousands of crickets carried a steady tenor line to the rhythm of katydids' call and response, back and forth, bass notes from bull frogs now and then, here and there.

Ben's mind drifted back to the delightful evening with Claire Elise, the ease of their conversation, the touch of their bodies at the piano, the deep green of her eyes, the softness of her lips. He pushed away all thoughts of Rachel Schumann, Virgil Wade, and the challenges that lay before him. This night, he was at peace.

As he drained the snifter and lay aside the remnants of the cigar, gentle rain began drumming lightly on the tin roof. He undressed and stretched out on his bed, a soft breeze cooling his naked body as he drifted into sleep. A soft knock startled him. Then another. Ben rose, confused, and quickly donned the bathrobe Jewel had provided. He opened the door. *Claire Elise.*

She stood in the hallway in a white cotton nightdress, a wine bottle in one hand, a small oil lamp in the other. "Ben," she said softly. "I ... I hope I am not disturbing you." Holding up the bottle, she added, "You see, there was some Malbec left after dinner. It will soon go bad in the heat."

Without a word, Ben motioned her inside. Claire Elise set the wine and the lamp on the side table and turned to face him. They were only inches apart, her fragrance in the air. Ben reached out, took her head in his hands, and kissed her, softly at first, but then more urgently as she responded. As they looked into each other's eyes, Ben gently removed the cloth belt holding her nightdress together. Spreading the garment open, he reached inside and cupped both breasts in his hands, feeling her nipples harden. Claire Elise closed her eyes, turned her head, gasped.

Her breaths coming quicker now, she looked deep into Ben's eyes and put both hands on his shoulders. At first, Ben thought she was pushing him away, but then realized that she was instead slowly pressing him back, back toward the bed. Claire Elise kept up the pressure as she opened his robe, touching him. Ben sighed with anticipation as he fell back onto the bed, looking up as Claire Elise joined him.

Shedding the nightdress, she put one knee across his body and lowered herself gently down, her eyes never leaving his. As he entered her, she drew a sharp breath and smoothly and languidly began to move. She slowly increased her pace, eyes closed, lips parted, rising and falling to the rhythm of their bodies. Her breath came in short, shallow gasps until finally she arched her back in pleasure, exhaling a deep groan, causing Ben to cry out his own release.

They lay together for long moments in silent embrace as their breathing slowed. Then Claire Elise slowly began to rise from the bed. "But?" whispered Ben, on his elbows, reaching for her.

"*Shhhh,*" she murmured, putting a finger to his lips and pressing him down.

Ben watched as she pulled the nightdress together and began to step away. As she opened the door, her face warmly lit by the small oil lamp cupped in her hands, she turned again to Ben and smiled. And then she was gone.

For a long moment, Ben stared at the closed door. Collapsing on the bed, looking up at the slowly turning blades of the ceiling fan, he considered what had just transpired. *What have I done?*

Chapter 27

Ben awoke from a fitful sleep, hungover, his head pounding, his mouth dry. With a start, he remembered, he remembered it all. *Shit!* he thought. *Shit, shit, shit!* He put on his robe and walked to the bathroom. As he looked in the mirror, razor in hand, he shook his head angrily. *Stupid! What was I thinking?* He finished shaving, washed himself in cold water, and returned to his room. As he packed his valise, he thought, *I have to handle this carefully. Somehow I must make this right.*

Ben entered the lobby, carrying his suitcase and satchel. All traces of the evening before had been removed. Claire Elise greeted him with a shy smile. "Good morning, Ben. I trust you slept well? Jewel will be out with your breakfast in just a few minutes."

Ben held up a hand. "About that. I'm afraid, Claire Elise, that I have no time for breakfast this morning. I need to be on my way."

Confused, she tilted her head to one side, eyed the suitcase. "So early, Ben? Why, the train doesn't leave until—"

Pulling himself fully upright, taking a deep breath, Ben interrupted, "We need to talk, Claire Elise. About last night."

Eyes wide, Claire Elise said, "Yes?"

Looking nervously around the room, Ben confirmed they were alone. "Well," he began gently and in a quiet voice. "Last night was . . . wonderful, Claire Elise. Please know that. But it was . . . I'm afraid it was a mistake. A very bad mistake."

The warmth and color of her face drained away. "Mistake? Mistake? Why, Ben, whatever can you mean?"

"Well, you see, it's like this. I . . . we . . . both had too much to drink, I'm afraid. It . . . shouldn't have happened, Claire Elise."

Her jaw set, she replied coolly, "I see. And why, may I ask?"

"Fond as I am of you, Claire Elise—and you must believe that—we must realize that you are deeply involved in the Rachel Schumann case. You will be a *witness*, for God's sake! An important witness. Taliaferro will make you testify about the . . . murder."

"But what does that have to do with . . . *with us?*"

"Please understand, Claire Elise. I told you before that there are certain aspects of this case that I am not at liberty to discuss. It is likely that these aspects will put us on different sides of the case. I fully expect that inevitable and unavoidable . . . conflicts, in the legal sense, of course, will develop."

"Conflicts?" she said guardedly.

Ben took another deep breath, exhaled. "You must trust me on this, Claire Elise. Until this matter is resolved, any . . . relationship between us would be highly inappropriate. I'm so sorry. You must know how this pains me—"

"Inappropriate," she snapped. *"Inappropriate!"*

"Claire Elise, please. Perhaps when all this is over and done—"

"Stop! Just stop, Ben. I see you have made up your mind." Nodding toward the door, she spat, "So, go then. Just go! Take the sulky. Leave it at the station. I'll have Ruby fetch it later. Goodbye, Ben," she concluded, her eyes on fire. "What do you lawyers say? 'See you in court.'" She turned abruptly and walked briskly into the kitchen.

W

In a black mood, and with a heavy heart, Ben pulled Maybelle to a stop in front of the Trogdon Opera House and tethered the pony. Tink Beasley, as always, greeted him with a warm smile. "Come on in, Ben," she said, shaking her head. "Breakfast's almost ready."

"So, you're off to Raleigh, then?" said McGee, finishing up his pork tenderloin and fried eggs, over easy.

Coffee mug in hand, Ben replied, "That's right, Ros. On the afternoon train."

Looking over at the wind-up clock on the kitchen counter, McGee said, "You've got plenty of time. Train doesn't leave until—"

Shaking his head, Ben said, "Don't start, Ros."

This brought McGee up short. "Well, it's good you've come by, Ben. Got some news for you."

"What's up?"

"Seems like yesterday's paper struck a nerve with ol' Razor."

"What do you mean?"

"Grand jury," replied McGee. Ben spread his hands, waited.

"Couple friends of mine, they're members. Got sworn in a while ago. Well, I saw them around town yesterday. Both of 'em tell me that Sheriff Poindexter's been to see them. Served 'em with a grand jury summons. Taliaferro's calling them back in next week."

"Next week? In the middle of the summer?"

"That's right," nodded McGee. "Gotta be for the Wade boy. You 'member he said something about it at his big *do* at the jail. And get this, Judge Transou's not even in town. Gone off to Asheville, not coming back 'til the end of the month."

"So, how did Taliaferro—?"

"He just *did* it, Ben. Don't ask me how. Told everybody to show up at the courthouse next Wednesday morning."

Ben pondered that for a moment, then smiled. "Well, well. Looks like he's pulling a fast one. But like everything he does, this is going to come back and bite him on the ass."

"How so?"

"Oh, I have no doubt that Razor will get his indictment. Probably take him about thirty minutes. And once there's a formal indictment, well, that means there's an active case against the boy. *State v. Wade.*"

"So?"

"See, now that the Wade boy is in Raleigh, and once he's indicted, I'm done trying to *protect* him. Frees me up to *represent* him. I can finally resign and take up the case, all out in the open. And most important, Ros, as his *attorney*, I can finally *talk* to the boy, get his side of the story, all under attorney-client privilege."

"How can I help you, Ben?"

"I want you to keep your eyes and ears wide open, Ros. There's a whole bunch of loose ends to run down before this thing comes to trial, a lot of work to do."

"Count on me, Ben," said McGee. "So, how're you going to spend your time waitin' on the train?

"Cairo. I'm going over there to see Reverend Bondurant and Pauline Oxendine. Tell them what I've got in mind."

PART II

THE TRIAL

Chapter 28

Ben Waterman sat at the big round table in the elegant, wood-paneled library of the governor's residence, drumming his fingers, staring at the marble fireplace across the room. The building was a large, sprawling pile of red bricks made from Wake County clay molded by prison convicts, many of whom inscribed their names on their work. When Maxwell moved in in 1897, he had invited Ben to come live with him. His room was on the third floor, under one of the many steeply pitched gables facing Blount Street.

Governor Maxwell entered with a broad smile. "Mornin', Ben!" he bellowed, reaching out a hand. Ben rose, shook it.

"Good morning to you, Judge," Ben smiled. "Good to see you."

"Guess you made it back last night?"

"Yes, sir. Got in late. The connection in Rural Hall was delayed a while."

"Well, good to have you back in Raleigh. Tell me what's up in Wilkes." Ben handed over his typed reports.

"What about the Wade boy?" asked Ben. "'He all right?"

"Bev Royster came by Wednesday night, all spit and polish in his fancy uniform. Said he delivered the boy safe and sound to Central Prison. Said everything went smoothly in Wilkes."

"You should know, Judge, that Taliaferro is moving ahead with the indictment. He's called the grand jury back next Wednesday. No doubt he'll get what he's after."

"Well, that's just what we've been waiting for, Ben. Frees you up to resign and take up the boy's case. Like we discussed."

"That's my thinking, too, Judge." Ben smiled and said, "Come next week, I guess I'll be a free man."

"Well, you know what that means, don't you?"

Ben raised his eyebrows.

"Why, means you've got to move out of here. Find your own place," said Maxwell. "Can't have a private citizen, a practicing lawyer representing a man indicted for murder, living here under my roof in the people's house. No, that won't do."

Ben realized Maxwell was right. "Hadn't really thought that through. I'll get right on it. Today."

"You aim to go see the boy? Over at the prison?"

"My plan is to wait, Judge. I don't want to speak to him until I file a notice of appearance. You know, attorney-client privilege."

"Smart, Ben. That's the way to do it. But, in the meantime, you still work for me. You know, the Suffrage Amendment referendum is coming up in August, and I'd like for you to connect up with some of our people in Charlotte and Greensboro, see if there's anything you can do to help them. Looks like the thing will pass in a landslide, but we still need to put some effort in it."

"I expect you're right, Judge. I'll do what I can. But now I think I'd better get out of here," Ben grinned. "Go find a place to live."

"Good luck, Ben. I'll surely miss you around here. But," he paused, "be careful out there."

Ben made a quizzical face. "Sir?"

"You know," laughed Maxwell, wagging a finger. "Friday the thirteenth, and all."

Chapter 29

Ben Waterman and Governor Maxwell were standing in Maxwell's office, maps before them, discussing the Suffrage Amendment. Ben shook his head. "Things don't look good, Judge. Negro registration has dropped off a cliff. This thing is sure to pass. And then . . ."

"Yes," said Maxwell sadly. "I know. I think we are moving into a dark place, Ben. A very dark place in North Carolina. Thank God I won't live to see the worst of it."

The door to Maxwell's office opened, and Peggy Alexander appeared. "Judge, sorry to interrupt, but I have Roscoe McGee on the line. From Wilkes."

Maxwell held the earpiece so that both could hear. "McGee! That you?"

"Yes, sir, it's me. Got some news. The grand jury met this morning for about an hour. They returned a true bill against the Wade boy. Got a copy of the indictment right here."

"What does it say, Ros?" asked Ben. "What are the charges?"

"Well, as far as I can make it out, once you get through all the legal mumbo-jumbo, there's just one charge—murder."

"Read it, please, Ros. Just the last part."

"Well, it says, 'The jurors for the State upon their oath present that on or about the date of the offense shown and in the County of Wilkes, defendant Virgil Wade unlawfully, willfully, and feloniously and of malice aforethought did kill and murder one Rachel Schumann, to wit, by infliction of a fatal knife wound to the victim's heart.'"

"So," Ben said. "Just one charge, then. Murder in the first degree. No other charges?"

"Don't look like it," answered McGee. "But there's more. Right after the indictment was released, ol' Razor filed some motions. In the Clerk's office."

"Motions!" bellowed Maxwell. "What motions?"

"Well, says here Taliaferro wants Judge Transou to vacate the declaration of emergency and order the Wade boy returned immediately to Wilkes for trial in the fall term. And he's asked for a hearing on Friday, August 3, right after Transou gets back from Asheville."

"Anything else?" asked Maxwell.

"Nope. That's about the size of it."

"Well, then, thanks, McGee. Appreciate the information. I'm sure Ben here will be back in touch soon about all this."

"Don't mention it, Governor. Good luck."

Maxwell hung up and sat back in his big chair. "Didn't take him long, did it?"

"We knew this day was coming, Judge. But these motions? There's no way I can let the boy be returned to Wilkes."

Maxwell waved a hand. "Don't worry about that, Ben. I'll speak to Transou. He's a lame duck like me. And he owes me, too. I'll make sure he knows what to do. But you'll need to stay sharp, Ben. Taliaferro knows every trick in the book."

"I've been thinking, Judge. I may have a surprise or two of my own."

Maxwell's eyebrows narrowed. "And?"

"It's not enough just to keep the Wade boy here, Judge, and then take him back for the trial. There's no way he can get a fair trial in Wilkes. Not with all the dirt Taliaferro has thrown up in the air, not with all the newspapers calling for Wade's scalp. He's as good as convicted in Wilkes before the trial even begins."

"I see your point, Ben, but what can you do about it?"

"*Move it,* Judge," Ben said firmly. "Move the trial. Move it to Raleigh."

Maxwell pursed his lips, narrowed his eyebrows, thinking. Looking up at Ben with a gleam in his eye, he shouted, "Now you're talking! *State v. Dula*, right?"

"Exactly, Judge. *State v. Dula*."

Slapping his thigh, Maxwell laughed, said, "Damnation, Ben Waterman! You have the makings of one fine lawyer!"

Reaching into his breast pocket, Maxwell pulled out an envelope, opened it, and withdrew a single typewritten page. He then reached for a pen on his desk and, with a flourish, scribbled his signature. Maxwell pronounced, "Your resignation from my service is hereby accepted, Benjamin Gordon Waterman. You are released, *counselor.* Now get on over to that rooming house of yours and get to work!"

"First things first, Judge," said Ben, smiling.

Maxwell shot him a puzzled look.

"First I need to get over to Central Prison. I need to speak with my *client."*

Chapter 30

Central Prison, Raleigh, Wednesday, July 18, 1900

Central Prison was an enormous, forbidding, castle-like fortress just west of downtown Raleigh. Prison labor was used to quarry granite from a nearby site, and construction took fourteen years.

Ben Waterman produced Pauline Oxendine's signed consent form and requested an immediate conference with Virgil Wade. After some bureaucratic back-and-forth, an armed guard escorted Ben to a dark, stifling prison cell reserved for lawyer-client meetings.

Virgil Wade sat at a table, handcuffed, his legs in shackles. The guard admitted Ben into the cell, locked the door behind him, and said gruffly, "You got one hour."

Ben removed his jacket and placed it on the back of his chair. He sat and retrieved a notebook and pencil from his satchel. The boy looked up at Ben with fear in his striking, intelligent blue eyes. He was a miserable sight. Small, skinny, and dressed in a prison uniform two sizes too big, Wade's skin was the color of creamed coffee, his hair a tangle of red curls. His narrow face was handsome, in a boyish way, almost pretty. Beads of sweat glistened on his freckled brow.

Ben smiled. "Virgil, do you remember me? I'm Ben Waterman. From the jail in Wilkes?"

Virgil nodded.

Ben held up a sheet of paper. "This has been signed by your mother, Virgil. She has given me permission to act as your lawyer, and I have agreed to do so. Do you understand?" Again, the boy nodded.

"As your attorney, nothing that you say to me can ever be repeated or used against you. That means that our conversations are private, confidential. My job is to defend you in connection with the Rachel Schumann thing. Please tell me if at any time you have questions or do not understand anything I might say, okay?" Another nod.

"Prosecutor Taliaferro in Wilkes has obtained an indictment, a formal charge against you for Rachel Schumann's murder. The trial will be sometime this fall. I am sorry to tell you that Taliaferro intends to seek the . . . death penalty in your case." Virgil's eyes widened in shock and terror, his mouth fell open, slack. Ben reached over to calm the boy, took his cuffed hands in his own. "I intend to fight this with every fiber of my body, Virgil. Are you ready to speak with me now?"

Virgil, his voice trembling and weak, whispered, "Yessir, I understand. You here to help me."

"That's right, Virgil. So, let's get started. How old are you, Virgil?"

"Sixteen, sir."

"Very good, Virgil. And how long have you lived in Wilkes?"

"All my life, sir. With my momma and Mr. Oxendine. Down in Cairo."

Ben took a deep breath. "Now, Virgil. Now I want you to tell me exactly what happened that night, after the fireworks."

Shaking his head slowly, Virgil said softly, "I cain't do that, Mr. Waterman."

"Why not, Virgil?"

"I told my story already to that Mr. Taliaferro. Him and the sheriff. After I got done, Mr. Taliaferro, well, he and the sheriff, they laughed at me. And then he, Mr. Taliaferro, he pointed at me, his face all red like. He told me that I was never to repeat it to anybody. Not a single soul, he said. Said if I ever did, the sheriff would turn me out. You know, to the Red Shirts. He said they would string me up." Shaking his head, Virgil whispered, "He's not a nice man, Mr. Waterman."

"Don't worry about that, Virgil. Nobody will bother you here. Please, now, tell me."

Virgil shifted in his seat, working things out. Then he began.

"Well, see, at the fireworks, Miz Rachel came up to me. I know her from the tannery. I work there some, skinnin' hides. Well, anyway she said she and her friend were goin' to spend the night at the hotel, wanted to go ridin' up the Reddies River next morning. Told me I was to take her horse and another one from the Schumann place over to the hotel livery and make sure everything was ready for their ride. I said okay, took the horses over that afternoon. Put 'em in the stable. I told Miz Jewel about it, and then I walked back over to the fairgrounds. I was helpin' 'em get ready for the fireworks."

Ben nodded, taking notes. "And after that? Did you come back to the hotel?"

"No sir. I meant to spend the night in the stable, but I never made it. I stayed on after the fireworks and helped the boys take down the tents, clean things up. It was late when we got done."

"Tell me what happened after that, Virgil."

The boy's eyes began to water. "I swear, Mr. Waterman," he pleaded. "I never meant to hurt that girl. I swear it!"

"Go on, Virgil. We'll get to that."

"Well, I was walkin' back to the hotel, got down by the iron bridge, and that's when I saw it. Down there under the bridge, I saw a light. Didn't have no idea what was going on, so I decided to take a look."

"What did you see, Virgil?"

"Well, I got down there, and there she was."

"Rachel?"

Virgil nodded. "Yes sir, she was there, sittin' on a quilt. All by herself, in her ridin' clothes. Her horse, the one I brought over, was tied up. She had a lantern. Kinda like she was 'spectin' somebody or somethin'."

"What else did you see there, Virgil?"

"Well, there was a whiskey bottle." He lowered his eyes, said softly, "I think she had been drinkin'."

Ben nodded. "Go on."

"Well, she looked up at me, surprised like, and then she frowned. But then, just like that, she smiled real big and said, 'Why, Virgil Wade. Come on over here and sit down.' I was nervous, Mr. Waterman. Me down there, late at night. And her a White woman and all. But she patted the ground and said, 'Come on, Virgil, I won't bite.' So, I did. Sat down, like she said.

"Well, then she took that whiskey bottle and poured some into one of those little glasses, handed it to me. Poured herself one, too. She said, 'Drink up!' and so we did. I'm not much for likker, Mr. Waterman, but I figgered I better do like she said. And then she poured us 'nother one. I was feelin' a little woozy, I don't mind tellin' you."

"Then what happened, Virgil?"

Virgil sat silent for a long moment, shook his head.

"I don't like to talk about that," he said. "I'm not proud about it."

"It's important, Virgil. Like I said, private and confidential. Just you and me."

Virgil took a deep breath, looked to the side, continued. "Well, then, see, she put her hand on my leg. High up on it. She said, 'You ever been with a woman, Virgil?' I was scared, Mr. Waterman, and I said 'No, ma'am, never.'" He paused, closed his eyes. "Well, then she leaned over and, you know, *kissed* me, I mean right on the lips."

Ben tried to hide his astonishment, waited.

"Well, then she stopped and poured us another drink. My head was a-spinnin', Mr. Waterman. I didn't know what to think. I didn't know what was happenin'. So, then she took my hand, put it up against her, you know, up *here*," he said, touching his chest. "Began rubbin' herself up against it like. Said, 'Do you like that, Virgil?' I didn't say nothin', and then she took her hand and started . . . unbuttonin', you know, my pants. Then she started . . . workin' on me. Down *there*." After a moment, he continued, tears in his eyes. "Well, I just . . . I just couldn't *hold* it anymore. I messed up on myself, right there, in her hand."

Virgil's eyes darkened. His voice grew louder. "Well, she, she thought that was *funny!* She started laughin', *laughin'* at me. Said I was no man! Just a hopeless high-yeller boy, not able to satisfy a growed up woman like her. That made me *mad*, Mr. Waterman. I guess I was drunk, but that made me *real mad*. So, I stood up, and I told her to quit it. Quit talkin' like that. But she wouldn't quit. She stood up, too, just kept on laughin' and pointin' at my pants. She just kept *on*.

"So, like I said, I was mad, and I just slapped her face, you know, to make her *shut up*. Well, she didn't like that a bit, and so she slapped me right back, called me a *nigger bastard*. So, I hit her again, hard, with my fist, I guess. She fell down, hit her head on the ground. I guess she was knocked out. I stared down at her, waitin' for her to move, but she didn't. I took another drink of that whiskey, waitin' for her to move, but she didn't. Then I got real dizzy, Mr. Waterman. I guess I passed out, 'cause the next thing I knew, it was mornin'."

Ben cleared his throat and leaned in toward the boy. "The knife, Virgil. Tell me about the knife."

Virgil paused, looked away again. "Well, like I said, when I woke up next mornin', there she was, on her back, *dead*, with my skinnin' knife stickin' out of her ribs!" Holding up his cuffed hands as if in prayer, he cried, "I swear, Mr. Waterman, I didn't do *that!* I never stabbed that girl! I don't know what happened, but it wasn't me! I swear! Please, believe me!"

Ben stared at Virgil, waited.

"So, then I got scared, *real* scared. I knew I had to get away from that place, so I took her horse and rode off. I know it wasn't right, Mr. Waterman, what we was doin' down there. I know I shouldn't-a been drinkin' and messin' around with her, a rich White girl and all. And I know I shouldn't-a hit her like that. But God as my witness, Mr. Waterman, I passed plumb out, and I don't know what happened after that or who else stabbed that girl. But it wadn't me, I swear it! I did not do that!"

Ben sat back, speechless. *What a story! Unbelievable! But it fits. Two people there. With Rachel. It fits.*

"Thank, you, Virgil," Ben finally said. "Thank you for being honest with me. I think that's enough for one day. I'll be back to see you in a little while. We'll work together to get ready for the trial. You settle down, now, and make the best of things here. Anybody gives you any trouble, you tell me next time I come to visit."

Virgil nodded. "I 'preciate what you're tryin' to do for me, Mr. Waterman. I do. Don't feel like I've give you much to work with, though."

"Don't worry about that, Virgil. It will all work out."

As he called for the guard and turned to leave, Ben had an idea. Without warning, he spun and flung his pencil at Virgil Wade. The boy flinched, raised his cuffed hands, and caught it. In his right hand.

Ben smiled and reached for the pencil. "Yes, Virgil. I think it will all work out fine."

Chapter 31

Ben Waterman and Roscoe McGee were finishing up supper in the hotel dining room. After a few minutes of small talk, Ben reached inside his jacket, withdrew his wallet, took out a dollar bill, and handed it to McGee. Looking at the money, McGee asked, "What's this, Ben? What's this for?"

"Why, it's your fee, Ros. Go on. Take it."

Curious, McGee said. "Fee? What fee?"

"You, Roscoe McGee, are now employed by me, Benjamin Gordon Waterman, Esquire, attorney and counselor at law. You are now my, well, my *assistant*. My . . . *investigator.*"

Now thoroughly confused, McGee blurted, "What—?"

"Attorney-client privilege, Ros. If you work for me, well, then the privilege extends through me to you, too. This way I can share information with you. And you can help me think my way through this Schumann thing. But you have to keep your mouth shut, Ros. Everything stays between you and me. Nothing in the paper, like we agreed before. You in?"

McGee grinned, grabbed the money. "I *like* it, Ben! You just hired yourself a top-notch investigator!"

That settled, Ben then revealed the details of his meeting with Virgil Wade.

"Well, if that's not the damndest thing I ever heard in all my life, Ben!" exclaimed McGee.

"I agree, Ros. I've gone over it a hundred times in my head. But you know what? It *fits.* I keep coming back to it. It fits with what we already

201

know and suspect. *Two* people under the bridge! *Two* people with Rachel Schumann. And the pencil, Ros. He caught it with his *right* hand."

"But *who*, Ben?" snapped McGee. "Who else was down there with her? If you believe the Wade boy, then who stabbed her?"

"Well, that's the thing, Ros. I don't know. Yet. But I have an idea."

Ben then explained the theory that had slowly been working its way through his mind.

McGee whistled, shook his head. "Damn, Ben! Seems like a stretch to me. But still."

Ben nodded, *"But still."*

"So, how're you going to prove this, Ben, even if it's true?"

"I don't know, Ros. But, you see, I don't have to *prove* it. I just have to convince somebody on the jury that it *might* have happened that way. You know, reasonable doubt. I don't have much hope that twelve jurors will acquit the boy, but once I plant the seed about two people being there and drive it home, why, *one* juror can hang the jury, Ros, just one."

"And so, what does a hung jury buy you, Ben?" asked McGee, spreading his hands. "Just another trial, right?"

"That's right, Ros. But it buys me, and Virgil Wade, some *time*. If I can keep Virgil Wade off the gallows for a few more months, maybe something will fall out of the sky. Hell, I don't know. Maybe a miracle. But it buys me *time*, don't you see? Maybe after the election Taliaferro will be more reasonable. Maybe make a *deal*. Maybe take the death penalty off the table. The boy will do time, for sure, but I can hope to save his *life*."

McGee smiled, shook his head. "Well, I know one thing for damn sure."

"What's that?"

"Well, if I ever get in real bad trouble, I want *you* to be my lawyer!"

Ben smiled. Looking around the dining room, McGee changed the subject. "Tell me, Ben, why're you staying here? Instead of the Schumann Hotel, over by the courthouse?"

Ben paused, said hesitantly, "Well, now that I am officially Virgil Wade's lawyer, I didn't think it would look right, you know, to stay over there. Claire Elise will surely be a witness at the trial. It's best if I keep my distance, if you get my meaning."

McGee nodded, accepting his explanation. "You ready?" he asked abruptly.

Ben blew out a breath. "Ready as I'll ever be, Ros. I filed my notice of appearance this afternoon, at the Clerk's Office, right after I got off the train. Filed my motions, too."

"Well, look here, Ben," said McGee. "I'll come by in the morning. Give you a ride over to the courthouse. Can't wait to see how this thing plays out."

"Don't forget, Ros. Bring your box."

McGee smiled. "All packed and ready, Ben. Ready to go."

Chapter 32

Wilkes County Courthouse, Wednesday, August 3, 1900

R oscoe McGee, lugging a cardboard box, grunted his way up the steps to the courtroom, accompanied by Ben Waterman and Tink Beasley. Entering through the swinging double doors, they stopped to take in the scene.

The courtroom was a large and imposing ceremonial space, two stories high. The room was lit by five tall and narrow windows running down each side, all thrown open to catch the cross breeze, as well as gaslight chandeliers hanging from a ceiling decorated with white punched tin panels. The judge's bench and the witness stand sat on a raised dais, flanked by counsel tables below. Behind the gated railing, spectators sat on curving rows of pews, each with baskets underneath to hold men's hats, spittoons placed here and there.

The courtroom was packed with mostly men, many waving small fans conveniently provided by a local funeral home, their conversations creating a restless murmur in the room. Ben could see a large group of Black folks in the balcony above, including Reverend Bondurant and Pauline Oxendine. Ben made eye contact, nodded to them.

"Well, Ben, looks like you've drawn quite a crowd," said McGee. He put down his box, reached out his hand and shook Ben's. "Good luck, Ben. See you afterwards."

Tink touched Ben's arm. "Give 'em hell, Ben. Show ol' Razor who's boss!"

As McGee and Tink took seats in the front row behind the defendant's table, Ben noticed a familiar face entering the courtroom. "Good morning, Mr. Gruenwald," said Ben.

"Good morning, Mr. Waterman," replied Gabriel von Gruenwald stiffly.

"I guess I am surprised to see you here," said Ben.

"Mr. Schumann asked me to be here," said Gruenwald gruffly. "I have remained in Wilkes longer than intended, to inspect a shipment of hides arriving on the midday train." Gruenwald looked around the courtroom, then fixed his eyes on Ben's. "I must say that Mr. Schumann was very disappointed to learn that you would be here, defending the boy who murdered his daughter."

"I can understand that, Mr. Gruenwald. It's . . . complicated. I respect Mr. Schumann's feelings, and I hope that one day—"

Gruenwald cut him off. "We all have choices to make in life, Mr. Waterman. You have made yours."

They were both silent for a moment. Then Ben, an idea forming, said, "After all this is over this morning, I would like to speak with you . . . privately. It's about the case. I think you will be interested in what I have to say."

Gruenwald made a face, thought about it. "Are you sure that is absolutely necessary, Mr. Waterman? I can't imagine—"

"Please. It's important. And it involves you, as well."

"Me?" said Gruenwald, perplexed.

"Yes," replied Ben. "You."

The two men stood facing each other. "Very well, then," said Gruenwald sharply, curious and thinking that perhaps he might learn something useful. "I will come to you when court is adjourned. We can talk then."

Gruenwald turned to find a seat, and Ben made his way to the defendant's counsel table, on the left side facing the judge's bench. As he was unpacking his satchel and arranging his papers, McGee walked up and set his box beneath the table. Ben leaned into McGee, whispered, "He's here, Ros. Gruenwald. Did you see?"

"Yeah, I saw."

"I told him I wanted to talk to him after the hearing. Privately. He didn't like it, but he agreed."

McGee looked around the courtroom, found Gruenwald sitting about three rows back. "So, you're going to talk to him about—"

"Yes, Ros. What we talked about last night. I'm going to put it to him. Directly."

McGee shook his head, whistled under his breath. "Whew, Ben. You sure? High wire, no net, my friend."

"I'm going to spring it on him, Ros. See how he reacts. Trust me on this. I know what I'm doing."

McGee winked. "You're the boss, Counselor."

"So, wait for me, Ros. We can talk on the way back to your place."

"I'll be right here, Ben."

A sudden rise in background noise drew Ben's attention. Nodding and with smiles for everyone, Vincent Taliaferro, elegantly dressed, proud as a Roman emperor, made his way confidently down the aisle, trailed by Sheriff Poindexter and Crip Goins. He pointed to the prosecutor's table, and Poindexter and Goins ambled over. Taliaferro then strode over to the defendant's table and planted himself before Ben. He did not offer to shake hands.

"Well, well, *counselor*," he sneered. "Just like a bad penny, you keep showing up in the oddest of places. All the way from Raleigh, you are. Just to get a taste of Wilkes County justice?"

Ben, without a word, turned his back on Taliaferro and sat.

At precisely nine o'clock, with the lawyers and court personnel in place, the bailiff rose and loudly commanded, "All rise! Oyez, oyez, oyez! All persons having business before the Honorable, the superior court of Wilkes County, North Carolina are admonished to draw nigh and give their attention, for the court is now sitting, the Honorable Judge Richard Transou presiding. God save the State of North Carolina and this Honorable court!"

As the spectators settled in, Judge Richard Magnus Transou strode purposely to the bench, his black robes swirling about him like an Oxford don. A descendant of German Moravians, Judge Transou was in his mid-fifties, a six-footer, slightly stooped, with large, raw-boned hands more suited to plowing than paperwork. His full head of wiry gray hair was close-cropped, and round, rimless spectacles magnified his steely blue eyes. His pursed lips pulled his narrow, clean-shaven face into a serious mien that informed those appearing before him that he was not a man to be trifled with.

Judge Transou, a staunch Wilkes Republican, was elected to serve the remaining six years of Judge "Cotton Bob" Maxwell's term after his election to the North Carolina Supreme Court. Some found him aloof and austere, but he was nevertheless well-respected in legal circles for his even-handed approach to the law. He ruled his courtroom in a disciplined, businesslike manner and had little patience for pomp or show.

Transou was also a realist. He could read the tea leaves and understood that his chances for re-election in the political climate of 1900 were slim indeed. This realization had brought with it a calmness and an uplifting, liberating sense of independence, confidence, and fearlessness that often surprised, and sometimes vexed, litigants, defendants, and their counsel.

As he finished shuffling through papers on his desk, Judge Transou looked up at the assembly before him, then rapped his gavel sharply. "This court is now in session in the matter of *State v. Wade.* I'm interested to see what sort of *emergency* has brought us all out in this infernal heat, so let's get started. Counsel, state your appearances for the record."

Taliaferro stood, bowed deeply, smiled. "Vincent Taliaferro, your Honor. For the *people.*"

"Ben Waterman, your honor, for the defendant Virgil Wade."

The judge nodded, "Thank you, gentlemen. Now—"

"Your Honor?" interrupted Taliaferro.

"Yes, what is it?" snapped the judge, irritated.

"Your Honor, I regret that it is my duty to object. On behalf of the people of Wilkes, I object to Mr. Waterman's appearance as counsel for the defendant in this case, and I move to have him disqualified. You see, during his recent tenure as an employee of Governor Maxwell, Mr. Waterman has done nothing but stir up trouble here. He was the architect and chief proponent of the travesty of justice that brings us here today. He is personally responsible for the declaration of emergency that has undermined and corrupted the judicial process here in Wilkes, and I—"

Judge Transou held up a hand to stop him. "That's enough, Mr. Taliaferro. Save it for the campaign trail." Turning to Ben, and holding up a piece of paper, he asked, "Mr. Waterman, it says in your notice of appearance that you are now an attorney in private practice in Raleigh, is that correct?"

Ben stood. "Yes, sir. I resigned from the governor's office on July 18, and thereafter agreed to undertake Mr. Wade's defense in this case. With the permission of his mother, of course, given that the defendant is a minor. You have her signed consent before you."

The judge nodded and banged his gavel. "Good enough for me. Mr. Taliaferro, your motion is denied." Chastened, his face reddening, Taliaferro took his seat.

"So, what's next, gentlemen?" asked the judge. Ben and Taliaferro both rose, declared "Your Honor" simultaneously. The judge frowned, looked back and forth, pointed at Ben. "You first, Mr. Waterman."

Ben nodded. "Thank you, Your Honor. I, too, have a motion, one that may be dispositive in this case."

"Go ahead."

"I move to quash the indictment, Your Honor. The whole thing. To dismiss the case in its entirety."

Bedlam in the courtroom, as Judge Transou furiously banged his gavel. *"Silence! Silence in my courtroom!* I will not have it! I will clear every living soul out of here if you folks can't keep quiet. I mean it!" he scolded, pointing the gavel at the spectators. The restless crowd settled down.

"Now then, that's better." Pointing the gavel at Ben this time, the judge asked, "On what grounds, Mr. Waterman? What could justify such an extraordinary request?"

Ben held up a copy of the indictment. "It is manifestly clear, Judge, that the indictment in this case was improperly obtained by Mr. Taliaferro. You see, he called the grand jury into session, solely on his own questionable authority. And, as Your Honor well knows, you were away from the jurisdiction that entire week. Mr. Taliaferro was therefore powerless to have the clerk issue the grand jury subpoenas, Your Honor, and was without authority to convene the grand jury in your absence. As a result, the defendant contends that the indictment in this case is fatally defective and must be dismissed."

Taliaferro shot to his feet, faced Ben squarely. "This is outrageous, Waterman! How dare you come in here—"

Again, the gavel banged. "Stop! Mr. Taliaferro, I remind you that any comments you may wish to make shall be addressed to the court and not to opposing counsel. Do you understand?"

Gritting his teeth, still seething, Taliaferro could only nod.

"Say it!" thundered Judge Transou. "Answer my question!"

Taliaferro lowered his head, said meekly, "Yes, Your Honor, I understand. Sorry."

Turning to Ben, the judge said evenly, "I get your point, Mr. Waterman, and technically speaking, you are probably correct. It would normally be extremely irregular for Mr. Taliaferro to proceed in the way he did, and I assure you that he and I will have a conversation about his methods and tactics later.

"But here, it must be said that Mr. Taliaferro was dealing with exigent circumstances, acting in response to a declaration of emergency that, if I understand things correctly, you had a hand in procuring."

"But Your Honor—" Ben pleaded.

"No," said Judge Transou, shaking his head. "No. If there was overreaching in obtaining the indictment, then I am prepared to excuse Mr. Taliaferro's breach of procedure as harmless error. It looks to me like the indictment against your client, Mr. Waterman, was never a case of *if*, but only *when*. Your motion, sir, is denied. The indictment is ruled proper, and the case will proceed."

Taliaferro sat back in his chair with a satisfied smile. Ben also took his seat. *Well, no surprise,* he thought. *Worth a shot.*

Judge Transou looked down at his papers, found what he was looking for, and addressed the lawyers. "We will now move on to the State's motion to vacate the governor's declaration of emergency and to have the prisoner Virgil Wade immediately returned to the Wilkes County Jail. Mr. Taliaferro?"

Taliaferro rose and summarized details of the Rachel Schumann murder, the capture of Virgil Wade, his incarceration in the county jail, and the evidence against him.

"There *is* no emergency in Wilkes, Your Honor. There never *was* any emergency here. Governor Maxwell's declaration is an insufferable insult to law enforcement in our county, Judge, an outrageous affront to your Honor's jurisdiction, and a grievous infringement of home rule! The declaration of emergency must be vacated, and Virgil Wade must be returned here to face a jury of his peers!"

Ben started to respond, but the judge's glare stopped him.

"What about the attack, Mr. Taliaferro? The attack on the jail? You didn't mention that. But it made all the Asheville papers, and I'd like to hear more about it from Sheriff Poindexter. Why don't you get him up here so we can all hear what he has to say?"

Startled, Taliaferro stuttered, "But Judge! It was just a minor incident, quickly put down!"

"I said I would like to hear from him," repeated Transou firmly. "He's sitting right there. Get him up here."

Eyes blinking, Taliaferro motioned for Poindexter to come up and take the witness stand. Taliaferro took Poindexter through the events of the night of Monday, July 9. Poindexter dutifully downplayed the attack as just "some boys raisin' a little Cain. Nothin' to worry about, Judge. Me'n Crip, we had it all under control. Then Mr. Taliaferro showed up, told 'em to git, and they rode off. That's all. That was it." He did not mention Ben's role.

"All right," said Judge Transou, "Thank you, Sheriff. I expect you have some questions, Mr. Waterman?"

Ben nodded, rose, and approached the witness stand. Slowly, Ben prodded and probed, peppering the sheriff with questions. *Weren't crowds of unruly men milling around the jail ever since Wade's arrest, calling for him to be lynched? Weren't you and Mr. Goins badly outnumbered on Monday night? Weren't the Klansmen disguised in white robes and hoods? Didn't they blasphemously profane a sacred Christian cross by burning it? Didn't they call for Virgil Wade to be released to them? Weren't they armed? Didn't they set fire to the jailhouse with Virgil Wade in it? Didn't you and Mr. Goins recognize the Red Shirt outlaw Luther Wade as the leader of the vigilantes?*

With a pained expression, Poindexter reluctantly admitted it all.

Ben looked down at his notes, then asked, "You testified that the attack on the jail was just 'some boys raising a little Cain,' right?"

"That's what I said," Poindexter nodded. "A whole lot of nothin', really."

"I see," replied Ben, taking a step toward the witness box. "So, tell me, Sheriff, who is Rufus?"

"Rufus?" said Poindexter, pulling a face. "Why, Rufus is just a dog, a Plott hound, 'belonged to Crip. We used him and some other dogs to, you know, find the Schumann girl. Down by the river."

"*Belonged,* you say? Past tense? What happened to Rufus, Sheriff?"

Before Poindexter could answer, Ben continued, his voice rising, his raised finger cutting through the air. "Isn't it true that Luther Wade, the leader of that gang of thugs just 'raising a little Cain,' as you put it, isn't it true that Luther Wade coldly took out his pistol and mercilessly *shot* Crip Goins' dog *dead*, right there in front of the jailhouse? Shot Rufus deader'n a doornail?"

An uneasy murmur moved through the courtroom. This was new information. Poindexter lowered his eyes, nodded. Looking up, he replied, "Well, that's true. The head man did shoot the dog. But—"

"And wouldn't it be fair to say, Sheriff Poindexter, that you know, you personally know some of those men? Those hooded, cross-burning cowards? Maybe Red Shirt friends of Luther Wade? Maybe the same men that were with Luther Wade at the jail when Mr. Taliaferro made his public announcement earlier that same day?"

Taliaferro started to object, made eye contact with the judge, thought better of it. Poindexter shuffled his feet, squirmed in his chair. "Maybe," he answered. "Maybe I know some of them."

"And you remember, do you not, Mr. Taliaferro having a conversation with Luther Wade right after his big show that Monday morning? Right there on the steps of the jail? *Just hours before the attack?*"

Taliaferro shot to his feet. "Objection!" he shouted. "I resent his insinuation, Your Honor! This is not proper cross-examination. This must not be permitted!"

"Overruled. Sit down, Mr. Taliaferro. I'll decide what is permissible in my courtroom and what is not. You would do well to remember that. Now, answer the question, Sheriff."

Poindexter was silent for a moment. Then he blew out a breath. "Yes. Yes," he repeated solemnly. "I saw them talking." Judge Transou frowned, shot a look in Taliaferro's direction.

"Thank you, Sheriff." Ben then moved on. "So, let's assume the judge grants Mr. Taliaferro's motion and the Wade boy is returned to your jail. It's just you and Mr. Goins there, right? To guard the boy? Keep him safe? Twenty-four hours a day, seven days a week?"

"Well, yes, that's right, but—"

"And," Ben interrupted, talking faster now, in the flow. "Let's suppose the Klan comes back for the boy, with even more men this time. Are you telling this court that you are prepared to use *force* to protect him? That you *can* protect him? That you will, without hesitation, take your Winchester rifle and open fire on the Klansmen, some of whom may be sitting in this very courtroom? Some of your friends, your neighbors? Trade their lives for Virgil Wade's?"

"Objection!"

"Overruled. I instruct you to answer Mr. Waterman's question, Sheriff Poindexter."

Poindexter sat silent, his jaw working. Ben turned, faced the spectators. "Take a look out there, Sheriff. They're all here, right in front of you. All good citizens of Wilkes. Tell me, Sheriff. Point them out to me. *Call their names*. You said you know them. Tell me which of these men you would shoot first, and how many, just to save the life of a poor colored boy?"

An uneasy rumbling filled the courtroom as spectators looked nervously left and right, fixed their eyes on the sheriff, waiting for his answer.

Poindexter gazed into the crowd before him, turned to Taliaferro with a helpless look. Then he looked to the judge, but there was no relief to be had there. Shaking his head, his jaw firmly set, his shoulders slumped, Poindexter slowly rose, stepped out of the witness box, and started back to his seat at the prosecution table.

The sharp *rap* of Judge Transou's gavel echoed like a rifle shot through the courtroom. "Sheriff Poindexter! Get back up here! Take your seat, sir!" Poindexter kept walking.

Ben threw his hands in the air, blew out a sigh. "No more questions for this witness, Your Honor," he said grimly.

Judge Transou sat stone-faced, quiet, for a long minute, brooding. "All right, then," he said. "I've heard enough. Seems to me the issue is pretty straightforward. The deed is done, after all. The Wade boy is already in Raleigh, locked up, at State expense. And as long as he is *there*, none of what Mr. Waterman is so rightly worried about can happen *here*. I see no need to muddy things up. No need for the State to spend the time and money just to bring him back. And no need to make things hard on Sheriff Poindexter and Mr. Goins."

Sensing things slipping away, Taliaferro rose. "But, your Honor, this is—"

Again, the judge raised a hand. "Sit down, Mr. Taliaferro. I'm ready to rule. Your motion to vacate the governor's declaration of emergency is denied. The defendant will remain in State custody at Central Prison in Raleigh until his trial."

Again, the courtroom exploded. Cries of *"No!"* *"Bring him back!"* *"Hang him!"* *"Bring him back!"* filled the air. Taliaferro, defeated, slumped in his chair. Poindexter looked down at his shoes. Crip Goins looked around the room, wide-eyed. Ben sat silent, eyes fixed straight ahead.

The judge's gavel quieted the room. "Now, then," he pronounced. "I've made my ruling. Is there anything else, gentlemen, or can we wrap things up and get out of this furnace?"

Slowly Ben rose. "Your Honor, the defense has one additional motion."

The spectators groaned. Judge Transou glared at Ben, sat back in his leather chair, pushed up his spectacles. "Go ahead, Mr. Waterman. State your motion. Make it quick."

As Ben reached for the box beneath his desk, beams of sunlight shone through each of the tall windows on the east side of the courtroom, illuminating motes of dust floating in the still and muggy air. Taliaferro sat at his desk, restless and fidgeting.

Judge Transou leaned forward, placed his elbows on the judge's bench, steepled his large hands, glanced down at Taliaferro. "I can see, Mr. Taliaferro, that you are ready to pounce, sir. I suggest that you keep your powder dry and let Mr. Waterman say his piece. Whatever he's got, you'll get your chance. Understood? Now, Mr. Waterman, get on with it."

Placing the box on the table before him, Ben began. "May it please the court, and as Your Honor well knows, every defendant in a criminal case has the constitutional right to have his case heard and determined by a fair and impartial jury of his *peers*." Looking at his notes, Ben continued, "Your Honor, this is exactly what Mr. Taliaferro demanded at the outset of this hearing. Virgil Wade must be returned here *to face a jury of his peers*. Those were *his* words."

Ben gestured toward the spectators. "Here, today, we can count well over a hundred Wilkes County citizens. Where, Your Honor, are Virgil Wade's *peers* in this courtroom? In this jurisdiction? My client is but a boy, a poor colored boy, never before in trouble, and now on trial for his life!

"Where in this room, where among these spectators are we to find twelve potential *peers* of Virgil Wade to sit in judgment of him? Peers?"

Pointing up, Ben said solemnly, "Certainly not up *there*, Your Honor, not in the balcony. I'll wager that not one of those folks' names appears on the jury roll for Wilkes County. Think, Your Honor, when was the last time a colored man sat on a jury before you in a criminal case?" Shaking his head, Ben said, "No. No *peers* to be found up there. So, where to look?" Turning and drawing his arm before those seated behind him, Ben said, "Here? I don't think so. First, we must exclude all the women, none of whom are deemed fit by our state constitution to sit on a jury *propter defectum sexus*, because of their *defective gender!*"

Drawing himself up to full height, Ben continued. "So, who are we left with, Your Honor?" Ben said softly. "Who remains to sit in judgment of Virgil Wade, to cast the first stone against him? *Men!*" he shouted. "That's right. All *men*. All *White*. And all of them riled up because Your Honor refuses to bring my client back to Wilkes in chains to face vigilante justice!

'Peers?'" said Ben, shaking his head sadly. "I don't think so."

At this, Taliaferro raised his hand like a schoolboy, stood. "Your Honor, if I may?" Spreading his hands, "Your Honor, Mr. Waterman has done nothing more than describe the current legal situation in all ninety-seven counties in North Carolina. There is nothing different about Wilkes. If Mr. Waterman wants to run for the legislature and try to change the way to do things, why, he is free to do so. But in the meantime—"

The judge looked down at Ben. "He's got a point, Mr. Waterman. You make an eloquent plea for reforms of our jurisprudence that I, a mere trial judge, am powerless to implement or even consider in this case. Where are you going with this?"

Ben's shoulders sagged for just a moment. But then he continued with greater confidence.

"Thank you, Your Honor. I don't like it, but I understand. But, you see, there's more. State and federal constitutional law and case precedents also guarantee every criminal defendant the right to have his case decided by jurors that are *impartial,* free of bias or prejudice. Prepared to hear and weigh the *evidence,* and *only the evidence* admitted in open court. To consider that evidence with clear and open minds, Your Honor, minds not swayed by rumor, innuendo, public opinion, or stories in local newspapers."

With growing interest, Judge Transou placed his chin on his hands. "Go on. Get to the point."

Taking a deep breath, Ben said firmly, "Your Honor, it is manifestly clear that it is now impossible for Virgil Wade to get a fair trial in Wilkes County. There is simply no way that an unbiased and impartial jury can be seated in this case given the level of public attention and rank speculation that the matter has provoked in the community and in the papers."

Again, an uneasy rumbling in the courtroom. Taliaferro was quickly on his feet. "Your Honor! I know you told me to wait, but this . . . this is absolutely intolerable! To suggest—"

"Sit down!" snapped the judge, banging his gavel. "Let him finish."

Ben removed the lid from the cardboard box, took out a tall stack of newspapers, and dropped them onto the table with a loud *thud.*

"Your Honor, Wilkes County is blessed, surprisingly and perhaps uniquely in our state, with a vibrant and highly competitive newspaper industry. Depending on which day you count, it looks like there are somewhere between ten and fifteen weekly papers published here, each one clamoring for the attention of a fickle public. These local publications claim to reach a combined circulation of more than *ten times* the county's entire population, which today stands at a little over twenty-five thousand men, women, and children.

"If Virgil Wade is to be subjected to the judgment of a Wilkes County jury, why, then we must surely consider the impact of these newspapers and their sensationalist coverage of the Rachel Schumann . . . incident."

Pointing to the stack on the table, Ben explained, "These are all of the newspapers that have been published in Wilkes in the short few weeks since the Rachel Schumann murder." Handing up copies, one by one, to Judge Transou, Ben said, "Please take a look, Judge, just the headlines and the photos, just the front pages, and you'll see what I am talking about."

Judge Transou examined each of the publications, then handed them down to Taliaferro. As this was going on, Ben continued. "*MURDER!* is the most common headline, in big, black letters. This is to be expected. But, as they say, the devil is in the details. I have read these papers, Judge, every last one of them. I can report that the word *Negro* is used to identify Virgil Wade no fewer than fifty-six times. Other repeated, personal references to him are 'murderer,' 'monster,' 'killer,' 'bastard,' 'savage,' barbarian,' 'high yeller,' 'criminal,' 'hang him,' 'string him up' . . . and worse.

"I must also bring to the court's attention that even the prosecutor, Mr. Taliaferro, has personally aided and abetted this feeding frenzy in the papers. On Monday morning, July 9, just hours before the attack on the jail, Mr. Taliaferro summoned the public and the press to the jailhouse steps, where he read a lengthy statement. He spoon-fed his so-called *evidence* to a large group of angry men, all of them potential jurymen in this case. He presented it all as proven fact, knowing full well that his *facts* were incomplete, misleading, and, in some cases, totally false, as I will demonstrate at trial."

Suffering under the judge's admonition, Taliaferro squirmed in his chair, fuming, licking his lips. Hitting his stride, Ben continued. "Worse, he proclaimed my client to be a 'half-breed, drunken, merciless monster.'" Handing up a document, Ben said, "Please read it yourself, Your Honor. This is Mr. Taliaferro's statement, copies of which were conveniently provided to all members of the press.

"Mr. Taliaferro, the ringmaster of this vile and base public spectacle, then revealed the alleged murder weapon, grinning and holding it high above his head, like a trophy." Ben paused, poured a glass of water from the pitcher on the table, took a sip.

"As the final act of his hateful circus, and yielding to the fevered demands of the crowd, Mr. Taliaferro then produced the poor and helpless Virgil Wade for all to see, in chains and shackles. Displayed like a wild animal at a carnival show, a triumph captured in front-page photographs like those Your Honor has just seen. I know, Judge, I was *there*. I saw it with my own eyes.

"As Your Honor noted earlier, Mr. Taliaferro is in the midst of a heated political campaign, seeking election as the solicitor and chief prosecutor." Pointing at the prosecution table, Ben spoke, sarcasm in his voice. "Mr. Taliaferro will surely be pleased to learn that, in the stack of newspapers before him, his name is mentioned even more often than Virgil Wade's!"

"I get the picture, Mr. Waterman," said Judge Transou sternly. "Move on."

Nodding, Ben said, "Your Honor, the presumption of innocence until proven guilty is a sacred and foundational principle of our jurisprudence, but to anyone reading those newspapers, and I reckon that means most every man in the county, Virgil Wade has already been tried and convicted in the press. This unprecedented level and degree of negative, highly prejudicial pre-trial publicity has clearly poisoned the minds of potential Wilkes County jurors against my client, Judge. There is no remedy in Wilkes for that.

"We must also remember that the victim of this crime was the beloved daughter of a wealthy and powerful local businessman. Jakob Schumann and his enterprises directly employ more than two hundred men in Wilkes, Your Honor. Countless other small businesses, suppliers, vendors, loggers, wagon builders, wheelwrights, blacksmiths, and their families likewise depend upon Mr. Schumann for their livelihood. He will understandably expect their loyalty in this case, and many will conclude he has earned it."

Another round of murmuring and nodding heads in the gallery.

"So, let's wrap this up, counselor. What relief are you seeking here?"

"There is only one remedy, Judge. Virgil Wade must not be tried in Wilkes County. My motion is for a change of venue. I move that the trial of Virgil Wade be relocated to Wake County, where he is currently incarcerated, and set for the fall term of court there."

As Taliaferro jumped to his feet, objecting, pandemonium erupted in the courtroom. Several men in the gallery rose, shook their fists at Ben. Cries of *"No!"* ... *"Never!"* ... "Hang him in Wilkes!" ... "Bring him here!" ...

As Ben turned to face them, a large, bearded man in bib overalls suddenly sprang from the crowd and barged through the gate separating the gallery from the counsel tables. Red-faced, furious, his fists clenched, the man advanced on Ben, grabbed him by the shirt front, shook him hard, and with spit flying, snarled, "Nigger lover! You goddamned nigger lover! Who in the hell do you think you are, you sorry-assed son of a bitch! Git on home! Git, I say!"

As Ben struggled to free himself, Judge Transou banged his gavel, hard, three times. "Bailiff! Bailiff! Arrest that man! Right now!"

Billy Ray Hill, the portly bailiff, moved as quickly as he could to break up the fracas. "Come on now, Jesse! Knock it off!" he cried, pulling the men apart. Panting, eyes on fire, the attacker backed away.

"Bailiff, you and Deputy Goins escort that man immediately to the jail and confine him there! I will deal with him . . . *severely* . . . later. Now," Judge Transou scolded, pointing his gavel, "Anybody else out there want to keep him company?"

As Billy Ray Hill led the man away, and as the spectators settled down, Ben turned to the judge, his hair askew, his suit jacket rumpled. He made no effort to compose himself or correct his appearance.

"*There it is*, Your Honor. Right there! There goes the very *face*, the *impartial voice* of your Wilkes County jury pool!" Flipping his hand at the crowd, Ben demanded, "How many potential Wilkes jurors witnessed this outburst? How many share that man's *hate*? How many times will folks repeat the tale of what happened here, in this courtroom, not just now, but throughout this proceeding, as you have observed? And oh, what stories the newspapers will print, Your Honor!"

Calming himself, Ben concluded, "You have *heard* it with your own ears, Judge. You have *seen* it with your own eyes. There is no justice to be had for Virgil Wade here. This case must be moved!" And with that, he sat.

Judge Transou responded in a steady voice. "Okay, Mr. Taliaferro. Your turn."

Taliaferro rose, steadied himself. "Your Honor, no doubt emotions are running high in this case. I see that. We all do. And for good reason! An unspeakable crime has been committed in Wilkes, Judge, and the people cry for justice. And, by God, they shall have it!

"And Mr. Waterman, why, he cries instead for *impartiality*. Impartiality? Who can remain impartial in the face of this savage affront to the peace of our community? The heinous crime that Mr. Waterman callously refers to as an *incident?* There is no justice in depriving twelve good Wilkes men of their rightful opportunity to hear my evidence, the overwhelming *evidence* that Mr. Waterman so flippantly disparages, the *proof* against this . . . this *defendant,* and to render the awful judgment this case demands.

"Mr. Waterman pleads that constitutional rights must be respected, Your Honor. And I join him in insisting that the constitutional right of the people to have this trial conducted right here, in Wilkes, must be respected! Defendant's motion should be *denied,* Your Honor!"

Judge Transou looked to Ben. "For the reasons cited, and on behalf of my client, Virgil Wade, I renew my motion for a change of venue."

"You've made your point, Mr. Waterman. Any law to back it up?"

"Yes sir," replied Ben, handing up a law book to the judge. "*State v. Dula,* from right here in Wilkes, a North Carolina Supreme Court case directly on point."

Waving him off, the judge said, "Keep your book, counselor. I know the case."

"Then Your Honor is well aware that in that case the defendant, Tom Dula, a resident of Wilkes, was charged with the murder of a woman, one Laura Foster. And just like in this case, the Dula prosecution created a sensation, to the point that Dula's lawyer, former North Carolina Governor Zebulon Vance, objected to a trial in Wilkes and made a motion, as I am doing in this case, to transfer the case to another venue.

"His motion was properly granted, Your Honor, and the case was moved to Statesville, where the trial was successfully completed, and a unanimous verdict was handed down by an *impartial* jury there, a judgment that was summarily upheld by the North Carolina Supreme Court. Defendant cites *State v. Dula,* Judge, as binding precedent for the relief sought here, under facts and circumstances that are even more compelling."

Judge Transou then turned to Taliaferro. "Anything else from your side?"

I need this trial, thought Taliaferro, desperate to slow things down, to change the direction of the hearing. "Your Honor, changing the venue means *delay.* It means a new *judge.* A new *prosecutor.* And for what? And think about the *witnesses,* Your Honor, the people who must testify, why, they are all *here.* Why must they be inconvenienced so? Why must they travel all the way to Raleigh? I can tell you now, Judge, here today in this courtroom, that the people are *ready*, Your Honor. I am ready to try this case right now. Today. There simply is no good reason—"

"I hear you," interrupted the judge. "And I am sympathetic to your concerns about delay." Pausing, he thought for a moment. "If there is nothing more, I am ready to rule." Both lawyers sat silent.

Leaning forward, looking at the spectators, Judge Transou spoke slowly and clearly. "Now, you people listen to me. When I announce my ruling, there will be no disturbance or ruckus. No outburst of any kind. If I have to, I will have Sheriff Poindexter arrest the whole lot of you and haul you off to jail to join Jesse Wilburn until you cool off and I decide what to do with you. Anybody fail to understand me?"

The courtroom was quiet as Judge Transou sat back in his chair, thinking, getting organized. Finally, he spoke. "First of all, I am persuaded by Mr. Taliaferro's argument. There will be no delay in the trial of this case." A satisfied murmur moved through the spectators, many nodding their heads and smiling. Ben's heart sank. Taliaferro turned to Poindexter, grinned.

"However," continued the judge, "Mr. Waterman makes a good case concerning the undeniable impact of all the publicity and attention this case has ginned up, much of it provoked by Mr. Taliaferro's own grandstanding. As we lawyers say, it is not possible to unring a bell, and this bell has been tolling loudly for some time now. I am satisfied that it will not be possible to seat a fair and impartial jury here under these circumstances."

Ben looked up, hopeful, still unsure. Taliaferro, stricken, eyes wide, looked up helplessly, knowing what would come next.

"Therefore, in the interests of justice, and for good cause shown, Defendant's motion for a change of venue is *granted*." The murmur rose in volume, changed in tone. Judge Transou looked threateningly at the spectators, raised his gavel. The crowd fell silent.

"The court notes for the record that, in order to address Mr. Taliaferro's legitimate concerns, only the *venue* of the trial in this case is affected, nothing else. Mr. Taliaferro will remain as prosecutor, and I will retain jurisdiction over this matter until the trial is completed. And, since the defendant is already in Raleigh, and not going anywhere, venue will be the Wake County Courthouse in Raleigh." Looking down at his calendar, he declared, "The trial in the matter of *State v. Wade* will commence at nine o'clock on the morning of Tuesday, September 4, 1900.

"We'll start with final motions in the morning, and then pick a local jury Tuesday afternoon. Opening statements and testimony on Wednesday morning. That way the witnesses won't have to travel over the Labor Day holiday. Y'all just have them in Raleigh Tuesday night, ready to go. I do regret that we will all have to make such a long trip, but personal convenience can never trump the constitutional right to a fair trial." Looking up, he concluded, "Now, are there any questions?"

Ben, who had been holding his breath, exhaled sharply and said, "No, Your Honor." Taliaferro could only whisper, "No, sir. No questions."

Judge Transou rapped his gavel one last time. "Court is adjourned."

Chapter 33

As the muttering, unhappy spectators exited, Ben caught a glimpse of Claire Elise Montgomery. Their eyes met for a moment, but she quickly turned away and disappeared into the crowd.

Ben put the newspapers back in the cardboard box. Roscoe McGee and Tink Beasley joined him at the table. With a big smile McGee started to speak, but Ben held up a finger. "Not here, Ros. Not now. We'll talk later."

McGee nodded, picked up the box. As he and Tink turned to leave, he said, "We'll wait for you downstairs, Ben. And good luck."

As they left, Gabriel von Gruenwald approached. With a sour face, no trace of the famous smile, he grumbled, "So, you wanted to see me?"

"There's a small room back there," Ben pointed. "Behind the judge's bench." He led them back and opened a window. It was cooler there.

"You must be very proud of yourself, Mr. Waterman," said Gruenwald. "Although I am not sure what you have accomplished. Mr. Schumann will be very disappointed."

Ben let it go. "Thank you for meeting with me, Mr. Gruenwald. I will not keep you long."

Gruenwald shot the cuffs of his dress shirt and looked at his watch. On his right wrist. "I must be on the afternoon train, Mr. Waterman. But first I will report to Mr. Schumann, so I do not have much time."

Ben looked at the timepiece. "That's a handsome watch, Mr. Gruenwald. On your wrist."

Gruenwald held out his right arm, gazed at the wristwatch. "It's something new. Made in Switzerland. A gift from my wife. Before she

221

died. But now," he said impatiently, "let's get on with it. You said you had something important to discuss with me. Something you say involves me?"

Slowly. Take your time. "Mr. Gruenwald," Ben began cautiously. "As you now know, I will be representing Virgil Wade in this case. It is therefore my duty to aggressively, to *zealously* we lawyers say, defend my client."

Gruenwald nodded stiffly. "I understand that."

"I have some professional experience, Mr. Gruenwald, with the law most familiar to you. German law. And I can tell you that here, in the United States, we do things a little differently. Here, criminal defendants are entitled to a *presumption of innocence*, meaning that, under the law, every man is deemed to be innocent until the prosecution *proves* him to be guilty, guilty beyond any *reasonable doubt*. Do you follow me?"

"Yes, yes. And—?"

"Please understand, then, that the burden of proof is on the prosecution. Mr. Taliaferro must prove my client's guilt beyond a reasonable doubt. And the verdict of the jury must be *unanimous*. Each and every one of the twelve jurors must vote, without exception, to convict.

"Virgil Wade is not obligated to prove anything. He cannot even be compelled to testify. It is *not* my job to prove that Mr. Wade is *innocent* of the charge against him. It *is* my job to show the jury that the evidence presented by the prosecution is insufficient to prove guilt beyond a reasonable doubt. If I can do that, why, then there can be no conviction."

"So how will you do that, Mr. Waterman?" Gruenwald asked. "After all, the evidence cited by Mr. Taliaferro seems—"

"Yes, I know," Ben interrupted. "The case presented to the public by Mr. Taliaferro seems strong. *But,* you see, I have uncovered additional evidence, facts that Mr. Taliaferro knows about, but has not yet disclosed. Evidence that causes me to *doubt* Mr. Taliaferro's story and that may cause a jury to have doubts as well. *Reasonable* doubts."

"Are you possibly suggesting that the Wade boy is *innocent*, Mr. Waterman? Why, his knife was used to kill poor Rachel Schumann!"

"I realize that, Mr. Gruenwald. And that is why I wanted to speak with you. Privately."

Gruenwald shrugged. "Please go ahead."

Ben moved ahead, cautiously. "I am trying hard to understand what happened that night under the iron bridge. Tell me about Rachel Schumann, Mr. Gruenwald. What was she like?"

Tilting his head, perplexed, Gruenwald said, "Well, Miss Schumann was a beautiful, intelligent, cheerful young woman, Mr. Waterman. Everyone who knew her can confirm this."

"And my understanding is that you knew her well, Mr. Gruenwald, is that right?"

Gruenwald looked at Ben and spoke guardedly. "She . . . she and I were . . . friends. She lived in Tanner's Rest, in the Schumann home, just across from the guest house where I reside during my trips to Wilkes. So, we saw each other often. I very much enjoyed her company."

Careful, Ben thought. *Careful.* "In fact, you were with her the afternoon before her death. Isn't that right? At the fairgrounds?"

Gruenwald's eyes narrowed.

"You were there with her," Ben pressed. "She was observed in conversation with you that day. What has been described as an *intense* conversation, isn't that right?"

Gruenwald did not speak.

"Please tell me about that, Mr. Gruenwald. What were you and Rachel Schumann discussing?"

Gruenwald's expression darkened. "I am not sure I understand what you are suggesting, Mr. Waterman. I have had many conversations with Miss Schumann, many of them in public. What of it?"

Here we go, thought Ben. "Mr. Gruenwald, when this case comes to trial, in September, please understand that I will be fighting for Virgil Wade's *life.* It is important that I understand every aspect of this case, from beginning to end. So, I ask for your indulgence, please."

Gruenwald nodded.

"You have acknowledged a close, friendly relationship with Rachel Schumann, Mr. Gruenwald. You have often been observed with her in public, sometimes arm in arm. You reside near her home when you are here. It may perhaps come as a surprise to you to learn that there are some in the community who regard your relationship with Rachel as perhaps *too* close, *too* familiar. Perhaps even *inappropriate?*"

"What do you mean, *inappropriate*?" Gruenwald scoffed. "What are you suggesting?"

Ben changed the subject. "Mr. Gruenwald, what Mr. Taliaferro has not revealed publicly are things, elements of the crime that do not exactly fit his theory of the case. There are photographs, sir. I have seen them."

"Photographs? Of the murder? What do they show?"

"A strange scene. Rachel's body, dressed in riding clothes, lying on a family heirloom quilt, a turned over lantern beside her. She had a precious necklace around her neck, money in her pocket, so robbery was no motive. And there was an almost empty bottle of whiskey, two small shot glasses. Why, Mr. Gruenwald? What was going on there? It's as if she was *expecting* someone. Someone to *join* her."

"Are you trying to say that Miss Schumann was waiting . . . expecting *Virgil Wade* to join her? At the river?"

"Virgil may have been there. He has admitted as much to Mr. Taliaferro. But he adamantly denies stabbing her, claiming that he passed out and awoke to find her dead. But, like you, I find it difficult to believe that Rachel *invited* him there, that she *expected* him." Shaking his head, Ben said, "No. Rachel was not expecting Virgil Wade."

"Then who?" exclaimed Gruenwald. "And why?"

Ben fixed his eyes on Gruenwald. "I have a theory about that, Mr. Gruenwald. A theory that, if true, could actually exonerate Virgil Wade. That could at least create reasonable doubt in the minds of the jury. I expect you will not like it."

"Tell me," said Gruenwald.

Ben counted on his fingers. "*First*, as discussed, you admit a close, friendly relationship with the victim, a relationship that others described as *inappropriate*."

Gruenwald moved to interrupt, but Ben raised a hand. "Let me finish, please.

"*Second*, you were seen in an intense, animated conversation with Rachel at the fairgrounds the day before her murder.

"*Third*, there are also photographs from the coroner's office. I have seen them. These show severe bruising on the *left* side of her face, suggesting that her assailant was right-handed. But the angle of the knife handle protruding from her chest would indicate that the stabbing wound was inflicted by a *left*-handed person," said Ben, glancing down at the watch on Gruenwald's right wrist.

"*Fourth*, you, sir, were the person who identified Rachel Schumann's body at Dr. Burleson's office. It was you, Mr. Gruenwald, who pressured Burleson to finish his examination quickly, to fix the cause of death and release the body to you without delay.

"*Fifth*, the autopsy photographs further support the possibility, the likelihood, in fact, that there were *two people* with Rachel Schumann at the river that night. *Two people* involved in her murder."

Ben paused to take a breath, then calmly asked, "Was that second person *you*, Mr. Gruenwald?"

Gruenwald left his chair. *"No! No! Of course not!"* he exploded. "You are accusing me of *murder*, Waterman. *Murder!* Why in God's name would I want to take Rachel Schumann's life?"

"Please sit down, Mr. Gruenwald," said Ben evenly. "Lawyers, Mr. Gruenwald, are born skeptics and trained cynics. This is why so many laymen dislike us. Our minds work in strange ways. So, let me tell you what my skeptical, cynical mind is suggesting to me. Suppose your *friendship* with Rachel had become too close, too familiar, too *intimate?*"

Gruenwald's eyes widened, the color draining from his face.

Ben bored in. "What would your fiancée in Wilmington think if word of this . . . *affair* made its way back to her? What if Jakob and Rebekah Schumann discovered that you, their trusted friend and business partner, had taken such callous advantage of their beloved young daughter?

"Perhaps you came to your senses, Mr. Gruenwald? Maybe you decided to end it? Told her that at the fairgrounds during your *intense* conversation? I expect that Rachel did not react well. I understand she had a temper. What if a spiteful Rachel Schumann threatened to expose your relationship to her father? Or perhaps she had some other, more important reason to meet with you that night by the river? Some piece of urgent news that would surely cause you to change your mind?"

Ben sat back, let Gruenwald's imagination work. In a weak, stricken voice, denying nothing, Gruenwald pleaded, "Who . . . *who* has so poisoned your mind against me, Mr. Waterman? Why would you even consider, *believe*, such a thing?"

Ben sat, waited as Gruenwald grimaced. "Now I see. Now I understand. You were staying at the Schumann Hotel. You have obviously been speaking with Mrs. Montgomery about me."

Wagging a finger, he continued, "You must not be fooled by her, Mr. Waterman. She is a bitter, manipulative woman, and you must not allow her charms to seduce you. She has been, and she remains, how do you say, *obsessed* with me. Since our days in Argentina. I have always tried to behave in a friendly way to her, to help her, but she has always wanted *more*.

"Things only worsened when she and her husband arrived in Wilkes. She thought that when fate and Jakob Schumann brought us together here, well, she took this as a *sign*. After her husband's suicide, she became even more aggressive, more delusional about the potential of our relationship. This, of course, made me very uneasy. To the point that I was no longer comfortable staying in the hotel, so I moved to the guest house."

Stunned, Ben turned away, looked out the window, thinking about his time spent with Claire Elise, not recognizing the stranger described by Gruenwald.

Gruenwald then said sheepishly, "Rachel and I were . . . close, as you say. This made Claire Elise insanely jealous. She believed that Rachel was . . . pursuing me, that Rachel had somehow stolen me away from *her.*"

So, now it's Rachel, thought Ben.

Gruenwald said sadly, "Claire Elise Montgomery has obviously planted an evil seed in your head, Mr. Waterman, one that no doubt appeals to your skeptical, cynical mind. This is a mistake!"

Ben leaned forward. "Evil seed or not, Mr. Gruenwald, I am prepared to let the jury decide. You see, the purpose of this meeting is to inform you that I intend to subpoena you, Mr. Gruenwald, to call you as a witness at the trial in September. You will be required to answer my questions, under oath, about your relationship with Rachel Schumann. Perhaps this will create reasonable doubt in the minds of the jurymen, perhaps not. But this alternative theory of the case will, I promise you, be put to the jury and will be forever on the public record."

Panicked, Gruenwald blurted, "You cannot do that! Doing so would ruin my reputation, destroy my upcoming marriage, forever spoil my friendship and my business relationship with Jakob Schumann! And all for nothing!"

"What do you mean, nothing?" asked Ben.

"I was never at the river with Rachel Schumann!"

Tilting his head, Ben asked, "So, tell me then. What did you and Rachel talk about at the fairgrounds?"

Gruenwald took a deep breath, exhaled. "All right, then. I confess that Rachel and I had developed a close relationship over the past months. Rachel had clearly become infatuated with me. Perhaps our relationship had become too close, too personal, *inappropriate,* as you say. She was, after all, a most beautiful woman, Mr. Waterman, mature and . . . willing, beyond her years. I was not immune. More than this, I will not say.

"The truth is, you are correct. At the fairgrounds, I told Rachel that I was engaged to be married, that the wedding would take place in Wilmington in the fall. This upset her greatly. She was angry. She told me that she had important news that would change my plans. She demanded that I meet her at the river around midnight. She said that if I failed to show up, she would go to her father.

"I made plans to go. I had saddled my horse and was preparing to leave Schumann Village late that night. But there was suddenly a huge disturbance coming from inside the tannery. A steam boiler had sprung a leak and severely scalded one of the night workers. Along with some men, I rushed into the tannery. Another worker, in his haste, knocked over a lantern, which started a fire. I helped put the injured man into a wagon, and we delivered him to the company infirmary. He was terribly injured, not expected to live.

"I then returned to the tannery and blew the whistle to bring the fire brigade. I helped them put out the fire." Snapping his fingers, Gruenwald said excitedly, "You can ask your friend Mr. McGee! He was there. He saw me! Ask him!"

Ben made a note. "What happened after that?"

"By the time things returned to normal, it was almost two o'clock. I then sat with Jakob Schumann in his home to give him the details. He can confirm this. Then I checked on the injured worker at the infirmary. Thank God, he survived.

"I walked to the guest house and went to bed. In all the confusion, I completely forgot about Rachel and the meeting at the river. But I planned to talk to her the next day, early, before she had a chance to say anything to her father. But, as you know, by then she was dead."

Ben sat for a moment, thinking. Then, shaking his head, he said, "So, you think you have an alibi. But the time of Rachel's death was never determined. Who's to say that you didn't ride over to the river after all the commotion at the tannery? There was still time for you to get there and back to Schumann Village before daybreak."

"Me? You mean to *kill* her? How? The autopsy confirms Virgil Wade's knife was the murder weapon. And from what you say, the boy admits he was there with Rachel."

"You're right about that. But he says he was drunk, passed out cold. You could've arrived late, sized up the situation, and taken your opportunity with Virgil Wade's knife. Rachel Schumann dead means no trouble with her father, nothing to explain to your fiancée. And no further *complications* with Rachel."

His mind racing, Gruenwald searched for some way, any way, out of this. Finally, he looked up at Ben. "Look," he pleaded. "I have an idea. I may know a way to prove, without any *doubt*, that I was not at the river, that I did not kill Rachel Schumann."

Ben frowned. "I'm listening."

With growing confidence, Gruenwald said, "First, I need a promise from you. I need you to promise me that, if I can satisfy you that I had nothing to do with Rachel's murder, you will then do two things: first, you will never put me on the witness stand during the trial, and second, you will never reveal to anyone—*anyone*—what I have just told you. Nothing about my relationship with Rachel. Jakob and Rebekah Schumann must never know any of this. And third, no word of any of this must ever get back to my fiancée in Wilmington."

Startled at this sudden shift, Ben asked, "That's a big 'if,' Mr. Gruenwald. So, how will you do that? Convince me?"

Shaking his head, Gruenwald said firmly, "I may not be able to prove *who* killed her, Virgil Wade or someone else, but I can prove that *I* did not. Hear me out, Mr. Waterman. If you are not convinced by what I am about to suggest, why, then, you remain free to do what you have to do."

"But how . . . how will you get this 'proof?'"

Gruenwald thought about it. "It will take me some time to arrange things. I leave for Wilmington later today. The trial is not until September. I think I can pull it all together. Here is what I am going to do . . . ."

Gruenwald explained his plan. It took some time. As he laid it out, Ben's eyes grew wide. When Gruenwald finished, Ben leaned back in his chair. Incredulous, he said, "You can do that? You can get all that done between now and September?"

"I'm not sure, Mr. Waterman. But I think so. I will try my best. If I am not successful, you are no worse off. And if I am successful, the result could help your client. What do you have to lose? The burden, as you say, is on me."

"But understand, Mr. Gruenwald nothing like this has ever been done in North Carolina. Not ever. I'm not sure that I can get Judge Transou to agree."

"Not my problem, Mr. Waterman. That's what lawyers are for," he said, smiling for the first time. "As I said, if I can deliver what I have promised, to *your* satisfaction, not the judge's, why, then I will have kept my promise. And I will then expect you to keep yours."

Ben considered Gruenwald's remarkable proposal, one he knew could backfire. If Gruenwald really was innocent, he could never put him on the witness stand, drag him through the sordid details of his relationship with Rachel.

After weighing his options, Ben looked Gruenwald squarely in the eye. "If, and I mean *if*, Mr. Gruenwald, if you can do what you say, then I agree." He reached out a hand and the men shook.

W

Over lunch at McGee's Emporium, celebrating with Tony Moretti's pizza and cold draft beer, Ben, McGee, and Tink reviewed the events of the day. Raising her mug, Tink offered a toast. "You sure reamed ol' Razor a new one, Ben. That was quite a thumpin'!"

"Nice to see him get a taste of his own medicine," McGee agreed.

"Thanks," said Ben, smiling and taking a sip. "But best not get carried away. Taliaferro is still good for a few surprises in Raleigh, I'm sure of that. This will be a tough fight."

"So, how did it go with Gruenwald?" asked McGee.

Ben quickly summarized the meeting. "He denies being at the river, of course. Swears he had nothing to do with the murder. But he does admit that he and Rachel were . . . *close,* as he put it. *Too* close, if you get my meaning. He came right up to the line but didn't actually admit it out loud."

"Did you tell him Rachel was . . . you know, *expecting*?" asked Tink.

"No. No need to mention that. Rachel never had a chance to tell him, so I guess he couldn't have known. He's almost surely the father, but I got what I needed from Gruenwald without it."

Ben then explained Gruenwald's attempt at an alibi. McGee nodded. "He was there all right, at the tannery, like he said. I saw him helping put out the fire. But, like you say, he still had time to get over to the river and back. He could still be the *second* person there with Rachel."

"I get that, Ros," Ben agreed. "He's not off the hook in my view. And get this. He's got a fancy watch. Wears it on his *wrist*. On his *right* wrist."

McGee looked confused. "On his wrist, you say? Not a pocket watch?"

"Nope. It's evidently a new thing. They make them over in Switzerland. Judge Maxwell's got one. His daughters gave it to him, a birthday present. Well, he's right-handed and wears his on his left arm. He's says that's the way they do it. If you're right-handed, you wear it on your left wrist. And—"

"And," interrupted McGee, "If you're left-handed . . . " He let the thought trail off, pointing to his right arm.

"Exactly," nodded Ben.

"Well, that settles *that*," said McGee firmly. "Another piece of the puzzle."

Ben shrugged. "But just one piece, Ros. Lots of left-handed people in Wilkes. But now, listen to this . . . ." Ben then explained Gruenwald's audacious plan to prove his innocence.

McGee whistled, said, "Golly Pete, Ben! You ever heard of such a thing? I'm no lawyer, but—"

"I know, I know. It seems mighty far-fetched, Ros, but like Gruenwald says, what do I have to lose? He can either deliver or he can't. If he can, why, that might go a long way to getting Virgil Wade out of this mess. If he can't, well, then I put him on the stand and let the jury think about it. *All* of it."

They were silent for a while. An idea forming, Ben asked, "Ros, you'll be in Raleigh, right, covering the trial?"

"Wouldn't miss it, Ben. I'll be there."

"Well, see, the thing is, I'm going to need some help at the trial. As Judge Maxwell says, it's always good to have two people sitting at the defense table. While I'm up *talking*, well, somebody else needs to be *thinking*, taking notes and such. And I'll need someone to help me with all the documents, exhibits, that sort of thing. It can't be you, Ros. You'll be busy, and everybody will figure you for a newspaperman. But you," he said, pointing at Tink. "*You* could be just what I need."

"Me?" blurted Tink. "You want me there, sitting beside you in the courtroom? Helpin' you out?"

"That's right, Tink," nodded Ben. "You're smart, and you know nonsense when you hear it. You'll be there anyway. If I know you, wild horses couldn't keep you away from Raleigh in September. Will you do it? For me?"

Without so much as a glance at McGee, Tink quickly answered, "Damn right I will! I'll do it!"

Smiling, Ben reached for his wallet, took out a dollar bill, and handed it to Tink. Taking the money, Tink asked, "What's this? What's this for?"

Looking first at McGee, then back to Tink, Ben said, "It's your fee, Tink. Ros can explain. You have just joined the Benjamin Gordon Waterman law firm. You're on the team. You work for me now."

Tink shot him a sly smile and a quick salute. "Yes, sir, *boss man!*" McGee threw up his hands, took another swig of beer, rolled his eyes, and laughed, *"Naarh! Naarh! Naarh!"*

Chapter 34

At Maxwell's invitation, Ben joined the Governor for lunch to bring him up to date on developments in Wilkes. "So, looks like congratulations are in order, Ben. Judge Transou kept the Wade boy here in Raleigh, and you got his trial moved. Good work, son!"

"Thanks, Judge, but there's still a lot of work to do."

Maxwell nodded, said, "So what now, Ben? What's your strategy? For the trial?"

Ben had to be careful not to divulge confidential information from his talk with Virgil Wade. "Well, Judge, it's a tough row to hoe. Virgil spoke at length with Taliaferro and Sheriff Poindexter after his arrest, so I am sure that Redbone will take the stand and tell the worst of it. He evidently admitted that he had been with Rachel Schumann at the river. Redbone will say that an argument broke out and that Virgil confessed to beating her, knocking her out."

Maxwell frowned. "That's bad, Ben. Really bad. What about the knife? What about that?"

Treading cautiously, Ben replied, "Well, if he's honest, Redbone will admit that Virgil denies stabbing the girl. I'll get that out in cross-examination if Taliaferro slides past it on direct."

"So what, Ben? Isn't the beating enough to convict the boy?"

"Well, that's the thing, Judge. Taliaferro has, I think, outsmarted himself again. He didn't charge the boy with that. It's not in the indictment, either. He's put all his eggs in one basket, first-degree murder. The indictment specifies that it was done with Virgil's hunting knife." Ben shrugged. "So the beating is, well, legally irrelevant."

"But the jury will hear all about it, Ben. And they'll likely not agree with you."

"I understand that," admitted Ben. "And the rest of the story Virgil told them, well, Judge, it's just quite frankly hard to believe. But, like I told you before, I've developed some strong evidence that there were *two* people at the river that night. I can't exactly prove who it was, but I'll get it to the jury. Let them think about it."

"Going for reasonable doubt, then?"

Ben nodded. "Unlikely I can get a not-guilty verdict, Judge. But you know it only takes one—"

"To hang the jury. I get it." Maxwell thought about it. "But what does that get you, Ben? Just kicks the can down the road, right? Taliaferro will surely retry the case."

"I hear you, Judge. But, as I've said before, a hung jury buys me, buys Virgil Wade, well, some *time*. I hope to use that time to make Taliaferro see reason. If I can hang the jury once, why, I can do it again. And again, if I have to.

"After the election is over and Taliaferro gets the big job, well, maybe I can make a deal with him, get him to accept a plea on something less than capital murder. Get him to take the death penalty off the table. The longer this goes on, people will get tired of hearing about Virgil Wade. The Schumanns are leaving town, so that lowers the temperature in Wilkes. My way, Taliaferro gets his conviction, his trophy, and can move on to other things."

Maxwell gazed out the window, thinking. "So, then. *One* juror. One. One stubborn juror buys you what you need. The time you need?"

"That's right, Judge. Just one."

Maxwell walked over to a side table, opened a drawer, and took out paper and a pen. He made a note to himself, turned back to Ben. "You've been dealt a lousy hand, Ben. I really hope you can find your stubborn juror, Ben, I really do."

Ben smiled. "Speaking of cards, Judge, I just may have an ace in the hole."

Maxwell's bushy eyebrows raised as he took his seat. "How's that?"

Ben then explained Gabriel von Gruenwald's plan. "Mother of God, Ben!" Maxwell exclaimed. "I never heard of such a thing."

"I agree, me neither. But if it works, well—"

"What if it works *too* well, Ben? What if the Wade boy really did stab the girl?"

"Well," Ben sighed, "That's the big gamble, isn't it? But it's a calculated risk, Judge. Nothing says that I have to use Gruenwald's information at trial. If it all goes sour, well, then I just bottle it up and keep it to myself. *But,* if things go my way, why, then I'm much closer to reaching that one stubborn juror."

"*If* Judge Transou even allows it, Ben."

Ben nodded. "That's true, Judge. For this to work, I will need Transou's cooperation."

"Dick Transou would have to go out on a limb for you, Ben. A mighty long limb." Pausing, Maxwell scribbled another note. "But you know, Dick's a good man, and a short-timer. Like me. He might go for it. Go out in a blaze of glory and let the state supreme court sort it out later."

Ben nodded. Rising, the lunch over, Maxwell set his jaw. "Maybe he just needs a little . . . nudge."

Chapter 35

Ben sat at the desk in his large corner room on the second floor of the comfortable Victorian boarding house on South McDowell Street, just a couple of blocks from the Wake County courthouse. The owner, Myrtle Davis, was a pleasant, cheerful spinster who provided soft linens and tasty meals for her boarders. Importantly, her home had a telephone, which Ben utilized more than his landlady would like.

Tall, open windows brightened the room and caught a cross breeze, ruffling the papers on Ben's desk. The late-summer heat had yet to break, so he was working in his shirtsleeves. In the weeks since the court hearing in Wilkesboro, Ben had kept busy preparing for the trial of *State v. Wade*. Judge Transou had set Tuesday, September 4, for final motions and jury selection, with the trial to begin the next day.

Ben would indeed have a motion, and he was hard at work putting it together. *This will drive Vincent Taliaferro absolutely crazy.* The more he got into it, the more confident Ben became that Judge Transou would see things his way.

On the desk were several thick books Ben had checked out from the municipal library, dense and complex science books. Ben was determined to learn all that he could about Gruenwald's scheme and the revelations he promised it could produce. There were also a couple of modern novels, but they were not for Ben's entertainment.

Ben stayed in telephone contact with Gruenwald in Wilmington. Each time they spoke, Gruenwald insisted that he was making progress and that Ben should be patient. Ben decided Gruenwald needed a little incentive.

At Ben's request, the Wake County clerk of court issued a subpoena to Gruenwald, commanding him to appear in Raleigh on Wednesday, September 5, to give testimony in *State v. Wade*. After being served in Wilmington, Gruenwald telephoned Ben, furious and complaining. "Remember our deal, Mr. Waterman!"

Ben responded firmly. "As you said, the burden is on you in this. The subpoena is just a little reminder from me. An insurance policy, if you will. Now, I suggest that you get busy and take care of your end of things."

Gruenwald, still miffed, grumbled, "I will have an answer for you soon, Mr. Waterman. But, in the meantime, there is something I must have from you, something from the Wade boy." As Gruenwald explained, Ben smiled and said, "No problem. I'll take care of that."

W

Ben had not neglected Virgil Wade. Once a week, all that was permitted by prison rules, Ben faithfully visited Central Prison. Except for the Gruenwald angle, there was little to report. Taliaferro was right. Ben knew just about everything there was to know about the case, and he had gone over it all, honestly and in detail with Virgil. Still, Ben thought that it was important to keep the boy's spirits up.

Virgil was relieved to hear that he would not need to testify. He was most reluctant to repeat his story publicly, still fearful of Taliaferro's promised retaliation. He was also interested in Gruenwald's plan. Ben explained it in the simplest terms he could, but the boy could not quite grasp the essence of it. Nevertheless, he could sense Ben's optimism, and that was enough to cheer him up.

Ben had one final point to clear up. "Virgil, I need you to know something. We don't have to do this Gruenwald thing. There's a risk."

Pulling a face, Virgil asked, "How's that?"

"Well," said Ben, "if we go ahead, we could get the . . . wrong answer. And that . . . well, that would hurt your case, Virgil. So, I need *you* to make the final decision. You need to tell me what you want to do, and I will follow your lead, understand?"

Virgil dropped his head, thought it through. Raising his eyes to Ben's, he smiled. "Naw, sir. No risk. That Mr. Gruenwald, he come through for you, he do what he say he can, how you say he do it, well, I got nothin' to worry about." Nodding, Virgil said in a clear voice, "You go on ahead, Mr. Waterman. Do it."

W

The trial just a week away, Ben was as ready as he could be. Judge Transou had intervened with the chief judge of the Wake County Superior Court, who had graciously offered his courtroom for the trial and had made small workrooms available for Ben and Taliaferro.

Roscoe McGee had reserved rooms for him and Tink Beasley at the elegant Park Hotel, walking distance from Ben's boarding house and the courthouse. "A little splurge for the old lady," McGee explained. "She'll be working hard." They would arrive over the long holiday weekend so Tink could help Ben prepare. At Ben's suggestion, Tink had agreed to purchase a suitable outfit for Virgil. Nothing fancy, just a new white shirt, dark trousers, and black shoes.

Ben completed a draft of his opening statement and organized his witness list. It was a short one. He anticipated likely threads of cross examination of Taliaferro's witnesses and had his outlines ready. He was also prepared, if necessary, to take Gabriel von Gruenwald to the woodshed.

There was a soft knock on his door. Miss Davis stood there, exasperated. "There's *another* telephone call for you. Wilmington again." Turning away, she muttered, "You can take it in the hallway downstairs. *Again.*"

Ben hurried down the stairs, grasped the earpiece, and said, "Ben Waterman."

Through the crackling static, he heard Gruenwald's voice. "Mr. Waterman? This is Gabriel von Gruenwald speaking."

"Yes?"

"It's done, Mr. Waterman. He's coming. He will arrive in Raleigh on Friday afternoon. I will pick him up at Union Station and bring him to you. You will no doubt have much to discuss."

Nodding, Ben replied, "That will be fine, Mr. Gruenwald. Let's meet at six o'clock in the lobby of the Park Hotel. Do you know it?"

"Yes, of course. An excellent restaurant. I will reserve rooms for us there. We can work through the weekend if necessary. Is that acceptable? And are you ready?"

"It is, and I am, Mr. Gruenwald. I look forward to seeing you both on Friday."

The line went dead. Replacing the earpiece, Ben thought, *well, there it is, then. Cutting it mighty close, but it will have to do.*

Chapter 36

The Wake County courthouse was an imposing three-story, late-Victorian red brick structure. The ceremonial courtroom, on the second floor, was configured much like its counterpart in Wilkes, only larger and more ornate. Judge Transou swept into the room at precisely nine o'clock and took his seat behind the bench, ready to begin. Billy Ray Hill called the court into session with his usual cry of "Oyez, oyez, oyez!"

Vincent Taliaferro, Sheriff Poindexter, and Cobey Goins sat at the prosecution table nearer the jury box, to the judge's left. Ben Waterman and Tink Beasley were in place at the defendant's table to his right. The gallery was sparsely populated, mostly newspapermen, including Roscoe McGee, and a few habitual court watchers. Seated in the front row were Gabriel von Gruenwald and beside him a small, balding, nattily dressed man with a pointed grey beard covering his prominent chin.

Judge Transou looked first to Taliaferro, then to Ben. "All right, gentlemen, this morning is reserved for any final motions you may have. I presume you are ready to proceed?"

"Yes, Your Honor," purred Taliaferro, standing, elegantly dressed as always. "The people are ready to go."

As Taliaferro sat, Ben rose. "The defense has but one motion, Judge, and that is a request to physically examine a piece of evidence critical to the prosecution's case." Taliaferro pursed his lips, raised his eyebrows, stared at Ben.

"I'm listening," said Transou.

"Judge, the indictment charges that my client is guilty of murder in the first degree, to be specific, 'defendant Virgil Wade unlawfully, willfully, and feloniously and of malice aforethought did kill and murder one Rachel Schumann, to wit, *by infliction of a fatal knife wound to the victim's heart.*' Mr. Taliaferro will surely display the alleged murder weapon to the jury, Your Honor, much as he did for the newspapermen at his public announcement in Wilkes."

"Water under the bridge, Mr. Waterman. What about the knife?"

"A simple request, Your Honor. The defense would like an opportunity to examine it before the trial begins. Under proper supervision, of course," said Ben.

"For what purpose?" asked the judge.

Turning to the gallery, Ben motioned for the man seated beside Gruenwald to rise. The man stood, cleared his throat, squared his shoulders, and looked at the judge.

"Your Honor, I would like to introduce to the court Mr. Juan Vucetich. Mr. Vucetich is a world-renowned criminal forensic scientist. The defense strongly believes that Mr. Vucetich's examination of the alleged murder weapon will likely reveal information of great benefit to the defense and to the cause of justice. Facts the jury should hear."

Taliaferro rose slowly and scoffed, "What's this, Your Honor? The evidence will indisputably establish the knife, known to be the property of the defendant and marked with his initials, as the murder weapon in this case. Why, it was protruding obscenely from the victim's chest! It's in the autopsy report. It's in the *indictment.*"

"So, if you're so sure of that, what's the harm in having Mr. Waterman take a look at it? Do you have it with you?"

Taken aback, Taliaferro sputtered, "Why, yes, sir. It's here. But—"

"Let's see it," said the judge.

Taliaferro sighed, motioned to Poindexter, who retrieved a small, brown paper sack from a cardboard box beneath the prosecution table. "It's in this bag, Your Honor," Taliaferro explained. "It was placed in there and taped shut after the Wade boy's arrest. I can attest that it has been opened and displayed only the one time, during my . . . announcement. In Wilkes. Mr. Waterman was there, saw the whole thing. I then replaced the weapon in the bag and resealed it. He saw that, too."

"No need to reopen it now, Judge," Ben offered. "I accept that, with the one exception, the knife has been in the prosecutor's possession, under seal. Defense stipulates to the chain of custody. It's actually better this way. For Mr. Taliaferro, and for the defense."

"So, you want your Mr. Vu-ce-tich to examine the knife?" asked the judge. "Today?"

"I realize that we are on the eve of trial, Your Honor, but Mr. Vucetich has traveled a long way to be here. He lives in a foreign country, Judge, and was not available earlier."

There was a low rumble from the small crowd of spectators, now suddenly interested.

"I warn you, counselor, I will brook no delay in commencing the trial."

"Your Honor, Mr. Vucetich's examination will not take long. He has his equipment with him. I am confident he can be finished no later than close of business today. So, there will be no delay." Vucetich nodded his agreement and sat.

Taliaferro, on his feet again. "Your Honor, what sort of game is Mr. Waterman playing here? Does he intend to call this, this *foreigner* as some sort of *expert* witness? I have a right to know."

"Good point," agreed the judge. "What say you to that, Mr. Waterman?"

"I'm not sure, Your Honor. Not until the examination is complete. However, if I do call Mr. Vucetich, I will present Mr. Vucetich's full credentials in matters of criminal forensic science relevant to this case. Your Honor will then determine whether he may offer testimony to the jury. As an expert."

"Your Honor, this is very irregular," objected Taliaferro. "Counsel is trying to have it both ways. If he likes what this *witness* comes up with, then he puts him on the stand. If not, well . . . "

"That's also a fair point, Mr. Waterman. If I grant your motion, let your man examine the knife, and for some reason you don't like what he has to say, why, then, seems to me that Mr. Taliaferro ought to have access to that same information.

"What about this. I grant the motion, permit the examination under court supervision, to be completed not later than three o'clock this afternoon. Mr. Vucetich will prepare a report of his findings and share it with both sides before we finish up today. Then you both can figure out on your own what to do with it. And," the judge leaned forward, pointing a finger, "I will reserve judgment on whether Mr. Vucetich is qualified to testify as an expert, either way. How about that?"

This was not what Ben wanted. He looked back at Vucetich,

who shrugged and nodded again. Ben struggled to decide, but then remembered Virgil Wade's final, clear instructions: *"That Mr. Gruenwald, he come through for you, he do what he say he can, how you say he do it, well, I got nothin' to worry about. You go on ahead, Mr. Waterman. Do it."*

Ben took a deep breath and rolled the dice, hoping that he was not condemning Virgil Wade to the gallows. "Yes, Your Honor," he sighed. "Those conditions are acceptable to the defense, thank you."

"Your Honor," sneered Taliaferro, "This is some kind of trick! We are starting a capital murder trial tomorrow morning, and I have better things to do than to—"

Shaking his head, Judge Transou said, "No, Mr. Taliaferro. Now it's you trying to have things both ways. When it was good for you, back in Wilkes, you couldn't wait to pull out that knife, parade it all around. Only fair that Mr. Waterman gets his shot now, though Lord only knows what will come of it."

Taliaferro scowled, slumped, his eyes on the floor.

"So, here's what we're going to do. Billy Ray, you take the bag from Mr. Taliaferro, and you never let it or the knife out of your sight, not for one second, understood? Escort this Mr. Vucetich to the prosecution work room down the hall and help him set up whatever gear he's got. Watch him like a hawk.

"Now, we're going to have monitors, *observers* if you will, from both sides while Mr. Vucetich does whatever with the knife. Mrs. Beasley, you will represent the defendant. Sheriff Poindexter, you will represent the prosecution. The lawyers may also sit in but must be back in here when we start to pick the jury.

"Now, listen to me. Mr. Vucetich will be permitted to examine the knife in the presence of all of you, and to take notes, whatever. Mr. Vucetich, you are not to damage, tamper with, or alter the knife in any way. Nobody, not a soul except the lawyers, will leave the room until he's finished. None of you will interfere in the slightest with his work.

"And you, Mr. Vucetich," said the judge, pointing his gavel. "Seems like you are not from around here. That right?" Vucetich stood, smiled, nodded. "But you speak good English?"

Vucetich nodded, bowed stiffly. "I am fluent in English, sir. I am, in fact, just completing a professional speaking tour on scientific matters here in the United States. There is no language barrier." He spoke with a slight accent Ben could not place.

"Good," said the judge, impressed. "Can you finish your work by three o'clock?"

"Yes, sir, I think so."

"So, by five o'clock then, when we get through here, I will expect you to complete your written report and deliver copies to both lawyers and to me, is that understood?"

Vucetich bowed again. "Yes, sir. I understand what I am to do. Now," he said quietly, "I should get to work, please."

Ben and Taliaferro remained as the group left the courtroom, Gruenwald and Vucetich carrying a small steamer trunk between them. A knot of clamoring newspapermen moved to follow, but Billy Ray backed them off.

Judge Transou raised his gavel. "If that's all then, we'll stand in recess until one o'clock this afternoon, when we will pick a jury. I'll let Central Prison know to have the defendant over here by then. And I'll have the clerk of court bring in the first twelve folks from the jury pool. I expect this to go quick. I moved this trial for a reason, gentlemen, and I will not tolerate any grandstanding or showboating from either of you. We *will* have a jury today, and we *will* start this trial tomorrow morning at nine o'clock sharp. Now, I expect you both will want to join the party. Court is adjourned."

The *bang* of his gavel resonated throughout the cavernous room as Ben and Taliaferro rushed to leave.

Chapter 37

U nder overcast skies, threatening rain, Ben, Tink, and McGee approached the steps of the courthouse. "You ready, Ben?" asked Tink.

Smiling, Ben answered, "You know me, Tink, I was—"

"Yep, I know, Ben," grinned Tink, playfully punching his shoulder. "You were born ready."

Leather satchel in hand, Ben turned to McGee. "Now, look, Ros. I need you to get over to that photographer's studio. Nothing much will happen here for a while. Get the film to him right away so I can have the pictures when I need them, okay?"

"Got the plates right here, Ben," said McGee, waving a large manila envelope. "I'll be back in a jiffy. Good luck in there."

The courtroom was already half full of spectators, some all the way from Wilkes. "Looks like a big crowd coming," whispered Tink.

Ben scanned the room, pleased to note that none of the expected witnesses was in the gallery. To prevent any tailoring of testimony, Judge Transou had ordered all witnesses to be sequestered in a smaller courtroom down the hall until it was time for them to take the stand.

With that in mind, Ben saw Gabriel von Gruenwald seated in the front row, again flashing his famous smile. Yesterday had been a good day for him. And for Virgil Wade. Ben, for his part, was still trying to absorb the startling revelations provided by Juan Vucetich. Now, for the first time, Ben allowed himself a glimmer of hope, not just for a hung jury, but perhaps for an outright verdict of acquittal. But he would need to play out his hand carefully, skillfully. And he would need a little help from the bench.

As Ben and Tink took their seats at the defense table, there was a commotion as the door beside the jury box opened. Two burly prison guards appeared on either side of Virgil Wade, handcuffed and shackled. A murmur moved through the crowd as the trio made its way haltingly to the defense table. The guards removed the handcuffs but left the leg restraints.

Virgil looked around the majestic room with its impossibly high, decorated ceiling, his blue eyes wide with wonder and panic as the pointing, gawking crowd of strangers settled in. Ben leaned down and placed his hands on Virgil's shoulders. "I know you're scared, Virgil. I understand. Remember, we talked about this. Just pay attention to me and Mrs. Beasley and try not to let it all get to you. You'll be just fine. I'll see to it."

"Thank you, Mr. Waterman," said Virgil weakly. "I'll surely try."

"And you look mighty fine in your new duds," grinned Tink, patting him on the back.

Vincent Taliaferro walked in, dressed to the nines, in intense conversation with Sheriff Poindexter and Crip Goins. Out of Ben's earshot, Taliaferro hissed, "What do you mean, he's not here?"

"Just that, boss. Jakob Schumann ain't here."

"But he's under subpoena! He's my first witness. I need him to tell the jury what a wonderful daughter Rachel was, how her murder has caused such grief and pain to the family."

Pointing to the gallery, Poindexter shook his head. "Gruenwald says he's gone. Took himself and the family back to the Old Country. Somethin' about Hebrew holidays. Says Schumann and his wife just couldn't face the trial. Left Claude Vestal, the foreman, in charge of the tannery."

"Damn!" vented Taliaferro. "Okay, then, we'll start with Mrs. Montgomery. Crip, go tell her to get ready."

Right on time, Judge Transou took his seat while Billy Ray Hill called the courtroom to order. "Bailiff, please bring in the jury."

The jurymen filed in, all men, all White, and took their seats in the jury box. The judge had kept his promise. Jury selection had not taken long. Refusing both attorneys' requests to question the prospective jurors, Judge Transou had conducted the *voir dire* himself. After confirming to his satisfaction that none of the initial twelve men knew either of the attorneys, Virgil Wade, or anything relevant about the case, the judge opined, "Looks like a fine jury to me, gentlemen. Any objections?" he asked, clearly expecting and receiving none.

The twelve men consisted of one doctor, one dentist, an animal husbandry professor from the North Carolina College of Agriculture and Mechanic Arts, a piano teacher, a traveling shoe salesman, three factory workers, two store clerks, a blacksmith, and a state employee working as an assessor of internal revenue for the North Carolina State Treasurer's Office.

Judge Transou perfunctorily welcomed the jury and apologized for taking them away from their daily routines. He reminded them of their sacred duty to do justice with impartiality, instructed them not to discuss the case until the proper time, not to read the papers, and thanked them for their service.

"We are now ready for opening statements in the case of *State v. Wade*. Mr. Taliaferro, for the prosecution."

During his time as a trial judge, Governor Maxwell often reminded Ben that criminal trials were like a locomotive or a steamship—heavy, ponderous, slow to start, but gradually gaining speed and momentum along the way before finally moving, inexorable and unstoppable, toward journey's end. Ben was eager to get there. He could see the pathway clearly before him, but realized he must be patient, take his time, let it all play out.

Taliaferro rose, eyes roving over the jurymen, making eye contact with each one, a solemn expression on his face. "Gentlemen of the jury," he began. As Taliaferro droned on, working himself up, spinning his fingers, Ben noted with satisfaction that he was sticking closely to the script of his earlier public announcement in Wilkes. Nothing new. Amid passionate and repeated pleas for "justice," Taliaferro dropped plenty of epithets: "horrendous crime," "savage," "brutal," "killer," "unspeakable," and, finally, pointing at Virgil, "drunken, merciless monster!" Ben had heard it all before. But the jury had not.

Taliaferro then turned to his evidence, pledging to the jury that they would learn about Virgil's meeting at the fairgrounds with Rachel, his delivery of her horse to the livery stable, his admitted presence at the scene of the crime, his physical assault, and his theft of poor Rachel's horse and tack.

Approaching a crescendo, Taliaferro suddenly lowered his voice to a conspirator's whisper, causing the jury to lean forward. "And worst of all, gentlemen, we have the murder weapon—the defendant's despicable, hideous, and ungodly skinning knife bearing his own damnable, hand-carved initials and covered with Rachel Schumann's life blood!" Louder now. "The wicked weapon he plunged deep into the heart of poor, defenseless Rachel Schumann!" he shouted, making repeated stabbing motions in the air.

"Gentlemen, I have promised the people of Wilkes County, I have promised Jakob Schumann and his grieving family, I have promised them *justice* in this case. Justice for Rachel Schumann! And I call on each one of you to pronounce your awful and final judgment here in this courtroom. And, for the murderer Virgil Wade," pointing him out, Taliaferro thundered, "justice can be found in only one place. At the end of a rope!"

Perspiring, satisfied, Taliaferro snapped a nod to the jury, turned with a flourish, and sat, his hands clasped on the table and his chin held high.

In the uneasy silence that gripped the courtroom, Ben looked over to the jury. *Taliaferro did well,* he thought. *His opening had an impact, landed a punch.*

The judge broke the spell. "Mr. Waterman? For the defense?" Ben did not move, thinking. After a moment, Judge Transou said again, "Mr. Waterman? Your opening statement?"

Slowly Ben rose, smoothed his jacket, shot his cuffs. "Thank you, Your Honor."

Eyes on the jury, with a serious look, Ben walked past the prosecution table to the railing of the jury box, grasped it with both hands, paused. Some of the jurors leaned back, shifted in their seats, waiting. Finally, Ben set his feet, spread his hands, smiled, and began.

"Well, then, gentlemen. I guess that settles it." Curious looks from the jury, mumbles from the spectators.

"Why, if what Mr. Taliaferro says is true, well, we can just wrap this up and all get home in time for lunch. Surely, there is nothing more to be said. Just go ahead, convict Virgil Wade, and be done with it, right?" Suddenly, raising a finger, Ben's smile disappeared. "Ah, *but,*" he cautioned, "*but,* you see, that's not the way we do things. That's not how it works.

"I must concede that Mr. Taliaferro is indeed a skilled prosecutor, a persuasive advocate, but the fact is, nothing Mr. Taliaferro has said to you is worth a plug nickel. That's right, you heard me." Several jurors exchanged glances, confused.

Pointing at his chest, Ben continued, "And, for that matter, same is true for me. You see, we both have our jobs to do, to help you gentlemen reach an understanding of the *truth*. And there is only one way you get there, and that's by listening to the *evidence* presented in this case. The *evidence*, gentlemen. Nothing more, nothing less. And no words coming out of my mouth or Mr. Taliaferro's constitute evidence in this case.

"Mr. Taliaferro has said a lot of bad things about my client, Virgil Wade," said Ben, pointing to Virgil. "He's made a lot of promises to you. And you should hold him to it, make sure he delivers. With *evidence*.

"Mr. Taliaferro's speech sounded convincing, didn't it? Well, that's because he presented just one side of things. *His* side. But the beauty and majesty of the law is that it recognizes that there are always *two* sides to things. *Two* sides. And that oath that each of you took, with your hand on the Bible, that oath *requires* that you keep an open mind. All the way to the end. That is your *duty*.

"Here's what I know, and what you will soon learn. Because the evidence will show it. Here's *my* promise. I will show you that what Mr. Taliaferro has told you is only half of the story. Maybe less than half. There's a lot about this case that Mr. Taliaferro failed to mention, neglected to tell you. I *promise* you that I will fill in the gaps, complete the picture. I want you to remember that and hold *me* to it. And once you have heard both sides, once you have heard all of the evidence, well, then it will be up to you to decide. Keep an open mind. That's *all* I'm asking, but it is *what* I'm asking, because it's what the law requires you to do. It's your duty, and you swore to do it.

"So, here's the deal. Like the judge says, I have the right to make an opening statement, sort of a preview of Virgil Wade's defense, just like Mr. Taliaferro did for the prosecution. But I think it's best to wait. Let's all wait and see what Mr. Taliaferro has to offer. And then let's see what comes out during my cross-examination of his witnesses. Don't accept what Mr. Taliaferro says as Gospel. Keep an open mind."

Turning to the prosecution table, Ben pointed. "And while Mr. Taliaferro lays out his case, I want you to keep your eyes open, too. You see that box underneath the prosecution table? Keep your eyes on that box. Think about what might be in there. You'll see it soon enough. And I promise you this . . . at the end of the day, you will be surprised."

Ben turned and walked slowly back to his seat, his left hand trailing loosely behind and pointing down to the box beneath Taliaferro's table. Ben looked up at the judge. "Your Honor, the defense elects to defer its opening statement until the conclusion of the prosecution's case."

Taliaferro jumped to his feet. "Your Honor, I object! *Defer* his opening statement? Why, Judge, he just made it!"

Judge Transou steepled his fingers, thought about it. "No, Mr. Taliaferro. Although it took him a while to get there, Mr. Waterman certainly has the right to defer, and he is entitled to some leeway in explaining to the jury what he's doing, and why. No, sir. Your objection is overruled."

Taliaferro scowled at Ben and sat.

"Now, gentlemen, if there is nothing else, we will proceed. Mr. Taliaferro, call your first witness."

Chin up, jaw set, Taliaferro declared in a clear voice, "Your Honor, the State calls Mrs. Claire Elise Montgomery."

Chapter 38

Wake County Courthouse, Raleigh, Wednesday, September 5, 1900

Head held high, her carriage erect, Claire Elise cut a striking figure in her elegant, forest green silk dress as she walked into the courtroom, advanced slowly to the witness stand, and took her seat. Ben had seen the gown before.

As she promised, in her proper English accent, to tell the truth, the whole truth, and nothing but the truth, Ben attempted eye contact, but her gaze seemed far away, her green eyes dark and empty. There was nothing in them for Ben.

Taliaferro led Claire Elise through a brisk and straightforward summary of the events of July 4 and 5. She described Rachel Schumann as a lovely, kind young woman and devoted daughter. She remembered speaking to Mr. Schumann at the fairgrounds on July 4, about a birthday celebration later that night for his younger daughter Leah, the preparations for it, and the success of the party.

She also recalled seeing Rachel speaking with Virgil Wade. Rachel, she said, later approached her and explained that she had asked the Wade boy to deliver two horses to the hotel so that she and her friend Eloise could take an early morning ride up the Reddies River to see the Giant Flume. She then described Virgil Wade's role as a part-time stable hand and his delivery of the horses that afternoon.

Her voice trembling, Claire Elise then recounted young Eloise's alarm at finding Rachel missing the next morning, the frantic search for the girl, the call to Sheriff Poindexter, his telephone call to Schumann

Village, the organization of the search party, and, finally, the terrible news of Rachel's murder.

As Claire Elise wiped away tears with a lace handkerchief, Taliaferro somberly concluded, "Thank you, Mrs. Montgomery, I know these are difficult memories for you, and I appreciate your willingness to testify." Turning to Ben, he declared, "Your witness, counselor."

Ben rose, maintained a polite distance, and faced the witness. Claire Elise met his gaze, her previously vacant eyes now filled with defiance and malice. Ben winced inwardly, but pressed on, gently at first.

"Mrs. Montgomery, in your direct testimony, you mentioned someone named Eloise. You said she was present at the hotel on the evening of July 4, and the morning of July 5. Who is that, please?"

Claire Elise nodded, answered formally. "That would be Rachel's friend, Eloise Vestal, daughter of the tannery foreman, Mr. Claude Vestal. The Schumanns and the Vestals are neighbors in Schumann Village. Rachel and Eloise were planning to take a ride the next morning, as I testified."

"And you also testified that you first learned from Eloise that Rachel was missing on the morning of July 5, correct?"

"That's right. She came downstairs, concerned that Rachel was missing, not in their room."

"What exactly did she tell you, Mrs. Montgomery?"

"Objection! Hearsay," asserted Taliaferro, on his feet.

Ben started to respond, but the judge waved him away. "Nope, sorry. Mr. Waterman patiently allowed you to go way down that road in your direct. Good for the goose, good for the gander. I'll allow it. Answer the question, Mrs. Montgomery."

"Well," Claire Elise began nervously, "she was . . . worried. She and Rachel were sharing a room, you see, and sometime during the night Eloise was awakened by movement in the room. She saw Rachel, dressed in her riding clothes, moving toward the door. Eloise asked her what she was doing, and Rachel said that she had trouble sleeping, heard noises down the hall, and thought she should check on the other girls."

"Go on, please."

"Eloise then said that she asked Rachel why she was already dressed. Rachel replied that she was also going to check on the horses, in the stable, to make sure that the Wade boy had fed and watered them."

"What next?"

"Well, Eloise said she was sleepy, so she went back to bed. She said that Rachel wrapped herself in a quilt she had brought with her, and then she left. That's it."

"So, then," said Ben, "The last time Eloise saw Rachel, she was fully dressed in riding clothes in the middle of the night, wrapped in a quilt, on one of the hottest nights of the summer? Is that right?"

Her jaw set firmly, Claire Elise nodded. "That's what I said, Mr. Waterman."

"Did you hear her leave?"

"Excuse me?"

"Rachel Schumann. In the middle of the night. Coming down the stairs. Leaving the hotel. Opening and locking the door behind her. Surely you heard something?"

Her eyes fixed on Ben, Claire Elise declared, "I did not. My room is at the back of the hotel, behind the kitchen."

"Now, if Sheriff Poindexter's theory is to be believed, Virgil Wade abducted Rachel Schumann in the livery stable, but then somehow took the time to use her key to enter the hotel, steal a bottle of whiskey and two shot glasses, and lock the door behind him, all before riding off to the river. All without a single scream, no cry for help from Rachel? And you say you heard none of that going on?"

Claire Elise nodded firmly. "I heard nothing. I was asleep in my room."

Looking at the jury, Ben then asked, "What about the bell?"

"I beg your pardon?"

"I was recently a guest in your hotel, Mrs. Montgomery. There is a bell attached to the entrance door. It rings every time the door opens or closes. So that you or your housekeeper will know when someone comes in or leaves. Isn't that right?"

Claire Elise paused, answered. "There is a bell."

"So, your testimony, under oath I remind you, is that you slept through the whole thing? By my count, the bell had to ring at least three times, in the middle of the night. Once when Rachel left, and then again when Virgil supposedly entered to steal the whiskey, and then again when he closed and locked the door behind him. You heard nothing?"

"Objection," said Taliaferro wearily. "Asked and answered."

"Yes," agreed Judge Transou. "Move on, please."

Ben paused, glanced at the jury, pleased that two or three were taking notes. *Here we go,* he thought, nodding to Tink. Reaching down to a small suitcase beneath the defense table, Tink took out a tall, green wine bottle with a fancy white label. Holding it carefully by the bottom punt, like a wine steward, she handed the bottle to Ben.

Ben took the bottle, holding it carefully, and raised it so that the label was facing the witness box. "Mrs. Montgomery, please take a look at this wine bottle. Do you recognize it?"

Puzzled, Taliaferro rose. "Objection, Your Honor. Relevance? Also, outside the scope of direct examination."

"He's got a point, counselor," said the judge. "What's this all about?"

"Your Honor, if you will permit me a little leeway here, the relevance will become clear to the court and the jury soon enough."

"It better, Mr. Waterman. I'll hold you to that. The witness will answer the question."

Unsure where Ben was headed, Claire Elise blanched. "I have never seen that bottle before."

"No?" asked Ben patiently. "You do not remember serving me wine from this bottle during my stay in the Schumann Hotel back in July?"

Claire Elise did not respond.

Approaching the witness box, Ben continued. "Please take a closer look, Mrs. Montgomery. Here," he offered, holding the bottle out to her. "Take it. Please look carefully before you answer."

Looking up at the Judge, Claire Elise pleaded, "Must I do this, Judge? I see no point."

Ben and Taliaferro were both on their feet, but Judge Transou fixed them with a stern look. "I see no harm in it, Mr. Taliaferro. The witness will take the bottle, examine it, and answer defense counsel's question."

Ben extended his right hand, and Claire Elise grasped the bottle by the neck in her left. She gave the label a cursory look, and then fixed her vivid green eyes on Ben as she handed the bottle back to him. "I do now recall serving you wine during your stay. It could have come from this bottle. Or not. Frankly, I do not remember. Red wine is readily available in Wilkesboro, as you well know."

"Yes, Mrs. Montgomery, true enough. But this bottle, well, this is special, isn't it? The label suggests it's a rare wine, a Malbec red wine, from Argentina, correct?"

Claire Elise squirmed. "Yes."

"And didn't you tell me that bottles of this particular wine had been imported by a friend of yours, a friend from Argentina who gave it to you so it would be available during his regular visits to your hotel? A special, rare wine from Argentina, not sold anywhere else in Wilkes?"

"And what of it?" snapped Claire Elise. "What does this have to do with anything?"

Taliaferro rose, "Exactly the point, Your Honor. I renew my objection."

Staring intensely into Claire Elise's eyes, Ben said simply, reaching for the bottle, "No further questions of this witness, Your Honor."

"Then the witness is excused."

Claire Elise sat silent, still, her eyes unblinking, meeting and holding Ben's.

"Mrs. Montgomery," repeated Judge Transou, "You may step down."

At last Claire Elise broke eye contact. She rose, walked through the spectators with as much poise and dignity as she could muster, and disappeared through the swinging doors at the rear of the courtroom.

As Ben watched her leave, he recalled Shakespeare. *"Beware of jealously, my lord! It's a green-eyed monster that makes fun of the victims it devours."*

W

"Call your next witness, Mr. Taliaferro," instructed Judge Transou.

"The State calls Wilkes County Sheriff Jimmy Poindexter, Your Honor."

Poindexter strode through the gallery into the courtroom, hatless, a line across his brow showing pale skin above where his Stetson normally rested.

Poindexter's testimony tracked Taliaferro's opening statement. He told the jury about Mrs. Montgomery's distraught telephone call on the morning of July 5, reporting Rachel's disappearance and his call to Schumann Village confirming Rachel had not returned home during the night. He testified he had taken Rachel's pillowcase from Mrs. Montgomery, organized a search party with dogs, and began looking for the missing girl.

Poindexter described in gruesome detail the scene beneath the iron bridge where Rachel's body had been found, Virgil Wade's skinning knife in her chest. One of the men recognized it from the tannery. He then recounted how Deputy Sheriff Cobey Goins and other townsmen had ridden off with the dogs, tracking Virgil Wade. They found him, with Rachel's horse, hiding out at the old Cleveland cabin near Purlear.

Reaching down into the cardboard box, Taliaferro withdrew a large manila folder, opened it, and spread several glossy photographs on the prosecution table. "Now, Sheriff, about the crime scene . . . "

Alarmed, realizing what was about to happen, Ben jumped up. "Your Honor! Sidebar, please."

Tilting his head, Judge Transou motioned the lawyers to the bench. "Judge," Ben whispered so the jury could not hear. "I believe that it is Mr. Taliaferro's intention to offer into evidence photographs of the crime scene. Photographs that would be highly prejudicial to the defense if submitted to the jury. I strenuously object!"

"That right, Mr. Taliaferro?"

"Exactly right, Your Honor," nodded Taliaferro. "That is my plan."

Looking up at the clock on the balcony railing in the back of the courtroom, Judge Transou then announced, "Ladies and gentlemen, members of the jury, the lawyers and I have some housekeeping business to attend to. This is a good time for a break, so court will now stand in recess for fifteen minutes. Bailiff, please escort the jury to the jury room, and," pointing at the jurymen, "I remind you gentlemen not to discuss the case among yourselves." He rapped his gavel and said to the lawyers, "In my chambers. Now."

W

Seated behind his office desk, Judge Transou reviewed the crime scene photographs with undisguised disgust. "Damn, fellas! These are terrible, just awful. What do you want to do with them, Mr. Taliaferro?"

"I intend to introduce them into evidence, Your Honor. A heinous, despicable crime has been committed, and the jury has every right to see with their own eyes the consequences of the defendant's depravity."

Ben shook his head, protesting. "Judge, defense stipulates that Rachel Schumann was the victim of a vicious, violent attack that took her life. That is not in dispute. But these photographs, they will do nothing but inflame the jury, Judge, rile them up, poison their minds, before they have even heard the prosecution's full case or anything from the defense! I implore Your Honor to exclude this evidence."

Judge Transou again sifted through the pictures, separating them on his desktop. "Sorry, Mr. Waterman, but I'm with Taliaferro on this one. This is a death penalty case, and the prosecution must convince the jury not only that your client is guilty, but that he deserves to hang. That's a high bar, and these photographs are relevant evidence."

"But—"

The judge held up a hand. "Now, having said that, I see no need for overkill. Mr. Taliaferro, I will allow you to submit one, *and just one,* of these pictures. And you, Mr. Waterman, get to pick which one it'll be. That seems fair. I know this is tough medicine, Mr. Waterman, but there it is. Understood?"

Defeated, but truthfully not surprised, Ben nodded.

"So, then, which one will it be?"

Ben studied the pictures, finally put his finger on what he believed was the least appalling among the array of damning images.

"All right, then," said the judge. "Mr. Taliaferro, there will be no release of any of these pictures to the public or the press. I want to be clear about that. You may introduce this single photograph and circulate it to the jury. Once they have all had a chance to look it over, you'll then put it away. I don't want to see it again, and neither will the jury. You can rant and rave about it in your closing, but the jury gets just the one look. Clear?"

"Yes, Your Honor," said Taliaferro. "There is one more thing. We might as well get it out of the way now."

"What are you talking about?" sighed Judge Transou.

"Well, Dr. Burleson, the coroner, he will be my next witness after Poindexter. And, you see, there are also photographs of the autopsy."

"The autopsy?" gasped Judge Transou. "You took pictures of that girl's *naked dead body?* And you want to show these to the jury, too?"

"Well, Judge, the photographs are . . . well, evidence, and—"

"Let me see them," snapped the judge. Taliaferro took out another manila folder, spread new photographs on the desk, and waited.

"Good God!" shouted Judge Transou, removing his spectacles. "I can't believe you would even consider admitting these . . . these *obscenities* into evidence! Show them to twelve upstanding men on the jury, desecrate the memory of that poor young woman! For God's sake, Taliaferro, have you lost all sense of decency?"

Suddenly the judge swept up all the photographs save one into his hands. Ripping them into small pieces, he snarled, "There! There is your ruling, Mr. Taliaferro. One photograph. That's it!" Jabbing a finger at Taliaferro, he added, "And if I hear or read one word about this in the press, you'll be sorry. Don't cross me!" he exclaimed, wagging a finger in Taliaferro's face.

Ben looked on in amazement. Taliaferro, chastened, hung his head. Judge Transou, breathing hard, sat silent for a good long while. "All right, then," he declared. "Let's get back in there. The jury's waiting."

W

Back in open court, the jury in place, Taliaferro skillfully and effectively bracketed Poindexter's remaining direct testimony between two evidentiary bombshells.

The first was the crime scene photograph. As the jurors, one by one, examined People's Exhibit 1, Ben could see their faces cloud first with horror and revulsion and then anger as they shifted their eyes to Virgil Wade.

The second, People's Exhibit 2, was Virgil Wade's blood smeared skinning knife. Taliaferro repeated his performance in Wilkes, strutting and holding it high above his head for the jurors, spectators, and newspapermen to see.

In between, Poindexter recounted how he and Taliaferro had questioned Virgil Wade after his arrest and that the boy admitted he was at the river with Rachel, that the knife was his. That Rachel had said something that angered him, and that he had struck her.

This revelation evoked uneasy chatter from the spectators. There was nothing Ben could do but sit and take it. Virgil began to tremble, on the verge of tears. Tink touched his arm to calm him.

As Taliaferro triumphantly lowered the knife and replaced it in its paper sack, he declared, "No further questions, Your Honor."

Ben rose, retrieved Exhibit 1 from Taliaferro's desk, and holding it out to the witness, began his questioning. "So, this photograph. Do you agree, Sheriff Poindexter, that it accurately captures the crime scene?"

"Yessir," drawled Poindexter, "It sure does."

"Well, let's talk about that. Let's discuss some things that Mr. Taliaferro didn't ask you about." Pointing to the photograph, Ben asked, "Other than the victim's body, what else do you see there?"

"Say what?" asked Poindexter.

"Her body is lying on a quilt, correct? A fancy quilt neatly spread out. Sort of like a . . . picnic?"

"Well, I don't know about that, but, yes, she was on a quilt."

"And do you see a lantern there? Overturned, on the quilt?"

"Yeah, I see it."

"And do you also see a whiskey bottle? Looks like it's about half empty, right?"

"If you say so."

This drew a sharp look from Ben. "And beside the bottle, what else do you see there? Take your time."

Poindexter squinted at the photo. "Looks like a couple of little glasses."

"Shot glasses, right?"

Poindexter shrugged.

"How many shot glasses, Sheriff?"

"Well, looks like . . . two."

"So, *two* shot glasses," said Ben.

"Objection," responded Taliaferro. "Asked and answered."

Ben moved on. "Anything else? What about the bag?"

Poindexter took another look. "Well, yes, there's a sack, with handles. I see that."

"Now, while you were waiting for the wagon to take the victim to the coroner's office, did you search the body? For evidence?"

Poindexter nodded. "I did."

"So, you saw a necklace around Rachel Schumann's neck, right? An expensive gold necklace with a jeweled pendant hanging from it? You can see it right there, in the picture."

Shifting in his seat, Poindexter answered, "There was a necklace, yes."

"And did you check her pockets? The pockets of her riding britches?"

"Well, yes, I checked."

"And what did you find?"

"There was folding money in one of her pockets. Twenty dollars or so, as I recollect."

"Anything else?"

"Well, there was a key. On a fob. Said Schumann Hotel on it."

"In your testimony on direct, Sheriff, you told the jury that, in your opinion as an experienced lawman, you figure that Rachel Schumann went to the livery stable in the middle of the night to check on her horse and was surprised to find Virgil Wade there. That the defendant saw an opportunity, attacked and overcame the victim, lifted her up onto her horse, climbed up himself, and rode off to the river to have his way with her . . . isn't that what you said?"

"Yep. That's the way I see it."

"So, let me get this straight," said Ben, pointing at Virgil. "Rachel Schumann, fully dressed in the middle of the night, walks out of the hotel, locks the front door behind her with her key, proceeds to the livery stable, surprises Virgil Wade, a small, skinny boy of sixteen years, maybe a hundred pounds dripping wet, who then decides on the spur of the moment to kidnap Rachel Schumann and haul her off to the Yadkin River bridge.

"Then he saddles up her horse, wraps her in a quilt, and, oh, stops along the way to grab a lantern, enters the hotel through a locked door to steal a bottle of whiskey and two shot glasses, puts all of that in a sack, locks the door behind him, lifts a terrified, fully grown young woman up onto her horse, mounts up himself, and rides off. All this without making a sound? No screams from Rachel Schumann? No cries for help? No bell ringing? No racket in the hotel to wake Mrs. Montgomery? That what you're saying?"

Poindexter thought about it, nodded. "That's about the size of it."

"Listen to yourself talking, Sheriff! A *lantern?* Why a lantern? It was almost a full moon. Wouldn't a lantern draw attention down at the river? Why risk being spotted? And the quilt? In the midst of this alleged violent attack, Virgil Wade turns Rachel loose, just so he can lay a quilt on the ground, all nice and tidy? No screams for help from the girl? No effort to run away?"

"Nothing that boy says or does makes any sense to me, Mr. Waterman," said Poindexter, heat in his voice. "He *confessed,* for God's sake!"

"And the necklace, the *money,*" continued Ben, ignoring the remark. "Poor colored boy like Virgil Wade, he's going to leave all that behind? After he's already *murdered* the girl? Are you serious, Sheriff?"

"Objection!" shouted Taliaferro. "Argumentative."

"Sustained," declared Judge Transou, "Move on."

Ben changed the subject. "Let's talk about your conversation with Virgil, Sheriff. You and Mr. Taliaferro, at the jail, after you captured him. Did Mr. Taliaferro threaten to turn Virgil loose, turn him out to the Red Shirts, to the Klan, if he didn't cooperate? Didn't answer your questions? Didn't *admit* to murdering Rachel Schumann?"

Poindexter looked to Taliaferro, muttered, "He might'a said somethin' like that."

"Excuse me, Sheriff. I don't think the jury could hear you."

"I said yes! Yes. We were just trying to get the truth out of the boy."

"Ah, yes, the truth. From the boy. So, Sheriff, what about the knife? Did you ask him about that? Did he admit to knifing the victim to death? What did he say?"

Poindexter shook his head, scowled. "Just a bunch of lies. He claimed he never touched his knife, never stabbed that girl. Said he passed out, woke up to find her layin' there, dead, his knife in her chest! Pure unadulterated bull crap, Your Honor. I paid him no mind," countered Poindexter, looking at the jury, "and you gentlemen shouldn't neither!"

"Objection! Move to strike," shouted Ben.

"Sustained!" snapped the judge, frowning. "The jury will disregard Sheriff Poindexter's intemperate outburst."

Ben looked at his notes, glanced at Tink, who gave him a tight smile. *That's enough,* he thought. *Better stop here.* Throwing up his hands, Ben declared, "I'm done, Your Honor. I'm through with this . . . witness."

Taliaferro made a desultory effort to repair any damage from Ben's cross-examination, but nothing much changed. In truth, and overall, Poindexter's testimony had been devastating to the defense, and Taliaferro knew it. Ben knew it, too.

W

When Judge Transou declared the midday break, guards arrived to take Virgil to the holding cell in the basement. As they replaced the handcuffs, Ben looked into Virgil's eyes. "That was the worst of it, Virgil. We'll get through this. Remember what I told you. You'll see. Stay strong."

As Virgil was led away, Tink glanced around the mostly empty courtroom. "Well, that was somethin', Ben. You set up Claire Elise, all right. And you did good takin' Redbone down a notch or two, but still."

"I did what I could, Tink, but the jury now knows that Virgil admitted being at the river, with Rachel. Admitted striking her. Admitted the knife is his. Admitted stealing her horse and fleeing the scene. We've got our work cut out for us, I'm afraid."

"Confidence, my man!" grinned Tink. "Buck up! The best is yet to come, boss. You said so yourself." She paused, looked around, whispered, "By the way, somethin' else is bothering me."

Ben gave her a quizzical look.

"Well, like you told me, I've been keepin' an eye on those jurymen. One of 'em, that guy on the end of the back row, the one with the moustache? You know, the government fella, works in the treasurer's office?"

"What about him?"

"Well, I don't like his look. Somethin' makes me think he's not buyin' what you're sellin'. He's paying real close attention, but not taking any notes. He just sits there, sorta creepy, with a little smirk on his face, kinda like he's, you know, enjoying all this."

Ben made a mental note, just as Roscoe McGee walked up. "Good job, Ben, given the cards you were dealt. Look, I got the plates to the studio. The guy says he can have the pictures ready this afternoon. I paid him and told him to deliver them to me, here at the courthouse. That all right?"

"Perfect, Ros. Now let's go get something to eat."

Dr. Noah Burleson sat comfortably in the witness box. He had done this many times before. His gentle eyes and ready smile projected solid credibility. Responding to Taliaferro, Burleson adjusted his spectacles, cleared his throat, and with dispassionate, clinical precision, told the jury about his postmortem examination of the body of Rachel Schumann.

He began with the large, dark bruise on the side of her face, between her left eye and left ear. He opined that this was the result of a heavy blow from a closed fist. He then moved on to the knife wounds, ten slashing, painful, but nonfatal cuts on the victim's chest and abdomen, indicating rage and fury. Finally, he described what he concluded was the fatal wound, allegedly inflicted by the knife that Taliaferro again eagerly displayed. The knife, he testified, was buried to the hilt in Rachel's chest, straight through the heart, so deep that its point protruded clear through the skin on her back.

Taliaferro then produced a copy of Burleson's official autopsy report, introduced as People's Exhibit 3. Cause of death: knife wound penetrating the heart. There was no mention of photographs. Taliaferro finished up and offered the witness for cross examination.

There were many questions Ben could have asked about the autopsy. But there was no point. Gruenwald was in the clear, at least for Rachel's murder. Vucetich confirmed it, as Gruenwald predicted. So, Ben went with what he had. "Dr. Burleson, you mentioned a large bruise on the side of the victim's head. On the *left* side of the face, is that correct?"

"Yes, that's correct, counselor. It appeared to be a heavy blow, consistent with a closed fist."

"And the fact that the bruising was on the *left* side of the victim's face, wouldn't that confirm, in your professional opinion, that the blow came from a *right*-handed assailant?"

Burleson hesitated. "Well, confirm is a strong word, Mr. Waterman, but I won't quibble with you. The evidence would, in my opinion, strongly *suggest* that the blow came from the attacker's right hand."

"Now, I note in your report, Dr. Burleson, that you offer no opinion as to which hand inflicted the knife wound through the victim's heart."

Confused, wary, Burleson said, "I'm sorry. I don't understand."

As hard as he fought to exclude the autopsy photographs, Ben now desperately wished he could show them to Burleson. "Work with me, Dr. Burleson. Think back on it. Imagine the victim's body on your examination table, lying on her back. Now, facing the body, focusing on the handle of the knife, buried to the hilt, as you testified, was it sticking straight up? Or was it leaning, in one direction or the other?"

Burleson closed his eyes, considered it. Ben took a deep breath, held it. "No. No, it was not straight. Now that you mention it, it was, it was in fact leaning, leaning to one side, pretty sharply as a matter of fact."

"So, now, again facing the body, standing at the feet, in which direction was the handle leaning, Doctor?"

Realizing where Ben was headed, Burleson hesitated again. Slowly he answered, "Well, to be honest, it was leaning . . . sharply as I said . . . leaning to the left. To the left side of the body as I would face it."

"And again, in your professional opinion, Doctor Burleson, wouldn't that strongly *suggest* that what you describe as the fatal knife wound, an act which the State claims was committed by the defendant, wouldn't that mean the wound was inflicted by a *left*-handed person? A left-handed person strong enough, furious enough to brutally push that knife clean through the victim's body? Up to the hilt?"

Burleson sat for a moment. "Yes, counselor, I take your point. Yes. The evidence of the leaning knife would be consistent with a strike from the left side, from a left-handed perpetrator, as you say."

"And, so, taking things to their logical conclusion, Doctor Burleson, wouldn't that further suggest that there were *two* people with Rachel Schumann that night? *Two* attackers? One right-handed, inflicting a blow to the head? The other, a left-handed person guilty of the knife wound?"

Grumbling and stirring erupted in the courtroom as the implications of Ben's examination began to sink in. As Judge Transou banged his gavel for order, Taliaferro was on his feet. "Objection! Calls for speculation, Your Honor!"

"I instruct the witness not to answer that question. Mr. Taliaferro's objection is sustained."

Too late. Ben smiled inwardly, felt the tension in his body melt away.

With a tight smile, he looked to the jury. "No more questions, Your Honor."

For several seconds, Taliaferro sat at his table, fuming, thinking, his arms crossed over his chest, legs crossed at his ankles. Finally, he rose. "Your Honor, I request that the defendant be instructed to stand. To stand and to hold his hands in the air."

Ben stood to object, but the judge shrugged and spread his hands in a helpless gesture. "The defendant will rise and do as instructed."

Virgil, eyes wide, not comprehending, grabbed Ben's arm in panic. "It's all right, Virgil. Just do as he says." Virgil obediently rose, the clanking leg shackles making him unsteady on his feet. Slowly, he raised both hands in the air, as if surrendering.

"Now, Doctor Burleson," Taliaferro began, his voice dripping sarcasm, "Take a look at the defendant. How many hands do you see?"

Staring at the helpless Virgil Wade, Burleson slowly answered, "Why, two of course."

Raising his own hands, wiggling them around, Taliaferro addressed the judge. "Your Honor, please instruct the defendant to move his hands like this, both of them."

Judge Transou pointed his gavel at Virgil. "Do it, sir. Do like he says." Ben sighed, dropped his head, as Virgil complied.

"Take a good look, Doctor. See any problem? *Both* hands look in good working order to you? In your *professional* opinion? Left hand, right hand?"

Unaccustomed to disrespect from lawyers and irritated by Taliaferro's gamesmanship, Burleson replied curtly, "The defendant appears to suffer no impediment in the use of his hands."

Chuckles ran through the courtroom and in the jury box as Noah Burleson was excused. Taliaferro sat grinning. Judge Transou stared at Taliaferro for a long minute. "Do you have additional witnesses, Mr. Taliaferro? It's getting late."

"Just one, Your Honor." He paused a beat. "The State calls the defendant, Virgil Wade!"

Astonished, Judge Transou's jaw dropped as he stared at Taliaferro, not believing what he had just heard. The jurymen, confused, silently sought clarification from one another with their eyes and hands. "Your Honor!" shouted Ben, struggling to be heard over the clamor from the gallery. "This is outrageous! Mr. Taliaferro knows better!"

Rattled, the judge admonished, "What do you think you're doing, Mr. Taliaferro? The jury is right here!"

Smiling innocently, Taliaferro said, "Your Honor, I am, of course, aware that the defendant cannot be compelled to testify against himself. That is his right. But it is his obligation to assert the privilege. If he doesn't want to talk, why then, the jury needs to hear him say it. Who knows, he might decide to open up?"

Ben, incensed at this flagrant breach of professional ethics and courtroom protocol, rose to argue, but the judge's look held him back. Gripping the gavel tightly in his rough, raw-boned hand like an ax handle, Judge Transou said through gritted teeth, "Mr. Taliaferro, I warn you: you are right on the edge. The very edge." Turning to Ben, the judge shook his head in exasperation. "Mr. Waterman, I know what you're thinking, and I don't disagree. But," pointing at the jury, "now that the cat is out of the bag, take a minute. Write something up, and then get your client up here so we can get this thing over and done."

Smoldering, Ben turned to Virgil, whispered, "Virgil, can you read?" The boy nodded. Ben quickly scribbled something on his notepad, showed it to Virgil, who nodded again. Ben took Virgil by the hand and led him awkwardly to the witness box, the chains rattling every step. The jury paid close attention, as Taliaferro intended.

Virgil, so small, sat low and deep in the witness chair as Billy Ray Hill administered the oath, Ben standing close by. "I do," the boy croaked.

Under Ben's watchful eye, Taliaferro asked Virgil for his name and place of residence. Ben nodded. "My name is Virgil Wade, and I live in Wilkesboro. In Cairo."

Turning to the jurymen, his eyes boring in, Taliaferro demanded in a loud voice, "Virgil Wade! Did you murder Rachel Schumann with your skinning knife under the iron bridge in Wilkes County in the early morning hours of Thursday, July 5 of this year?"

As Judge Transou banged for order, Ben gestured to the piece of paper in Virgil's hand. In a halting voice, Virgil looked down and read aloud the words written for him. "I res—pect—ful—ly decline to answer under rights guar—an—teed by the consti—tutions of the United States of America and the State of North Carolina."

A broad, satisfied smile crossed Taliaferro's face. His eyes still fixed on the jury, not the boy, Taliaferro declared, "Your Honor, the People rest."

Chapter 39

Ben and Tink sat at the defense table with Virgil, waiting for Judge Transou. Roscoe McGee was in the gallery, notebook in hand. Gabriel von Gruenwald sat in the front row, the heel of his right foot nervously tapping the floor. Juan Vucetich waited in the spare courtroom down the hall. Glancing over his shoulder, Ben noticed that, her testimony concluded, Claire Elise Montgomery had joined the spectators.

Taliaferro strutted in and took his seat, Sheriff Poindexter and Deputy Goins following. After Taliaferro's bold and clumsy, but dramatic and impactful, effort to pressure testimony from Virgil Wade, Judge Transou had wrapped things up for the day. *So, the jury had all night to think about it,* worried Ben.

Ben, Tink, McGee, Gruenwald, and Juan Vucetich had enjoyed a working dinner the night before in the sumptuous dining room of the Park Hotel. Still in high spirits, Gruenwald picked up the tab. The group reviewed Vucetich's upcoming testimony and Taliaferro's expected pushback. Ben also had a new task for Vucetich, who confirmed he could take care of it after dinner. McGee had the photographs from the studio. Ben was satisfied, ready.

Billy Ray Hill commanded everybody to rise. Judge Transou sat and motioned for Ben to proceed. Ben faced the jury.

"Good morning, gentlemen," he began. "I trust you all had a restful night." Several nodding heads, a couple of tight smiles. "I have good news. I only have two witnesses, and unless I'm mistaken, we should be able to get this trial over with today, so you can begin your deliberations this afternoon." More nods and smiles, enthusiastic this time.

"Now, you remember yesterday morning I told you that I would defer, postpone, my opening statement until Mr. Taliaferro got through presenting his case. I warned you that Mr. Taliaferro would not shoot straight with you, that he would leave out a lot of things that he didn't want you to know. And that's just what he did. But I promised you that I would fill in the gaps, bring out all the facts that Mr. Taliaferro tried to hide from you."

"Objection!" cried Taliaferro. "This is not proper argument!"

"Overruled," snapped Judge Transou. "Do not interrupt Mr. Waterman again."

Ben took a breath, resumed. "I promised that I would work hard to help you get to the *truth* in this case. 'The whole truth, and nothing but the truth.' A wise judge once told me that no substitute has ever been found for cross-examination as a means of separating truth from falsehood. And he was right."

Ben took the jury through his examination of Sheriff Poindexter. The quilt, the lantern, the whiskey bottle and shot glasses, the necklace, the cash money and hotel key in Rachel's pockets, no cries for help. He scoffed at Virgil Wade's *confession* as coerced under threat of lynching.

Spreading his hands, shaking his head, Ben said, "The truth, gentlemen, is that it doesn't add up. The prosecution's case doesn't make sense. It just doesn't. And now you can see that." Ben then reviewed his examination of Noah Burleson. He stressed the left-hand, right-hand testimony, *two* people with Rachel that night.

Ben then turned to Virgil, motioned for him to stand. "Look at the boy, gentlemen. Because there, standing before you, is an *innocent man*. Innocent until proven guilty. A foundational principle of our jurisprudence. Unless and until each and every one of you decides otherwise, an innocent man. Keep that in mind."

Making eye contact with each juror, Ben explained, "You see, Virgil Wade is under no obligation to prove anything to you. He doesn't have to *prove* his innocence. It's the *State's* burden to prove guilt, guilt beyond a reasonable doubt, a judgment that requires a unanimous verdict from you. The State's burden is a heavy, heavy one."

Ben threw up his hands. "Why, we could just quit right now. Stand down. We have already shown the State's case is as full of holes as Swiss cheese. Leaks like a sieve." Lifting a finger, his voice rising, Ben said, "But we won't do that. Instead, the defense will, in fact, *prove* to you, beyond any doubt, that Virgil Wade did not commit the crime he is accused of. That he did *not* use his knife to take the life of Rachel Schumann. We'll help you get to the right decision. And we will do it with *evidence*. Just wait.

"A boy's life is at stake here, gentlemen. Keep an open mind. An open heart. Be willing, be ready, to accept the truth." Looking up to the balcony, Ben announced, "The defense calls Reverend Napoleon Bondurant."

W

It took some time for Bondurant to make his way down from the balcony where Black spectators were required to sit. Dressed in his Sunday preaching suit, Bondurant strode purposefully through the courtroom, his head held high, a book in his hand. As Billy Ray Hill held out a Bible, Bondurant shook his head, held his own book in his left hand, raised his right, and smiled. "Brought my own," he offered.

Billy Ray blinked, continued, "Do you solemnly swear . . . "

"Affirm," said Bondurant, coolly.

"What?" asked Billy Ray, confused.

"*Affirm*, sir. I do not swear. But I do indeed solemnly affirm that I will tell the truth, the whole truth, and nothing but the truth, so help me God." That said, he took his seat.

Responding to Ben's questions, Bondurant confirmed he was pastor of Mount Zion AME Church in the Cairo district of Wilkesboro, and that Virgil Wade and his mother were both committed Christians and respected members of his congregation. He described Virgil as a smart, quiet, shy, industrious, and well-behaved boy who attended church faithfully. No, he had never been in any trouble to Bondurant's knowledge, and his arrest had come as a shock to the entire church. No, he could not imagine anyone less likely to have committed such a terrible crime.

Taliaferro slowly rose. "This all makes for a good bedtime story, Judge, but what does it have to do with Rachel Schumann? We are, after all, in the middle of a *murder* trial here."

"Mr. Waterman is certainly entitled to call a character witness on defendant's behalf, Mr. Taliaferro. You know that. But, Mr. Waterman, we all get the picture. Please move on now."

Ben nodded to Tink, who reached down and opened the small suitcase. She withdrew two medium-sized picture frames, handling them carefully by the foldable stands on the back, and set them on the table, arranging them so as to be visible to Bondurant, the judge, Taliaferro, and the jury. The frames were finished in glossy black lacquer, and clear glass covered the two photographs.

"Do you recognize these photographs, Reverend Bondurant," asked Ben.

"I surely do, Mr. Waterman. One is a picture of our church in Cairo, and the one on the right is a portrait of Mrs. Pauline Oxendine. She's Virgil's mother." Pointing to the balcony, he said, "She's sitting right up there, with her husband and several other members of our congregation."

"And have you seen these particular pictures before?"

"Why, yes sir, I have. You asked me to send them to you. You told me that Virgil, well, he said he misses his mother, misses going to church. You said it might cheer him up some if I sent those pictures. So you could take them with you when you visited Virgil in . . . in the jail down here. I was glad to do it, Mr. Waterman. And from what you tell me, Virgil was mighty grateful."

Taliaferro struggled wearily to his feet. "Your Honor, please."

Judge Transou looked at Ben. "Where is this going, counselor?"

"If Mr. Taliaferro will just be patient, Your Honor, the relevance of the pictures will become obvious when I examine my next witness. If you agree, to save time, we'll just leave them where they are, here on the table."

The judge looked at Taliaferro, who just shrugged.

"Very well, Mr. Waterman. Finish up then."

Ben smiled and asked his final question. "This may sound a little odd, Reverend, but do you happen to know whether Virgil is right-handed or left-handed?"

Laughing, shaking his head, Bondurant replied, "I sure do. See, the colored churches in Wilkes, we have a baseball league for the young boys. Mount Zion has a team, and I try to coach it. We play other church teams around the county. Well, Virgil Wade is a baseball nut. Just loves it."

Looking at the boy, Bondurant, said, "I've got to say, no offense, Virgil, well, the boy's not much of an athlete, but we still let him play. Can't hit worth a lick, so he bats last, right-handed. He's not much better in the field, so we put him on first base. He sure 'nough throws with his right hand, 'cause the only first baseman's glove we have is for a right hander. That what you mean?"

Ben grinned along with the judge and several of the jurymen. "Yes, Reverend, that's exactly what I meant. Thank you and," looking up to the balcony, "please thank Mrs. Oxendine and your other congregants for being here to support Virgil. No further questions, Your Honor."

"Mr. Taliaferro?"

Eager to get to the jury, Taliaferro just shook his head, and the reverend was excused.

"Next?" asked the judge.

Bracing himself, Ben stood. "Your Honor, the defense calls Mr. Juan Vucetich."

W

Vucetich strode confidently into the courtroom, all eyes on him. His face, gray beard neatly trimmed, was open and friendly, his attire and demeanor formal and professional. He nodded a respectful bow to the judge and took his seat.

Taliaferro jumped up. "Your Honor, as you know, the State objects to testimony from this witness and asks that it be excluded."

Judge Transou pulled a face. "Yes, Mr. Taliaferro, we have been over this. Your objection is on the record and is overruled. Again."

"Exception," muttered Taliaferro.

The judge nodded. "Duly noted. For the record. Now, Mr. Waterman, please proceed."

Ben walked toward the witness box, stopped, and smiled. "Good morning, Mr. Vucetich, and welcome to Raleigh." Vucetich returned the smile, nodded to Ben and then to the jury. "Please state your name and occupation, sir."

"My name is Juan Vucetich, and I am director of the Center for Dactyloscopy in Buenos Aires, Argentina. As a forensic scientist, I am in charge of criminal identification for the provincial police department there."

"Yes, we will get into more detail about that a little later. But, sir, and with no disrespect, I note that you speak with a slight accent. Just to be sure, do you have any problem testifying in the English language?"

Vucetich smiled again. "No, sir, not at all. I am, you see, fluent in several languages in addition to my native Croatian. These include Spanish, French, and, of course, English."

"So, Mr. Vucetich, please be so kind as to summarize for the jury your professional background and experience."

Vucetich explained that he had been born in the Dalmatian region of Croatia, at that time part of the Habsburg Empire. He emigrated to

Argentina and began his career in police work, rising steadily through the ranks. His particular focus and expertise is the science of forensic criminal identification.

"You described yourself as director of the Center for Dactyloscopy in Buenos Aires. *Dactyloscopy.* That's a mighty big word, Mr. Vucetich. Could you please explain it to the jury, in layman's terms?"

"Certainly. Dactyloscopy is the science of personal identification based on fingerprints. Fingerprints are known to have been used for this purpose since ancient times. As early as the 3rd century BC, the Chinese used fingerprint identification in court proceedings and to authenticate official documents. Official records from Persia in the 14th century also bear fingerprint authentication. The practice is even known here in the United States. In 1882, for example, a New Mexico surveyor named Gilbert Thompson affixed his own prints on documents to prevent forgery. So, you see, the practice and the science behind it are well documented."

"But how does this carry over to criminal proceedings? To trials like this?"

Vucetich recounted that, drawing on earlier work by Dr. Henry Faulds and Sir Francis Galton in the United Kingdom, he had developed his own method and system of fingerprint classification and identification. His system was officially adopted by the Buenos Aires police department in the early 1890s, replacing the discredited and unreliable Bertillon method of anthropometric identification, which relied on measurement of various body parts.

"So, your system uses fingerprints to identify criminals? To solve crimes?"

"That is correct," replied Vucetich.

"Please explain how this works."

"Yes, of course," said Vucetich. Holding up a hand to the jury, fingers spread, he described how tiny friction ridges and valleys on each human fingertip form patterns of loops, arches, and whorls that are unique to every person in the world. "Such friction ridges are useful in enabling humans to grasp and hold objects and to appreciate their texture. Fingertip impressions, for example, allow us to differentiate the feel of smooth silk from that of, say, rough concrete."

"So," said Ben, "These *friction ridges.* Can you see them? With the human eye?" Members of the jury began looking at their fingers.

"Without doubt," said Vucetich. Reaching into his jacket, he took out a small round magnifying glass. "If you move the glass over your fingertips, like this, the ridges and patterns are clearly visible."

"Your Honor," said Ben, "I request permission to pass Mr. Vucetich's magnifying glass to the jury. So they can see for themselves." The jurymen passed the instrument from one to another, moving it back and forth, excited to see the very ridges, whorls, loops, and arches described by Vucetich on their own fingers. "So, Mr. Vucetich, what does all this have to do with police work? How does it help you identify criminals?'

Vucetich explained that fingertip friction ridges, formed in the womb, remain constant throughout life. More importantly, since their patterns are unique to each individual, they provide a reliable and scientifically proven means of positive identification. He also noted that human fingertips are also covered in minute sweat glands that coat the friction ridges with moisture.

"So, when human beings touch things," Vucetich continued, "the moisture leaves behind an imprint of the fingers involved. A *fingerprint*, as we say. Fingerprints from the object touched can then be examined and compared to those taken from a person suspected of a crime. If the prints match, the suspect is thereby identified as the person who deposited the prints on the surface in question. In a criminal context, this method can provide irrefutable proof of guilt."

"Are you saying that your system has actually been used to solve crimes?" asked Ben. "To positively identify and convict criminals? In a court of law?"

"Oh, yes," answered Vucetich. "Many times." He described the first known case where fingerprints had been used to obtain a criminal conviction. In 1892, a man named Velasquez was arrested for the murder of two boys in a village near Buenos Aires.

"Using bloody fingerprints lifted from the door post of the family home, I was able to demonstrate that the actual killer was the boys' mother, Francisca Rojas, who used the same knife to wound herself to deflect blame to Velasquez. Confronted with this evidence, she confessed to the crime.

"Soon after this case was solved, fingerprint identification was adopted throughout Argentina and most other countries in South America. A system very similar to my own, developed by Sir Edward Henry in England, has been adopted by Scotland Yard and several other countries in the British Commonwealth as a court-approved means of criminal identification."

Ben walked back to the defense table and picked up a thick, heavy book. Showing it first to Vucetich and then to the jury, he asked, "Mr. Vucetich, do you recognize this book?"

Vucetich nodded, smiling. "Yes, sir, I do. The book is a treatise that I wrote and published earlier this year. The title, in English, is *Comparative Dactyloscopy.* The book, which has been translated into several languages, contains a detailed description and analysis of the theories, methods, and findings that constitute what has become known worldwide as the Vucetich Classification System."

With Judge Transou's permission, Ben handed the book to the jury for their inspection.

"So, your book has received attention around the world? Please, Mr. Vucetich, do not be modest."

Somewhat shyly, Vucetich nodded again and smiled. "I have been most fortunate, Mr. Waterman. This book has led to a number of professional and scientific awards and invitations to speak at scholarly conferences in many countries, including India, China, the United Kingdom, and now, the United States."

"So, Mr. Vucetich, how did this particular case come to your attention? How is it that you are here today?"

"For the past several weeks I have been on a speaking tour here in the United States, delivering lectures on my system of dactyl—, excuse me, *fingerprint* identification to several law enforcement agencies. For example, I have spoken to police officials in New York City, and I am currently in discussions with the New York Civil Service Commission about adopting my system statewide. I have also been invited to meet with officials at the Leavenworth Federal Penitentiary in Kansas, and next week I will speak with the St. Louis Police Department."

"But why Raleigh, Mr. Vucetich? Why this case, this trial?"

Nodding toward the spectators, Vucetich said, "A friend of mine from Argentina, Mr. von Gruenwald, sitting there, has business dealings here in North Carolina with the father of the victim. He contacted me in New York, concerned that justice be done in the case of Mr. Schumann's daughter. He suggested that perhaps I might be able to assist in confirming the identity of the person responsible for the crime.

"The case interested me, particularly given its similarities to the Rojas case in Argentina and other similar cases I have been involved in. There was availability in my schedule to travel here and provide whatever assistance might be appropriate. Mr. von Gruenwald's request was a favor I was pleased to grant."

Anticipating Taliaferro's likely line of attack, Ben asked, "Mr. Vucetich, are you being compensated for your services today? Are you being paid to be here?"

Shaking his head, Vucetich said, "No, sir. Mr. von Gruenwald has kindly agreed to cover my travel expenses, but otherwise my participation in this trial is on a *pro bono* basis, that is, without charge."

"Thank you, Mr. Vucetich." Ben faced the judge, took a deep breath.

"Your Honor, the defense requests that the court accept Mr. Vucetich's credentials as a world-renowned criminal forensic scientist and that he be recognized and permitted to testify and provide his professional expert opinions on matters relevant to these proceedings."

It all comes down to this, Ben thought, looking at Virgil Wade.

Judge Transou leaned forward, steepled his fingers. "Mr. Taliaferro, I expect you have some questions before I rule on this?"

Taliaferro rose. "Indeed I do, Your Honor. Indeed I do." He strutted to the jury box and picked up Vucetich's book. Shaking his head, he lifted it a couple of times, exaggerating its heft as he ambled over to the defense table. Holding the volume in both hands, he dropped it with a loud *thud*. Virgil Wade visibly flinched. "So, Mr. *Vu-ce-tich*, you wrote a book?"

Perplexed, Vucetich tilted his head, narrowed his eyebrows.

"Take a look behind the judge's bench, please. What do you see there?"

Vucetich turned his head to see and then looked at Taliaferro. "There are bookshelves there, filled with books."

"Exactly," said Taliaferro. "Many books. Those books contain published North Carolina Supreme Court opinions for cases going back over a hundred years. On the top shelf are more books, the General Statutes of North Carolina passed by the General Assembly. Now, Mr. Vucetich, if we had time to read through all these books, do you think we would find any mention, any reference at all, to the term *fingerprints?*"

"I am quite sure that I do not know the answer to that question."

"Ah, but *I* do, sir. After I learned that you would be coming to Raleigh, I consulted with the chief librarian at the School of Law at the University of North Carolina in Chapel Hill. He confirmed that, during his entire career as a practicing lawyer and now as an academic, he never in his life heard the word *dac-tyl-os-co-py* or the term *fingerprints*. And he knew of no such references in either the statutes or the case law of this state."

Ben could have objected, but he felt confident that Vucetich could hold his own.

"That would not surprise me, sir," replied Vucetich evenly. "Fingerprint identification is indeed relatively new technology, but, as described in my book and now in my testimony, the science is rapidly being accepted and adopted by police departments and criminal courts around the world. I am confident that the United States will soon follow suit."

Changing the subject, Taliaferro asked, "Mr. Vucetich, have you ever been to North Carolina before? Have you ever been allowed to provide your so-called *expert* testimony in any criminal case here?"

"No, I have not had an opportunity to visit your state before, nor have I ever testified in a court case here."

"Well, then, what about those other places you claim to have visited? Are you aware of any situations where *dac-tyl-os-co-py* evidence has ever been accepted in any criminal case in the United States?"

"No," Vucetich admitted. "Not yet. But, as I testified, the system has been adopted in the United Kingdom and elsewhere in the Commonwealth, as well as throughout South America. And my system is currently under active review in other places in the US that I mentioned."

Turning to the jury, Taliaferro sneered. "So, let me get this straight. You come all the way from *Ar-gen-tin-a*, from *New York City*, you waltz in here with your big *book* and all your fancy *foreign* awards, and you now presume to lecture this court and this jury about how we should do our business? Do you take us for a bunch of ignorant hillbillies, sir? In your arrogance, you would now presume to turn our system of justice upside down based on your *personal opinions?*"

Vucetich patiently replied, "No, that is not my intention. My *personal* opinions, as you say, are not relevant here. I am a man of *science*, sir, and my system has withstood rigorous, independent, scientific review in scholarly publications and jurisdictions throughout the world. There are many cases of record where this *science* has been relied upon to provide irrefutable evidence of guilt in criminal cases.

"And I can also tell you this, sir," Vucetich continued, looking directly at the jury. "In no case that I have been involved in, and in no case where my fingerprint system has been applied, anywhere in the world, in none of these cases has the verdict or the court's judgment ever been overturned on appeal. Never. Not once.

"So, to answer your question directly, I have no personal opinions about this case. However, I am prepared to offer my *professional* conclusions, as a man of science, to this court and this jury, regarding the identity of the person responsible for the knife wound inflicted on the victim in this case."

A low, rolling murmur moved through the gallery as Taliaferro again changed the subject. "Tell me, Mr. Vucetich, isn't it true that *gorillas* also have these things you call *fingerprints?*"

"I beg your pardon?"

"Come on, Mr. Vucetich," said Taliaferro, leaning way over, jutting out his jaw, and moving his arms and fists around threateningly. "You know. *Gorillas. Ummph! Ummph! Ummph!*"

"Order!" shouted Judge Transou, pounding his gavel to quiet the laughter in the courtroom.

"Well," Taliaferro asked scornfully. "Do they or don't they?"

Vucetich didn't like the question, but he answered. It was plain that Taliaferro's research had gone beyond the law library. "Scientists have established that primates such as gorillas do exhibit friction ridges, much like human beings."

Pleased, Taliaferro then asked, "What about *monkeys?* Don't they also have *fingerprints*, like people?"

Vucetich narrowed his eyes. "Monkeys, like gorillas, sir, are primates, and so do exhibit friction ridges."

"And isn't it also true, Mr. Vucetich, that monkeys also have so-called *fingerprints* on the ends of their *tails?*"

Uncomfortable, Vucetich answered, "It has been noted that monkeys' tails, due to their prehensile characteristics, do exhibit friction ridges."

"So," sneered Taliaferro triumphantly, "this so-called *science* of yours, why, sounds like to me that you can't even tell a human being from a *gorilla!* Can't tell a *fingerprint* from a *monkey's tail!*"

"Your Honor!" shouted Ben. "That was not the witness' testimony. There are no monkeys on trial here!"

Taliaferro stared directly at Virgil Wade and smirked, "So *you* say, counselor." With a wicked smile to the jury, Taliaferro declared, "Fine. I withdraw the question. And I'm through. I'm done with this . . . *expert.*"

"So, Mr. Taliaferro, Mr. Waterman's motion is pending. What would you have me do?"

"Your Honor, I would like for you to put an end to this carnival sideshow, to dismiss this witness and his *voo-doo science*, and let us get on with our business. We've wasted enough time already."

Ben rose and said earnestly, "Your Honor, I must admit that I am flabbergasted by Mr. Taliaferro's efforts to discredit this witness in the minds of the jury and this court. Mr. Vucetich, known and respected around the world, is here today, without compensation, to help us, to use the power of modern science to discover the *truth*, to identify the *real* person who took the life of Rachel Schumann.

"Mr. Taliaferro has obtained a grand jury indictment alleging that the culprit is my client, Virgil Wade, and that Virgil should pay with his *life*. If he has confidence in his indictment, if he is sure beyond a reasonable doubt that he has the right man, well, then, I would think he would welcome Mr. Vucetich's evidence to confirm it, to prove his case.

"But," Ben said, facing the jury and wagging a finger, "if Mr. Taliaferro is *wrong*, if the evidence proves in fact that someone else committed this heinous crime, why, certainly Mr. Taliaferro should welcome that information as well. I am confident that the gentlemen of this jury would not want to participate in a horrible miscarriage of justice by convicting the wrong person!

"Your Honor, the jury deserves to hear from Mr. Vucetich, to hear his testimony, so that we may all learn the truth. So that the justice that Mr. Taliaferro cries for can truly prevail in this case." Turning to the judge, Ben concluded, "Your Honor, the defense renews its motion with respect to this witness."

Judge Transou leaned back and stared at the ceiling for a long moment. The lawyers, the defendant, the witness, the jury, and the spectators could only wait. Finally, he tilted his chair forward.

"Gentlemen, this is indeed an unusual situation. Mr. Vucetich presents a dilemma for the court in that, so far as I know, nothing like this has ever come before a trial court in North Carolina, as Mr. Taliaferro correctly points out. However, Mr. Vucetich presents impressive credentials, and his scientific and professional background and experience are most compelling. And so, even in a case of first impression like this, I believe the witness should be allowed to testify as an expert with respect to relevant matters in this case. If this be legal error, then the supreme court can fix it."

Pointing his gavel at the jurymen, the judge added, "Gentlemen, now y'all listen up. The credibility of this witness and any testimony he may give, well, that's up to you to decide, not me. Again, whether you believe a word he has to say or not, that will be your decision. I'll be listening carefully, too, and if Mr. Waterman or the witness get out of line, I'll reel them in right quick. Now, with all that in mind, the defense motion is granted. Mr. Waterman, you may continue your examination of the witness."

$$W$$

Ben let out a long breath as Taliaferro slumped, scowling. He walked to the evidence table below the judge's bench, opened the sealed bag, and withdrew People's Exhibit 2. Holding the knife in his hands, Ben asked, "Now, Mr. Vucetich, have you seen this before?"

"Yes, sir. That is the alleged murder weapon in this case."

"And have you had an opportunity to take a look at this exhibit?"

"Yes. I was permitted to examine it, in the presence of witnesses, last Monday."

"And what were the results of your examination?"

Vucetich paused, cleared his throat. "My purpose, of course, was to look for fingerprints on the knife handle. In an effort to identify the last person to hold the knife, the person who used the knife to stab the victim." Judge Transou overruled Taliaferro's objection, and Vucetich continued. "There were, of course, older fingerprints on the knife, prints that I was able to identify as belonging to the defendant, Virgil Wade."

The spectators' collective intake of breath echoed throughout the courtroom, followed by uneasy mumbling and muttering, nodding of heads.

"But these older prints are irrelevant. The knife is said to be the property of the defendant, so his prints are to be expected. What was compelling, decisive in fact, were the most recent prints overlaying the older ones. These fingerprints were the most prominent, clearly visible, brownish red in color. It is my professional opinion that these prints were formed from the blood of the victim and deposited onto the knife handle by the person responsible for the final strike."

"Were you able to preserve these bloody fingerprints, Mr. Vucetich?"

Nodding, Vucetich replied, "Yes. Using specialized equipment that magnifies the images, I was able to take photographs of the prints."

Tink reached down again into her suitcase and took out a folder. Ben withdrew several photographs and handed them to Vucetich. "Are these the photographs, sir?" Vucetich examined them and confirmed their authenticity. Ben marked them as Defense Exhibits 1-4 and passed them to the jury. "Now, Mr. Vucetich, turning to the defendant, have you had an opportunity to examine *his* fingerprints?"

"I have."

"And how did that come about?"

Pointing to the defense table, Vucetich replied, "Those two picture frames. It was represented to me that the surfaces of the frames and the glass covering the photographs contain the fingerprints of the defendant, who touched them on multiple occasions while in jail."

"Your Honor," Ben said, "Defense offers these two picture frames into evidence as Defense Exhi—"

Taliaferro jumped up. "Objection, Your Honor! Lack of foundation. Nothing in evidence links these frames to the defendant other than counsel's unsubstantiated claims."

Ben had anticipated this bump in the road, but it was Tink Beasley who came up with the solution. They exchanged a tight smile as she once again reached into the small suitcase and took out several items, including a stack of white notepaper.

"Your Honor, I concede the point. If Mr. Taliaferro is not satisfied, then I am prepared to respond to his objection in another way. I request permission for the witness to take a sample of the defendant's fingerprints right now, here in the courtroom, so that the jury may see Mr. Vucetich's system in action and remove any doubt about the issue."

Taliaferro objected again, to no avail. With the judge's permission, Vucetich stepped down, walked over to the defense table, and lifted a small rectangular object. "This," he said to the jury, "is an ink pad, like the ones used with rubber stamps." As he patiently explained things, he slowly rolled each of Virgil's left hand fingers onto the pad before rolling them again on a blank sheet of paper, leaving behind five clear, black ink imprints. He then labeled the paper *Virgil Wade—Left Hand* before repeating the procedure with the right hand.

"So, Mr. Vucetich, you now have clear, indisputable imprints from both of the defendant's hands, correct? Fingerprints from the defendant that you can now compare against the images from the knife?"

"That is correct."

"Then, please, by all means, do so."

Taliaferro, realizing the trap he had fallen into, objected again, but was shut down by the judge. Vucetich took the magnifying glass and took several minutes to compare the two sheets of paper against the photographs of the bloody knife handle. He then asked to examine the two picture frames. Finally, he looked up and nodded at Ben.

Ben took the photographs and the sheets of paper from Vucetich. "Your Honor, in addition to Defense Exhibits 1-4, the images of the bloody knife handle, I ask that the picture frames be admitted as Defense Exhibits 5 and 6, and that the labeled fingerprints of Virgil Wade be admitted as Defense Exhibits 7 and 8." Ben then requested permission to circulate the exhibits to the jury.

"Mr. Vucetich, now that you have had an opportunity to carefully examine People's Exhibit 2, the knife, and Defense Exhibits 1 through 8, and to compare the bloody fingerprints on the knife against those of Virgil Wade, do you have a professional opinion, sir, a firm conclusion based on science and your own expertise, with respect to these different sets of fingerprints?"

"I do. And that opinion is set forth in the written report I submitted yesterday afternoon to you, Mr. Taliaferro, and the court." Tink produced a copy of the document, signed by Vucetich, and Ben handed it to him. Vucetich reviewed it carefully, looked up, and confirmed that this was indeed his report. But then he raised a finger.

"Before we get into the report, Mr. Waterman, I must clarify something." Ben's heart skipped a beat. "You see, my report is based on a comparison of fingerprints taken from the two picture frames against those on the knife handle. But, after careful examination, I can now confirm that the prints on the frames are identical to those taken just now from the defendant. They are from the same person, the defendant Virgil Wade."

Ben looked at Tink, breathed a sigh of relief. "So, Mr. Vucetich, your report is very detailed and comprehensive and contains many scientific terms that may be beyond the comprehension of laymen like myself. I wonder if I might ask you to skip to the bottom of the report. To the section marked *Conclusion*. Would you read that aloud, please, for the jury?"

Vucetich turned to the jury as he read. "'*Conclusion: It is my professional opinion as a criminal forensic scientist, stated with one-hundred percent certainty, that the bloody fingerprints on People's Exhibit 2, deposited by a small left hand, do not match those deposited on the two picture frames provided to me. The fingerprints were therefore deposited by two different people.*'"

Taliaferro slumped and shook his head as Judge Transou vainly tried to quell the uproar in the courtroom. When things quieted down, Vucetich continued. "I should also add that, now that I myself have had the opportunity to take fresh fingerprint samples from the defendant today, in open court, my confidence in my conclusion as stated in my written report is all the more strengthened and confirmed."

Ben had the report marked Defense Exhibit 9 and handed it over to the jury. Taliaferro stood, thinking it was time for his cross-examination. "Excuse me," said Ben. "I am not yet finished with the witness."

Ben gestured to Tink, who took the green wine bottle from the suitcase, handling it carefully. Ben held the bottle by its punt and showed it to Vucetich. "Mr. Vucetich, have you seen this wine bottle before?"

Vucetich reached into his jacket pocket and pulled out a pair of white cloth gloves. As he fiddled with them, Ben heard a gentle whisper of rustling fabric behind him. Tink tugged on his sleeve and passed him a note. *She's leaving.* Ben wheeled around to see heads turning and straining to see Claire Elise Montgomery pushing through the courtroom doors.

Vucetich finished putting on the gloves and gestured to Ben for the bottle. He examined it carefully, nodded. "Yes, sir. This is a bottle that you showed me yesterday evening. I see your initials, written on the label."

"Objection, your Honor!" cried Taliaferro. "I renew my objection as to the relevance of this object. And testimony about it goes far beyond our understanding concerning this witness."

"Your Honor," said Ben. "I promised to demonstrate the relevance of this bottle yesterday, and that is what I am about to do. And our agreement concerning Mr. Vucetich's testimony only dealt with his examination of People's Exhibit 2."

Judge Transou nodded, intrigued. "All right, Mr. Waterman, proceed."

"Now, Mr. Vucetich, I note that the neck of the bottle appears to be covered in a white substance, like powder, correct?"

"Correct. You asked me to examine the neck of the bottle for fingerprints. I did not have time to take photographs and have them developed, so I used a different method. In cases such as this, I use a soft brush to apply white powder to the surface in question. The powder reveals fingerprints in sharp detail, which can then be examined visually using a magnifying glass."

"And did you see any fingerprints on the neck of the bottle, sir?"

"I did. There were several fingerprints, from the left hand of a person, a small hand, suggesting they were from a young person, or perhaps a woman."

"Objection! Speculation!"

"Your Honor," replied Ben patiently, "you have already ruled that Mr. Vucetich is an expert in criminal forensic science, fully competent to testify as to such matters."

"Overruled. Proceed."

"Now, Mr. Vucetich, do you know who deposited these fingerprints on the neck of this bottle?"

"I do not."

"But did you have an opportunity to compare those fingerprints with other evidence in this case?"

"I did. Again, at your request, I compared the images from the bottle against the bloody fingerprints left on the knife, People's Exhibit 2."

"Objection!" shouted Taliaferro, panic now in his voice.

"Your objection is again overruled, Mr. Taliaferro," replied Judge Transou sternly.

Ben paused for effect, turning to the jury. "And what were the results of your comparison, Mr. Vucetich?"

"In my professional opinion, again with one-hundred percent confidence, the prints from the neck of the wine bottle are a perfect match for the left-hand images, the bloody fingerprints, from the alleged murder weapon."

The spectators erupted as the jurors looked to one another, astonished, the implications of Vucetich's testimony sinking in.

Ben waited a long moment, and then reached for the bottle. "Your Honor, I ask to have this bottle marked as Defense Exhibit 10 and introduced into evidence."

Taliaferro did not bother to rise as he muttered, "Objection." Judge Transou shot him a look as he declared, "Overruled. Anything else, Mr. Waterman?"

"Nothing further, your Honor."

"Mr. Taliaferro?"

Taliaferro, anxious to get Vucetich off the stand, stood and pleaded, "Your Honor, the People renew our objection to this witness's testimony and ask to have it stricken from the record in its entirety! This circus has gone on long enough!"

"Overruled and denied. Now, Mr. Taliaferro, do you have any questions for this witness, or are we done here?"

"No, sir," seethed Taliaferro, working his jaw. "I will not participate further in this charade. What we have witnessed here today is the work of a kangaroo court, an egregious breach of criminal law and procedure and an affront to the cause of justice and the people of Wilkes County and the State of North Carolina!"

Judge Transou banged his gavel. "Watch your mouth, Mr. Taliaferro! Your disrespect for this court is intolerable and highly unprofessional. I will deal with you later in consultation with the North Carolina State Bar." Pausing to catch his breath, the judge turned to Ben. "Anything else, counselor?"

Shaking his head, Ben responded firmly, "No, sir. Nothing." Turning to the jury, taking a deep breath, Ben stated, "Your Honor, the defense rests."

Still trembling with fury, Judge Transou said as calmly as he could, "Very well, then. The witness is excused. We will break for the midday meal and reconvene at one o'clock. Then we will hear closing arguments."

W

Ben skipped lunch to work on his closing. Shortly before one o'clock, Billy Ray Hill told him that Judge Transou wanted to see both lawyers in chambers.

Ben and Taliaferro sat across from the judge, waiting. Judge Transou, without mentioning Taliaferro's intemperate outburst, shifted his chaw of tobacco from one cheek to the other, spit out a brown stream into the spittoon at his feet, and got right down to business.

"So, what I want to know, Mr. Waterman, is what in the hell happened in there this morning? Am I missing something, or did a cold-blooded murderess just sashay her way out of my courtroom, free as a bird? And you, Mr. Taliaferro, you and Poindexter just sat there and watched it, without so much as a by-your-leave? Well?"

Ben cleared his throat and said, "Your Honor, I played a hunch. You see, I saved the wine bottle as sort of a souvenir of a pleasant evening in Wilkesboro. But the more I got into the case, the more I learned, well, let's just say I began to have doubts about Mrs. Montgomery. I had . . . have reasons to suspect her, reasons to believe that she may have had . . . some animus against Miss Schumann. I believe she was at the river that night. I believe she is the person who struck Rachel Schumann with the knife. And I think I know why. But I had no way to prove it. Until Mr. Vucetich arrived, that is, and I learned what fingerprints could do. So, with your permission, I had Mrs. Montgomery handle the bottle, and then I asked

Vucetich to compare her fingerprints to . . . well, you heard what he said on the stand."

"*Pffft*," snorted Taliaferro, shaking his head. "What a bunch of hogwash! You got us into this mess, Judge, by allowing this Argentine snake oil salesman to testify at all. You said it, Judge. You said it yourself. It's up to the jury to decide whether or not to believe anything this South American grifter said. Me? I don't believe a word of it, and when I'm done with the jurymen, none of them will either. Virgil Wade killed Rachel Schumann, Judge, and he will hang for it! I do not need to waste my time, or Sheriff Poindexter's, chasing shadows."

Judge Transou sat still for a moment, frowning. "So be it, then. The only thing connecting Mrs. Montgomery to anything is Vucetich. And, Mr. Taliaferro, as you correctly point out, his credibility is for the jury, and I will so instruct them. Let's get in there and wrap this up, gentlemen. My sense is the jurymen have heard enough and are ready to get to work. Closing arguments next. Keep it short."

W

Because the prosecution bears the burden of proof in criminal trials, Taliaferro was entitled to make his closing, followed by the defense. The prosecution is then allowed to make a rebuttal statement, a final appeal to the jury. Taliaferro elected to waive his initial closing, choosing instead to respond to Ben during rebuttal. This surprised Ben, but he was prepared. It was clear to everyone that Vucetich's explosive testimony would hover over it all.

"Go for it, Ben," encouraged Tink. "Bring it home."

Ben walked slowly to the jury box, spread his hands, and smiled. "Well, gentlemen, as they say, 'it's all over but the shouting.' The evidence is all in now, and soon it will be up to you to decide Virgil Wade's fate. What's left is what lawyers do best—argument. Again, I remind you that nothing that Mr. Taliaferro or I say in closing counts as evidence. Both of us will summarize the case as we see it and ask you to render a verdict accordingly. Here are some things you should keep in mind."

Ben then reminded the jury of their oath, their solemn pledge to render impartial justice. He stressed the prosecution's heavy burden of proof, that any vote to convict must be beyond any reasonable doubt, and that their verdict must be unanimous.

Counting on his fingers, Ben then reviewed the gaps and inconsistencies in the prosecution's case. He scoffed at Virgil's coerced confession and recalled Dr. Burleson's testimony strongly suggesting that there were two people with Rachel Schumann at the river. "That's right, gentlemen. *Two* people. And now you know who. Because one of the preeminent criminal forensic scientists in the world has proven it! He proved to you that Virgil Wade did not handle the knife that took Rachel Schumann's life. But he did more than that."

Walking over to the exhibit table, Ben reached for the wine bottle, held it aloft. "You watched me present this bottle to Mr. Taliaferro's first witness. You saw her flinch as I asked her to hold it, to examine it closely. You must have been wondering why I did that.

"To be honest, I myself did not know exactly what would come of it. But something told me to do it. To ask Dr. Vucetich to compare the images on the neck of this bottle against those bloody fingerprints on the knife that killed Rachel Schumann. He did, and you heard the results." He replaced the bottle on the table.

His voice rising, Ben declared, "Using the tools of twentieth-century science, he demonstrated, *with one-hundred percent certainty,* that a *second* person was at the river that night, the very person you heard speaking from the witness stand, a person who violated her sacred promise to tell the truth, an attractive, well-dressed vixen so cold-blooded that she was prepared to send a young boy to the gallows for a crime that she herself committed! And when it became clear that her secret would be revealed, you saw her casually saunter out of this courtroom, head held high.

"She has a name, of course, this woman. Everybody from Wilkes knows her. But I will not speak the name, not here, not in this courtroom. Why? Because she is not on trial here! Justice cries out, *why not? Her* fingerprints, on the knife! Yet she struts out of here like the Queen of England, not a care in the world.

"Now, you might think that Mr. Taliaferro, who has repeatedly demanded justice in this case, you might think that he would do the right thing, do something to stop her, *arrest* her. But no. Mr. Taliaferro and the sheriff just sat there and watched her leave. Did Mr. Taliaferro demand that the trial be stopped, the charges dismissed, call for a halt to this miscarriage of justice? Sadly, no. Instead, he did everything he could to muzzle Mr. Vucetich, to keep him quiet. From proving Virgil Wade's innocence!

"You will recall a while ago I asked you to keep an open mind. Well, now I'm asking you to focus, to accept the *truth*, to wrap your minds around the inescapable *fact* that Mr. Taliaferro has made a terrible mistake. He has relentlessly and without mercy prosecuted, and now, without humility, without embarrassment, without *shame*, he asks you to take the life of an *innocent person!*"

Taking a deep breath, Ben again spread his hands. "What really happened at the river that summer night? I must admit, I don't know the whole story, and Mr. Taliaferro has done precious little to enlighten us. Perhaps we will never know.

"I also asked you to keep an open heart, and I now renew that plea." Pointing to the defense table, Ben continued, "Put yourself in Virgil Wade's place. Stand in his shoes for a moment. Imagine how you would feel if you faced a jury like this, falsely accused of a crime you did not commit? Think about it. What would you do, how would you decide this case if Virgil Wade were a *White man?*"

Reaching into his jacket pocket, Ben took out a document. Holding it out, he said, "This is the indictment against Virgil Wade. This is the document that brought y'all here, the formal charge that you must consider, the only document that you *may* consider."

Ben read it to the jury. "The jurors for the State upon their oath present that on or about the date of the offense shown and in the County of Wilkes, defendant Virgil Wade unlawfully, willfully, and feloniously and of malice aforethought did *kill and murder* one Rachel Schumann, to wit, by infliction of a *fatal knife wound* to the victim's heart.'

"Two things to think about. *Kill and murder,* and *fatal knife wound.* That's it. You know in your hearts that these charges are false. The evidence is clear, beyond any reasonable doubt. You know that Virgil Wade did not stab Rachel Schumann to death. And now you know who did. As promised, we proved it to you.

"Gentlemen, I do not ask for mercy for Virgil Wade. I ask for *justice.* Virgil Wade, whose very life is at stake here, is innocent of the charge against him, and I respectfully ask you to confirm that by your unanimous verdict of *not guilty.* Thank you for your service and your attention during this trial."

W

The lawyers crossed paths as Taliaferro eagerly approached the jury. His gaze roving over the jurymen, he smiled and spun his fingers around his ears. "Confused?" he asked. "Me, too. So, like Mr. Waterman, I want y'all to focus now."

Taliaferro then meticulously summarized the evidence against Virgil Wade—Virgil talking to Rachel at the fairgrounds, the gruesome crime scene photo, Virgil's knife buried in Rachel Schumann's chest, the autopsy report, the theft of Rachel's horse and Virgil's flight to the old Cleveland place, his admission that he was with Rachel under the iron bridge, that he struck her.

"Gentlemen, that's all you need to know to convict Virgil Wade." Spinning his fingers around his ears again, he said, "All the other rigmarole from Mr. Waterman is just noise, lawyer talk designed to mix you up. As Mr. Waterman says, now is the time to *focus*. To focus on the *evidence*. You do that, and you will surely know what to do."

He paused for effect. "I can tell you this. In all my years as a prosecutor, I have never seen a more open-and-shut case. *Never* have I seen evidence so compelling, so overwhelming. 'But what about Vucetich?' you ask. Ah yes, the famous Mr. Vucetich. The *foreigner*. The *stranger*. What to make of him and his testimony? Well, I say, *nothing!* Nothing at all.

"Like Judge Transou said, nothing that man said, with all his *credentials*, is to be taken as Gospel. It is for *you*, and you alone, to decide what weight and credibility to give to his *expert* opinions. I suggest that you should ignore everything he said. Every last word. I tried to get the judge to dismiss his testimony, but he decided it was up to you. So, do the right thing and put it all out of your mind.

"*Scientist?*" Taliaferro scoffed. "More like a fortune teller, a carnival barker, if you ask me. Why, as he was spinning his yarn, I halfway expected him to produce a crystal ball or a Ouija board. Oh, he was very clever, I'll give him that. Using big words like *dac-tyl-os-co-py* to distract you, to mesmerize you into some sort of trance, to accept his two-bit, Argentine quack science instead of relying on your own good common sense! Don't fall under his magic spell. Don't be seduced by that charlatan, gentlemen. No sirree. Don't be fooled into disbelieving what you saw with your own eyes, what you heard with your own ears.

"So. Finger. Prints. Ridges on your fingers, like an ape or a monkey. Are the courts of North Carolina to substitute monkey-science for the wisdom and good judgment of twelve upstanding men like you? No, I say! Even Judge Transou admits that no such evidence has ever contaminated a criminal trial in the long and distinguished history of North Carolina jurisprudence. I expect that our own supreme court will soon set him straight. I'll see to it.

"Mr. Waterman begs for the truth. But you already know the truth. In your hearts, as he says. You know, I know, and soon the people of Wilkes County will know that boy," pointing at Virgil, "that boy sitting right there brutally and savagely murdered poor Rachel Schumann. He. . . is . . . *guilty!* Guilty as charged, gentlemen. Beyond *any* doubt. And he must pay for his crime. With his life, as the law requires.

"It is time now for you to do your duty. It should not take you long. Focus, gentlemen. *Focus.* I have every confidence in you as I once again ask you to return a unanimous verdict of guilty. Thank you."

W

The courtroom was silent as Judge Transou shuffled through papers. Clearing his throat, the judge dutifully read out the final jury instructions required by law. He closed by reminding the jury once more that it was up to them what credence, if any, to give to the testimony of Juan Vucetich.

Ben and Taliaferro stood as the twelve jurymen rose and Billy Ray Hill led them into the room behind the jury box. As the door closed tightly behind them, Judge Transou banged his gavel. "Pending word from the jury, this court stands in recess."

The prison guards came for Virgil Wade. Before they could handcuff him, he placed both hands on Ben's arm. "Thank you, Mr. Waterman. That was good. Real good. I surely do 'preciate what you done for me."

The courtroom slowly emptied as the guards led Virgil away. Roscoe McGee walked up to Ben and Tink. "That . . . that was mighty fine, Ben. Mighty fine. I never thought I'd say this, but I think you got a shot. That Vucetich fella blew a hole right through ol' Razor's case."

Exhausted, Ben nodded. "It's out of our hands, Ros. Now we wait."

"So, Ben, how long you think this will take?" asked Tink.

"Who knows, Tink? A quick verdict, well, that would be bad news. But tomorrow is Friday, so I would bet that they will want to finish up and get out of here for the weekend. We'll see."

"Gruenwald is all excited," said McGee. "Says he wants to take us and Vucetich out to dinner."

Shaking his head, Ben replied, "Sorry, Ros. Judge Maxwell has asked me to dinner tonight at the Mansion, but maybe tomorrow night? One way or the other, I'll be ready for a stiff drink and a big steak."

Chapter 40

Over dinner at the mansion, Ben told Governor Maxwell about the day's events. Shaking his head, Maxwell said, "What a trial, Ben! Is this guy Vucetich for real? Can he be believed?"

Ben sighed. "His credentials are real enough, Judge, and he was a good witness. But whether the jury will buy it or not—? Taliaferro did a good job with his cross-examination and his closing. I'm not sure a North Carolina jury is ready for this new science. Taliaferro made Vucetich sound like some kind of a witch doctor."

Maxwell nodded. "Transou went way out on a limb letting him testify. Took guts to do that. Taliaferro will appeal, no doubt, and I expect the new supreme court will reverse. Do you really think you have a chance at an acquittal?"

"It all comes down to Vucetich, Judge. If the jury believes him, then maybe. If not, well."

"Worst case, maybe a hung jury? Remember, it only—"

"It only takes one," Ben finished, smiling. "Surely, given Vucetich's testimony and the wine bottle evidence, Taliaferro will be more reasonable if there's a mistrial."

"I wouldn't bet on that, Ben. And this Montgomery woman! What to make of that? Who'd've thought it?"

Ben shrugged. "Taliaferro has a tough decision to make, Judge. Without Vucetich's testimony about the wine bottle, it would be tough to convict her. She may just get away with it."

Taking a long pull of bourbon, Maxwell changed the subject. "So, Ben, like we discussed, have you given any thought to your future? What you'll do after this case is over?"

"To tell you the truth, Judge, I haven't had time to think about it. I just want to get through this thing."

"Well, I've been working on it, Ben," smiled Maxwell. "I told you I would take care of you. And I have an idea."

Curious, Ben tilted his head, waited.

"I got a call last week from Lester Hogewood. Down in Wilmington." Hogewood, a staunch Republican, had been elected a superior court judge for New Hanover County in the Fusionist landslide of 1896. "He told me that Needham Gulley is starting up a law school over at Wake Forest College, near Raleigh. He says that Gulley wants his help. Offered him a job as law professor.

"Well, to make a long story short, Hogewood is worn out. Tired of all the politics. Appalled by the violence and hatred back in '98. He told me that he accepted Gulley's offer and would be resigning from the bench."

Ben's brow furrowed. "So, what's that got to do with me?"

Maxwell leaned forward. "Think, Ben. Think about it. Hogewood's got four years left on his term. If he resigns, why, that creates a *vacancy*. A vacancy on the superior court in Wilmington. A vacancy *I* get to fill. A judgeship with four years left.

"You'll never win in '04, I know that, but you'd have a good job until then. And you'd make a great judge, Ben. And wouldn't Ben Waterman taking a judgeship in *Wilmington* just drive those Democrats crazy?"

Ben nodded, warming to the idea. "Me? A superior court judge? In Wilmington? Why, that would be just too fine!"

"So, then, you'll take it?"

"If you can pull this off, Judge, it would be an honor."

"Good, then. I'll fix it. I already got Hogewood to wait. He'll quit after the election. The Democrats will be riding high then, but this lame-duck governor will have a little surprise for them. Oh, the irony!" he laughed. The men stood, lifted their glasses, and shook on it.

Chapter 41

B en and Tink huddled around the defense table, doing what they could to comfort Virgil Wade, to reassure him that things would all work out, as he held his head in his hands, bent over the table. Ticks on the clock slowed to a crawl. Taliaferro and Poindexter were playing cards as Crip Goins fiddled with a gee-haw whimmy-diddle, spinning the propeller first right, then left.

The jury filed into the courtroom at nine o'clock, their faces expressionless, and retired to the jury room. Lunchtime came and went. About 3pm, Ben stood up and declared, "This is torture, Tink. I'm going to get some fresh air. I'll be at that bookstore across the street. If anything happens, come get me quick." Tink nodded and said that she would hold down the fort.

W

Ben found what he wanted and asked the clerk to wrap his purchases in festive paper, tied with a bow. As he handed over his money, the bell above the bookstore entrance tinkled, and Tink Beasley strode in. "Ben!" she whispered. "They're coming back. The jury. Better hurry."

Ben and Tink arrived in the courtroom just as the jurymen were sitting down. As the guards settled Virgil into his seat, Ben tried to read the jurors' faces, but gleaned nothing.

Judge Transou took the bench, put on his spectacles, and looked to the jury box. "Well, gentlemen, have you elected a foreman?"

The college professor rose and faced the judge, a sour expression on his face. "Your Honor, my fellow jurymen have asked me to speak for them."

Nodding, the judge then asked, "Well, sir, what say you? Has the jury reached a verdict in this case?"

The foreman shot a look down to the end of the back row, to the state employee Tink had cautioned Ben about earlier. That man sat looking, with a slight smile, directly at Ben, appearing to enjoy the proceedings immensely.

"No, Your Honor. I'm afraid not."

A low rumble moved through the now-filled gallery.

"I see. Please explain."

"Well, as you know, we worked 'til suppertime last night, and then all day today. But we were unable to come to a unanimous verdict."

"How far did you get?" asked the judge.

"Well, sir, we took a straw vote at the very beginning, and the vote was 11-1 in favor of conviction. We then began to . . . deliberate. We went over the evidence again and again, but I regret to inform you that the . . . dissenter would not be moved." Looking down the row again, he continued. "He's stubborn as a mule, Your Honor, and he wouldn't give in. Said we could talk and talk 'til the cows come home, but he would not be changing his mind." Shaking his head, the foreman declared, "And I . . . and the others, well, we have to take him at his word at this point. We are deadlocked, Your Honor, and I see no way out of it."

"You are very close to a verdict, sir," said Judge Transou patiently. "Are you sure that working a little harder, a little longer, might not produce a definitive outcome? I remind you that the people are depending on you to finish what you have started. Considerable time and resources have been consumed in this trial, and you all on the jury have a job to do. A duty to come to a unanimous verdict if at all possible."

The foreman shook his head sadly. The man at the end of the row leaned back, crossed his arms in front of him, set his jaw, and frowned. "No, sir. We tried. We tried every way from Sunday to get him to see reason, but he's firm. I do not think he will change his mind, Your Honor, and it's for sure that none of the rest of us will. That's where we're at, sir, much as I hate to say it."

The judge pursed his lips, leaned forward. Taliaferro slumped in his chair, put his elbows on the table and grasped his head in his hands.

"Very well, then. You leave me no choice. Mr. Waterman, do you have a motion?"

His heart pounding, his mouth dry, Ben rose and said, "Your Honor, the defense moves for a mistrial in the case of *State v. Wade*."

Judge Transou looked to Taliaferro, who shrugged and shook his head. The judge took up his gavel, paused a moment, and blew out a deep breath. He tapped his gavel gently and pronounced, "Motion granted, counselor. Now, until Mr. Taliaferro can decide his next move, the defendant will remain in Central Prison until further order of the court. I thank the jury for your service. You are now dismissed, and this court is adjourned."

As Judge Transou stood and slowly made his way back to his chambers, chaos erupted in the courtroom. *"No! No mistrial! Hang him! Hang him!"* came the chorus from the spectators, some rising and shaking their fists at Virgil Wade. "Justice for Rachel Schumann!" Billy Ray Hill walked toward the gallery. A warning.

As the muttering crowd finally began to disperse, Taliaferro and his team rose to leave, but Ben intercepted them. Taliaferro, his face sweaty and red as a ripe tomato, snarled, "What have you done, Waterman? Just what do you think you have accomplished? I'll get him, Waterman, on my mother's grave, I promise you that! Now get out of my way!"

"Wait," commanded Ben. "We should talk. Tomorrow, after you've had a chance to think things through. You have some big decisions to make, and you need to hear me out."

"Talk? Talk, talk, talk! That's all you're good for. But sure. I'll talk to you. Tomorrow. Ten o'clock in that room down the hall there. I can't wait to tell you what I have in mind for your murdering high-yeller bastard! I'm not through with him, Waterman. No, sir. Not by a long shot!" With that, he turned sharply and marched away.

Ben returned to the defense table just as the guards appeared. As they snapped the handcuffs tight, Virgil looked to Ben, his eyes pleading. "What just happened, Mr. Waterman? Am I free? Can I go home now?"

Ben put a comforting hand on his shoulder, shook his head. "No, Virgil, no. Not today. But this is good, Virgil. The jury couldn't agree. I'll come to the prison and explain it all, after I've had a chance to talk to Taliaferro. Now, you stay strong, Virgil, you hear me? Keep your spirits up, and I'll see what I can do." Gripping Virgil's shoulders, his eyes fixed on Virgil's, Ben repeated, "Stay strong."

As they led Virgil away, Tink approached Ben with a big grin. "Well, Ben Waterman, I've a gre't mind to give you a big ol' hug!" And she did.

Roscoe joined them, smiling. "Good job, Ben! Good work!"

"It's not what we wanted, Ros, but I'll take it. I'll see Taliaferro in the morning. See if we can work something out. Something that keeps Virgil Wade *alive.*"

As they packed up their things, Tink glanced over to the jury box and tugged on Ben's sleeve. The state employee in the Treasurer's office, a patronage position, smiled and reached under his chair for his fedora. The last juror to leave, his eyes never leaving Ben's, he placed the brown, wide-brimmed hat on his head, adjusted it, and, with a final wink and a nod, walked out, whistling.

Chapter 42

Park Hotel Dining Room, Raleigh, Friday, September 7, 1900

Ben, Tink, McGee, Gruenwald, and Vucetich sat in a private dining room around a candlelit table covered with starched white linen and elegantly set with polished silver, fine china, and lead crystal wine glasses from Ireland. As the dinner drew to a close, Ben walked away from the table and returned with a small package, smiling. He placed it on the table before Vucetich. "This is for you, sir. A present, with our thanks." As Vucetich removed the wrapping paper, Ben said, "I found these in the bookstore near the courthouse."

The package contained two leather-bound books. "Even if North Carolina is not yet ready to accept your research, Mr. Vucetich, there are some in our country who already appreciate the value of *comparative dactyloscopy.*" Vucetich examined the volumes, his face breaking into a broad smile.

"The first book is *Life on the Mississippi*, by Samuel Longhorne Clemens. He writes under the pen name *Mark Twain.* In Chapter 31, *A Thumbprint and What Comes Out of It*, he tells of a murder solved using *fingerprints.* The story was written just a year after you moved to Argentina."

"I know of this man!" exclaimed Vucetich. "I have heard of his work, but never read it. But how?"

"I came across it during my research for the trial. And the year after you solved the Rojas case in Argentina, he wrote a whole book about fingerprints, *The Tragedy of Pudd'nhead Wilson.* In this novel, a lawyer," Ben closed his eyes, lifted his eyebrows, and made an extravagant bow, "a lawyer used fingerprints to exonerate his client. You will like this passage." Ben opened the book and read aloud:

"'May it please the court, the state has claimed, strenuously and persistently, that the bloodstained fingerprints upon that knife handle were left there by the assassin of Judge Driscoll.' . . . *He turned to the jury: "Compare the fingerprints of the accused with the fingerprints left by the assassin—and report."*

The comparison began. As it proceeded, all movement and all sound ceased, and the deep silence of an absorbed and waiting suspense settled upon the house, and when at last the words came, "THEY DO NOT EVEN RESEMBLE," a thunder crash of applause followed, and the house sprang to its feet . . .'"

Ben grinned and handed the book back to Vucetich as the company broke into laughter and applause. "Not exactly the result in our case, Mr. Vucetich, but I am confident that your work will soon set the standard throughout the United States."

Vucetich stood and vigorously pumped Ben's hand. "Thank you, Mr. Waterman. I am flattered by your gift and your words, and I will treasure these books forever."

Over glasses of port wine, the party continued. All were in a celebratory mood, save Vucetich, who observed the animated exchange with reserved detachment. At a break in the conversation, he intervened. "Mr. Waterman, I now understand, of course, why you had me examine the wine bottle and why you asked me to compare the prints to the knife. But what led you to do this? What gave you the idea?"

Ben and Gruenwald exchanged looks. Gruenwald spoke first. "I expect that I planted the seed, Juan," he said. "When Ben first confronted me with his . . . theory . . . of the case, I realized that his ideas could perhaps suggest that *I* had something to do with Rachel's murder. This, of course, was absurd, but from Ben's perspective, there was a certain logic to it. Then it came to me. Claire Elise Montgomery had been poisoning Ben's mind against me, creating and feeding suspicions borne of her own madness, her own insane jealousy."

"She was very . . . convincing," Ben continued. "When you and I talked, Gabriel, I confess that I had you at the top of my list for the murder. But, of course, you had an alibi. You were fighting a fire at the tannery that night, and Ros confirmed it.

"When you told me about Claire Elise's longstanding infatuation, her *obsession* with you, going all the way back to Argentina, well, something clicked. I remembered her unkind, even vicious, remarks about Rachel. Comments that I now see were fueled, as you say, by jealousy, pure and simple. She just could not tolerate Rachel's interference."

"I had the wine bottle, I had Claire Elise right there, I had the knife, and, most importantly, Mr. Vucetich, I had *you*. So, I took a chance. And Judge Transou went along."

"But what if there had been no match?" asked Vucetich. "What then?"

"Then no harm done. Your written report established that Virgil Wade was no match for the bloody knife. So, clearly *two* people. Proving that Claire Elise held the knife was just icing on the cake."

"Here's how we figure it happened," offered Tink. "Rachel made some noise and woke up Claire Elise. She got dressed and up in time to see Rachel riding off down to the river with the whiskey and the quilt and all her stuff. That was weird as all get-out, so she decided to follow her. On foot. It's not far."

"She watched through the trees as Rachel laid out the quilt and got ready for whoever she was expecting there," added McGee. Ben shot Gruenwald a look, and he dropped his head, looked away. "But nobody shows. Rachel gets mad, starts drinking. Then, out of nowhere, here comes Virgil Wade. It's not who she's waiting for."

"That's right," nodded Ben. He then outlined Virgil's story about what happened at the river with Rachel. Choosing his words carefully, he presented it as a *what if* hypothetical— Rachel's disappointment at her paramour's failure to appear, her spur-of-the-moment invitation to Virgil, his hesitation. The drinking, the sexual overture, the fight and the blow from his fist, leaving Rachel unconscious. Virgil passing out and waking up to find Rachel's dead body on the quilt.

"So," said Vucetich. "Mrs. Montgomery. She was there?"

Ben shrugged. "Had to be. You proved it, Mr. Vucetich. She was there, hiding in the bushes. For the whole thing. And with both Rachel and Virgil on the ground unconscious, she saw her chance, and, in a jealous rage, she took it. A perfect opportunity to get rid of her beautiful young rival once and for all and blame it all on some poor, mixed-up colored boy. It almost worked." Ben shook his head. "And, sad to say, it still might. She could very well get away with it. All of it. It's up to Taliaferro."

Vucetich nodded. *"Los celos. La envidia.* Jealousy. Envy. Powerful human emotions that many times have provided motivation for . . .

murder. I see your point, Mr. Waterman."

"So," said Ben, rising and holding his port glass high. "A toast to Mr. Juan Vucetich, who provided the evidence that exonerates Virgil Wade, that proves his innocence!" The others rose, smiling, glasses in hand.

Vucetich remained seated, however, with a grim expression. "That was not my testimony, Mr. Waterman."

Confused, his glass in mid-air, Ben said, "Excuse me?"

"I am afraid you have misunderstood me. My testimony was only that Virgil Wade did not hold the knife during the attack."

"But . . . " sputtered Ben.

Vucetich held up a hand to stop him. "I do not mean to disappoint you, Mr. Waterman, but hear me out. My specialty is comparative dactyloscopy, but my expertise and experience in forensic science extend far beyond that. I am not a medical doctor, but I am well versed in many aspects of forensic pathology."

An uneasy silence filled the room as the group sat, waited. "Last weekend, as we were preparing for trial, you showed me photographs, pictures of the crime scene and the autopsy. These led me inescapably to the conclusion that the knife wounds on Miss Schumann's body were most certainly postmortem."

Stricken, Ben whispered, "What do you mean?"

Vucetich took a breath, spread his hands. "Mr. Waterman, I am saying that Rachel Schumann was already dead when the knife wounds were inflicted."

Ben and the others recoiled in surprise and astonishment. "Could you . . . would you please . . . explain that?" Ben said softly.

Vucetich nodded. "The photographs, you see, show little blood around the knife wounds, almost none. A penetrating puncture wound to the heart while still alive would produce massive amounts of blood as the organ continued to pump in its death throes. The pictures contradict this.

"This is also true of the other, less dramatic slashing wounds to the chest and abdomen. There was some leakage, of course, enough to transfer blood to the knife and the hand of the perpetrator, but insufficient to support a conclusion that the stab wounds were antemortem and thus the cause of death."

Struggling to breathe, Ben asked, "So what killed her, Mr. Vucetich? How did she die?"

"Most likely from the blow to the left side of her cranium, compounded by her head striking the large stone visible on the ground. The enormous bruise around her left eye suggests a powerful blow from a right-handed person, no doubt causing massive hemorrhaging and internal bleeding. In essence, Rachel Schumann was dead, or dying, when she hit the ground. The lack of substantial antemortem blood flow from the knife wounds demonstrates conclusively that her heart had already stopped beating by the time they were inflicted."

Working to maintain his composure, Ben countered, "But Dr. Burleson, the coroner, testified that the wound to the heart was the cause of death. It's in his report."

Vucetich again shook his head, replied with confidence. "The coroner was mistaken, Mr. Waterman. The photographs do not lie. I suggest that the coroner's lack of experience in such matters led him to what appeared to be an obvious, but incorrect conclusion.

"I have personally investigated many stabbing cases in Argentina, most antemortem, where knife wounds were indeed the cause of death. And some, like this case, where the wounds were postmortem. The differences are manifest. Here, I am afraid that the coroner saw what he expected to see, surely what he *wanted* to see. But to be blunt, the knife wounds are quite irrelevant in solving this murder."

"So, who killed Rachel Schumann, then?" asked Ben weakly.

Vucetich hesitated, continued. "The person who struck her head and knocked her to the ground."

Ben stared into space, unable to meet Vucetich's eyes. "Are you saying, sir, that Virgil Wade is in fact guilty? Guilty of the murder of Rachel Schumann?"

"That is not for me to say, Mr. Waterman. But the proof, the evidence in this case as I understand it, strongly suggests it."

"But why have you waited until now to tell me this?" Ben demanded.

Vucetich smiled tightly. "Because you did not ask, counselor. And quite frankly, I did not think you wished to know. And Mr. Taliaferro chose not to go into this during his cross examination. I was surprised by that.

"In my view, Mr. Taliaferro also made another mistake. In his indictment. In his rush to judgment, and as you very astutely reminded the jury, Taliaferro charged the boy with only one offense—murder by knife wound. There was, for example, no allegation of manslaughter, an unintentional death. So, in my view, Virgil Wade is indeed innocent of the crime charged in the indictment, and the jury was correct not to convict him."

Sitting up straight, he concluded, "My testimony confirms that Virgil Wade was not the person who handled the knife. I further established that the person who handled the wine bottle was also the person who did take the knife in hand. That is all. If your theory is correct, Mr. Waterman, then Mrs. Montgomery may be guilty of an unspeakable desecration of an already-dead corpse, but certainly not murder."

For long moments, an icy silence filled the room as Vucetich's audience stared at the tablecloth. Finally, Vucetich spoke. "I see I have spoiled the party. I am sorry for that. Perhaps it would be best if I retire. I must pack for my journey tomorrow." Without a parting word from anyone, he rose and walked slowly out of the room.

After a moment, McGee whistled softly. "Son of a bitch, Ben. What now?"

Ben sat slumped in his chair. "I don't know, Ros. I just don't. I've got my meeting with Taliaferro tomorrow. I need to think this through."

The party was over.

Chapter 43

Raleigh, Saturday, September 8, 1900

M orning trains took people in different directions. Vucetich north, Gruenwald east to Wilmington, McGee and Tink westbound to Wilkes.

A violent morning thunderstorm, the remnants of an Atlantic hurricane, provided a fitting climax to Ben's sleepless night. Torrential rainfall lashed the windows, and bolts of lightning cast shadows on the walls as Ben sat brooding in his room. Staring out at the rain, Ben worked his way through his options.

What about Virgil? he mused. *What do I say to him? Do I tell him about Vucetich's revelations?* He thought long and hard. *What would that accomplish? And why torture the boy and his mother further? No, better to keep quiet about this. Virgil still faces a retrial. Just leave it alone. Maybe make some kind of deal with Taliaferro.*

And what about Claire Elise? What if Taliaferro decides to charge her with the murder? Do I push that? How could I just sit on what I know? She tried her best to kill Rachel Schumann and thinks she did. But she failed. Just wait and see what Taliaferro has in mind.

All roads lead through Taliaferro, he concluded. He reached for his umbrella.

Taliaferro sat at the table in the prosecution workroom, drumming his fingers. He pulled out his watch, impatient. After yesterday's surprise in the courtroom, Furnifold Simmons sent him a terse message summoning him to a meeting at Democratic Party headquarters. This morning. Before lunch. Taliaferro was worried about that. The air in the cramped room was heavy and damp. Taliaferro tried to open the window, but it was painted shut. There was a hard knock on the door. "It's open."

Ben walked to the table and sat across from Taliaferro. "So," the prosecutor began. "What's on your mind? What's so important?"

"I'm here to discuss next steps. What you intend to do about Virgil Wade. After yesterday."

"That was a pretty clever trick you pulled. With your Argentine *expert*."

"Good enough to hang the jury," countered Ben. "I was hoping that you might be open to some sort of . . . arrangement."

Taliaferro waved a hand. "*Pffft!* A *deal?* You want me to make some kind of a *deal?*"

"Look," Ben said evenly. "Vucetich proved Virgil Wade never handled the knife, and he also proved who did. Under the circumstances, Mr. Taliaferro, it would be unconscionable for you to press your murder charge against the boy. Why—"

"Stop!" Taliaferro shouted, slapping the table. Jutting his jaw, he sneered, "For all your smarts, Waterman, you are one naïve son of a gun. Let me paint you a picture how this thing will play out.

"First, I will most certainly retry Virgil Wade. If you hang another jury, which you won't, well, then I'll try him again. And again, if I have to. I will not stop until I get a guilty verdict. Your little magic show bought you delay, that's all. So, your boy can stay here in Raleigh until I decide it's time for the retrial. In the meantime, I will appeal Transou's ridiculous decision to let your monkey-science foreigner testify. The supreme court will set him straight. They'll never stand for it.

"After the supreme court reverses Transou, I will let a little time pass. Say, until the election is over and the Democrats take over. New governor, new judges, new everything. Aubrey Absher will whip Transou like a rented mule in November. When Absher's on the bench, he won't be so sympathetic to your tricks, counselor.

"Then, I'll get the boy moved back to Wilkes. Absher will see to that. Virgil Wade will stand trial in Wilkes County, the jury will take about five minutes to convict him, and he will hang. End of story."

"But the evidence!" Ben reached into his satchel, pulled out a document. "I have Mr. Vucetich's report—"

"*Report?* Wake up, Waterman! Here's the only evidence the jury will hear. I've got Wade at the scene. I've got Rachel's battered body and his knife sticking out of her chest. I've got the *photographs.* I've got Doc Burleson's autopsy report. I've got the boy stealing her horse and fleeing the scene like the sorry bastard he is."

Taliaferro reached for the report. "This?" he snorted, flinging it back at Ben. "This worthless piece of paper? The jury will never see it. Absher won't consider it, not after the supreme court rules. The jury will not hear one word about *fingerprints!*"

Ben removed the wine bottle from his satchel, sat it on the table. "But what about this, Mr. Taliaferro? What about Mrs. Montgomery's role in all this? You know what she did. How can you—?"

"You can put that thing away," Taliaferro interrupted dismissively. "Now, listen to me very carefully, Waterman." In a measured cadence, he pronounced, "*I . . . don't . . . give . . . a . . . damn.* I've got a no-good, high-yeller colored boy mixed up with a rich young White woman. He stalked her, beat her within an inch of her life, and took off. Maybe he stabbed her, maybe he didn't. No matter. The jury won't care, and neither do I. I'm going to hang Virgil Wade, Waterman. I'm going to put him in the *ground.* And you, sir, can take that to the bank!" His voice easing, Taliaferro leaned back. "'Sides, she's gone."

"What? What did you say?"

Fluttering his fingers like a bird, Taliaferro repeated, "Gone. Like . . . away."

"But how do you know—"

Taliaferro grinned, showing teeth. "After she left, I had Crip follow her out. Told him to tell her that I might need to talk to her later. Well, she didn't go back to her hotel. Seems she hailed a buggy and lit out for Union Station. Crip followed her there.

"She met up with that colored maid of hers, Jewel or something. Crip saw a porter load up two or three big steamer trunks onto the train. She climbed in, and the maid got in the colored car. The train pulled out, and it didn't look like they were coming back any time soon. So, she's gone, out of reach," he sneered. "Too bad."

For a moment, Ben couldn't speak. Then he offered one final appeal. "You know this is not right, Mr. Taliaferro. This is not the *justice* you speak of so passionately. I beg you to reconsider. You hold the life of a young boy in the palm of your hand. Please, don't do this."

"Beg all you want, Waterman," snarled Taliaferro. "It suits you. But it won't change a damn thing. The boy will hang, sir. And I will sleep like a baby. Now," he concluded, looking at his watch, "if there's nothing else, I have an important meeting across town and can't be late."

Chapter 44

New Hanover County Courthouse, Wilmington, Friday, May 3, 1901

S uperior court Judge Benjamin Gordon Waterman, leaning back and smoking his pipe, relaxed in his chambers in the Victorian courthouse on the corner of Third and Princess Streets. A civil trial involving a waterfront warehouse lease had unexpectedly settled the day before, freeing his schedule. He would read his mail and then take the rest of the day off.

A soft knock on the door. Emily Whitaker, Ben's secretary, entered with her usual bright, sunny smile. "Here's the mail, Judge. Anything else for me this morning?"

Ben reached for the stack and shook his head. "No, Emily. I'll sort through this, and then we'll close up shop for the week." Grinning, he added, "Work for you? Get an early start on the weekend?"

Pleased, Emily answered, "You're the boss, sir. Whatever you say." Emily, a childless widow, had been Judge Hogewood's secretary when he was in private practice, and she followed him to the bench. Her husband, who owned a local feed and seed store, had been killed by a stray bullet during the violent uprising in 1898, one of the many innocent victims of the Wilmington Massacre.

Despite the crushing loss that forced her into gainful employment, Emily managed to maintain her pleasant good humor and optimistic outlook. She was pretty, intelligent, a charming young woman. She ran Ben's office with cheerful efficiency and had been especially helpful in guiding Ben's transition from practicing attorney to superior court judge. He had come to depend on her down-to-earth judgment and solid common sense.

"I hope that you have something fun planned for the weekend," said Ben. "The paper says the weather should be fine."

W

As Ben absent-mindedly sorted through the mail, his thoughts drifted back over the past months. The Suffrage Amendment passed easily in August, effectively erasing Black registration and participation in the November election. Continued violence and intimidation by the Red Shirts kept many White Republican voters away from the polls.

In an enormous victory for the White Supremacy campaign, Democrats swept the state and would dominate North Carolina politics for the next hundred years. Charles B. Aycock was easily elected governor, and even in Republican Wilkes, Vincent Taliaferro and Aubrey Absher won by slim margins.

Furnifold Simmons proudly proclaimed that the state had, at last, been "redeemed from the grip of Reconstruction carpetbaggers and scalawags." In March of 1901, a grateful Democratic legislature elected him to the United States Senate, where he would serve for thirty years.

Sheriff Jimmy "Redbone" Poindexter bucked the Democratic tide and was re-elected, leading the Republican ticket in Wilkes. Deputy Crip Goins bought a new dog, a blue heeler he named Lucky.

Judge Richard Magnus Transou, defeated at the polls, retired and moved to Asheville to be near his children and grandchildren.

In early December, Judge Hogewood submitted his resignation and, true to his word, Governor Maxwell promptly appointed Ben to fill the vacancy. Maxwell held the Bible as Ben took the oath of office on Christmas Eve. Democrats seethed and gritted their teeth, but there was nothing they could do.

Maxwell refused to attend Aycock's inauguration and vacated the Executive Mansion at the last possible moment, vexing Aycock and his staff mightily. He moved back to Wilkesboro and set up a one-man law practice in his fine home on East Main Street.

Gabriel von Gruenwald returned to Wilmington and married his fiancée, but tannery business regularly brought him back to Wilkes. Ben and Gruenwald lived only a few blocks from one another in Wilmington, but their paths never crossed.

Jakob and Rebekah Schumann, unwilling to face the trial, moved the family back to Alsace, taking Rachel's remains with them. They never returned. Jakob appointed Gruenwald as his agent to sell the tannery and the hotel. Gruenwald brokered a deal with Golden Empire Shoe Company, which operated the tannery until the devastating Yadkin River flood of 1940 swept away its buildings and much of the town. As Roscoe McGee reported in *The Lost Province*, "the familiar tone of *Old Sam*, the tannery steam whistle, which for decades roused generations of Yadkin Valley workers, farmers, and tradesmen to their labors, will be heard no more." Despite his best efforts, Gruenwald was unable to find a buyer for the Schumann Hotel. It was finally put up for auction and was bought for a song by a local entrepreneur who owned a well-known chain of dry goods stores.

Roscoe McGee and Tink Beasley continued to publish *The Lost Province* and hosted rowdy gatherings at McGee's Emporium. Pizza became a favorite "Eye-talian" food everywhere.

In 1919, a WWI veteran barnstormer landed his Curtis "Jenny" biplane on an open field by the Yadkin River. Tink and McGee joined the crowd, marveling at the pilot's daredevil maneuvers. Ever the adventuress, Tink paid five dollars for a joyride. As the pilot, encouraged by Tink, attempted an inside loop, one of the wing spars snapped, sending the aircraft into an uncontrollable spin. Both were killed instantly. McGee never got over it.

Juan Vucetich returned to Argentina after his American tour and continued to promote the science of comparative dactyloscopy. As Ben predicted, the Vucetich/Henry systems of fingerprint identification were soon adopted by law enforcement agencies around the world, including the United States.

No one heard anything from or about Claire Elise Montgomery or Jewel Ponder. Ruby, Pearl, and Opal prayed for their mother's safe return.

Luther Wade, in a drunken stupor, was shot and killed in a barroom fight on New Year's Eve. And what of his illegitimate son, Virgil Wade?

After the futile and fruitless meeting with Ben in Raleigh, things worked out much as Taliaferro predicted. As promised, Taliaferro appealed Judge Transou's ruling to the North Carolina Supreme Court. In a stinging reprimand, the court unanimously reversed Transou and barred fingerprint evidence from North Carolina courtrooms.

Soon after Aubrey Absher was sworn in, Taliaferro moved to have

Maxwell's emergency decree vacated. Absher agreed, and ordered Virgil moved back to the Wilkes County Jail. The Klan stayed quiet as Virgil awaited his retrial.

Now a superior court judge, Ben was barred from acting as Virgil's lawyer. As the new trial loomed, Ben hired Charlie Odell, Taliaferro's unsuccessful opponent, to defend Virgil, paying him out of his own pocket. It was a doomed effort. Odell tried valiantly to present Vucetich's report to the jury, but, citing the supreme court decision, Absher sustained Taliaferro's strenuous objection and excluded the document.

It all went as Taliaferro had foreseen. About lunchtime, the jury retired to deliberate, and sandwiches were brought in. An hour later, they returned a unanimous guilty verdict. Judge Absher solemnly sentenced Virgil to "hang by the neck until dead." Taliaferro personally oversaw the construction of the scaffold on the courthouse lawn, near the Tory Oak.

Ben and Reverend Bondurant persuaded Pauline Oxendine to stay away from her son's public execution. Ben, McGee, Tink, and Governor Maxwell were there to witness the event, along with a throng of citizens from Wilkes.

It was the worst day of Ben's life. Poindexter led the bound and shackled, terror-stricken boy up the thirteen steps. Just before the sheriff put the hood over his head, Virgil's eyes, wild with fear, met Ben's. Helpless, Ben crossed his arms over his chest and bowed. As required, Poindexter asked if the boy had any last words. As Virgil slowly opened his mouth to speak, his whole body shaking, Poindexter roughly pulled the hood over the boy's head, muffling him.

Taliaferro himself jerked the lever, and the trapdoor opened with a loud *thunk*. Virgil's hooded body dropped straight down, the noose breaking his thin neck cleanly with a sickening *crack*.

As the crowd roared its approval, Ben turned his head, bent over, and vomited on the grass. Virgil Wade's execution would forever torment Ben, an unhealing canker sore on his soul.

Virgil's lifeless body was hauled away to Cairo for burial in the Mount Zion AME Church cemetery, Reverend Napoleon Bondurant presiding.

Public revulsion against the barbarity and obscene spectacle of public hangings led the state to take over administration of capital punishment in 1910.

The last piece of mail was a letter postmarked New Bern, addressed to The Honorable Benjamin G. Waterman and marked *"Personal and Confidential."*

Curious, Ben took his silver letter opener, a gift from Judge Maxwell, and slit the envelope. The correspondence bore the engraved letterhead *A. Buford Caudle, Esq., Attorney and Counselor at Law, 211 Broad Street, New Bern, NC.*

Dear Judge Waterman,

This will inform you that I represent the estate of the late Claire Elise Montgomery.

You are mentioned in her Last Will and Testament, prepared and witnessed by the undersigned.

Certain aspects of the estate are of a sensitive nature, best discussed privately and in person.

I would, therefore, respectfully request that you contact me at your earliest convenience. I can be reached at number 429C, New Bern Exchange.

I remain, sir, with respect,

Sincerely,
Buford Caudle, Esq.

Stunned, Ben read the letter again, the words swimming before his eyes. Finally, he looked up, smoothed the paper with his hands, his thoughts a jumble in his mind. Holding the letter, Ben approached Emily's desk. "Emily," he said in a weak voice. "Something's come up. I need you to make a telephone call, right away. To New Bern."

Chapter 45

As he walked from the train station to Caudle's office near the Craven County courthouse, Ben's mind was filled with a mix of curiosity and foreboding. Claire Elise dead? How could this be? The lawyer had been evasive on the telephone, urging him to come to New Bern. He promised to explain everything.

Caudle welcomed him warmly as they took seats around his conference room table. Papers were spread out. "I realize that my letter must have come as somewhat of a surprise, Judge Waterman. I appreciate your willingness to travel on such short notice, given your busy docket, but I think you will agree that a private meeting is in order." Gesturing to the papers, he continued, "I understand that you and Mrs. Montgomery were acquainted."

"That is correct, sir," agreed Ben. "We met last year. When she was working in Wilkesboro. She was also a witness at a trial in Raleigh last September. I represented the defendant."

"I am aware of that. She came to me shortly afterwards and asked me to represent her. Shortly before her . . . unfortunate death, she asked me to prepare her Last Will and Testament."

"But how, *how* did she die, Mr. Caudle?"

"Mrs. Montgomery was, shall we say, a troubled woman. She and her housemaid—"

"Jewel?"

"Yes. She and Jewel were living on Ocracoke Island, on the Outer Banks. Very remote. She intended to move back to England, but she chose Ocracoke for her confinement."

"Confinement?"

"Yes. You see," Caudle hesitated. "Mrs. Montgomery was . . . expecting . . . when she arrived here."

"Expecting?" Ben asked, the lawyer's words not making any sense. "I'm sorry, but I don't understand."

"Mrs. Montgomery passed away as a result of . . . complications during her pregnancy. She died shortly after giving birth last month, leaving no known relatives either in the United States or England. She had a son, Judge, a baby boy. She listed the father on the birth certificate as Charles Randall Montgomery."

"But, but he—"

"Yes, I am aware. I know that now. She was very ill, Judge. She knew she was dying. She sent a telegram, asking me to come right away. So, I journeyed to Ocracoke and met with her on her deathbed. She was very weak, but her mind was clear. She gave me precise instructions about her will, which I prepared and she signed shortly before her death. She left everything, including a sizable legacy from her father to her son. The will also mentions you, sir."

"Me?" Ben whispered.

"Her testament specifically states her desire that you, Judge, assume legal guardianship of her son. She also requested that you use the inheritance to provide for the baby and for her housemaid, Jewel Ponder. She expressed her hope that you would keep Jewel on. To help raise the boy." Caudle handed Ben the Last Will and Testament. Ben scanned it, confirming Caudle's astonishing summary.

"She died the next day, Judge. She also left a message for you. As I said, she was very weak, but she insisted on preparing a note to you, in her own hand. She made me swear I would deliver it." Caudle handed Ben a small, sealed envelope, bearing a single word, *Ben.* "I have not, of course, read this."

Ben took the envelope with trembling hands, opened it. The message, in uneven handwriting, was brief:

> *He's yours, Ben. Take care of our son.*
> *His name is Michael. CEM*

Overwhelmed, Ben let the note drop from his hands.

"I realize that all this must come as a shock to you, Judge," Caudle added in a comforting tone. "Now you know why I sent for you."

Ben, breathing deeply, said, "Yes. Well, yes, a shock. But now, Mr. Caudle, what is to be done?"

"Jewel and the baby are here, Judge. She would very much like to see you."

"Here? Now?"

"Yes. In the next room. Shall I bring them in?"

Ben could not speak. He could only nod.

Caudle left the room, leaving Ben disoriented, unbelieving. Soon he returned, Jewel by his side. Tears in her eyes, she held a tiny baby, swaddled in her arms. Jewel walked slowly to Ben, extending her arms. "Here, Mistah Waterman. Take him." As Ben gently cradled the child in his arms, Jewel leaned in, whispered in his ear, "He's your'n, Mistah Waterman. He's shore 'nuff your'n."

Ben looked down at the sleeping infant. It was plain to him. In the baby's face, he could see his own. Tears streaming, Ben looked to Caudle, his voice trembling. "Of course. Of course, Mr. Caudle. I will take the baby, as Mrs. Montgomery requested. I will be his guardian. I will care for him. Raise him. And," he added, looking earnestly at Jewel, "you would do me great honor if you would help me, Jewel. Come to Wilmington. Join my household. Help me with the boy. Please."

Taking the baby back, Jewel smiled through her tears. "Don't you worry, Mistah Waterman. You'n me. We'll get it done. We'll raise him right. We'll do Miz Claire Elise proud."

Ben reached out, sobbing, and wordlessly embraced his new family. After a while, Ben disengaged and addressed the lawyer. "Mr. Caudle, please prepare the guardianship papers. Right away. When they're filed with the court, let me know immediately."

Facing Jewel and the baby, Ben said, "Jewel, I need to get back to Wilmington. To prepare for you and . . . Michael. Mr. Caudle here will make arrangements for you here in New Bern until I can send for you."

"Don't you worry none, Mistah Waterman. I'll be waitin'," Jewel grinned.

Ben took the baby again, gazed at the tiny, peaceful face and pressed a gentle kiss against his son's forehead. "You're coming home, Michael. Soon."

Lightheaded, Ben rushed back to Wilmington. Before leaving Caudle's office, he borrowed his telephone. "Emily! This is Ben. Listen, something's come up here in New Bern. I need you to clear my calendar. For the next two weeks. I have some important personal matters to take care of."

"Excuse me?" Emily asked, concerned. "Clear your calendar? But, Judge, you have that trial coming up!"

"Postpone it!" Ben shouted, sharper than he intended. Softening his tone, he apologized, "Sorry, Emily. That came out wrong. Look. What are you doing for dinner tonight?"

"Dinner? Me? Tonight? You want to take me to dinner?"

"Yes, yes. Pick someplace you like. I'll be back on the afternoon train. I'll meet you at the office, and we can go from there. I really need your help."

"Help? Whatever for?"

"It's a long story, Emily. But I've got to buy a house. Tomorrow."

W

Emily listened carefully to Ben's amazing story. She did not interrupt. Ben explained everything but withheld any mention of the child's paternity. Emily, of course, was aware of the Virgil Wade trial and Claire Elise Montgomery's role in it. Like Ben, she received the news of her death, Michael's birth, and Ben's agreement to the guardianship with a mix of disbelief and astonishment. But she agreed to help him.

The next day, they went house hunting. Emily's keen and practical eye for detail focused on a large, three-story mansion in a row of fine homes on Third Street, just a block away from the courthouse. The house had been on the market for some time. Ben made an offer that was immediately accepted. With Emily's assistance, Ben filled the house with suitable furniture and prepared for the arrival of Jewel and the baby.

Caudle filed the guardianship papers and offered the English bank book to Ben. Ben instructed Caudle to delay transferring the money until he could figure out what to do with it.

Jewel inspected her new home and pronounced it acceptable.

Ben returned to work, leaving Michael in Jewel's able care. Emily was a frequent visitor in his home, smitten by the infant's cooing smiles and periwinkle blue eyes. Everything went smoothly, and Ben was pleased.

A few weeks in, Ben walked into the kitchen one Saturday morning, looking for coffee. Jewel stood at the sink, humming and stringing snap beans. Michael was sound asleep in his bassinet. Without looking up, Jewel shook her head, stopped humming. She turned and looked directly at Ben. "Mistah Waterman, I been thinkin."

"What's on your mind, Jewel?"

"Well, suh, here we are in this big ol' house. Just you'n me. But seems to me they's somethin' missing."

"Missing? Is there something you need? Just tell me and the boy—"

Jewel interrupted, "I can take care of the baby, shore 'nuff, and I can keep your house, cook your supper. But they's one thing ol' Jewel cain't do, suh." Pointing at the crib, she declared, "Mebbe none'a my bidness, but that boy needs a momma. Ever' boy does. You'll see. And you, suh," she raised her eyebrows, "well, seems like you could use a woman in the house."

"A woman? What are you getting at, Jewel?"

"Jus' 'zackly that. A woman. A *wife*, Mistah Waterman. And don't you try to tell me you don't know what I'm talkin' 'bout. You a good-lookin' man, Mistah Waterman, goin' to waste, 'you ask me."

Ben furrowed his brow. "Well, I thank you for the compliment, Jewel, but I've been a little busy lately. No time for courting. And who in the world would have me?"

"I'll swanney, Mistah Waterman, sometimes you 'just as blind as a bat!"

Taken aback, Ben blurted, "Blind? What on earth do you mean?"

"Hmmph!" Jewel snorted, placing her hands on her hips. "Why, Miz Emily, of course! Cain't you see it? Open your eyes! She's done fell in love with you, Mistah Waterman! Plain as the nose on your face. And that baby? Why, she love that boy like her own! I was you, I'd jump on a stick. 'Fore some other lawyer man come along and sweep her off her feet. Ask me, you won't do no better." Turning back to her beans, Jewel said, "There. I've done said my piece. Up to you, now."

Dismissed, Ben ambled into his study, his thoughts racing. He turned Jewel's remarkable speech over in his mind but could find no flaw in her logic. And he realized just how fond he had become of Emily, how easily she had become a soothing and calming fixture in his home life, how her gentle, affectionate touch and mellow voice could immediately comfort Michael. And, for perhaps the first time, he allowed himself to see Emily as a woman, to feel his pent-up desire for her touch, her body. Jewel was right. He'd better get busy.

A week later, Ben and Emily sat in the parlor of his home, playing with Michael. As the baby cooed and gurgled on the quilt on the floor between them, Ben took Emily's hands in his.

"Emily, I have something to tell you." Slowly and patiently, Ben told the story of his time in Wilkes, his brief affair with Claire Elise, the birth of the baby boy. "I'm more than his guardian, Emily. He's my son. He's mine."

Emily stared into Ben's eyes, tears forming in her own. "Oh, Ben. Thank you for sharing that . . . that wonderful news! You're a father!"

Taking her into his arms, Ben said, "And you, dear Emily, I would like you to become his . . . mother."

Emily broke the embrace, looked at Ben, her eyes wide. "Are you saying—?"

Ben forced a crooked smile, dropped clumsily to one knee. "Yes, Emily Whitaker. I am asking you to marry me. To be my wife. To be the mother to our son."

W

The wedding was the social event of the season. Among the guests was Jewel Ponder, beaming in her new dress, Michael in her arms. Later, Ben lifted Emily and kissed her as he crossed the threshold of their new home on Third Street.

Soon after the wedding, Ben contacted Buford Caudle in New Bern. He asked him to prepare and file formal adoption papers for the baby. Michael Montgomery became Michael Gordon Waterman. Ben requested that the guardianship and adoption files be placed under permanent seal. The New Hanover County Clerk agreed, as a matter of professional courtesy to the judge, and placed the sealed files in a dark corner of a little-used storage room, behind dusty boxes of old case files.

Ben then asked Judge Maxwell to set up an irrevocable trust in Michael's new name and file the papers with the clerk in Wilkesboro. Caudle then arranged a wire transfer of Michael's inheritance to the Bank of North Wilkesboro, where the funds were deposited to the trust account. Ben never touched the money.

Time passed quickly and happily as Michael grew into a toddler. Fortune was kind to the Waterman family. As the end of Ben's term approached, he had a decision to make. As a Republican in Wilmington, despised and reviled by the Democratic establishment, Ben stood no chance in the upcoming election. As Ben sat in his chambers, pondering his future, Emily, still his secretary, announced that Judge Maxwell was on the line.

Delighted, Ben picked up. "Judge! Good to hear from you. What can I do for you today?"

Maxwell got right to the point. "It's 1904, Ben. You're done down there. Time for you to come on home. Time for you to come back. To Wilkes."

Epilogue

As Roscoe McGee stood over the box, late afternoon sunlight broke through the storm clouds. Still not ready, he sat down again. He allowed his mind to wander, recalling the personalities that, over all the long years, had left such vivid, indelible footprints in his memory.

Ben, his best friend, dead now. Emily, claimed by breast cancer five years ago. Jewel Ponder, born a slave, died in 1929, a free woman and beloved Waterman family member, age seventy-nine, surrounded by her cherished daughters, Ruby, Pearl, and Opal, comforted by Reverend Napoleon Bondurant.

Tink, killed in an airplane crash. Robert Rousseau "Cotton Bob" Maxwell died in his sleep in 1915, eighty years old. George Vincent Taliaferro and retired Judge Richard Magnus Transou, victims of the Spanish Flu Epidemic of 1918.

Gabriel von Gruenwald, German-born but traveling aboard the *RMS Lusitania* under a passport issued by neutral Argentina, perished along with 1,197 others off the south coast of Ireland when his ship was sunk, ironically, by a single torpedo from a German U-Boat on May 7, 1915.

Amos, beloved only son of Jakob and Rebekah Schumann, was conscripted into the German Army in January of 1915. He threatened to flee to France with his wife and young children, but was persuaded by his father to remain and comply. He perished in August 1918, three months before the Armistice, in the Second Battle of the Marne, the last major German offensive on the western front during the Great War. Juan Vucetich passed away peacefully in Dolores, Argentina in 1925.

Charles B. Aycock, dead of a heart attack while making a speech extoling White Supremacy in Birmingham, Alabama in 1912. Senator Furnifold M. Simmons, hero of the Ku Klux Klan and unsuccessful candidate for President of the United States in 1920, dead at age eighty-six back in April.

Drawing on his cigar, McGee took another sip of whiskey. Picking up Ben's handwritten note, he read it again.

Dear Ros,

If you are reading this, then I am dead. This means that you are the last one, the last man standing.

He doesn't know, Ros. He doesn't know anything.

It's all in here. I trust you. You decide . . . .

Your friend,

Benjamin Gordon Waterman

He's right, thought McGee. *I'm the last one.* McGee opened the box. Reaching in, he took out the contents and arranged them on the desk. First, there was a blue-bound legal document labelled *In the Matter of Michael Montgomery—Guardianship.* Leafing through it, McGee saw confirmation of Ben's original status.

Next, another blue-bound set of papers. *In the Matter of Michael Montgomery—Adoption.* McGee turned the pages until he came across the court order formally changing the infant's name to Michael Gordon Waterman. When Ben, Emily, and Michael moved back to Wilkes in 1904, the deed was done, the original documents tucked away in New Bern. Michael was, of course, accepted as the natural child of Ben and Emily Waterman. No one was the wiser, and nobody gave it a second thought.

A final set of legal papers bore the heading *Irrevocable Trust for the Benefit of Michael Gordon Waterman.* McGee was amused to read that Michael had become fully vested and entitled to the assets free and clear several years earlier. *How about that?* he mused.

He then picked up a bank book bearing the seal of the Bank of North Wilkesboro. The account was registered to *Michael Gordon Waterman Irrevocable Trust.* McGee whistled as he read the amount on deposit. There was no record of any withdrawals.

Finally, there was the last item, an old, green wine bottle bearing a fancy label printed in Spanish. What appeared to be traces of white powder still clung to its neck. McGee let out a deep breath, shook his head, and put it down.

McGee placed the trust indenture and the bank book in his breast pocket. He would need these later.

Picking up the guardianship documents and the adoption papers, McGee thought a moment. *He doesn't know, Ros. He doesn't know anything. I trust you. You decide . . .*

Eyeing the potbellied stove, McGee made his decision. He walked over and swung open the front grille. He again drew deeply on the cigar and touched the glowing tip to the documents. They soon caught fire. Holding the flaming papers by the corner, he carefully laid them inside the stove and watched, bent over, until they burned into black ashes.

Rising, McGee grasped the wine bottle and moved slowly toward the front door of the Finley Law Office. Closing it behind him, he walked through the early evening air, cooled by the storm, up the hill to his black 1939 Ford coupe parked below St. Paul's Episcopal Church. Turning to face Ben's grave, he saluted his friend, cranked up his car, and drove slowly downhill to the old iron bridge.

Pulling to the side of the roadway, he opened his door and walked to the railing. Taking a deep breath, and with a final look through the trees at the small strip of beach where Rachel Schumann was found, McGee took the bottle in both hands, extended his arms, sighed, and dropped it into the river.

For a moment, the bottle floated in the slow current, bobbing along before gravity took hold. Once, twice more, the bottle fought stubbornly against the force. McGee watched as it finally surrendered, silently slipping and disappearing into the dark, swirling waters of the Yadkin.

Historical Notes

*T*he *Tannery* is a work of historical fiction set in Wilkes County, North Carolina in 1900. In my experience, fans of this genre are keen to know where the *historical* ends and the *fiction* begins, the line between reality and imagination. Wilkes, the *Lost Province*, takes pride in its rich and compelling history, and many of its people, places, and events play roles in the book.

The Tannery introduces many characters, some real people who lived at the time, the rest imagined. For the historical figures, I have done my best to capture their personalities and motivations in a purely fictional context. For the others, well, they are as described.

Historical Personalities

- **William Franklin Trogdon:** Visionary entrepreneur, savvy real estate developer, and enthusiastic promoter of the new town of North Wilkesboro.

- **Furnifold McLendel Simmons:** Chairman of the North Carolina State Democratic Party, advisor to gubernatorial candidate Charles B. Aycock, and mastermind of the White Supremacy campaigns of 1898 and 1900; served as US Senator from NC from 1901 to 1931 and was an unsuccessful candidate for the Democratic Party presidential nomination in 1920.

- **George Henry White:** African American US congressman from North Carolina's 2nd congressional district from 1897-1901, the only Black member to serve during his term and the last Black member of Congress to serve at the beginning of the Jim Crow era.

- **Dannie N. Heineman:** Charlotte native, successful businessman and financier in New York City and abroad, legendary philanthropist in Charlotte, founder of the Heineman Foundation for Research, Educational, Charitable and Scientific Purposes, Inc.

- **Major Wade:** Leader of the notorious Fort Hamby Gang of Union deserters and marauders that terrorized Wilkes County in the dark days after the Civil War; paramour of Meg Hamby, who provided refuge to the Gang at her home near the Yadkin River.

- **Beverly S. Royster:** Granville County native, Adjutant General of the North Carolina State Guard.

- **Juan Vucetich:** Croatian-born Argentine police official and world-renowned criminal forensic scientist and pioneer in the development of criminal identification using fingerprints.

The towns of Wilkesboro and North Wilkesboro, separated by the Yadkin River, and their landmarks, streets, and buildings were as described in *The Tannery* (some dates of construction have been modified to fit the narrative), and most can be visited today.

If you drop by the Wilkes Heritage Museum in the old courthouse in Wilkesboro, Jennifer Furr, the museum director, will provide you with a map showing locations of St. Paul's Church and graveyard, the courthouse and jail, the site of the original Tory Oak, the Finley Law Office, the Smithey Hotel (Schumann Hotel in the book), Ferguson's Store, and lovely Main Street heading east to the former Cairo community. The 1780 Cleveland log cabin, Virgil Wade's hideout, was originally located west of town, but in 1986 was moved next to the county jail and is now open to visitors.

The iron bridge so zealously monitored by Sheriff Poindexter is shown on Trogdon's 1907 map of North Wilkesboro. Today there is a new pedestrian bridge, part of the Yadkin River Greenway, at the confluence of the Yadkin and Reddies Rivers. Steps on the north end of the bridge lead down to the spit of sandy beach where Rachel Schumann's body was found.

Roscoe McGee's newspaper, emporium, and apartment are set in the

Trogdon Opera House at 5th and D Streets in North Wilkesboro, uphill from the rail depot on Cherry Street and Brame's Drug Co. in the center of town. Sadly, Trogdon's pride and joy burned years ago and is now a vacant lot.

Jakob Schumann's business was inspired by the C.C. Smoot and Sons Tannery, which operated in North Wilkesboro from 1897 until its destruction by the Yadkin River flood in 1940. Tannery operations in the novel are drawn from historical descriptions of the Smoot enterprise. Ruins of the old tannery, including the towering smokestack and the remnants of Tanner's Rest, are now part of Smoot Park east of town. A mostly flat trail leads visitors from the park along the Yadkin River where Jakob Schumann took his walk.

The descriptions of the successful Fusionist campaigns of 1894 and 1896, Black voter suppression and intimidation, Red Shirt violence, the White Supremacy campaigns of 1898 and 1900, the Wilmington Massacre of 1898, passage of the Suffrage Amendment, and the rise of Jim Crow are all based on historical fact. While it is true that the Ku Klux Klan was mostly dormant in 1900, the fictional attack by Luther Wade's henchmen on the Wilkes County Jail demonstrates that former members had not disposed of their terrifying regalia. Robert Rousseau ("Cotton Bob") Maxwell is a character based very loosely on the real Fusionist governor at the time, Republican Daniel Lindsay Russell, Jr.

The storyline about Jews in Alsace in the late 1800s and their engagement in the leather tanning business is also based on historical fact. Emperor Joseph II did indeed issue his "Universal Decree" in 1787 demanding that "each Jew should have a constant surname," and many Jews simply accepted their occupation as their new family name.

The New Canaan Project in Argentina and the roles of Baron von Gruenwald and his son, Gabriel, are based on the remarkable story of Moises Ville, the first Jewish agricultural colony in South America, established in 1889 by Russian Jews fleeing oppression in Ukraine. The colony was supported by *Moritz Freiherr von Hirsch auf Gereuth*, a German Jewish financier and philanthropist who founded the Jewish Colonization Association, which sponsored Jewish emigration to Argentina. Many of the colony's cattle hides were exported to the Smoot Tannery in North Wilkesboro.

The history, geography, and economy of Wilkes and the Yadkin River valley, and the personalities mentioned in *The Tannery* (Christopher Gist,

Sequoyah, Daniel Boone, John Wilkes, Colonel Benjamin Cleveland and the Overmountain Men, Eng and Chang Bunker, Tom Dula, and the Fort Hamby Gang) are accurately described.

The arrival of the Northwest North Carolina Railroad in Wilkes (tracking the route of modern-day Highway 268 beside the Yadkin River) and W.F. Trogdon's "theft" and placement of its terminus on the north bank of the Yadkin happened as set forth in the book.

Public hangings in North Carolina were banned in 1910.

Acknowledgments

I have learned that folks in Book World refer to the process of bringing an author's draft manuscript to bookshop shelves as a "project." Projects are always a team effort, but *The Tannery* required an entire village.

I could not have completed *The Tannery* without the unfailing support and encouragement of my wonderful wife, Helen Ruth. For many years HR endured my preoccupation with historical research and later patiently and lovingly reviewed each day's new pages, providing insightful input and comments. And once the book was accepted for publication, she managed the marketing strategy that brought this copy of *The Tannery* into your hands.

Prodded by Helen Ruth, I spent my days of pandemic isolation here at Almond Springs Farm completing the manuscript between May and October 2020. But, as noted above, the scene-setting historical research extended over several years. When I began this project, I never envisioned that the historical setting of *The Tannery* would prove so relevant to current circumstances in the US.

Thanks and appreciation to Jennifer Furr, Director of the Wilkes Heritage Museum, and my friends Mara Lynn Tugman and Deborah Beckel at the Wilkes County Public Library for their support. The list of books, newspaper and magazine articles, and other historical sources I relied upon is too long to list here, but I am grateful to all the chroniclers of Wilkes County and North Carolina history who set the stage for me.

As I worked through the writing process, I was fortunate to have a plucky band of early readers who agreed to read the emerging manuscript in installments and offer comments and suggestions along the way, most of which ended up in the final text. Many thanks to Donna Lampke, Millie and Tom Cox, Jimmy Caughman, Bill and Frances Thompson, Pat Mitchell, Hilma Prather, and Aubrey Almond. I couldn't have done it without you.

Mark Ethridge and Mark de Castrique, friends and fellow novelists from Charlotte, warned me that, once the draft manuscript was completed, "the hard work really begins." They were right. Kim Wright, an award-winning novelist and writers coach, agreed to provide developmental editing, and her suggestions made the book so much better.

The next challenge was to get the thing published. I was amazed how generous fellow authors and others were with their time in providing advice and guidance. Kudos and thanks to Kimmery Martin, Tracy Curtis, Tommy Tomlinson, Leslie Hooton, Bess Kercher, John Russell, Myles Thompson, Charlotte Hanes, Webb Hubbell, and Elizabeth Leland.

I will be forever grateful to my old friend and law school classmate Walter Dalton for his introduction to Kathie Bennett and her husband Roy of Magic Time Literary Publicity. Kathie first introduced me to John Koehler, and she has proven to be an intrepid and tireless promoter of *The Tannery*. Thanks, Kathie!

It is an honor to have *The Tannery* published by Koehler Books. Publisher John Koehler, Executive Editor Joe Coccaro, and their colleagues have guided me every step of the way through the publishing process, and I sincerely appreciate their support and encouragement.

I was fortunate to entice a wonderful group of fellow authors, journalists, and professionals to read the finished manuscript and provide advance reviews. I appreciate so much the contributions of Frye Gaillard, Fred Kempe, Jeffrey Blount, Kim Wright, Jimmy Caughman, Emeritus Professor Bill Thompson, Vince LoVoi, Bob Bamberg, Judy Goldman, Landis Wade, UNC Charlotte Professor Dr. Mark West, and Harvey B. Gantt.

Invaluable marketing advice was provided by Karen Beach, Deputy Director of the Charlotte Mecklenburg Library Foundation, and Judith Sutton, retired Deputy Director of the library, as well as Jeremy Powers, who developed my author website www.michaelalmondbooks.com.

Finally, many thanks to my son, Aubrey, who brought his considerable technical skills to the online marketing effort, and my daughter Sarah, who years ago first demonstrated the creative gene that runs through the family DNA.

About the Author

Michael A. Almond, a retired attorney, was raised in the small town of Pilot Mountain in the Piedmont foothills of North Carolina. He received his undergraduate and law degrees from the University of North Carolina at Chapel Hill, and was a Fulbright Scholar in political science at the University of Mannheim, Germany. During his years as an international business lawyer, he was awarded the prestigious Order of Merit of the Federal Republic of Germany for "outstanding commitment in fostering relations between the United States and the Federal Republic of Germany." An avid reader and student of Southern history and literature, he currently lives on a farm with his wife, Helen Ruth, in the beautiful Blue Ridge Mountains of North Carolina. *The Tannery* is his debut novel.

www.michaelalmondbooks.com